Livin' on a Prayer

The Untold Tommy & Gina Story

Jody Clark & Sue Roulusonis

DEDICATION

Jody:

For Erica and Owen – for your endless support and encouragement!

Sue:

My daughters, Deren Parisi and Brynn Pione, for their patience.
My mother, Susan Cherry, for her patience and her babysitting.

ACKNOWLEDGMENTS

Thanks to all our friends and family for their support over the years.
Thanks to Sue Roulusonis for taking me up on my offer to help
transform my screenplay into a novel! ~ Jody
Thanks to Jody Clark for inviting me to play along! ~ Sue
Thanks to all of our early readers who offered great feedback.
A special thanks to my old friend and classmate, Ian Horne for his
funny, clever, and invaluable additions during the screenwriting process of
this story… York High Class of 88' Rules!

TRACK 1

York, Maine 1988

Walking through a high school cafeteria in the 80's was like taking a world tour in one room. Each table seemed to be their own country, recognizable by age, hair length, cleanliness, and accoutrements. At the center table sat the Cheerleaders. Their perky ponytails were held high by scrunchies, and they wore the latest high fashion outfits. Their table was cluttered with trays, pom-poms, cute purses, and Bonne Bell Lip Smacker Lip Glosses (cherry). Of course, their table was usually void of bodies, as the pattern of the social butterfly was to never remain in one place for too long. When they did land back at their center table, their conversations were usually one of two things.

If their voices were at a high pitch dolphin-esque shrill, they were talking about their recent shopping spree to Merry-Go-Round.

If their voices were almost whisper-soft, and they were huddled closer together, you knew exactly what they were talking about: Which of the jocks they hoped to *make love* to at the big party (paraphrasing).

As you would expect, the table directly next to them was the Jocks. Their short hair was plastered to their forehead with sweat, and each one wearing dual-colored numbered jerseys and varsity jackets. Depending on the season, their conversations were always the same and always loud. Their topics also fell into two categories:

(1) Rehashing and highly exaggerating the plays from the previous game. It's amazing how they could remember every detail about a silly game yet couldn't remember what the capital of their own state was (Augusta).

(2) Discussing which of the hot cheerleaders they planned on *boning* at the big party this weekend (not paraphrasing).

Residing at the next table were the side-parted, well-groomed, brushed-by-their-mothers hair, "serious students." AKA - the Nerds. They sat with perfect posture with their shirts neatly buttoned and properly ironed (also by their mothers). A few sported the cliché, yet requisite, pocket protectors, which consisted of a black pen, blue pen, red pen - in that order. A stack of paper bag-covered textbooks sat to the left of each lunch tray.

This was by far the quietest of the tables. If this was a Friday, they'd all be deep in concentration in a game of Dungeons and Dragons. But being a Monday, most of them had their noses firmly planted in some type of college-prep book. A few were entrenched in solving an equation for their Advanced Physics class (extra credit, of course).

Far off to the side, was the Band Geeks (not to be confused with the nerds). It was always off to one side to accommodate all of their cased instruments. So much so, that you could barely see the kids sitting there or even get to the table, for that matter. You always knew it was the day of a big game, because they all dressed in the same polyester uniforms. Their headgear was piled together in the middle of the table to protect the Shakos.

Scattered among the more prevalent clique tables were less definitive tables of seemingly random students attached by one distinguishing feature. For instance, the table of girls whose actual height was belied by the height of their hair. They were the ones who kept Aqua Net in business for so long, even as aerosols were considered dangerous to the ozone layer. Luckily, nobody at this table owned a lighter.

Another random table-group was the not-so-defined circle of baby-faced freshmen, thrown together like leftovers before they were even part of a real meal. Their table was covered with an assortment of paraphernalia which combined a little bit of every outer region. These mixed-race-different-hair-length babies were still unsure of their nationalities and spent much of their lunch break looking around, trying to decide who they wanted to be. They seemed to belong nowhere (at least until their visas were approved).

The room also had a color scheme from light to dark. The darkest regions of the cafeteria were occupied by the New Wavers,

Punk Rockers, and Goths. As far as everyone else was concerned, they were all somewhat of a combined group back then, but *they* knew the difference. Their divisions were by degrees of extremity, hair, makeup and music. The new wavers had the strangest and highest hair; Flock of Seagull-esque.

The punk rockers sported either buzz cuts or colorful Mohawks. Their attire consisted of dark colors, combat boots, studded bracelets, and either a Ramones or a Misfits shirt. The one common thread among these groups were they all preached nonconformity and individualism, which the rest of the school found ironic, considering they all dressed like one another.

In the slightly darker regions lounged the Deadheads, which was also ironic, considering the brightness of their tie-dyed clothing. Their bodies slumped across chairs as they munched on bags of chips. There was never a book in sight. Instead, they spent their time doodling Grateful Dead symbols; either the red & blue skull or the multi-colored bears (gummy bears??). When they weren't doodling or sleeping, they were defending their causes to anyone who would listen.

Their causes were simple:

(1) to legalize pot.

(2) to add hacky sack as an Olympic event.

Their hair was longer than most of the females at school. It was unkempt, unclean, and retained the scent of the various leaves they smoked in the school parking lot or bathroom earlier.

That same smell was shared in the air and in the hair of the occupants of the nearby table of the hair band rockers. AKA the Burnouts. This is where our story really begins. Their table was also messy and sans books. Their hair was longer than that of the deadheads, fuller than the aqua-nets, and bouncier than the cheerleaders. If genders had been reversed, they would have done more shampoo commercials than all of Charlie's Angels combined. No one 'hated them because they were beautiful.' Their attire was simple; ripped acid washed jeans and jackets covered by hair band pins. Not one of them owned a shirt that wasn't purchased at a concert (or washed).

The table was headed by four quintessential hair band rockers. Even though they were all friends and band mates, there was definitely a hierarchy of power. Otto Kringeman was the self-appointed leader of his crew. He was a walking stereotype of a bully, from the top of his greasy mullet, past his scowling face, over a black concert T-shirt and dirty jeans, down to his half-unlaced construction boots. Despite not being able to play an instrument, or carry a tune, or capable of writing an original song, Otto was also the self-appointed leader of their band.

Now, every good or even not-so-good leader needs a sidekick - a second in command, if you will. That was Tommy Stevens. Tommy was a walking poster child for Glam Rock. He was tall, slender, big permed hair, and he wore an acid-washed jean jacket with Bon Jovi's Slippery When Wet emblem on the back. His jeans were ripped, bleached, and accented by a blue bandana tied around his thigh.

The other two friends were Ricky Martell and Brett Cormier.

Even though they dressed like Otto and Tommy, and even though they could rock just as hard (actually, better), they seemed to be relegated to more of a minion status. You might say they were the original Wayne and Garth. They talked less than Otto & Tommy, not because they had less to say, but because their thoughts and ideas were usually drowned out or ignored by the two *leaders*. Somehow, the dynamic worked.

On that particular day, their conversation centered on the release of the new Poison record - "Open up and Say... Ahh." With all four Walkmans cranked up, they debated which song was the best. It didn't take long for Otto to get annoyed with everyone's wrong opinions, and his attention drifted over to the nerd's table. It had been at least two hours since he bullied, embarrassed, or had made fun of anyone. In other words, he was overdue.

He slipped off his headphones and motioned to Tommy to join him. They walked, no, they strutted their way over to the *nerd's table*. Otto watched two of them engrossed in a heated game of chess. Their concentration, seriousness, and pure nerdiness were too much for Otto to take. He reached over and knocked one of the chess pieces off the board.

"Check Mate, ya losers! Otto wins!" (The sign of a true leader is one who speaks in the third person. Right?)

No eye contact was made from the two innocent boys. They remained with heads down and still. It was almost like they were playing dead. A tactic which not only works well in the animal kingdom, but seems to work on Otto too, as his attention then turned to a chubby, geeky freshman sitting next to the chess players.

"Hey look, Tommy, speaking of losers, it's your baby brother, Alan."

Being Tommy's little brother, Alan was used to being picked on, especially by Tommy and Otto. Alan didn't look up. His face remained planted in his science book. Sadly, the 'playing dead' tactic never worked for Alan. More times than not, it only made things worse. This was proven when Tommy reached over and snatched up Alan's lunch bag and asked, "What did Mommy pack her favorite, perfect, geeky son today?"

The first item he pulled out was an olive loaf sandwich (with crust cut off). With zero interest in this, Tommy squished it. The next item he pulled out was a Ziploc bag which caused Tommy to shout, "Hey, those are my Chicken in a Biskits, ass face!"

Tommy shoved a handful of them into his mouth. Alan shook his head in disgust but said nothing. Instead, he glanced back down at his book while Tommy and Otto exchanged high fives.

Out of the corner of his eye, Otto noticed little Timmy Colwell giving him a look. "What are you looking at, you Phil Collins-lovin' mother fucker?"

Timmy's head and eyes quickly sank down. Otto was a rude and mean son of a bitch, but in this case, he spoke the truth (minus the *mother fucker* part). Timmy Colwell really was infatuated with anything Phil Collins (Genesis). Case in point, on that particular day, Timmy was wearing an *Invisible Touch* concert shirt. He didn't purchase it at the actual concert, of course. Timmy's parents would never have let him attend a rock & roll show.

A high schooler wearing a band shirt wasn't all that unusual. It was actually commonplace. What made little Timmy Colwell's situation a little weird was the other stuff; the other stuff being - his academic book covers. It was nerdy enough that some kids in high school still covered their books with brown paper bags, Timmy's covers were collages of everything Phil Collins. His science book was an ode to the aforementioned *Invisible Touch* record. His math book was an ode to *Face Value* (In the Air Tonight). His history book was an ode to *No Jacket Required*, and scribbled on the back of the books were random lyrics. So basically, if you ever found a book with a giant *Sussudio* written on it, you knew it belonged to Timmy Colwell.

Not wanting to leave anyone out, Otto turned his attention to the nerdiest of the bunch, Stuart Barnes. Stuart was a spitting image of Wormser from Revenge of the Nerds. Otto stared at Stuart's oversized geeky glasses, then reached over and snatched them off of his face and put them on.

"Wow," Otto mocked, "I feel so much smarter! I think I could even recite Newton's Theory of Relativity now."

As Tommy, Ricky, and Brett all laughed, Otto flicked the glasses to Stuart then turned, heading back to his table.

"It's Einstein's Theory, you burn out," Stuart blurted out.

With Stuart's words still hanging in the air, Otto stopped dead in his tracks. You could have heard a pin drop as all eyes fell on the two boys. Stuart immediately regretted his outburst. His face was bright red, and as he sat there trembling, he knew it was only a matter of time before a warm sensation flowed down his leg.

Before turning around, Otto smirked and pounded his fist into his hand. Finally, after what seemed like an eternity to Stuart, Otto turned and made his way back to the nerd's table. All at once, Stuart's friends slid their chairs back out of the way.

Meanwhile, Ricky and Brett were grinning ear to ear trying to guess Stuart's punishment.

"An atomic wedgie?" asked Ricky.

"Nah. I'm thinking a punch to the nuts," said Brett.

They both looked over at Tommy, who smiled with authority. "Nope. Otto's got a new move. *The Smiley*. Watch and learn."

Stuart continued to tremble in his chair, his eyes fixated on Otto's clenched left fist. With Stuart's attention distracted, Otto discreetly submerged his right hand down the back of his own pants running his finger up his butt.

Disgusted, Ricky and Brett curiously turned to Tommy.

"Did Otto just run his finger up his own ass?" whispered Ricky.

"Shhhh, keep watching," Tommy said.

All three guys, along with the whole lunch room, watched Otto cock his left fist back. Although scared shitless, Stuart still had the wherewithal to take off his glasses (after all, they were super expensive). Stuart placed his glasses on the table, closed his eyes, and braced himself. As soon as Otto saw Stuart's eyes shut tight, he turned and smirked at the entire cafeteria. He then lowered his left fist and instead of punching him, Otto rubbed the finger that was down his pants above Stuart's upper lip.

Still confused, Brett and Ricky chuckle. "But why is it called a Smiley?" questioned Brett. Tommy motioned for them to keep watching.

When Stuart realized that Otto didn't actually punch him, he slowly opened his eyes and let out a huge relieved exhale. But when he inhaled and caught the smell of what was on his upper lip, his face contorted in a mouth-open, teeth-baring smiling grimace.

The entire cafeteria burst out laughing. Tommy turned to Brett and Ricky and said, "And that my friends, is why they call it the Smiley!"

Brett and Ricky stood and gave Otto a standing ovation and bowed down as he strutted back to their table. After the many congratulatory high fives, they looked over to see an extremely embarrassed Stuart using a napkin to wipe off his shit-eating-grin.

***

In the mornings before school, the hallway floors would look shiny and pristine with the lockers reflecting off of them. Everything seemed the same color, and when the quietness bounced off of the walls, it was almost − religious.

Once school started, the quiet was broken, and the noise and conversations became almost sacrilege; unless one's idea of religion is the open worship of the Red Sox, Dungeon Master, George Michael (because you gotta have faith), or the tightest ass in jeans − and depending on who is talking, the last two could be the same.

After being trodden on by hundreds of feet, the floor's shine was quickly lost. Most of the male scuff marks were made by Air Jordans – ironically, the shoe Nike created for the man whose feet never stayed on the ground long.

Because locker assignments were based on homerooms, status boundaries weren't as clear in the school hallways. In the five minutes between classes, the hallways became a frenzy of bodies in a kaleidoscope of color. Some of them darted back and forth visiting neighbors across the way, while others formed small circles, standing around one open locker door. There was also the fervent two mashed together (almost *in* the locker), sucking as much face as they could in the minutes between classes.

The aromas wafting through varied by chance and proximity. One could get a mouthful of Love's Baby Soft if occupying the locker next to the cheerleader who was primping before study hall, or Drakkar, if one is unfortunate enough to have the locker next to the boy whose showering ritual could only be described as 'occasional'. Neither of them tasted good. Fortunately, one learns the routines of their locker neighbors before the first month of school ends and learns to work around it.

On that particular day, the noise level was an eleven on the loudness scale. The deeper tones were from the serious students comparing test scores. The higher-pitched squeals were either from certain girls or prepubescent boys (hard to tell which). There were various locker stereo systems (a boom box squeezed in sideways at the bottom), all punctuated by the regular beat of slamming locker doors, dropped books, high-fives, and dope-slaps.

Going from one end of the hallway to the other, conversations blended into a mish mash of, "Like, ohmygod, he's totally cute but I don't think that the distance from the y axis equals *ex* boyfriend because he didn't know what a microchip is gangsta, man he totally fuckin' rocked it hard!"

As the mish-mashed sentence ended, a smoke machine filled the hallway. Through the thick smoke, Otto and his crew emerged, strutting their shit. Their big hair was windblown by a giant fan, all the while Twisted Sister's "We're Not Gonna Take it" blared in the background. Well, that's how they pictured it in their heads, anyway. Pretty much the only part that was true was their attempt to strut their shit. Basically, this consisted of them ripping down random posters, shooting puny freshmen evil glares, and giving chicks creepy winks (followed by the perverted tongue wag).

Otto spotted Alan talking to a girl. He nudged Tommy, "Yo, check it out, your brother's talking to *a girl.*"

Tommy cracked a devious smile and he and Otto strutted closer. Otto placed himself between Alan and the girl and draped an arm over each of their shoulders.

"Lookie here, Tommy, your baby brother is talking to a chick. A cute one. You must be the chick that's been getting Alan's socks all sticky and stiff this past month." A puzzled look appeared on the girl's face. Otto was quick to clarify, "Alan uses socks for a nutrag." The poor girl cringed and looked at Alan. Otto shook his head, "I know, disgusting, right?" Why can't he use tissues like the rest of us."

Repulsed, the girl threw Otto's arm off of her shoulder and stormed away in disgust. Alan's face was red with embarrassment.

Watch out, Otto," Tommy warned, "when Alan gets nervous or embarrassed he gets awful gassy, and it looks like he's about to blow!"

Alan glared at the two bullies and almost yelled at them, but he didn't. Instead, he stormed off, with Otto and Tommy's sneering laughter echoing from behind.

The inside of Tommy's locker was a mess. On the top shelf were a couple of lighters, a dirty pink eraser, and one black, dusty Converse Hi-top sneaker with the laces dangling. Oh, and don't forget the obligatory can of Aqua Net. The bottom of his locker was filled with a mixture of dirty laundry, aerosol cans, and untouched homework assignments. Magazine pictures were plastered all over the inside of the locker door. There were scantily-clad pictures of Brinkley, Schiffer, Macpherson, and Locklear scattered about, but they weren't the centerpieces of his make-shift collage. That was reserved for pictures of Bon Jovi, Whitesnake, Poison, Motley Crue and Van Halen (Roth not Hagar).

A jagged shard of a mirror was stuck to the top inside corner. Tommy peered into the mirror and sprayed a long, steady fog-o-Aqua Net into his hair. When he finally finished, he admired himself one last time, gave a satisfied grunt, and then slammed the locker door shut. As the door closed, Tommy came face to face with Gina Cassidy.

Gina faked coughing and waved her hands in front of her face in an attempt to waft away the haze of hair spray. Tommy took in her appearance from top to bottom; from her stick-straight, blown-out, spiky hair, down to her tight black mini-skirt over black leggings, and military-style chunky black boots. His gaze paused twice on the way down — once on her midnight blue lips and then a second time over the swell at the top of her long black shirt. Gina jabbed him in the ribs when she noticed where his eyes were stopping.

"Lemme guess," Tommy began, "you wear black on the outside because black is how you feel in the inside?"

Without missing a beat, Gina responded with, "Lemme guess, you wear acid-wash on the outside to match all the acid you've done on the inside?"

"Lemme guess, you're really a colorblind girl who thinks that black is actually pink?"

"Pfft, that's the best you got?" Gina rolled her eyes at his lack of creativity.

They held their ground, giving each other a stare-down. Finally, they both cracked a smile, and Tommy yanked her in for a long, deep, and loud sloppy kiss.

They pulled apart long enough for Tommy to utter, "I'll see ya tonight."

Gina nodded. They kissed once more, putting their all into it (after all, it had to last them 'til later). With one last smile at Tommy, Gina turned and walked over to where her friend Heather was waiting.

Otto's voice interrupted Tommy's admiration of Gina's stride, "I can't believe you and Elvira are still dating."

"You've been saying that for two years now, Otto," chuckled Brett. "Besides, I think they're kinda good together."

"Shut up, Pud!" Otto barked, giving Brett a cold stare before turning back towards Tommy. "You do realize if she bites you three times, you'll turn into a vampire, right? You should be dating in your own species." And with that, Otto gazed down the hall.

Tommy, Ricky, and Brett all looked toward where Otto was leering, and there, standing with her friends was Jill MacNamara. Jill and her friends had the reputation of being the sluts of the school (reputation well-earned). Her back was to them and all you could see was a large head of hair flowing down to the bottom edge of a tight cropped tee with an expanse of bare back. Her even tighter acid-washed jeans barely held in her curvy bottom. Jill's slim legs tapered down into slouchy black leather heeled boots. As if she knew they were gawking at her, she turned and flashed them a smile before whipping her hair around as she turned away.

"She can Tawny Kitaen my car any day," Otto drooled. He turned again to Tommy, "Your little vampire must really know how to suck your … blood, if you choose her over that." This was Otto's way of blatantly challenging the order of their friendship.

Tommy had every intention of defending his choice of why he dated Gina. His eyes raised up and met Otto's. A smug and cocky look came over Otto's face as he awaited Tommy's attempt to stand up to him. Tommy's eyes lit up with anger. Ricky and Brett looked at each other wondering (hoping) if Tommy was actually going to stand up to Otto this time. Their curiosity was quick-lived. For all Tommy could muster was, "Whatever, Otto." Tommy stormed off and Otto just laughed. All was right in the hierarchy of power.

Across the hall, Heather gave Gina the same interrogation. "I can't believe you and Jon Bon Bonehead are still together?"

"Oh come on, Heather, not this again."

"Seriously, Gina, they're nothing but bullies and losers."

Gina and Heather watched Otto ogling Jill MacNamara and the slut squad.

"Look who he hangs out with," Heather continued. "They don't get any more disgusting than Otto Kringeman!"

"He's nothing like Otto! He's different."

"Uh huh. Like when you guys are alone?" Heather interrupted.

"Well…yea," Gina answered.

"And how often has that been lately?" Heather asked.

Gina's gaze swung back to Tommy. It was just in time to see him get angry at Otto and then see him back down. She sighed.

"Who are we looking at? Jon Bon burn out?"

Gina and Heather turned to see their friend Kelley Lambert. Kelley smiled then reached over to borrow Gina's lipstick. Kelley's magenta–dyed hair was put up in multiple tiny pigtails, and she was rockin' a "Meat is Murder" tee shirt by "The Smiths."

"I was just asking Gina, for the thousandth time, what exactly she sees in Tommy Stevens," said Heather.

"Did you mention he's a bully?" questioned Kelley.

Heather nodded.

"Did you mention that his friends are"…

"Losers?" The two girls exclaimed in unison then laughed.

A pissed-off glare shot from Gina's eyes.

"Oh come on Gina, the dude uses more hairspray than all the cheerleaders combined." Kelley nodded at Heather's observation.

"You guys don't know the Tommy that I know. He's funny. And he can be sweet sometimes… in his own way. I mean, underneath all that hair spray… and hair … and ripped jeans, and the acid washed jackets… there's a really great guy." Sadly, Gina smiled as she watched him storm off from his friends.

TRACK 2

York, Maine is the classic seaside town. Its population nearly triples in the summer months. From Memorial Day through Labor Day, tourists flock there from New York, Connecticut, Vermont, and even Canada. Oh, and let's not forget the Mass-holes (affectionately). Yup, lots and lots of Mass-holes (less affectionate). From the huge harbor houses to the ones up on the cliff overlooking the Atlantic: If you were to judge the town based on these, you would assume it to be a super elite white collar town. Despite the wealthy areas of town, however, its median income is only just slightly higher than that of middle class. The fact of the matter is, the majority of the town is hard-working, blue-collar workers living in modest houses.

The Stevens' were one of those families. Their raised-ranch-one-car-garage-white-paint-peeled-picket-fence-house was in a quintessential neighborhood; 27 Flintlock Road, to be exact. The entire neighborhood was filled with similar style houses and quiet streets. The kind of streets you'd have no problem letting your little ones ride their bikes unsupervised. It was the type of neighborhood where it was commonplace to see twenty kids playing an after dinner game of Wiffle ball. It was also the type of neighborhood that was not only profitable (money-wise) for the Ice Cream man, but was very profitable (candy-wise) for the kids on trick or treat night.

It was nearly 5:00 PM, and Mrs. Stevens was in the kitchen happily preparing tonight's meatloaf dinner. Happily, not because of the meatloaf per se, but because tonight was the rare occasion that the whole family would be home for dinner.

Mr. Stevens, who would sometimes work late, came home on time and was already in the shower. Alan, who was usually at the library studying or at Stuart's house playing D & D, was sitting at the kitchen table doing homework. The fact that Tommy was also home made it the rarest of occasions. He was usually out with 'that Otto kid' doing God-knows-what or was out with Gina doing – *other* things. Not wanting to dwell on what any of that entailed, Mrs. Stevens decided to focus on her gratitude that they were all home together.

For tonight anyway, Tommy was content with spending a little alone time with his Nintendo system. He was sprawled out on the couch; his head on one armrest, his sneakers on the other. With the game pad clutched in both hands, and his thumbs moving feverishly, he intently stared at the TV (19" RCA).

From the kitchen, Mrs. Stevens called out, "Tommy?"

Tommy heard her but chose to ignore her. He ignored

everybody when he was in the Nintendo Zone.

Knowing that he was in 'the zone' made her yell even louder, "TOMMY!"

The zone was broken. Tommy threw the controller down in disgust and pulled himself up off of the couch and yelled back to his mother, "What? What Ma?!"

His irritation continued as he lumbered through the kitchen door. "What? Can't you see I'm busy blowing things up in there?"

"First of all, don't yell at me like that. I'm your mother, not one of your school buddies."

Tommy's scowl quickly turned to a smile as he burst out laughing, "School buddies? What am I, like in 5th grade?"

Mrs. Stevens simply rolled her eyes at her son. She was used to never saying the right or cool things around her kids.

Honey, I'm just saying, you've had your face in front of that television for two hours straight. Why don't you and Alan go outside and play ball or something?"

Alan, who was sitting at the kitchen table doing his homework, looked up at his mother in horror as Tommy belted out a loud, obnoxious laugh.

"Yeah, right! Alan play ball? Ha! Although, from what I heard coming out of his room last night, he does more *ball* handling than Larry Bird."

Alan's face turned beet red as he quickly fumbled to put his Walkman headphones on.

"Thomas! Watch your mouth!" his mother admonished.

"C'mon, Ma. Have you ever seen fat ass do anything athletic? Ever?"

"What did I just say to you? And that is no way to talk about your brother. Besides, he's not fat! He's just a little husky."

It was the classic parent euphemism. As the words 'husky' still hung in the air, it caused Tommy to laugh even harder, and caused Alan to crank his Walkman even louder. Seeing this, Tommy snatched the headphones off of Alan's head.

"What'cha listening to, there, husky boy?"

Alan feebly attempted to grab the headphones back, but Tommy easily fended him off. With his left hand on Alan's face, he kept him at arms-length while he placed the headphones to his ear. As a sole voice sang mournfully, Tommy's face turned to disgust.

"Who the hell is that?" exclaimed Tommy.

Before Alan could reach across the table, Tommy saw the cassette case - Richard *Marx*. Tommy released Alan's face, shook his head, and tossed the headphones back at his brother. "Queer bait!"

Mr. Stevens entered the kitchen, just in time to hear Tommy's last comment. "Hey! Enough, Tommy! You keep picking on your brother like that, and you'll be cruisin' for a bruisin'! You need to start showing him a little more respect."

"Him?" Tommy laughed in disbelief.

"Yes, him. He's your brother. As a matter of fact, you need to start showing all of us more respect. 'Friends come and go, but family will always be there.'"

"I know, I know. You can pick your nose, but you can't pick

your family," Tommy mocked. Tommy then proceeded to grab Alan's finger and force it up his nose. "But you can pick your family's nose!"

Alan angrily removed his finger from his nose, and all Mr. and Mrs. Stevens could do was to shake their heads at Tommy.

"One day, son, you will realize how important your family is. 'Family is a treasure chest worth more than a mountain of gold.'"

Mrs. Stevens smiled and nodded at her wise, clichéd filled husband. "Your father is right, Tommy."

Arrogantly, Tommy laughed, "'Cruisin' for a bruisin'? 'Mountain of gold'? Who the hell talks like that? You should quit your job and start writing fortune cookies! Save your stupid clichés for someone who actually gives a crap!"

With that, he stormed over and swung open an upper cabinet door and reached inside for a box of Chicken in a Biskit.

"Tommy, we're going to eat in twenty minutes," Mrs. Stevens pleaded.

"Yea, so?" He slammed the box down on the counter. He reached in the cabinet under the sink for a bottle of bleach. He then rummaged through one of the drawers until he found a pair of scissors. He gathered up the crackers and bleach in his arms, and with the scissors dangling from one thumb, he started to walk out of the room. Mr. and Mrs. Stevens looked at each other and shook their heads.

"I can't believe you keep ruining your jeans," said Mrs. Stevens. "They should sell them in stores like that, already bleached and cut."

Tommy stared at his mom as if she had three heads. "Pfft. Dumbest. Idea. EVER." And with that, he exited the kitchen.

Defeated and helpless, Mrs. Stevens looked over at her husband. He met her look with a reassuring smile and put his hand on her shoulder ad said, "He's just going through a phase." Slowly, Mrs. Stevens nodded in agreement. "And by the way, I think your pre-cut & pre-bleached jeans idea is a winner, dear."

"Aw, thanks," she smiled as she gave her husband a huge kiss.

Disgusted by his family's *PDA,* Alan returned the headphones to his ears and mumbled to the Richard Marx cassette case, "You, my friend, you are very much an underrated singer/songwriter."

***

Mr. Stevens was a simple man – not unintelligent, just not very complicated. He had a steady job as Head of Maintenance at the Portsmouth Navy Yard which provided him the means to feed, clothe, and house his family (with the opportunity for overtime when needed). He took pride in that work and what it allowed him to do. He took the same pride in his appearance, keeping his hair trim and combed, collars lightly starched, a not-for-power-tie neatly tied, and pressed pants. A solid worker, a solid *man.*

He was content, with no aspirations of grandeur and no desire to be anyone or anything other than who and what he was. There was no need, he had everything he wanted.

His sons felt differently, he knew. Alan wanted to succeed, to do something that would make him feel like he made a difference. Tommy, well, Tommy was a little lost right now, but Mr. Stevens was confident that one day he would find his way.

Mr. Stevens did everything he could to make sure his family always had what they needed, and when they didn't feel the same, he would recite something (anything) motivational or inspiring he'd ever heard or seen. Usually, they came from the motivational calendars and wall hangings he'd see in the offices of his higher-ups as he was emptying their trash barrels.

While these clichéd spoutings seemed trivial to his sons (especially Tommy), they were decidedly more well-received by the boys than his declarations of love. Mr. Stevens used them as proxies for the softer words, hoping they would read the underlining simple fact that they had his complete support and that there was nothing he wouldn't do for them. Nothing.

Mrs. Stevens lived to prove the example that people should be made to feel appreciated. She took special care of everyone; her clients at the Pine Ridge Nursing Home, the patrons at the public library where she worked part-time, and even better care of her husband and her boys. One could argue she spent more time with Alan, but that was just because Alan spent many hours studying in the library, and Tommy didn't even know there was one in town; if he did, he didn't know where it was.

She was an old-school mother, June Cleaver-minus-the-pearls, at home most of the time taking care of her family. Like her husband, she wouldn't have it any other way. Her disposition showed easy on her face - a face which was always smiling.

Right now, her smile was warmly directed at Alan, who was eagerly talking about the upcoming Odyssey of the Mind meet in Fryeburg. In between bites, he segued into a monologue about his college-prep trigonometry class, his excited speech slowing as he lamented his 96 average.

"Aw, I feel your pain," sympathized Tommy, "I have a 27 average in Gym."

Mr. and Mrs. Stevens glared at Tommy.

"Oh, come on guys, like we're supposed to feel sorry that poor Alan only has a 96 average in Triggernometry? Besides, you're a friggin' freshman, why the hell are you taking college-prep classes already?" questioned Tommy.

"Never too early to be thinking about your future," pointed out Mr. Stevens.

"I think it's wonderful," boasted Mrs. Stevens.

Tommy rolled his eyes in disgust, "Alan could take a major dump and you'd think it's wonderful."

Both Mr. and Mrs. Stevens shot Tommy a look. "Speaking of your future," said Mr. Stevens, "have you thought anymore about your plans after graduation? I really think you should consider that trade school I told you about."

"Dad, I'm not going to that stupid, retarded trade school you keep yapping about."

Before Mr. Stevens could yell at Tommy regarding his insolence, Mrs. Stevens interrupted, "Maybe your dad can get you a job at the

Yard?"

"Yea Ma, cuz I've always dreamt of becoming a janitor."

"Your father's not just a janitor, Tommy, he's the head of maintenance."

"Custodial supervisor to be precise," mumbled Mr. Stevens.

"Ohhhh, the boss of the janitors. Where do I sign up?" Tommy joked.

"Make fun all you want, Tommy, but that job puts food on the table and a roof over your head."

Again, Tommy rolled his eyes. The eye roll was a prerequisite of teenagers and Tommy had mastered it. The thought of Tommy attending any sort of school after graduation greatly amused Alan causing him to laugh, "I heard Cumberland Farms is hiring. Better yet, I think the Big Apple is looking for a gas attendant."

Tommy shot a glare Alan's way, "Shut up, ass wipe!"

"Hey! Language!" warned Mrs. Stevens.

"For your information, butt wipe, while you're taking your stupid little college-prep classes, my band will be rockin' clubs all over New England."

Again, Alan cracked up. "Yea right. You guys got booed off the stage at the winter talent show when your fearless leader, Otto, forgot the words."

Tommy was pissed, but he knew Alan spoke the truth. Otto was a disaster in the band, especially the day of the talent show. Not only did Otto forget the words, he tried to play it off by doing some sort of head bangin' dance then tripped into Tommy's drum set.

"Yea…well… our school sucks!" Tommy shot back.

"No, it's because Otto sucks," Alan mumbled under his breath.

"What did you just say, ya little sh"…

"Enough you two!" pleaded Mrs. Stevens. "Geez Louise, can't we just enjoy a family dinner for a change. You boys need to start being more supportive of one another."

"Your mother is right," said Mr. Stevens. "You should be proud of your brother's academic accomplishments, Tommy."

Alan proudly straightened his posture, looking over at Tommy.

"And you, Alan, you need to be more supportive of Tommy's musical ambitions," added Mrs. Stevens.

"But Ma"…

"No buts, Alan. "If they work hard and dedicate themselves, then there's no reason why their band can't be successful."

Tommy straightened and sneered over at Alan.

"And who knows, maybe one day his band will sell out the Fenway Park," Mrs. Stevens sweetly spoke.

Both brothers looked at each other and burst out laughing.

"They don't do concerts there, Ma," laughed Tommy.

"Well, they should. It would be a great venue for a show."

"And it's Fenway Park, Ma, not *the* Fenway Park," joked Alan.

As both brothers chuckled at their mom's expense, Mr. Stevens put his hand on his wife's and winked, "I think Fenway would be a great place to see a show, dear."

She smiled appreciatively at her husband, and for the next few minutes, all was right and quiet in the Stevens' household. There was no arguing, no sarcastic comments, no threats of sibling dismemberment…everyone was too busy chowing down on Mrs. Stevens' meatloaf(w/extra ketchup), her homemade mashed potatoes(w/dab of sour cream), and creamed corn(Market Basket not Jolly Green Giant).

Taking in the scene of her family at the table, Mrs. Stevens' mind flashed back to other family dinners when the boys were younger; Tommy sitting at the table, his feet unable to reach the floor from his chair, and Alan in the high chair next to him. She remembered pretending not to notice when Tommy would grab a handful of the detested peas and put them in front of Alan, who giggled when he pushed them off his tray and onto the floor. She remembered when they were both in elementary school, and first-grader Alan would listen with rapt attention to Tommy's dinner conversation about the perils of fourth grade, exaggerating for his little brother's benefit about the amount of homework they would get (because teachers got meaner as you got older). In those days, family dinners were every night and not an occasional event. She really missed those days, especially Tommy's sixth-grade year when he would help her cook, hoping to learn enough to have a conversation with little Lucy-from-the-other-side-of-town, whose favorite class was Home Economics …

Her nostalgic moment quickly faded as Tommy began to speak, "Hey guys, why don't you ask Alan about his new little girlfriend?"

With an equal amount of shock and excitement (well, 60/40), the Stevens' looked at each other, then over at Alan.

"You have a girlfriend, Alan???" Mrs. Stevens tone just changed the ratio to 80/20. The ratio wasn't lost on Alan as his face turned bright red.

"No, she's not my girlfriend. And thanks to Tommy and Otto, she'll probably never talk to me again."

Proudly Tommy chuckled.

"Are you guys picking on your brother at school again?" questioned Mr. Stevens.

"I'm really not a fan of you still hanging out with that Otto Kringeman," added Mrs. Stevens. "I think he's a bad influence on you. You used to be such a sweet boy before you started hanging out with him."

"Hanging out?" interrupted Alan. You mean before he started worshiping him. Otto is Tommy's hero.

"Shut up, faggot," snapped Tommy.

"Hey!" yelled Mr. Stevens. "You know we don't tolerate that kind of talk. I think your mother is right. Your attitude directly stems from hanging out with these unsavory types.

"Unsavory types? Who the hell talks like that?"

"This is exactly what we're talking about; your blatant disrespect for your family." Before Mr. Stevens continued chastising his son, his eye caught the kitchen clock. "Oh shit. We gotta get going, honey."

"Language!" sarcastically interjected Tommy.

Mrs. Stevens glanced at the clock and nodded in agreement to her husband.

"Where you guys going?" questioned Alan.

"Town Hall meeting," answered Mrs. Stevens.

"Whoa!" joked Tommy. "You guys are livin' on the wild side."

Pretending to ignore his sarcasm, Mrs. Stevens began clearing the table. "Honey, leave it. The boys can clean up in here," said Mr. Stevens.

Assuming this didn't apply to him, Tommy slid his chair out and started to leave. "*Both* of you boys can clean up in here. Understood?" The famous eye roll was quickly followed by the equally popular sigh. "It's about time you helped out around here."

Before Tommy could argue or make some sort of communist regime comment, his parents were gone out of the kitchen and out of the house. Alan, being the dutiful son, already started clearing off the table. Tommy let out another irritated sigh as he moved back towards the table. He glanced over at the bowl of mashed potatoes, and a sly smile appeared on his face. He then looked over to Alan and saw that he too had a sly smile on his face.

"You thinking what I'm thinking?" asked Tommy.

"It's been a while," smiled Alan.

A moment later, they each had a handful of potatoes and were competitively staring at one another. "Loser cleans the kitchen," Tommy instructed. Alan nodded. "One, two, three….go!" Go!"

Simultaneously, they flung their potatoes upward. Two squishy splat sounds were heard as they hit the kitchen ceiling. Both brothers giggled at the sound as they stared up at the potatoes stuck to the ceiling. They had been playing this 'whose potatoes can stick the longest game' since they were little kids. And although it had been a long time since their last match, their child-like competitiveness immediately took over. Profanities spewed from both brother's mouths as they cheered on their potatoes. In the throes of excitement, Alan broke character and yelled, "C'mon you dirty little whore, stick…stick…stick!"

"Whoa," exclaimed a shocked Tommy. "Language!" And with that, both brothers began to laugh out loud. It's the most they had bonded in months…years. Unfortunately, their little brotherly bonding moment would be short-lived. With their eyes fixed on the ceiling, they watched Tommy's clump of potatoes released its grasp on the ceiling and in one super slow motion, fell to the floor.

Alan jumped up and down relishing in his rare thrill of victory. Tommy clutched his fist, and with his hung his head low, mouthed the words, *Fuck me.* The agony of defeat was something Tommy wasn't used to, especially to his little geek of a brother. Tommy quickly composed himself and even reached out his hand for a congratulatory handshake.

"Congratulations, ya little shit."

Alan proudly smiled and returned his brother's gesture. He did it. Alan finally earned his brother's respect. Tommy grasped Alan's sweaty, chubby hand, gave him a nod of approval, then proceeded to pull Alan in close and kneed him in the nuts. Alan fell to the floor writhing in pain (testicles in the stomach kinda pain).

"Now clean up this mess before Mom and Dad get home!" Tommy ordered.

"But…but I won," winced Alan.

"And yet you're still the loser. Rock on little brotha!"

With that, Tommy gave the classic head bangers pose; tongue out, head thrusting forward, his long hair flying wildly to and fro, and topped off with the classic rock & roll hand gesture.

"I'll be in my room. Send Gina up when she gets here. And don't think of disturbing us. Got it?"

Alan was still nursing his wounds and didn't even acknowledge him. It wasn't until Tommy left that Alan finally picked himself off the floor and begrudgingly started to clean the kitchen.

***

It would be impossible for anyone to guess the paint color of Tommy's room. His walls, like his locker, were completely plastered by posters; Bon Jovi, Poison, Cinderella, Ratt, Ozzy Osbourne, Twisted Sister– no one without a glorious head of hair. The room was a mess, with bureau drawers open part-way to all the way (depending on the necessity of the items inside), and clothing strewn about the floor – except for his Bon Jovi jacket, which was carefully hung on the bedpost. A full, dirty ashtray and a bong sat in plain sight on his nightstand. In the place of honor, next to his bed on the other side, was a Pioneer dual-cassette with turntable stereo system in a glass cabinet. It was the only item (aside from the bong) in his room not surface-covered in dust and cigarette ash – and that was only because it was covered in fingerprints from his consistent use. The two large speakers on either side of the console, however, had enough dust and ash on them to show his finger-written 'FUCK'.

Tommy sprawled out on his bed idly flipping through a Sports Illustrated Swimsuit Edition (Covergirl -Elle Macpherson). Besides the smile on his face, he wore oversized headphones, which were plugged into the aforementioned kick-ass stereo system. With his eyes bugging out over Elle, and his head moving to the beat of the song, Tommy didn't even notice Gina enter his room.

Gina walked in and closed the door behind her. On the back side of the door were three mini posters: Madonna, Michael Jackson, and George Michael - all punctured with holes. George had a number of darts stuck in his eyes and nose while Madonna was punctured across her chest. MJ had been adorned with Sharpie devil-ears and a mustache, and the B in the poster had been darkly scribbled over with an S, now reading, "SAD."

Gina stood in front of the bed looking down at Tommy, who still hadn't acknowledged her coming in. Finally, she kicked at one of his legs that was dangling off the bed. Tommy gave her a quick nod of acknowledgement then went back to jamming and 'reading.' Gina threw a glare his way then headed over to his stereo and hit the stop button on the tape player.

"Gina! What are you doing? I'm trying to listen to the new Poison tape!

"So," exclaimed Gina, "I didn't come over to watch you listen to a tape...or to watch you drool over your trashy magazines either."

"It's not trashy. It's Sports Illustrated. The swimsuit edition," he smiled.

"No wonder why young girls have self-esteem and body issues, look at the crap you guys are looking at."

"Yea, they're pretty hot, huh?" Tommy said as he stared longingly at Elle.

"Pfft! They're nothing but fake, airbrushed, anorexic bimbos!"

"Yea, they're pretty hot, huh?" Tommy smiled up at Gina. It was the kind of smile that made it impossible for her to stay mad at him.

"Don't give me that smile, Tommy Stevens."

He pulled himself off the bed and crept over to his stereo. He unplugged his headphones then pressed the play button on the cassette deck. As Poison's *"Nothin' but a Good Time"* blared out, he turned and smiled wider. He shot Gina his sexiest bedroom eyes as he strutted towards her. The music was piercing her ear drums, and the sight of her headbangin' boyfriend sexily strutting towards her was absolutely ridiculous…yet she loved every minute of it.

Less than a second later, their lips were locked and making out (sloppily…always sloppily). Tommy backed her into the wall, pressing her against his Guns & Rose's *Appetite for Destruction* poster. As Brett Michael's vocals overtook the room, Tommy's hand overtook Gina's breast (the left one…always the left one first). His lips moved down her neck, just behind her ear - that was her spot.

"I've been thinking about you all day, babe," Tommy whispered.

"Really? What exactly have you been thinking about?" she whispered back.

"The taste of your lips…your soft skin…your sweet smell"…

Gina loved hearing him list his thoughts about her. What girl wouldn't, right?

"What else?" she whispered.

"Your big brown eyes…your big, perfect tits" (yup, he went there).

Surprisingly, however, his comment didn't kill the moment. Secretly, Gina loved that he loved her breasts. After all, they were pretty big, and she was proud of that! What girl wouldn't be? Not to mention, she loved that he called them *perfect*, especially considering she always thought her right nipple was slightly larger than her left. The truth was; she loved all his compliments – even the perverted ones.

As Gina basked in his compliments, Tommy's left hand made its way up her leg and onto her thigh. Gina met his hand with hers.

"Tommy, we can't," she said as she lowered his hand from her thigh.

In his best convincing voice, Tommy spoke, "Sure we can." My parents won't be home for a while."

Again, she thwarted his left hand from reaching her promised land. Undeterred, the horny headbanger attempted to conquer her other thigh with his right hand.

Gina smirked at his persistence, but again denied him access. Tommy knew he needed to unleash his secret weapon (Not *that* weapon. Get your minds out of the gutter!) Tommy's lips headed towards her neck, more specifically, behind her ear — Gina's spot.

Her defenses, along with her knees, were weakened. The momentum was his, and they both knew it. His troops were well on their way in accomplishing their mission. Gina gave a last ditch, feeble attempt to deny him.

"Tommy, we can't."

"Why, babe? You raggin' it?"

And just like that, Tommy's momentum came to a grinding halt.

"No, I'm not 'raggin' it, you idiot!" She snapped as she pushed him away.

"Then why aren't you succumbing to my charms?" he pouted.

He really was an idiot. A big, pathetic one. But he was Gina's idiot, and she adored him, despite his inappropriate comments.

"Oooh no. Don't go giving me your fake puppy-dog eyes, Mister." Gina couldn't help but to smirk at the sight of Tommy batting his eyes at her.

"You just got here. Where do you have to go that's so important?"

"I'm supposed to meet my mom at the mall in like ten minutes. She's taking me shopping for an early birthday present."

"Birthday?" questioned Tommy.

Irritated that her own boyfriend didn't remember her birthday, Gina glared at him in disbelief. When her irritated look changed to one of sadness, Tommy bursted out laughing, "Relax, Gina. I know your birthday is this Saturday. Man, you shoulda seen your face. You looked like you were gonna cry for Christ's sake."

Gina gave him a playful, yet hard, smack in the arm. "Idiot! You better have gotten me something good," she joked.

"Good? Dude, what I got you is borderline unbelievable!"

"Really?" Gina was intrigued. "What did you get me?"

Tommy shrugged, "Guess you'll have to wait until your birthday."

"Yea, yea, yea. You totally didn't get me anything yet, did you?"

"Maybe I did, maybe I didn't. Well, you better get going. Don't wanna keep Mommy waiting."

Gina shook her head, smiled, then leaned in for a good-bye kiss (yes, a sloppy one). "See you tomorrow," she whispered and headed towards his door.

Tommy's eyes went directly to her ass. Hypnotized. Mesmerized. Before she could open the door he caved, "Fine! I'll give you your present now."

Gina's ass – 1   Tommy – 0

"Really?" Gina smiled and blatantly adjusted her boobs in her bra. "You don't have to."

"No, it's okay," caved Tommy. "Besides, I've been so excited ever since I came up with the idea. I'm dying to see your reaction." He took her by the hand and sat her on his bed.

"Ready?" Tommy asked.

Gina excitedly nodded yes. Tommy reached under his pillow and pulled out a small package wrapped in what appeared to be a brown paper lunch bag.

"I wrapped it myself," he proudly boasted.

"Hmm, I would have never guessed," joked Gina. "Wait, this isn't the same thing as last year, is it?"

Tommy shrugged, "I don't even remember what I"...

"Condoms," Gina interrupted.

"Ohhhh ya," he smiled, "the Magnums. That was a good gift."

"That was a ridiculous gift," Gina corrected.

"What are you talking about?" Hello, don't you remember? They were ribbed - for *your* pleasure. Besides, I didn't hear you complaining later that night, now did I? Huh? Huh?"

She blushed slightly, then smiled as she snatched the present from him. Curiously, she examined the over-abundance of scotch tape used then checked the weight.

"Hmmm, definitely too light for the Magnums," she smirked. "Actually, it feels too light to be anything. You sure there's something in here?"

"I'll give you three hints," he said. "Summer. Great Woods. Front row!"

Gina's eyes widened. "Oh my God!" she exclaimed as she unwrapped the package faster. "You're taking me to see Depeche Mode this summer at Great Woods!!!"

Hurriedly, she ripped through the wrapper and pulled out two tickets. Upon closer examination, her excitement faded to disappointment.

"Whitesnake?" she asked, dejected.

"Yup! And with Great White as their opening act!" Tommy snatched the tickets from her to get an9other glimpse of the two beauties. He was so busy admiring them that he didn't even notice her disappointment. The more she watched his child-like excitement, the less disappointed she felt. She consoled herself with the fact that it's the thought that counts, and he *did* get her a gift ahead of time, instead of waiting until the last minute.

"And you saw where we are sitting, right?" Tommy shoved the tickets close to her face. "Your man got you a little front row action!!"

It was obvious by his enthusiasm and his proud look that he truly thought he had gotten her the perfect gift. Of course, part of her would have rather gotten the condoms (I mean, they *were* ribbed for her pleasure). But the other part of her was happy that he was happy. Anything they did together was fine with her. She glanced down at the tickets, smiling while she shook her head. She leaned over and kissed him on the cheek.

"Thank you. It'll be fun." Gina stood up, kissed him again then made her way to the door. She spied the Sharpie on the floor, picked it up and walked over to the wall where the Ujena Splash Swimwear calendar was tacked and made a bold circle around May 20th. "Two more weeks!" she smiled happily.

"What are you talking about, babe? The concert ain't until this summer."

"I'm not talking about the concert," Gina glared. "I'm talking about our prom? Remember?"

"Oh yea. That," Tommy sighed.

"Please tell me your tux is all set? You owe me big time for last year's prom." Tommy looked at her, stupidly. "Uh, *hello*, Tommy, you ditched me so you and the three stooges could follow Bon Jovi around for like two weeks?"

"Oh yeaaa. Right. Junior Prom vs. the *Slippery When Wet* tour." Tommy laughed, "Uh, *hello*? Can you say 'no brainer'? Not to mention, Cinderella was the opening act."

"Like I said," Gina began, "you owe me big time this year."

"Yeah, yeah. Don't sweat it, babe."

"Oh, I also have something I wanna run by you," Gina said.

"Yea, I thought you might." Tommy's face turned a bit more serious, and he prepared himself for the worse.

"I, um, kinda told Heather and Michael they could go to dinner and the prom with us. That okay?"

"That's what you wanted to run by me?"

"Yea. I didn't want you to be surprised that night, that's all."

"Are you sure there isn't something *else* you wanna share with me?" Tommy questioned.

"Like what?"

"I don't know. You tell me."

"Uhh, no? Why are you being so weird, Tommy?"

"Whatever. Forget it." Tommy's attention went back to his magazine.

"Umm, okay. I guess I'll see you tomorrow?"

Tommy gave her a nod that was nowhere near sincere. Before Gina exited the room, she stopped and reached into her purse. "Oh, I almost forgot. Here, I made this for you."

She handed him a mix tape. Tommy's face contorted as he read the titles, "The Cure? The Smiths? Echo & the Bunnymen? I've never even heard of this crap. Rem?"

"It's R.E.M." Gina corrected. "I just thought you could broaden your horizons a bit. You know, listen to some of the bands that I like."

Tommy chortled, "Do I have to dress all in black when I listen to it?" At Gina's stare, he turned pleading, "Come on, Babe, check out these names; Depeche Mode? More like, Depressed Mode."

"For your information, there, smart ass, their song, "Somebody" is the prom song this year."

"Somebody?" Tommy laughed. "As in, *somebody* slit my wrists so I don't have to listen to this crap?"

When he saw the disappointment in her eyes, he softened a bit. "Thanks, babe. I promise I'll listen to it."

"Uh huh. See you tomorrow, ya knucklehead," she affectionately said, "and make sure your tux is ready in time," she reminded him.

He gave her a thumbs up and smiled at her. When she was gone, he looked down at the mix tape and read some more names, "Jesus &Mary Chain? Joy Division? Siouxsie and the Banshees? Pfft." He shook his head in disgust and proceeded to toss the tape into a box of random tapes.

TRACK 3

The school bell rang, and the hallway was once again flooded with students. Gina exited her Psychology class and headed towards her locker. First-period Psychology with Mr. Layne was pretty much dreaded by most. Partly because most were still trying to wake up, and the last thing they wanted first thing in the morning was to be inundated with theories of Freud or Pavlov (or Pavlov's stupid dog). And partly because the last thing you wanted to deal with first-period (or any period) was the *in-your-face, take-no-shit* teaching style of Mr. Layne. Gina, however, loved his straight-forwardness and was immensely intrigued by psychology and sociology (Junior year-also with Mr. Layne).

Debating students on their views was his specialty. In Gina's sophomore year, he debated Adam Gosmer for 37 minutes straight about suicide. Adam's opinion: It's your own life, and you have the right to live or choose to die. We all come into this life alone and leave alone, so we should be able to live (or die) however we want. Gina tended to side with Adam (More on this later). And why wouldn't she, most of the music she listened to was dark and depressing and filled with introspective lyrics. Lyrics that praised individuality and at times even romanticized suicide.

Adam Gosmer started his high school career off as more of a 'New Waver/Alternative music type kid. His hair used to droop in front covering up most of his face. As his high school years went by, he slowly transformed into more of a Punker. Now, as a senior, his hair transformed into a jet-black Mohawk. He had multiple piercings on his ears (even his *right* ear) and wore a black studded leather jacket with emblems of the "Dead Kennedys" and "Suicidal Tendencies" on the back. Gina admired his non-conformist attitude and loved that he had such a passionate opinion about everything.

Adam also considered himself deeply profound. Case in point - the bath house at the beach. On its back wall was sprayed some of Adam's handy work - "What is life? Is it what you think? Or what I think? Either or it does not matter." (I told you- deeply profound). Adam loved taking the opposite point of view, especially when it went against the norm. Of course, this played right into Mr. Layne's wheelhouse. The more Adam disagreed with him, the louder Mr. Layne would get. And the louder he got, the more that vein in his forehead would bulge out. Their back and forth verbal battles were must-see-TV. The students were not only mesmerized, but were highly entertained by it.

On the particular day of the suicide debate, Gina was in

complete agreement with Adam. His conviction, his argument…it just made sense to her. We as individuals have the right to choose how we live our lives. We have the right to cover our bodies in tattoos or piercings. Hell, we even have the right to self-mutilation if we so choose. And we sure as hell have the right to choose how we end our life. But somewhere between Adam's initial sentence and when Mr. Layne's vein started to bulge, Gina found herself being swayed the other way; at least with regards to suicide.

Mr. Layne argued vehemently (and loudly) that suicide, was an extremely selfish act. He showed compassion at the loneliness and sadness someone must feel to commit this act, but he also painted a vivid picture of the aftermath. A picture of the friends and family left to deal with this tragedy.

By the end of the class, Gina went from being 100% in agreement with Adam Gosmer, to being completely on the fence. The fact that a 37-minute debate could make her rethink her beliefs; she looked at that as the sign of a great teacher. And from that day on, even though she didn't always agree with his opinions, she loved that he opened her mind to things.

It was here, at Gina's locker, between first and second period, that she got her initial daily glimpse of Tommy. They used to see other earlier in the morning back when Tommy used to pick her up for school every day. But ever since study hall became his first-period class, he chose to sleep in instead. There was definitely a part of her that missed him picking her up each morning in his old, beat up 1973 Pontiac GTO. Its original color was white, but by the time Tommy had purchased it was more like dirt and rust with a hint of white here and there. The price tag was 500 dollars, but he shrewdly haggled it down and walked away with it for 482 bucks. Like most guys, the sound system was worth more than the car itself. When he pulled into her driveway, the bass would be pumping with some sort of hair band song pulsating out. He'd always just sit there, beeping until she'd come rushing out. It wasn't just random beeps either. He'd always attempt to beep some sort of song to her, and once in the car, he'd excitedly ask her to name that tune. Of course, she never could name any...not a one. To her, it just sounded like a string of arbitrary Morse code-like beeps. This always pissed Tommy off to no avail. He couldn't for the life of him figure out why she couldn't hear the perfect beep symphony he was conducting. This silly little game went on for their entire junior year. Truth was, Gina missed it. She missed their seven-minute ride to school every morning. She even missed him singing (screeching) along to whatever glam rock song was cranked on that day.

Gina tossed her Psych book into her locker. A few papers flew onto the floor. She bent over to pick them up and two underclassmen stopped dead in their tracks, giggling as they admired her backside.

"Hey! Are you two dick wads staring at my girl's ass?" Tommy's voice boomed from down the hall. Both boys froze in fear as Tommy approached. "Do it again, and I'll have to introduce you to Mr. Backhand!" With that, Tommy raised his hand and pretended to strike the boys. Neither of them waited around to see if he was faking. They bolted down the hall, clumsily bumping into each other on their way out.

Fully amused, Tommy turned towards Gina. By now, she had picked up her papers and was glaring unapprovingly at him.

"What?"

"You're such a bully, Tommy. You're getting more and more like Otto every day."

Tommy smiled and proudly nodded.

"That wasn't a compliment, idiot!" Gina smirked.

"Aw, is that any way to talk to the guy who got you the best birthday gift ever?" Tommy made his way over to Gina and put his arm around her.

"Speaking of which," smiled Gina, "seeing as this weekend is my *actual* birthday, how about we do something special?"

Tommy looked a bit puzzled.

"You know, in addition to the great, great concert tickets you got me."

"Like what?" Tommy questioned.

"Well, I was thinking we could go on one of those harbor cruises around the Isles of Shoals? They even have one that'll take us out to Star Island and we can have a picnic. I've always wanted to go out there. I heard it's very romantic." She batted her eye lashes as Tommy skeptically looked down on her. "Or we could go out to the Chapman Stables up on the mountain and go horseback riding…also very romantic I'm told."

Tommy grimaced, "So my choices are seasick or sore ass?"

Gina slapped his shoulder. "Ha, ha. Maybe, if you play your cards right, afterwards we can park up at the lighthouse and I'll let ya get lucky."

This caused Tommy to perk up and throw a 'now we're talking' look at Gina. But, before he could agree to his girlfriend's request, a voice interrupted from behind.

"That's sounds very romantic, but unfortunately Tommy won't be able to make it." Tommy and Gina turned and saw Otto arrogantly standing there. "The Battle of the Bands is coming up soon, and we're practicing all weekend. Right, Tommy?" With that, Otto slouched his greasy arm on Tommy's shoulder. "Right, Tommy?"

"Um, yea, right. Band practice. Sorry, Gina, maybe another weekend?" Tommy couldn't bring himself to look her in the eyes.

"Yea, Gina, maybe another time." Otto condescendingly smirked. "Besides, the dude got you front row tickets to Whitesnake for Christ's sake. What more do you want?" Otto turned his attention back to Tommy. "I told ya, she's high maintenance, man."

Even though Tommy pacified Otto with a slight chuckle, in his heart, he knew this was furthest from the truth. Gina was probably a three on the high-maintenance scale. A three and a half at worst. Her low maintenance, cavalier attitude was one of the things he loved about her.

Part of him wanted to put Otto in his place, but, well, he didn't. He simply stood there, torn between defending his girlfriend and getting into it with his best buddy. Gina knew his dilemma, but hoped Tommy would stand up to Otto and defend her…just once. Tommy felt a surge of relief as the class bell rang.

"Yo, let's bail. Let's go grab some Flo dogs and head out to the rocks," Otto ordered.

The *Flo dogs* he spoke of were of course Flo's famous hot dogs (with Flo's special sauce). The small, faded red hot dog stand on Route 1 was a local institution. They say you can't come to York without seeing the Nubble lighthouse, and you can't leave without having a Flo dog or three.

The rocks Otto spoke of were up by the lighthouse. They were a bit of a hike, but were the perfect spot for drinking and smoking. The giant craggy rocks formed a cave-like formation that was completely out of sight from the cops or the hordes of tourists snapping their pictures of the lighthouse.

Tommy gave Otto a nod then slowly turned around to deal with what would surely be a dejected and disapproving glare from Gina. But there was no glare, Gina had given up all hope of Tommy standing up for her and was already halfway down the hall. All she left behind was the scent of her shampoo - Agree. Tommy was more of a Head & Shoulder's guy, but requested his mother to start buying Agree for him; not because it added volume and body to his hair, and not because of its repair of split ends, but simply because it smelled like Gina. Tommy breathed it in and couldn't help feel disappointed in himself. Of course, his disappointed look was exactly what Otto was going for. As Tommy watched Gina head to class, his disappointed look turned to one of anger…a jealous anger. Joining

Gina on her walk to class was Adam fuckin' Gosmer; Tommy's self-appointed arch enemy.

Otto took one look at Tommy's anger and patted him on his back and said, "I don't mean to keep harping on this, but you have to face the facts; guys like Gosmer are who she belongs with."

Tommy wanted to be pissed at Otto for suggesting such a thing, but he knew Otto spoke the truth. Again, Otto slapped Tommy on his back and said, "Eh, don't sweat it, Bro, she's not worth it. Let's go grab Ricky and Pud and get out of this shit hole.

The truth was Tommy did sweat it. It wasn't just the fact that Gina and Adam shared many of the same classes together, or the same taste in music, or the similar black attire…well, okay, it was all of those things, but more importantly, it was because they had a history together. Adam was the guy who dated Gina after her and Tommy's first go-around.

Tommy and Gina's first dating go-around was back in junior high. Of course, the word 'dating' had its own meaning back in those grades. Basically, it meant - you are the person who I talk to the most on the phone, or the person I sit with at lunch, or, (if you're a guy), the person who shows off for you at recess. Oh, and it meant that you are the only person of the opposite sex who I'll dance with (slow songs only) at the school dance. Actual dates consisted of parents driving you to either the movies, or the mall, or if the girl got her way, to Happy Wheels roller rink.

As an 8th grader, Tommy felt like he had it all. He was well-liked by his classmates, he got good grades, he was a burgeoning drummer in the school band, and most of all, he had the perfect girlfriend in Gina. It was as if they were the king and queen of 8th grade. Little did he know his reign would come crashing down that summer.

Believe it or not, back then, Gina's attire rarely consisted of anything black. It was actually quite colorful, and not only was she totally into pop music, but she was into cheering. That's right, once upon a time, little miss introspective, dress-all-in-black-girl was an aspiring Ra Ra, fake smile, full of spirit cheerleader. Ironically, it was the cheering clinic she attended the summer before her freshman year that would be the catalyst for her and Tommy's breakup.

The clinic was run by varsity cheering coach Sue Thibodeau. Sue was also a math teacher at York High School. Her trademark booming voice could be heard from all corners of the school. She was also famous for starting off a sentence with a 10 on the loudness scale and ending it with a 2. i.e.: "A-squared (10 on scale) plus B-squared (6) equals C- squared (2 on scale).

Tommy had her for Geometry his sophomore year. He spent most of the year getting yelled at for being late, and for talking too much, and for making fart noises. Despite all the yelling, and despite having a 69 average, he actually liked her as a teacher, and truth be told, she took a liking to Tommy as well (NOT a Pamela Smart-type liking).

One time, she interrupted one of Tommy's fart noises by asking him to stand up and tell her which theorem he would use to solve the problem on the board. Without missing a beat, Tommy stood and recited, "The dangle of the angle equals the size of my rise!"

Half the class cracked up laughing while the other half braced themselves for a 10+ on the loudness scale. Surely he'd get a week's worth of detention, and maybe even a trip down to the principal's office. Her booming, chastising yell never came, however. Instead, she semi-quietly (4 on scale) spoke to Tommy, "Very creative, Tommy, but wrong. Have a seat and start paying attention. Lisa, what's the right answer?" As Lisa stood and recited the correct answer, Ms. Thibodeau slowly shook her head at Tommy and threw a slight, yet amused smirk his way. From that point on, although his grades never improved, he had a new-found respect for her.

Anyway, back to the cheerleading clinic: It was run by Sue Thibodeau and was led by Megan Gosmer. Senior captain Megan Gosmer... quite possibly the hottest and most popular girl in school Megan Gosmer. Megan immediately took a liking to Gina, and just like that, even before she had officially entered high school, Gina was hanging with the cool and popular upperclassmen.

While Gina's new circle of friends certainly affected her and Tommy's *summer hangout time,* it was who she met a Megan's house that changed everything; Megan's freshman brother Adam. Considering they were both in the same grade, Gina knew of Adam, but over the years, they had never shared the same homeroom or circle of friends. Adam was always a quiet, keep to himself type of kid.

Throughout that summer, Gina's visits to Megan's house became less about Megan and more about hanging and getting to know Adam. They shared many of the same literary tastes, and Adam made it his mission to introduce Gina to, as he put it, *real music*. Some of which included: The Violent Femmes, The Cure, Echo & the Bunnymen, and U2. Gina loved hanging out listening to Adam talk about some of his interests. Whether it was Eastern philosophies, or poetry, or even politics, Gina was enamored with his passion. Being an aspiring writer herself, she loved that she could talk writing with Adam.

As the summer moved on, she found herself becoming physically attracted to him as well. She'd become intoxicated by the famous, age-old *new guy smell*. It wasn't that Tommy did anything wrong, or that she didn't still 'love' him. It's just, the shiny newness stage of her and Adam took hold.

If it's true that girls mature much faster than boys, Gina's new circle of friends reflected this. That summer, Gina's mental and physical maturity took two giant leaps forward while Tommy's maturity just stood still (maybe a step backwards).

Tommy and Gina's 'breakup' occurred late in the summer before their freshman year (Aug.21, 1984 to be exact). Tommy had just finished beating Brett in a game of foosball at the Fun O Rama. Following the foosball beat down, Tommy and Gina headed for the boardwalk for a victory stroll. Unfortunately for Tommy, this would be the exact opposite of a victory stroll.

He could tell something was on Gina's mind. As a matter of fact, he could tell something had been on her mind most of the summer. Even when she was with him, she wasn't really *with* him. Tommy sensed the end was near, and Gina sensed that Tommy sensed the end was near. With all this sensing going on, Gina finally opened up to him. And by opened up, I mean she broke the poor guy's heart. And for a guy, or a girl, there's nothing worse than getting dumped on the beach in the summer...nothing except hearing Gina's final, dreaded comment: "We can definitely still be friends though, right?"

To Gina's credit, it wasn't just a polite closing line. She actually meant it. Once in high school, she remained friendly towards Tommy; not fake-friendly, but legitimately heartfelt friendly. And never once did she attempt to throw her new relationship in Tommy's face. She was very conscious of Tommy's broken heart and did her best to respect that.

The start of their freshman year was extremely difficult on Tommy, more so than Gina. He found it much harder adjusting and fitting in at the new, bigger school. Not to mention, jealousy raged through his body with regards to Gina's new boyfriend. More times than not, he found himself pining for the good ole junior high days.

While Tommy lamented the loss of their relationship, Gina was enjoying the shiny, sparkly newness stage of her and Adam. They found themselves talking late into the night on the phone. Some of their conversations were: 1) Listening to Adam read his newest poem to her. 2) Deeply analyzing their assigned novel in English class ("The Heart is a Lonely Hunter"). 3) Equally analyzing lyrics of alternative albums ("Closer" by Joy Division being one).

Luckily, Tommy (and his broken heart), rarely saw Gina at school. Due to the fact they only shared one class their freshman and sophomore year, their encounters were mostly relegated to the hallways. Fortunately for Tommy (and his broken heart), his depression and pining only lasted for a couple of months. They say the best way to move on from someone is to find someone else. Tommy did just that. Kind of. Tommy's *someone else* came in the form of a new best friend...a best friend who could show him a whole new world. This new best friend would be, of course, Otto Kringeman.

TRACK 4

Over the weeks leading up to the prom, Tommy began slowly pushing Gina away. He'd pick fights where there was no fights to be picked. Gina's first impulse was to think he was just trying to get out of going to the prom. In reality though, it went deeper than that, much deeper.

One day, by complete accident, Tommy discovered an acceptance letter for a school in California. It was bad enough that she was going to college and he wasn't, but Califuckinfornia? He just assumed she'd go somewhere more local. What made it worse was she never mentioned the letter to him. The end was near and he knew it.

***

THE DAY OF THE PROM

Gina's house – 2 PM

Gina stood in front of the full-length mirror, her eyes inspecting the finished result. She kept half-turning this way and that, not out of vanity, but because she couldn't focus on her appearance while her thoughts were so worried.

She hadn't heard from Tommy since 2:00 PM on Thursday. Up until right now, she was very excited about this evening and confident (semi-confident) in Tommy. Now, at the final hour, she had more than her share of doubts. He'd been an especial jackass for the past two weeks, even when they were alone, and not hearing from him at all for a whole day only made her feel less confident.

Again, she did a half-pirouette in front of the mirror, and forced herself to focus this time on how she looked.

"Well, I wouldn't call that a traditional prom dress, Gina, but I must admit it's very you." Gina's mother stood behind her as she did a slow pirouette in front of the mirror, adding, "And very lovely."

Black was slowly becoming a popular choice for prom dresses, yet Gina still managed to maintain her individuality, working with the local dressmaker for months to create the right dress for her, paying for it with her own time and money. It was perfect; a fitted black bodice flaring out into an ankle-length tutu, a crimson bustier laced with black and gold strings, its gothic look softened by scalloped seams. For all of its severity of color, it was quite feminine.

"Thanks, Mom," Gina said with more than a hint of sadness.

"What's wrong, honey?" her mother asked, although she already knew the answer. Gina knew she didn't have to answer, and stayed quiet, but both looked at the clock on the wall.

Otto's garage – same time

Loud music echoed down the street from Otto's garage. Inside, in a haze of smoke, Tommy banged away on the drums, accompanied by Brett on guitar and Ricky on bass. Empty Stroh's cans were scattered around them on the floor. They finished the jam and smiled at each other, satisfied with how the sound is coming together. Tommy got off of his stool to grab another beer, and Brett began to play a slow instrumental ballad on his electric guitar. Not recognizing the tune, Tommy listened and watched intently until Brett finished.

"Wow. Is that an original?" Tommy asked.

Brett humbly nodded and Ricky added, "It's pretty amazing, huh?"

"I don't have any lyrics for it yet, but"…

"Play some more," urged Tommy. Ricky nodded in agreement, and they watched Brett fill the musty garage with the beautifully melodic sounds of his guitar. It didn't take long for Ricky to experiment with a bass line and for Tommy to join in with a soft beat. It was obvious by their smiles that they were creating something magical. The magic quickly ended when Otto burst through the door with a disgusted look on his face.

"What the hell kinda shit are you guys playing?"

"It's a new song Brett has been working on. Cool, huh?" Ricky interjected.

"Um, no! First of all, we are a rock band. We don't do sappy love ballads. Second of all, I'm the lead here, not Pud! Besides, we do covers, not originals. Isn't that right, Tommy?"

Tommy cringed. Whether it was Gina or Ricky and Brett, Tommy hated when Otto pinned him against his friends. Before Tommy could utter a word, Ricky spoke up, "You do know that the Battle of the Bands is originals only, right?"

Otto covered up his obvious oblivion by snapping back, "I fuckin' know that! Don't question me, ya dick weed. I'm actually working on an original as we speak."

"Cool. Let's hear what you got," exclaimed Tommy, trying to be the peacekeeper.

"Um, it's not ready yet...still working on the lyrics." Otto could feel the disbelief in their eyes. "But it definitely rocks! Way more than Pud's pussy love song." Otto reached in the case for a beer, but came up empty. Angrily, he smacked the box at Ricky. "Lemme go see if my old man has more," scoffed Otto. "When I come back, we're gonna play some real fuckin' music."

As soon as the door closed, Brett and Ricky glared over at Tommy behind the drums.

"What?"

"You know what," said Ricky. You gotta kick him out of the band. He's totally bringing us down."

"Me? Yea, right. Besides, where else are we gonna find a place to rehearse? Especially one that comes with free beers."

"C'mon Tommy. You have to admit, when we were jamming to Brett's song just now, it was pretty friggin' magical. And anyone of us can sing lead better than Otto."

"My Great Grandmother can sing better than Otto," joked Brett.

Tommy knew they were right. Otto couldn't carry a tune to save his life, and he sure as hell wasn't capable of writing an original song (or having an original thought). But the truth was, Tommy felt a sense of loyalty to him, which was ironic considering he had been friends with Brett and Ricky long before he had even met Otto.

Otto moved to York their freshman year. Even back then he was a bit menacing with his whole 'fuck the world' disposition. And even as a freshman, he came complete with tattoos and facial hair.... not peach fuzz, but a full-on beard and stache (ungroomed of course). Being a small town, rumors immediately followed his arrival.

The top 3 rumors:

1) Otto was kicked out of his last two schools for fighting and had served time in juvi for actually cutting a kid with a knife.

2) Otto was actually 25 years old and was working as an undercover narc (21 Jumpstreet type stuff).

3) Otto's drug-riddled mom went crazy and tried to burn down their house, so he and his dad moved here to get a new start.

When Tommy was a freshman, he was quite different than he was now. Tommy was gangly, awkward even, and hadn't yet grown into his body. As a senior, he only stood 5'8, not very tall, but a far cry from being only 5'2 as a freshman. Tommy was never the A+ student like Alan, but he at least used to be a solid B type student (well, maybe a solid B-).

His musical taste back then was more in the Classic-Rock genre: Zepplin, Deep Purple, Aerosmith (and if you shot him with truth serum – Reo Speedwagon). He was never really big or talented enough to make any of the sports teams, but he was still way more into athletics back then compared to now. It was actually down at the basketball courts at the beach where he had his first memorable encounter with Otto.

The three freshmen, Tommy, Brett, and Ricky were at the courts playing a game of horse (they spelled it *whores*). Over on one of the other courts were three juniors from their rival school, Marshwood. The three cocky juniors were all on Marshwood's varsity team. Tommy and his friends knew it was only a matter of time until they received the dreaded request. They hoped they could just finish their game of *whores* and head out unnoticed.

"Hey, you three Yorkies wanna wanna play a real game of three on three?" And there it was, the dreaded request…the dreaded condescending request.

"Um, no thanks. We were just leaving," Tommy answered timidly.

Ricky shot Tommy a look as if to say, 'I say we play them!' Not only was Ricky the most athletic out of the three friends, he was always up for a challenge.

The next thing Tommy knew, they were engulfed in a 3 on 3 game with the bigger, older, more talented dudes from Marshwood. Well, it wasn't much of a game as Tommy and friends found themselves down 13 to 1. It was bad enough that the Marshwood boys were humiliating them on the scoreboard, but they also began humiliating them verbally and physically. It quickly became a shit show that Tommy wanted no part of.

And then it happened: the 5'2 Tommy attempted to box out his 6'0 counterpart for a rebound. The next thing Tommy knew, he was being thrown to the ground. His head slammed onto the hard asphalt.

"What the fuck was that?" yelled Ricky.

"What? I was trying to get the rebound and Tiny Tim got in the way," laughed the Marshwood junior as he high fived his friends.

Tommy clutched the back of head and Brett helped him to his feet. "You okay, Tommy?" asked Brett.

A bit embarrassed, Tommy nodded. Ricky continued to give the Marshwood boys a stare down.

"What the fuck you looking at, loser?" The Marshwood boys taunted.

Ricky's blood boiled, but he knew they were no match for the older, bigger boys from Marshwood.

"Let's just go," urged Brett. Ricky reluctantly joined his friends, and all three began to walk off the court.

"Aw, the little babies from York are gonna go home and cry to their mommies."

Just then, a clinking sound was heard. It was slow and methodical, yet loud enough to catch everyone's attention. At the opposite end of the court, stood Otto Kringeman - the mysterious new student. Apparently, Otto had been watching the whole thing go down. He was wearing a faded, ripped jean jacket and had a cigarette dangling from his mouth. In his right hand, he held a beer bottle and was not-so subtly tapping it against the metal basket support. It was actually a bottle of Birch beer, but a real beer made for a better legend. The rhythmic tapping seemed to be some sort of Morse code, warning the Marshwood boys that it was time to pay the reaper. It was like a scene right out of "The Warriors" (minus roller skates).

"What are you looking at, ya burn out?"" exclaimed the biggest of the Marshwood boys.

Otto continued to tap... and to stare... and to smirk. Then, just like that, the clinking stopped. He pounded the rest of the beer, put his cigarette out (on his forearm), then slowly started walking towards the boys.

Before the Marshwood punk could utter another word, Otto's fist slammed into the kid's nose, breaking it and knocking him off of his feet and onto the court. (The blood stains are still on the court today). Otto then turned his attention to the other two. In one swift motion, not only did Otto pull out a switchblade, but he broke the bottle against the basket support. Tommy and his friends watched in awe. It was like a scene from the "Outsiders" (minus the pegged pants).

The two other Marshwood boys also watched in awe...and in

shock…and quite frankly, were scared shitless. They had no idea what just happened, but they took one look at their bloodied friend and at Otto's crazy eyes and quickly booked it out of there.

Less than an hour later, Tommy and his friends were sitting in Otto's house drinking a celebratory beer or three. It was obvious that Tommy and his friends were far less experienced than Otto. He pounded three beers to every one of theirs. Otto's life experience went much deeper than theirs; from tattoos to smoking cigarettes, to smoking pot, to being able to fight, like really fight. And last but certainly not least, the fact that Otto had not only already sex….he did it for the first time in 7th grade (unconfirmed).

Ironically, they did share many of the same likes.

Some of their mutual likes:

1)   Their love of heavy rock music. It was Otto, who really got the guys into Motley Crue. As a matter of fact, as they sat in his living room that day, Otto had Motley Crue's "Shout at the Devil" tape blaring in the background.

2)   Their love of horror flicks. The gorier and more disturbing the better. They guys were blown away when they found out Otto owned bootleg VHS copies of Faces of Death I, II, III.

3)   Their love/infatuation for senior Mia Carlson. More importantly, their love for how her ass looked in her tight Calvin's. Tommy and his friends labeled her as a 'UT' (Untouchable). Otto scoffed at that and made a bet that by the end of the year he would personally give her the hot beef injection. (Mission Failed).

As the four laughed and drank, nothing was spoken about the

fight earlier, and nothing was certainly spoken about the rumors which surrounded Otto's past. The guys were just happy to have someone like Otto have their backs. From that day forward, their little threesome turned into a foursome, with Otto, of course, taking the lead. And also from that day on, Otto seemed to take Tommy under his wing. It was no coincidence, from that point on, Tommy's grades started to decline. And it wasn't a coincidence that Tommy developed a sarcastic, smart ass mentality either.

It was also no coincidence that Tommy started to develop more self-confidence. He spoke a little louder, walked a little taller, and more importantly, Otto was the perfect distraction to help him get over Gina. So, in Tommy's mind, he owed this all to Otto.

...So yes, Tommy knew that Otto was totally bringing down the band.

...And yes, Tommy knew that Brett had more talent in his pinkie than Otto did in his whole body.

...And yes, Tommy knew that it was originally Brett's idea to form the band in the first place. He shared his idea with Tommy and Ricky at the start of their junior year. It was originally supposed to be a three-piece...Ricky on bass, Tommy on drums, and Brett on guitar and lead vocals, and they would all be equal collaborators on the songs.

Of course, as soon as Otto caught wind of this, he not only anointed himself as a member, but as the leader. This didn't sit well with the guys, but no one had the heart (balls) to tell him otherwise. The only, ONLY good thing was the spacious garage to rehearse in and the free beers.

...So yes, Tommy truly wanted to defend his two old friends by telling Otto they should pursue Brett's song.

Just then, the garage door swung open and Otto trounced in carrying another case of beer. A hush quickly came over the room. All eyes uncomfortably rested on Otto.

"What the fuck you guys talking about?"

"Um...actually, Otto," spoke Tommy, "we've been talking and have decided to practice Brett's new song, and we think Brett should sing the lead."

Well, that's what Tommy *wanted* to say.

"Um...actually Otto, we were trying to decide what to play next. Faster Pussycat or some Whitesnake?"

That's what Tommy actually said.

And yes...he immediately felt ashamed by his betrayal of his friends.

Gina's house - 4:30 PM

Sadly, Gina stood in front of the full-length mirror. She should have been admiring herself. She was fully dressed and made up and knew she looked absolutely gorgeous (even with the worried line between her brows). Unfortunately, how she looked and how she felt were two different things. Moments earlier, Gina's best friend, Heather, and her boyfriend Michael had arrived. They all had dinner reservations at the York Harbor Inn for five o'clock.

Every tick of the clock was like a loud reminder that there was a distinct possibility that she would be stood up by Tommy. Slowly, she picked up the phone and dialed. She was torn between angrily punching something or throwing herself on her bed and balling her eyes out. As the Stevens' answering machine turned on, she chose somewhere in the middle. With a tear in her eye, she slammed down the phone in anger.

"I really think you should draw the line at fifteen unanswered calls," Heather sarcastically suggested. "Besides, I think we both know where he is."

Heather was right. Gina knew exactly where Tommy was. A part of her wanted to march over to Otto's house and drag Tommy by his ear to their prom (while kicking Otto in the nuts in the process). But the more practical part of her knew if she had to physically drag her boyfriend to something as special as the prom then he probably wasn't worth being her boyfriend.

While Heather attempted to cheer Gina up, her boyfriend, Michael, was downstairs on the couch uncomfortably hanging out with Gina's parents. Gina's dad reclined in his La Z Boy stoically watching reruns of *My Three Sons.*

Michael wasn't sure what was worse, having Mrs. Cassidy talk his ear off about her and Mr. C's prom night back in '66, or dealing with the Cassidy's dog; some large, hairy mixture of German shepherd and … poodle? Whatever it was, Orville (Yes, they named it Orville) continually attempted to hump Michael's leg. Disturbingly, deciding which one was worse, was actually a closer call than you'd think.

Despite the babbling of Mrs. C and the humping of Orville, Michael's mind was firmly focused on the prom. Well, more like the after prom. He looked at the dog trying to wrap itself around his leg and thought, *I can relate*. Michael and Orville shared a brief look of understanding before Michael kicked the dog away.

Back in Gina's room, Heather did her best to console Gina – in her own best friend sort of way, "Can't say we didn't warn you, Gina. I thought you guys were totally adorable together back in junior high, but this isn't junior high anymore, and Tommy is a far cry from who he used to be. Face it, Gina, you guys are two different people heading in two different directions."

Again, Gina knew Heather was right. Of course, a little more sympathy and a little less 'I told you so' would have been nice, but yes, Heather was completely right. This was usually the part where Gina would defend their relationship with statements like: 'You don't know how it is when we're alone together', or 'Deep down, Tommy really has a kind and big heart' or…well, you get the picture.

Heather did her best to be inconspicuous about glancing over at the clock (4:50 PM), but Gina sensed her anxiousness.

"Why don't you and Michael go on without me?"

"Aw, Gina, no. If you're not going to the prom then neither am I (a polite, yet totally fake offer)."

"Thanks, but I just meant you two should go to dinner without me. I'm still going to the prom, I'll just be there later."

"Really? You're still going to the prom?" spoke Heather a bit shocked but hugely relieved.

"Damn right I'm still going! I don't need a guy to dictate my happiness (her quintessential "Pretty in Pink" moment). Besides, I spent a ton of money on this dress…and I look damn good." Heather nodded in agreement then gave her best friend a big hug.

After Michael pried Orville off his leg again, he and Heather headed off to their pre-prom dinner. After they left, Mrs. Cassidy attempted to console her heartbroken daughter, but Gina put on a strong, convincing face and told her mother that she was fine. Mr. Cassidy would have also attempted to console his daughter except, well…he really wasn't into the whole talk about your feelings sort of thing. Besides, a rerun of *All in the Family* had just come on.

As Gina sat alone in her bedroom, she felt strong, empowered, and fiercely independent. She even started boxing up some of Tommy's belongings. If this was 2006 instead of 1988, Beyonce's "Irreplaceable" would be playing in the background.

Over and over she repeated aloud, "I don't deserve this, I'm better off without him… I don't deserve this, I'm better off without him"… She would have repeated this mantra a third time except, she was kind of distracted by her fingers dialing Tommy's house…again. And for a sixteenth time, there was no answer; no Tommy, no Alan, no Mrs. or even Mr. Stevens. At this point, Gina would have been happy to hear any of their voices. Unfortunately, no one would be home for hours. Mr. Stevens was once again working a Saturday overtime shift, and Mrs. Stevens was way up in Fryeburg proudly watching Alan in the Odyssey of the Mind.

When Gina heard Mrs. Stevens' cheery voice on the answering

machine, she slowly hung up and mumbled to herself, "I don't deserve this, I'm better off without him."

Otto's garage

Back in the garage, the guys were heavily involved in a debate over the sound of one particular chord. There were more beer cans strewn around them, and it was obvious by the slurring of their words that the drinking had caught up with them.

Otto, who had zero desire to analyze chords or notes or anything for that matter, interrupted their banter, "I think it's time for a little weed break, boys." Otto reached into his pocket for a joint. "Actually, if I invite my old man to join us, he'll probably give us some of his good shit." Otto smiled at his genius idea, then stumbled through the door and into his house.

As you can probably guess, Otto's old man was also a piece of work. His idea of being a good parent was being best buds with his son. His idea of being best buds with his son was drinking, smoking, and partying with him. And due to his dad's loss of a license (DWI x 2 & driving with an expired license), Otto was his personal chauffeur.

While Otto hit his old man up for some pot, the boys, now drunk, began entertaining themselves. Ricky ripped, what just might be, a World's Record fart. A World's Record for its length (9.7 secs), and a record for its wretched smell. With his lighter in hand, Brett fought back the face-melting stench, and attempted to light Ricky's nuclear explosion. All three practically fell on the floor laughing.

When their laughter finally subsided, Brett gazed at his watch then curiously looked over at Tommy. "Hey, don't you have a Prom to go to?"

"Holy shit," exclaimed Ricky, "that's right, Tommy. The big prom is tonight."

Tommy just shrugged it off, "Whatever. I'll just have to be fashionably late."

"Dude, I wouldn't be late if I were you," warned Ricky. "Chicks take that prom shit serious.

Brett nodded in agreement, "If either of us had girlfriends we'd be there."

"Pfft, I tell ya what, if you guys wanna take my place, be my guest."

Tommy watched as Brett and Ricky gave each other a concerned look. "What? If ya got something to say, spit it out!"

"I know we give you crap all the time about having a girlfriend," said Ricky, "but the truth is, we're kinda jealous."

"What are you guys saying," joked Tommy, "you wanna bang Gina?"

"No, not at all. We're just jealous of the whole girlfriend thing. We've never had much luck with that sorta thing."

Brett and Ricky spoke the truth. It wasn't that they were bad looking guys, and it wasn't that they weren't nice enough. As far as headbangin' bullies go, they were actually quite friendly. Truth be told, they were more like spectators and commentators to the bullying dished out by Otto and Tommy. They were more the comic relief of the crew: The court jesters to King Otto, so to speak. And it wasn't that they didn't have their share of chicks to rock & roll into bed with, it's just, for some reason, those type of chicks (skanks) weren't exactly girlfriend material.

Tommy didn't show it, but he was touched, flattered even, that his friends were actually jealous of him. He might walk around all cocky and confident, but inside, he was still battling insecurities. Sarcasm and anger became his best defense for this.

"It just seems," continued Brett, "that lately"...

"Lately what?" snarled Tommy. (Anger defense)

"Well, lately it seems like you're kinda treating Gina like a....well, like a jerk."

Tommy slowly stood up from behind his drums and angrily cracked his knuckles, "What did you say, Pud?"

"What Brett means is, it almost seems like you're trying to sabotage your relationship."

"Sabotage my relationship? Dude, you've been paying way too much attention in Mr. Layne's Psych class." (Sarcasm defense).

Just then, Otto returned to the garage holding up a bag of weed. His smile quickly turned into a look of disgust as the remnants of Ricky's fart still lingered in the air. "For Christ's sake! Who the hell shit their pants?"

The four boys smoked some pot and drank a few more beers, but the gravity of the whole 'Gina conversation' continued to weigh on Tommy's mind. He knew his two friends were right. He had been slowly pushing Gina away the last couple weeks. It wasn't because he didn't want to be with her anymore, and it certainly wasn't because he didn't love her…because he did, but in Tommy's heart, he knew their days were numbered. Come September, Gina was heading to the University of California, and she STILL hadn't told him yet!

Ever since he found out she was heading to California, his mind was invaded with thoughts…thoughts of Gina getting banged by smart, artsy-type boys. College boys. College men even. He pictured her in an eclectic coffee house having deep conversations with dudes who dressed in black ribbed mock-turtlenecks. These images made him sick to his stomach. But what really made him sick to his stomach was while Gina was on the other coast improving her life, he would be back here in Maine, working some shitty dead-end job. While Gina was studying for an important test, he'd be banging on his drums getting drunk and high with Otto and the boys. More than sick to his stomach, he felt worthless, completely worthless. From this point on, he and Gina would be heading in different directions.

Tommy could never reveal these feelings to Gina or even to his friends. Instead, he handled it the only way he could; by acting like he didn't give a fuck, by getting drunk and high, and by pushing Gina away before she pushed him away. If their relationship was going to end, it sure as hell was going to end on his terms!

So Ricky and Brett were right, in his own twisted and self-preserving way, Tommy was slowly trying to sabotage his and Gina's relationship. Up to this point, Tommy had simply used sarcasm and rude comments to accomplish this, but not showing up to their prom was taking this to the next level. He knew this would cause a huge fight; one their relationship would surely not survive from.

TRACK 5

A high school prom is very similar to the whole cafeteria situation, but at the prom, the delineation of each clique is even more obvious. Throughout the prom, the students stood and gathered in small clusters (cliques). The group on the dance floor was determined by the song and/or artist. It is a written law that no male with shoulder length or longer hair be on the dance floor when anyone is singing "Wake Me up Before You Go-Go," and no male with shorter hair would be caught dead bopping to "Dude Looks Like a Lady."

For the girls, that musical line was slightly blurred. They are expected to be on the dance floor "if it's got a beat we can dance to." When the expected Cyndi Lauper female anthem played over the speakers, most of the girls were on the floor, bouncing around. Heather managed to get Gina to dance with her and the rest of the girls for a few minutes before she begged off, saying she was too hot.

Gina wasn't the only one without a date, but she felt like she was. Being dateless at a prom is much like being dateless at a wedding; watching all of the couples dance, kiss, and being over-the-top lovey dovey. She had only been there twenty-seven minutes, but she was already tired of all the sympathetic looks and of everyone asking if she was okay. And she was totally tired of people telling her she was better off without him. Basically, everything a person in that situation *doesn't* want to hear.

It wasn't long before Adam Gosmer made his way over to her. Adam was dressed in his true non-conformist and anachronistic fashion - Mohawk, 40's style zoot suit, and combat boots. Not only did he make it a point to tell her how beautiful she looked, he also made it clear that she deserved far better than Tommy. Adam also made it crystal clear that he and his prom date, Tanya Garrett, were completely plutonic. Adam even offered to whisk Gina away from the prom. He'd take her for a drive along the darkened beach where they could park and watch the waves crash into the rocks (he'd probably use that as a metaphor for her and Tommy's relationship). They could just sit and talk about deep, emotional things and when the moment was right, he would reveal that she had inspired him to write 31 poems about her. He would then take a dramatic pause…and claim that #32 was being created as they spoke.

Naturally, Gina was flattered by his compliments and by his offer to whisk her away from the prom. She would have also been flattered (and a little creeped out) if she ever found out about the 31 poems. As a matter of fact, less than two years ago, Gina would have been totally mesmerized by Adam's melancholic magnetism, but now, as he stood there in front of her, she felt absolutely nothing for him; that ship had long since sailed.

Their relationship lasted through the winter of her sophomore year. She used to love how introspective Adam was and how he'd make her think deep thoughts. She also used to love how Adam would take the time to read her stories, even if he was a bit over-critical. It wasn't just her writing either. She noticed that he was overly critical about pretty much everything – books, movies, music, and people. The truth is, he was always critical and cynical of these things, but she never really noticed it because she was caught up in the new-car smell of him.

The real tipping point came at Christmas 1986, when not only did he not get Gina anything, but he rejected each of her well-thought out gifts for him. Instead, he gave her a long, drawn-out speech about how Christmas was overblown, over-commercialized, blah, blah, blah, blah. Her decision to break up with him had less to do with Christmas presents and more to do with simply wanting to have fun again. She couldn't remember the last time she laughed…like really laughed. Actually, she could. It was back in 8th grade with Tommy.

It wouldn't be until the summer of 87' that Tommy and Gina would find their way back to one another. But when they finally did, Tommy made sure to make up for lost time in the fun/laughter department. At least in the beginning he did, until Otto's influence began to really take hold.

As Eric Clapton's "Wonderful Tonight" gave way to the Bangles

"Walk Like an Egyptian," Gina stood there holding out the slightest of hope that she still might get her John Hughes happy ending. And then it happened, there was a slight commotion behind her, and the muffled words of "Oh my God, look who showed up," hit Gina's ears over the vocals of Suzanna Hoffs.

Gina's heart raced as she slowly turned towards the commotion. A smile crept onto her face. She was actually going to get her "Pretty in Pink" moment after all. Unfortunately for Gina, the person stumbling in wasn't Andrew McCarthy or even Duckie...it was a very drunk and very stoned Tommy Stevens.

"Yo, Gina!" boomed Tommy's voice from across the dance floor. And just like that, Gina's hopeful smile turned to an evil, fire breathing glare. It took Tommy a moment to spot Gina, and when he finally did, he drunkenly started strutting through the middle of the dance floor in her direction. Knowing that all eyes were on him, Tommy paused in the middle of the dance floor and awaited Suzanna Hoffs to belt out the chorus, where, at that point, he joined in...sort of.

Tommy mocked the girls on the dance floor as he obnoxiously sang, "Walk like an *erection!*" With his pelvis thrusting forward, he used his arm to simulate a hard-on. His walk like an erection dance took him right towards Gina. Most of the kids in the crowd laughed, while some of the girls looked on in pity. By the time Tommy reached Gina, she was red with embarrassment and anger.

Using his thumbs to pull out the shoulders of his shirt, Tommy gloated, "See, I told you I had a tux!"

Gina looked in disgust at Tommy's outfit; ripped acid-washed jeans, and a black T-shirt screen printed to look like a tuxedo jacket.

"You're an asshole, Tommy!" Gina could feel the tears stinging behind her eyes.

Tommy shrugged, "Love hurts, babe."

Betrayal, anger, hurt, and confusion made the burning in her eyes even stronger. "I have no idea what I ever saw in you! My friends are right. You're just another burnout loser! Consider us through!" She said vehemently.

"Ha!" laughed Tommy. "Only a matter of time until you made it official, huh? I just figured you were gonna spring it on me graduation night or were you gonna wait until this summer and dump me on the boardwalk again."

Tommy's drunken statement left Gina a bit confused. "What the hell are you talking about?"

"Or were you gonna wait until you were out in California before you dumped me?"

Gina was taken aback. How did Tommy know about California? The University of California had an amazing creative writing program. Gina's biggest dream since she was little was to be a writer, and although she dabbled in poetry, her true passion was to be a fictional novelist. She practically worshiped Stephen King and had high aspirations of following in his footsteps.

Before she could ask how he knew about California, Tommy blurted out, "I found the stupid acceptance letter in your bag two weeks ago."

"What the hell are you doing going through my stuff?"

"I wasn't going through your stuff. I was looking for some paper to write down some new lyrics I was thinking of. What other secrets are you keeping from me?"

As cool and confident as Tommy seemed strutting around the hallways of school, he was full of insecurities. He knew he pissed away his four-year high school education, and he knew he was destined for some dead-end shit job. Gina never rubbed his nose in her good grades and never once made him feel stupid because of his *not so good* grades. Still though, Tommy constantly felt like he was never smart enough for her.

"What are you babbling about? I don't have any secrets. And for your information, idiot, I've been accepted to five schools so far and most of them are right here in New England. And secondly, you have to be a damn good writer to get accepted in their writer's program. A little congratulations from my boyfriend would be nice! Of course, you wouldn't know how talented a writer I am."

"What does that mean?"

"It means, idiot, have you ever read anything I've given you?"

He started to answer but hesitated. Busted.

"Yea, that's what I thought. If it's not lyrics or if it doesn't have pictures, then Tommy's not interested."

Through her anger and resentment, part of her felt bad for him. She knew how hurt he was when she broke up with him four years ago, and the fact that he still carried the fear of her doing it again caused her to take pity. She felt guilty about not telling him about the acceptance letter and wanted to apologize to Tommy for not finding out directly from her. She wanted to make it clear, that even if she was going to California, and even though she knew a long-distance relationship would be difficult, she had <u>no</u> intentions of breaking up with him.

That's what she wanted to say, but she didn't. For right at that moment, she found it nearly impossible to feel pity for the person standing (swaying) in front of her reeking of beer and weed. The person she defended the most over the years had just royally embarrassed her in front of the whole prom, so she was fresh out of pity.

With everyone's eyes on her, her voice quivered as she fought back tears, "I don't ever wanna see you again."

Even though Tommy knew the end-game was coming, and even though he facilitated it to end on *his terms*, he was still stung to the core with Gina's last sentence. He wanted to rush forward and wipe away her tears. He wanted to wrap his lanky arms around her, hold her tight and tell her how absolutely beautiful she looked...but he was too drunk, too stupid, and too concerned with everyone's eyes on him.

And to make matters worse, Adam Gosmer made his way next to Gina in a show of support. Gina's hand reached over and clasped Adam's. Tommy's anger boiled over. All he could think about was wrapping his hands around Adam's throat. Before he could act on his anger, Tommy spotted some of the chaperones making their way towards him, so he kept his response short and sweet.

"Good luck replacing this, babe!" His hands awkwardly parodied a game show hostess as he gestured to his full body.

Just then, one of the chaperones made eye contact with Tommy across the dance floor and angrily gave him a *come here motion* with his finger. Knowing they'd have him surrounded in less than thirtyseconds, Tommy headed towards one of the emergency exits in the back. As he stumbled through the amused crowd, he passed by Jill McNamara. Without hesitation, he grabbed her arm, pulled her into him, and planted a huge kiss on her. Before Jill or her date could react, Tommy was already at the exit door with his eyes firmly on Gina – the only reaction he cared about. Gina's eyes were filled with tears and her face was flushed with anger.

With an exaggerated and theatrical finger point in her direction, he loudly shouted, "Shot through the heart, and *you're* to blame! Darlin,' you give love a BAD NAME!" And just like that, he was gone.

***

Before any of the chaperones could chase him down, Tommy jumped into his GTO and high-tailed it out of there, making sure to lay some major rubber on his way out. Inspired by his final sentence, he reached into the messy passenger seat in search of Bon Jovi's "Slippery When Wet" tape.

Blindly, his hand sifted through old McDonald's wrappers and empty Marlboro packs until he finally clutched a handful of tapes.

Through his drunken haze, he squinted, giving the tapes a closer inspection: "Look What The Cat Dragged In" from Poison, "Round and Round" from Ratt, "Night Songs" from Cinderella. All great tapes but not what he was looking for.

As he approached a stop sign, he tossed the tapes into the backseat and continued his search on his passenger floor. His hand rummaged through empty Burger King wrappers, his drum sticks, a few crushed beer cans, and a pair of underwear...tightie whities...his tightie whities (which were neither tight nor white anymore).

Angrily, his foot laid on the gas, leaving exhaust smoke and rubber in his wake. After tossing his underwear out the window, he leaned down for one final search. With his eyes off the road, he swiped at the floor board again. Almost immediately, he felt his car swerving onto the gravel shoulder. Frantically, his eyes made their way back to the road. After he straightened his car out, he gazed down at what his hand had retrieved. He held two tapes and another empty pack of Marlboros. The first tape was "Theatre of Pain" from Motley Crue. The second – Bon Jovi's "Slippery When Wet." Score! Oh, wait, the Marlboro pack wasn't empty either. There was one cigarette nestled in its corner. Double score! Of course, finding his lighter was a whole other search.

Tommy inserted the tape and immediately fast-forwarded to "You Give Love a Bad Name." As he and Jon Bon Jovi belted out the opening lyrics, he sped down the dark and empty road along the beach. With no destination in mind, he just drove; through the beach and onto the back roads of York.

As Tico's drum beat filled the car, Tommy couldn't stop thinking about Gina. He thought of all the great times they had shared over the years. All the smiles, all the laughs, all the memories…all the hot & heavy sexual moments (Boobs can be included in nostalgic moments, right?). And as his car sped down the dark and winding back road, he thought of tonight. He thought of how beautiful she looked when he first spotted her, and how hurt and angry she looked as he left. He hated himself for how he treated her. He hated himself for being such a loser. A burnout loser. A burnout loser with no future plans. He wasn't anything what or where he'd thought he'd be. Blaming Otto for being such a bad influence would be the easy way out, but Tommy knew he was ultimately responsible for his own actions. What the fuck was he thinking showing up to the prom like that? What the fuck was he thinking breaking Gina's heart like that? More importantly, what the fuck was Adam Gosmer doing putting his hand on Gina's shoulder? And just like that, Tommy's introspective thoughts turned to Adam fuckin' Gosmer. By now, Adam had probably whisked Gina away from the prom to someplace quiet and dark. He was probably offering her his shoulder (or other body part) for her to cry on.

As Tommy pressed harder on the gas pedal, his drunken imagination got more graphic. He pictured Gina on all fours with Adam banging her from behind with his little non-conformist dick. Better yet, while he was pounding her, he was probably reciting his latest fuckin' poem. For a split second, Tommy found himself wondering if Adam left his combat boots on during sex. Probably, he thought. Those things must take forever getting on and off.

Tommy's imagination took a quick break as he passed by a small cemetery. Tommy knew that in exactly 3 tenths of a mile, he'd be headed over thrill hill. Thrill hill was the spot where the road abruptly dipped over a small hill causing you to get air if you hit it at over 50 MPH. The fastest Tommy had ever hit it was 70 MPH. It was in Otto's piece-of-shit car with Ricky and Brett. If it wasn't a piece-of-shit car before the jump, it certainly was after. The left tire blew, and the front end was ripped up on impact.

Tommy's foot pressed harder on the gas. His GTO raced closer to thrill hill. His thoughts also raced.

'Fuck Adam Gosmer! Fuck Otto! Fuck the world!'

As "You Give Love a Bad Name" was blaring its final chorus, Tommy was determined to hit thrill hill at over 80 MPH. Moments before hitting the hill, a loud garble filled the car. It was the unmistakable sound of his cassette deck eating his tape. Like a parent innately jumping into action to save their child from danger, Tommy's finger jumped into action and hit the eject button. He was determined to save the tape before it became totally unsalvageable. As he pulled it out, his heart sank. It was his worst nightmare come true; along with the cassette was a long twisted thread of tape. Before he could attempt *cassette* CPR (using your finger to carefully recoil the reel), he felt his heart jump out of his chest…weightless. In his panic-stricken cassette moment, he forgot about thrill hill.

Not only did he hit it at 91 MPH, but because he took his eyes off the road, he hit it from the other side of the lane. He turned his wheel to the right in mid-air, but it was useless. He was going far too fast and was far too drunk to regain control. His trusty ol' GTO came crashing down on the other side, and Tommy's seat-beltless body was thrown about. His foot quickly searched for the brakes, but it was too late. Directly in front of him was a large oak tree. He closed his eyes and braced for impact.

What happened next was quite possibly the loudest, heart-wrenching sound ever heard. It was said that the sound of mangled metal and glass shattering could be heard for miles. Even the sound of his spinning rims could be heard echoing throughout the night. When the rims finally came to a squeaky halt, all was quiet…deathly quiet.

TRACK 6

Even in the pre-internet, pre-cell phone age, news traveled quickly, especially in a small town. Whispers of Tommy's major accident on thrill hill filtered through the prom. Gina was sitting in a darkened corner still being consoled (hit on) by Adam when Heather approached her and broke the news. Already distraught from the earlier events, Gina lost it.

Heather's version of the accident came from Michelle LaBonte, and her version came from Joey Horne, which came indirectly from Tony Ewing. Usually, with this many people playing telephone, the end version was drastically different from what actually happened...not in this case, however. Descriptions of the accident were disturbing, and Tommy's prognosis seemed grim. Ignoring Adam's offer to drive her to the hospital, Gina bolted across the dance floor and out the door.

Gina was actually the first person to arrive at the hospital.

Unfortunately, because she wasn't family, she couldn't get a straight answer about what was going on in the ER. Because Ricky's cousin was an EMT, Ricky and Brett were next to arrive. They hadn't had nearly as much to drink as Tommy that day, but were still a bit buzzed and high.

As they entered the waiting room, they were 'greeted' with a stone-cold glare from Gina. How the hell could they let Tommy drive tonight? She wanted to jump up and strangle them both, but she didn't. There was no yelling or strangling. She took one look at the glazed, sad look in their eyes and realized they were just as scared as she was. Not to mention, she too was partially to blame. She saw how drunk he was, yet she made no effort to stop him from leaving. As a matter of fact, it was because of her that he left so angry. She should have never reached for Adam's hand. She only did it to spite him.

The more she sat and thought about it, she knew she had no right to be angry with either of them. Unsure of the right words to say, Ricky and Brett simply gave her a slight smile of support. Gina returned their look and watched as they nervously paced around the room.

A few moments later, Gina broke the silence, "Did anyone contact the Stevens?"

"I left a message on their machine," replied Ricky. "They must still be on their way home from Fryeburg."

"They're going to be devastated," Gina's words were followed by a fresh set of tears.

The guys immediately empathized with Gina's pain. "It's gonna be okay, Gina. He's gonna pull through," urged Ricky.

"Tommy's a tough son of a bitch," added Brett. "A stubborn son of a bitch too. He's not going out this way." Gina did her best to smile in appreciation of their positivity, but deep inside, she feared the worst.

By midnight, not only had the Stevens finally arrived, but so had a handful of family members and close friends. Heather and Michael were there in support of Gina. Ricky and Brett continued to pace. If it's the not knowing that drives people crazy, then the Stevens were going absolutely insane. Updates on their son's condition were few and far between. All they knew, was he was in critical condition.

Mr. Stevens tried his best to be strong, to hold it together for his family, but was becoming more worried and frustrated as the moments passed. With an extra squeeze to his wife and son's shoulders, he stood up and ostensibly walked over to the coffee machine. He had no desire for coffee. He just needed to move, to do *something*. He took his time preparing the coffee, trying his best to hide his tears. By the time he was done, he'd composed himself enough to turn back to his family and Gina.

Noticing how pale and afraid Alan looked, Gina reached over and grabbed his hand. Even though her head was bowed, it was still possible to see the tear streaks of mascara down her cheeks. Mr. Stevens heaved a sigh as he took in her once beautiful dress that was now all crumpled around her in the tight little waiting room chair.

He walked towards his wife, his hand holding the coffee

extended toward her. She sat quiet and still, but when she looked up at him, he could see the panic in her eyes. He scoured his mind for the right thing to say, but nothing came to his lips. Sadly, he realized there was nothing to say that would give any of them comfort. What kind of man was he that couldn't do that for his family? With that thought, he again fought back tears.

At the sound of a door, all of them anxiously looked toward a doctor who was striding towards them. His scrubs were covered in blood, and he was still wearing a surgical mask. The only thing that was visible of him was his slicked-back hair over dark eyebrows. When he removed his mask to speak, it revealed his perfectly capped teeth as he gave a smile of introduction.

"Mr. and Mrs"... he paused to read their names off the clipboard in his hand... "Stevens. I'm Doctor Hargrove."

A smile? What was this, a political fundraiser? There was zero sympathy on the young doctor's face. Mr. Stevens hated him on sight. He quickly felt guilty since this could be the man who would take care of Tommy.

"How is our son? Is he okay?"

"Mr. and Mrs. Stevens, your son"... again, he referred to his clipboard... "Thomas was in a very serious car accident. He was thrown through the windshield...face first."

The way he said *face first* was as if he thought it was cool or something. Everyone in the waiting room immediately shared Mr. Stevens' hatred for him.

"He suffered severe lacerations to his face, which will require extensive reconstructive surgery."

As Mrs. Stevens covered her mouth in emotional shock, another voice joined the conversation. "Unfortunately, that is the least of our concerns right now." All eyes turned to see another doctor enter the waiting room. He was older and more distinguished looking gentleman than Dr. Hargrove. He was in his mid-40's and had a strange resemblance to young Christopher Walken.

Doctor Hargrove provided an introduction, "This is Doctor Zimarchi. He is the head of our Brain Trauma Unit. More like the research part of it," he said condescending.

Mr. Stevens noted the eyes of the new doctor. They were carefully blank, as if hiding something, yet with discernable sympathy behind them. He immediately trusted him.

"What's wrong with Tommy's brain?" Mrs. Stevens fearfully blurted out.

"I'm afraid your son has zero brain activity," Dr. Zimarchi answered with heart-felt eye contact.

"But you can make him better, right?" Mrs. Stevens pleaded. Please tell us that you can make our son better, Doctor?"

With his hand on her shoulder, Doctor Zimarchi gently began, "We'll know more once the swelling goes down, but for now"...

"But the bottom line is," coldly interrupted Doctor Hargrove, "the prognosis doesn't look good."

The Stevens and Gina all reacted in shock with their eyes widening in fear. Just then, the loud, annoying buzz of Dr. Hargrove's pager went off. Without even noticing the reaction his words caused, he glanced down at his waist in irritation and grabbed his pager and looked at it.

"Great. There goes my coffee break," sighed Doctor Hargrove. "I'll leave you in Doctor Z's hands." With that, he flashed his fake Hollywood smile and left.

Doctor Zimarchi watched him leave then turned back to Tommy's family. "I'm truly sorry about that. I'm afraid his bed side manners are, well, pretty much non-existent. I promise I'll keep you informed, every step of the way."

"Thank you, Doctor," thanked Mr. Stevens. "But shouldn't we consider moving him to a bigger more specialized hospital? Maine Med or Boston maybe?"

Just then, one of the nurses who was walking by spoke up, "Doctor Zimarchi is one of the top brain specialists in New England...maybe even the whole country."

The doctor gave the nurse a modest, appreciative smile. She returned the smile and walked on. The nurse's comment seemed to satisfy and comfort the Stevens.

"Can we see our son?" begged Mrs. Stevens.

Doctor Zimarchi slowly nodded, "It will have to be brief, and unfortunately, immediate family only.

The Stevens sympathetically gazed at Gina. She was crushed by this rule, but nodded and resigned herself back in the chair. "Tell him I said hi, and ...and tell him that I"... Gina's voice broke as tears flowed from her eyes. Mrs. Stevens approached and gave her a big hug.

Gina slowly reached into her purse and pulled out the little boutonniere she made for Tommy, which matched her dress. It was a single black rose with thin red ribbons tied around the stem and the ends trailing loosely. Still trembling, Gina handed it to her. Mrs. Stevens sadly smiled, but it was enough to reassure Gina that Tommy would get it.

The doctor then escorted them into the emergency room. "I must warn you," cautioned Doctor Zimarchi, what Doctor Hargrove said was true, your son has suffered traumatic injuries throughout his body, especially his face."

Nothing can prepare a parent for finding out their child was in a serious accident. But hearing it and actually seeing them in the emergency room in critical condition is a whole different reaction. Within a split second of entering, Mrs. Stevens totally lost it. Her heart sank. Her knees buckled, and tears burst from her eyes. Her baby boy was connected to various machines through tubes running from his mouth and arms. Not only was his face covered in bandages, but with the exception for his right hand that laid limply on the bed, so was his body. Mr. Stevens propped up his wife, and with Alan hanging on his arm, all three slowly made their way closer to Tommy. Doctor Zimarchi watched from the doorway. No one said anything, the silence only interrupted by muffled crying.

Moments later, the same nurse from earlier entered the room and gently informed the Stevens they needed to leave for now so they could run more tests. Still shaking and crying, Mrs. Stevens leaned down and kissed his cheek through the bandages. Alan reached down and grasped his big brother's hand squeezing it in support.

Mr. Stevens was the last to say good-bye. As he kissed Tommy's cheek, he whispered into his ear, "If it were not for hope, the heart would break. I have hope, Tommy."

Out in the hall, Doctor Hargrove was laughing and flirting with a young nurse. The normally resigned and non- violent Mr. Stevens felt his blood boil as his hands clenched into fists. Visions of rushing over and shoving the stethoscope up the doctor's ass filled Mr. Stevens's head.

Before he could put his plan into action, he spotted Doctor Zimarchi. Doctor Zimarchi was also fixated on the touchie-feelie doctor and shared Mr. Stevens content and disgust. Mr. Stevens approached Doctor Zimarchi and with a quiet yet fervent tone spoke, "Please fix our son … whatever it takes. *Whatever it takes*."

Doctor Zimarchi took Mr. Stevens' hand in a firm clasp, staring intently into his eyes. The doctor appeared to see something that satisfied him and almost imperceptibly, he nodded. Strangely, this comforted Tommy's father, and with one last shake of his hand, he followed his family back to the waiting room.

TRACK 7

Over the next month, test after test was run by Doctor Zimarchi and although the swelling around the brain was reduced, his brain and body were still unresponsive. Throughout that time, a moment didn't go by that at least one loved one wasn't by Tommy's bedside. Family and friends came and went, but the one constant, the one fixture that never left his side was Mrs. Stevens. Many a night she'd sleep in the chair next to him with one hand clutching Tommy's hand and the other clutching her rosary beads.

Unfortunately, Mr. Stevens' hospital time was limited due to all the overtime he had picked up to help with the bills. When he wasn't at work or the hospital, he and Alan would visit their church. Nothing was spoken. They'd just sit quietly and pray.

As the days passed, the Stevens and Dr. Zimarchi had developed beyond just the patient-doctor relationship. There was always a mysterious air about him, but his kindness and compassion towards

Tommy and his family were unparalleled. Dr. Zimarchi was deeply moved by the love and dedication the family had towards Tommy. The Stevens were equally touched and appreciative of the day-and-night dedication shown by Dr. Zimarchi. Conversely, they were often angered and disgusted at the cold, cavalier antics of Dr. Hargrove.

The large oak beyond thrill hill served as a makeshift memorial for Tommy. Not only were there flowers, but there were dozens of liner notes of some of Tommy's favorite bands strewn about. Unfortunately, there were also obnoxious displays of disrespect; crushed beer cans encircling the large oak.

The memorials for Tommy didn't end there, during York High's graduation ceremony, the school had a moment of silence to offer positive thoughts and prayers to Tommy. While thoughtful, these memorials didn't set well with the Stevens or with Gina. It was as if they were treating Tommy like he was dead, which basically, he kind of was. But even so, the Stevens and Gina held tightly to hope and faith. This hope and faith didn't prevent tears from flowing from Gina's eyes throughout the entire graduation ceremony, especially when the Stevens chose her to accept Tommy's diploma (yes, he had enough credits to graduate).

It was no surprise that Otto, on the other hand, fell three credits short and failed to graduate. It would also be no surprise if he never did. Slightly less surprising was Otto never once visited Tommy in the hospital. It wasn't that Otto was completely heartless or even emotionless, because he did feel terribly for his sidekick. It just wasn't his style to visit the hospital, especially knowing how everyone felt about him. After the accident, Ricky and Brett's friendship with Otto slowly waned. After graduation, it pretty much was over for good. Otto left town and joined his uncle as a roadie for the band Kix.

As hard as it was, Gina made it a point to visit Tommy as much as possible. Actually, two Ginas would visit Tommy: Happy Gina and Angry Gina. Happy Gina would sit by Tommy's bed holding his hand while reading song lyrics to him (at first, she would bring in a few record albums and read directly off of the record sleeve; after a while, she would type the lyrics at home and come in with pages of them – this way, she could be more selective in the songs she would read to him). On some days, she would even sing them. Initially, she brought in albums/songs by Bon Jovi and all of Tommy's other favorite bands, and sneak in one or two of her own favorites in between; but as time went on, all of the songs were from her top artists, with only a token few of Tommy's hair bands.

Angry Gina would cry and rail, first at the injustice in the world and then at the unfairness of Tommy's accident – which would lead to full-on blame for the accident, and every event that led up to that night, starting back in the 8th grade.

On a daily basis, you never knew which Gina was going to show up, but it was easy to tell once she got there by looking at her eyes – or, more specifically, her eyeliner. If her eyeliner was neat, Happy Gina was here, if her eyeliner was streaked, Happy Gina was not here. Her carrying albums or a stack of papers wasn't always a good indication, either; she always carried them, following the grand traditions of the Boy Scouts preparedness and would make up her mind on the way in.

On some days both Ginas would visit. Happy Gina would walk in all neat-eyelinered, and later on, Angry Gina would come out of Tommy's room with most of it running down her face.

Alan visited daily – well, on the days he had nothing going on after school … which was pretty much every day … okay, Alan visited *regularly*, every Thursday at 4:00 PM, after he went home and changed out of his school clothes and before his newly scheduled 7:00 PM homework time.

Alan changed his homework schedule for Tommy. For Alan, this was momentous and significant.

During his visits, he would try to limit his conversation to only stuff that would appeal to Tommy – not that he really knew what that was, but he did have a good idea of what Tommy was *not* interested in. He set aside time to listen to the radio for a full half hour two non-consecutive days a week (to avoid listening to stupid stuff twice) to gather tidbits of things he felt Tommy would relate to (if he could hear him). When Tommy woke up, Alan had every intention of letting him know of the sacrifices he made for him.

When Tommy woke up …

The visits were tough on Alan. Some days he left earlier than his allotted 6:15 PM leave time (a half hour to get home and fifteen minutes to unwind before homework). It wasn't just that he was having a hard time seeing Tommy laid up and bandaged like he was (and it was not easy to see him like that), he was also feeling some heavy guilt – because he was much more relaxed at home with

Tommy out of the house. He was aware that he noticed the difference, and it felt *terrible*. He knew he loved his brother, but he also knew that lately his brother had been making things harder on him, making it harder for him to even *like* Tommy on some days.

And then there was his *so-secret-he-couldn't-tell-his-parents* anger: that Tommy's prom-night *fuck up* – yes, he said it (in his head) – caused all of this *and* made him and his family have to leave the Odyssey of the Mind competition before it was over. For fourteen-year-old Alan, this kind of guilt was crushing. What kind of kid cared more about a scholarly competition than *his own brother?*

Ricky and Brett usually showed up together. They said because it was easier to take one car, but it was probably more because they needed each other's support (even though they never admitted it). Their conversations in the car on the drive to the hospital never once covered how either of them was *feeling*. Brett had managed to sneak into the police impound lot right after the accident because he wanted to see Tommy's car. He was amazed that Tommy wasn't killed immediately, based on how the car looked.

Ricky had started reading about brain trauma and injury, secretly hoping to figure out an easy cure for Tommy, but when the words got too big, his attention turned towards 'foods that keep your brain healthy' – easier reading, because there were a lot of articles about that in the magazines at the checkout line in the grocery store. He had time to read a whole article waiting in line with his mother. He would sometimes even have time to run back through the aisles for a last-minute purchase to bring to the hospital for Tommy, if he woke up (blended, of course).

Knowing his wife hated to leave Tommy's side, even for a second, Mr. Stevens headed to the cafeteria to get his heartbroken wife something to eat. On his way there, he passed by Dr. Zimarchi. They exchanged a pleasant nod, but before Mr. Stevens entered the elevator, he turned back and spoke.

"Dr. Zimarchi, do you have a second?"

The doctor stopped and turned, "Of course."

As they approached one another, Mr. Stevens slowly spoke, "I need to talk to you about something I heard."

"If this is about Dr. Hargrove and that nurse getting caught kissing in your son's room, I promise you, I personally will take care of it," assured Dr. Zimarchi.

A disturbingly puzzled look appeared on Mr. Stevens' face. "Umm, no. It's about something I heard about you."

The doctor's face went carefully blank for a moment, but then he smiled as he replied, "Oh. And what might that be?"

"I was talking with one of the head nurses, and they mentioned that you were working on a new drug that might help our son? Is this true?"

The doctor's smile vanished. "I *was* working on a potential breakthrough."

"Was?"

"The government funding for our research was unfortunately cut back in January."

"What exactly would this drug do…in layman's terms?"

The doctor paused, then responded, "Well, in layman's terms, if perfected, it could restimulate the dormant brain waves."

Mr. Stevens' eyes widened. "What are the risks? Would he regain all his motor skills? Would his memory still be intact? Would"...

"I'm afraid I never got that far."

"But there must be a way to get new funding?" begged Mr. Stevens.

"I promise you, I'm working on it."

Disappointment filled Mr. Stevens' face.

"I'm truly sorry, Mr. Stevens. I know how hard this is on you and your family."

"With all due respect, doctor, you have no idea how hard it is…to watch your child lie there in a brain-dead coma…it's the most helpless feeling in the world."

***

At the end of the second month, with no improvement in Tommy's condition at all, the subject came up of "pulling the plug" – the exact words used by the ever-tactful Dr. Hargrove one morning in between the continuous buzzing notifications of his pager. Mr. and Mrs. Stevens both looked up at him in shock.

"Maybe he just needs more time to heal?" Mrs. Stevens' voice was soft.

"It doesn't matter if it's five years or twenty-five years, your son's condition won't change. The fact is, Tommy is brain dead and there's nothing more we can do. It's time you start thinking about pulling the plug."

Nurse Donna was in the room at the time, changing Tommy's IV. She was in her mid to late-50s, *very* professional and *very* capable. She seemed to be Dr. Zimarchi's right-hand man/woman, if he were to have one. Mrs. Stevens adored her, telling everyone who would listen how happy she was that such a wonderful woman was around to take care of her son when she wasn't there. While she wasn't much for chatty talking, "Nurse Donna" (that's what they all called her) was obviously very fond of Mrs. Stevens, too.

When she overheard Dr. Hargrove broach the subject, she immediately left the room, but not without first giving Mrs. Stevens' shoulder a reassuring squeeze.

Dr. Zimarchi was there in minutes and immediately called Dr. Hargrove out into the hallway. While the Stevens' weren't able to hear the actual conversation, they could hear that Dr. Hargrove was getting quite the talking-to from Dr. Zimarchi. Everyone in the hallway heard Hargrove curse as he stormed off.

When Dr. Zimarchi came into the room, his demeanor was somber. Tactfully and caringly, he discussed the subject that Hargrove had started. After a few minutes, Mrs. Stevens left the room with tears streaming down her cheeks. Mr. Stevens and the doctor talked a few more minutes before Mr. Stevens went out to see his wife.

Mrs. Stevens was sitting in a chair in the waiting room, Nurse Donna by her side and holding her hand. When the nurse saw him, she got up to leave, but he reached for her hand.

"Nurse Donna … thank you. While nothing short of a miracle could have changed this horrible situation, you were surely one of the brightest spots in it."

When the Stevens' got home that night, they sat Alan down and told him they made the decision to take Tommy off of life support the day after next.

Alan slept in Tommy's room that night.

TRACK 8

Gina's heart was heavy going into the hospital for the last time to see Tommy. As she walked into the room, she took a long look around, noting everything. She then began talking immediately.

"God, Tommy. I can't believe this is happening. This is not supposed to be how it all ended – it wasn't supposed to end at all! I know things haven't been too great this past year, but I still thought we could – would – work things out. It's just that you've been different lately ... not really lately ... it's been like this for a while. The band ... Otto ... has seemed to be more important to you than I was. You can't deny that."

She looked at his face still covered in bandages, and the endless tubes connected to the beeping and whirring machines. "I guess you really can't," she sniffed. "I don't know what to do anymore." She looked around at all the apparatus again. "But it looks like your decision once more, doesn't it?"

The tears began to fall faster, and she began to pace around the room just trying to keep it together. She wanted her last words to him to be kind and loving, not angry. She faced his bed again.

"Hey, do you remember Halloween a year ago when I convinced you to go to the old cemetery with me? You didn't want to go. I think you were even a little freaked out even though you wouldn't admit it. I remember Otto was trying to get you to go with him to Billy's keg party. Even when he said you were pussy-whipped, you told him you were going with me. I had a creepy little picnic all set up for us at the old headstone of that little boy. Remember? You kept looking over your shoulder at every noise – you were so jumpy!" She smiled through her tears. "After a while, a while you began joking about sharing the food with anyone who decided to 'appear'. We talked a lot that night. And then we started making out. That was one of the best nights" ... Gina's voice trailed off as a thought came to her. "Do you know what I remember most about that night? It was the last time you chose me over Otto... Right! That *was* the last time! What happened?" Gina's voice began to get a little louder. "What happened? For the past year everything you did was dictated by Otto! Why? And I hoped it was just a phase, figuring it wouldn't last long and I could wait it out. Waiting for you to show me that I was still important to you. I *waited!* For what? *This?* I waited for *nothing?*"

She began to cry in earnest, letting it all out. After a while, she rubbed her red and swollen eyes.

"You were a good guy – you *are* a good guy. Inside. I have always known that. That was one of the things I loved about you.

When we were together, *really together*, I felt like I could do anything ... that we could do anything. You made me feel so special ... I thought we would get through the 'Otto stuff' ... remember when we talked about getting older together? I would be talking about our house and kids and you were only worried about whether or not you'd have any hair ... and then for the next few days I'd see you sneaking looks at your father's head, checking for bald spots ... *every time*." She smiled at that thought.

She looked at the bandages wrapped around his head. "I wish I could touch your hair now, although they probably had to shave it all off ... I used to try to picture you with shorter hair – of course I never told you that."

Another thought crossed her mind. "Did you hear that? I used to picture you, older – *with less hair!* Wake up! Wake up, Tommy, and yell at me for that! *Please!*"

That was it. With one last plea, "Oh, Tommy!" Gina crumpled into the chair next to the bed, crying.

***

With a chaplain standing at the foot of the bed, Tommy's parents and Alan said their last good-byes. Drs. Zimarchi and Hargrove were both present in the far corner of the room. Doctor Hargrove frequently and impatiently checked his watch. As Mrs. Stevens and Alan begin to leave the room, Mr. Stevens leaned over Tommy's bed and whispered in his ear. He straightened and turned to Dr. Zimarchi. A look passed between the two of them as he reached out to shake the doctor's hand.

"Thank you, Dr. Zimarchi, for everything." Mr. Stevens didn't even acknowledge Dr. Hargrove when he left the room.

Gina, Brett and Ricky were in the waiting room. The three of them looked up when the Stevens came in. Mr. Stevens opened his arms, and the six of them stood together, holding each other.

TRACK 9

With the family out of the room, Dr. Hargrove coldly began to turn off the machines. He threw a sheet over Tommy's still unrecognizable face as soon as the monitor sounded its final tone. He then gestured to Nurse Donna to bring the gurney. At Dr. Zimarchi's nod, she wheeled Tommy's body out of the room, down the hallway and into the elevator. When the elevator door shut, she reached down to the bottom of the gurney under a sheet and pulled out a bag that contained a battery operated machine, which she quickly hooked up to Tommy.

The doors opened to the basement, and as Nurse Donna wheeled the gurney out of the elevator, a dark van pulled up in front of her. The back doors opened, revealing Dr. Zimarchi inside with a full emergency-vehicle setup. Together they put Tommy in the back of the van, and she hooked him up to more equipment and an IV. When she was done, she smiled warmly at Dr. Zimarchi, climbed out of the van, and walked back to the elevator like nothing happened.

Dr. Zimarchi closed the doors of the van, gave a slight rap on the partition separating him from the driver, and the van slowly pulled out of the garage. If anyone actually looked at the van as it drove down the street, it would have appeared that there was no one sitting behind the wheel, even though the driver, Paco, was sitting on a phone book just to be able to see over the steering wheel.

Paco loved driving the van. It made him feel taller. Without his 'special driving shoes' on, Paco stood exactly 4 feet tall (short). Because his feet barely reached the pedals, Dr. Zimarchi only let him drive it under unusual circumstances. These 'special events' were a real treat for Paco.

By the time he got to the back of the house, Dr. Zimarchi was already waiting for him. Together, they wheeled Tommy into the basement. As far as basement renovations go, Dr. Zimarchi's went beyond anyone's idea of a rumpus room. It was fully redone from one end of his enormous house to the other. From the back door they wheeled Tommy in from what appeared to be an office. There was a desk with a computer on it, two filing cabinets, a bar, and medical books lining built-in shelving.

Walking deeper into the room was a hospital bed and a complete setup of patient monitors; there was also a strange-looking device hooked up to the IV stand that looked like a high-schooler's science experiment using a blender as the main component. Past the medical Cuisinart, the walls on either side were flanked with stainless steel tables containing microscopes, burners, a sink, various surgical tools, beakers and test tubes. The furthest end of the room was equipped with a kitchenette, a large television, a stereo, and a bed that was covered by the flag of Mexico. Next to the bed was a nightstand with a lamp that looked like a bong. Fluorescent lights ran the length of the ceiling from the desk to the stainless tables, and separate tract lighting illuminated the apartment set up. The walls of the entire room were bare except next to and over the bed where they were covered with clippings and covers from TV guide. Basically, the room was a combination office, hospital room, laboratory ... and college dorm.

Paco and Dr. Zimarchi wheeled Tommy over to the hospital bed and transferred him onto it. Once they connected him to the various monitors, the machines whirred to life. During the few minutes it took to connect the IV to the odd blender-contraption, the doctor began to speak, "While the government funding was nice while it lasted, Paco, I think I'm happier funding my own research. Less limits that way." He walked over to the medical cabinet and pulled out a vial and syringe. "I'll call the plastic surgeon to come out next week. I don't believe your new roommate will give you any trouble," he continued as he transferred the liquid from the vial into the syringe and proceeded to then empty the contents of the syringe into the IV. "Don't get too attached to him," he warned as he turned to face Paco. "If this drug works as well as I expect, this young man will be home in time to celebrate Christmas with his family!"

The doctor walked to the desk and notated the time and date in a journal, then headed over to the bar and poured two shots of whiskey and handed one to Paco.

"To science!" The doctor toasted, and he and Paco downed their shots, slamming the glasses on the bar. "Now, we wait."

***

Months Later

By the time Thanksgiving rolled around that year, there was no change to Tommy's brain activity. Dr. Zimarchi flipped through a small stack of journals on his desk. Despite one failed drug after another, the doctor remained optimistic. He was positive that the next experimental drug would be *the one*. He and Paco still held out hope for the Christmas miracle he had predicted months earlier.

He walked over to Tommy's bedside, grabbing another vial and syringe on the way. After adding the medication to the IV, he spoke softly to the still-comatose patient, "I'm still not giving up."

***

Many Years Later

Now, ten years older, Dr. Zimarchi seemed less optimistic. He slumped at his desk in his basement lab. The stack of journals had now reached nearly 4 feet (or 1 Paco high). He glanced over to the bed where Tommy lay 'resting'. "I'm still not giving up, my friend."

***

Many, Many Years Later

The pile of journals on the desk was '2 Pacos' high. Dr. Zimarchi, now pushing 70 years old, sat at the desk, contemplating. More than just being older, the doctor seemed worn down and frustrated. Slowly, he got up and walked over to the computer monitor, absently tapping the table while it spit out its information. A cursory glance at the page caused his facial expression to contort into a grimace as he crumpled the page and tossed it in the wastebasket.

The passage of time and accumulation of disappointment added lines to his face. Paco, also a little grayer now, stood quietly nearby with a somber look on his face and listened as the doctor began to mumble.

"I don't get it. That drug should have worked. They all should have worked. They should have at least done SOMETHING!" He slammed down the print outs and put his hands to his face. He took a deep breath, composed himself, then turned to Paco, "I hate to say it, my little friend, but I think we've done all we can."

He walked the well-worn path to the bar, reached up to the top shelf and pulled down an unopened bottle of Tequila. He stared at the bottle for a moment, rubbing his finger across the label.

"I had planned to open this in celebration. Instead, I will open it and celebrate this poor boy's life. I really thought I had the cure this time"… his voice trailed off. "Tomorrow, we will do what needs to be done…probably what should have been done twenty-five years ago. Tomorrow we will officially pull the plug on this young man." With that, he broke the seal on the bottle and poured two shots. "To the Stevens."

They held up their glasses in Tommy's direction, tipped them to each other, and drank. The doctor gently placed his glass on the bar with one hand, and with the other, he patted Paco on the head before turning to leave. Sympathetically, Paco watched him head upstairs. When the door shut, Paco reached out to the bottle of Tequila and brought it straight to his lips.

TRACK 10

The first thing the doctor heard the next morning when he headed towards the basement was the television blaring loudly. The first thing he saw at the foot of the stairs was the bottle of Tequila he'd opened the night before. It was now on its side and empty. Curiously, he looked around the room and noticed several other bottles on the floor in the same condition - empty. They formed a trail, along with various wrappers, leading to a heap on the floor which turned out to be Paco, wearing nothing but his tightie-whities and sucking his thumb.

Despite his solemn mood, Dr. Zimarchi appreciated the small smile that came to his face. "Must've been some party," he said quietly. He put the newspaper he'd been carrying down on the desk then pulled a blanket out of a nearby cabinet and covered Paco with it before he walked over to the hospital bed.

Tommy's body was still, and his head was turned to the farthest end of the room. Dr. Zimarchi stared at him for a moment then walked around to the other side of the bed where the monitor was. Without looking at Tommy, the doctor reached out and began turning off the machine.

"I'm sorry, my friend. I really thought I could have helped you."

His hand paused, as a slight movement caught the corner of his eye. He turned his head towards the bed, but Tommy's body appeared still. *I must be going crazy*, he thought as turned his attention back to the machine. Again, before he could press any buttons, he saw some movement out of the corner of his eye. And again, his attention turned from the machine to Tommy's bed.

This time he stared intently at Tommy, slowly moving his gaze down the body until finally – the movement occurred again. It came from under the sheet in the middle of Tommy's body. Dr. Zimarchi stared in disbelief as he saw the unmistakable tenting of the sheet. *An erection?*

Momentarily confused, he looked around the room and saw Victoria's Secret angels prancing around on the TV screen. When he looked back at the bed, Tommy's eyes were now *open*, fixated on the television.

The doctor's triumphant joy was tempered with confusion. *What? How?* He looked back at the monitor and equipment and noticed Paco's trail of trash leading to the blender apparatus. A Dunkin' Donuts cup, empty pill bottles, Flintstone vitamins, 5hour Energy drink bottles, Viagra pills, and candy wrappers of Pop Rocks were just a few items he saw in his quick glance. When the scientist in him took over, he put that information aside for later review and focused on Tommy to see what he would do.

When the commercial ended, Tommy yawned and turned his head. He saw an old doctor at the foot of his bed, smiling as he stared at his junk. Still a little disoriented, he sat up and pushed his erection down. He looked around the large room, and then back at the doctor (who was still smiling).

Tommy began to speak, but was surprised that his voice was hoarse, "Where am I? Who the hell are you? And why are you staring at my morning wood?"

"I'm Doctor Zimarchi. You are in my laboratory in my basement. Do you know who you are? What's the last thing you remember?"

What ridiculous questions, Tommy thought. "Of course I know who I am. Umm, I was driving down Shore Road ... my Slippery When Wet tape got jammed, and then ... then ...that's all I remember." He looked up at the doctor, puzzled.

"You were in an accident. A very, very bad accident. Your car hit a tree and you were thrown through the windshield. You were actually declared brain dead."

"Brain dead? And you cured me?" Tommy interrupted.

Before the doctor could answer, Tommy attempted to stand up, but as soon as his feet hit the floor, his legs wobbled, and he fell back onto the bed.

"Whoa, take it easy, boy," the doctor warned. "It's been years since you've been on your feet. Paco did his best to keep your muscles loose, but I'm afraid his inventions aren't always the most effective. I'll give him credit though, his giant IV blender seemed to work pretty well, but I'm not so sure about his exercise contraption."

Basically, Paco's exercise contraption consisted of a series of modified pulleys above Tommy's bed. One end was connected to Tommy's legs and arms, the other end to a stationary bike. Of course, the bike itself also had to be modified as to accommodate Paco's size. Depending how fast he pedaled, the pulley system randomly lifted and lowered Tommy's legs and arms in hopes of giving him a good workout. To the doctor, Tommy simply looked like a break-dancing marionette.

"Um, what's a Paco?" Tommy asked.

Doctor Zimarchi motioned over to the tiny Mexican passed out on the floor... in his tightie whities...sucking his thumb.

Again, Tommy slid off the bed and attempted to stand. He noticed his legs were still wobbly, but this time he maintained his balance. As he stood there, he also noticed two other strange things: He noticed he was only wearing a pair of boxers with red chili peppers on them, and more importantly, he noticed how much weight he'd put on.

"Holy crap, Doc! What the hell happened to me?"

With a slight smile the doctor answered, "Your diet hasn't been completely 'conventional' over the years. Even though you were only feed through an IV, Paco's Super Blender allowed us to feed you anything. But I'm afraid my little friend didn't always adhere to the diet I had laid out for you. And judging by the look of things," the doctor gazed at the various wrappers on the floor, "last night's 'dinner' might not have been overly healthy. I'm fairly certain it wasn't the first time Paco fed you a few sweets over the years."

Tommy took his eyes off of his new, hefty size and asked, "Why do you keep saying over the years? How long have I been here?"

Dr. Zimarchi hesitated for a moment then answered, "Twenty-five years."

Tommy's eyes opened wide then burst out laughing, "Twenty-five years? Yeah, right!"

The doctor went over to the desk, picked up the newspaper and handed it to Tommy with a finger pointing toward the date: April 27, 2013.

Tommy's mouth opened, but nothing came out. Finally, he blurted, "Oh my God! I've gotta go! My parents must be worried sick about me!" Hastily, he looked around the lab for some clothing. When there was none to be found, he yanked the sheet off of the bed and wrapped it around him toga-style. He scanned the room for the door but stopped cold when he saw the mirror on the wall. He hesitantly approached it. His eyes opened even wider when he saw his new face.

The doctor spoke, "Like I said, you were in a very bad accident. You were thrown through the windshield. Your face was cut up so bad that it needed reconstructive surgery. Lucky for you, I had connections with a plastic surgeon, who... owed me a favor."

Tommy stared at himself in shock. Another moment passed before he could even look away from the mirror. He turned to the doctor, "Brain dead for twenty-five years? Love handles? A new face?"

"I know this is a lot for you to process, but before you go anywhere, I need to run some tests on you," Dr. Zimarchi said. "And then we need to have a talk."

"I don't have time for that now. I have to see my family. I have to see Gina."

"That's what I need to talk to you about. You see Tommy, everyone actually thinks... you're *dead*."

"Yeah, brain dead. You said that already."

"No, Tommy. They think you are *dead, dead*. As in dead and buried."

"Right. What did ya do? Kidnap my body?"

When Dr. Zimarchi didn't answer him immediately, Tommy's shock turned to horror.

"Oh my God! You did kidnap my body. You're like a mad scientist, aren't you? Like Doctor Frankenstien!" He then gestured to the Paco-pile on the floor. "And that's Igor!"

Tommy formed a cross with his fingers and began shouting, "Stay back! This is how it's gonna go down, Doc. I'm gonna walk out that door, go tell my family that I'm alive, then I'm coming back here with the cops. You and your little sidekick, Taco, are gonna spend the rest of your lives behind bars! Kidnapping, malpractice, improper nutritional meals. They're gonna put you in solitary confinement. Inmates don't take kindly to these types of crimes."

Tommy grabbed a handful of sheet, so he wouldn't trip on it, and walked purposefully to the nearest door, which turned out to be a closet. Tommy cursed under his breath then headed towards another door. *Another closet?* Still angry, but somewhat embarrassed, Tommy looked over at the doctor. Taking pity on his newly awakened patient, the doctor motioned his head toward the real door.

Tommy took one last look at himself in the mirror before opening the door. "And what the fuck kind of quack are you that you couldn't even *save my HAIR?*" With that, he slammed the door hard behind him.

The noise woke Paco, who squinted up in question at the doctor. The doctor smiled wryly at him and asked, "What did you *do* last night?"

Happily surprised, yet still hung over, Paco smiled and shrugged.

TRACK 11

Clad only in a toga sheet and chili pepper boxers, and feeling every single unused muscle and added pound, Tommy ran through the streets of his hometown until he came to 27 Flintlock Road – the only home he ever knew.

By the time Tommy got to his front door, he was doubled over in pain and practically wheezing. Exhausted, yet relieved he was home again, he looked at the house. The fence was gone, and the tree that used to get weighed down by the Christmas ornaments his mother would hang every year had grown enough to cast shade on half of the lawn and most of the sidewalk. He stared at that tree, then looked around at the neighborhood. Tommy noticed that *all* the trees in the neighborhood had grown, and the paint on most of the houses were fading.

Then he heard it - *nothing*. Why was it so quiet? Where were all the kids? No one was playing football in the street. There should have been a playpen in the front yard of Mrs. Picker's house – hell, she squeezed out a new kid every year – but there wasn't. No Big Wheels (with one side of the wheel flattened from spin-outs) in driveways, no banana-seat bikes scattered across lawns ... the neighborhood looked deserted ... older. If a tumbleweed rolled across his vision at that moment, he wouldn't have been surprised. It was exactly the way he remembered it, but completely different.

He looked back at his house. It looked smaller (or maybe it was the trees behind it). The antenna was gone from the roof, and there was a funny, convex disc in its place that looked like Marvin the Martian's ray gun ("Where's the Earth-shattering KABOOM?"). His mother's station wagon was not in its usual spot. Instead, there was a funny little squished version of the wagon with a bumper sticker on the back (MY KID IS AN HONOR STUDENT). His father hated bumper stickers, because they made the car look messy. Whose clown car was that?

As he walked up the driveway and past the car, he took a quick peak inside. The first thing he noticed was the stereo system. "No cassette player. Pfft." When he got to the front door, he reached for the knob and turned. Locked. Tired, frustrated, and with zero patience to search under the porch for the spare key, Tommy simply began pounding on the front door.

He pounded on it for what seemed like an hour. Finally, after twenty-seven actual seconds, the door swung open, and there stood Tommy's baby brother, Alan. Not the 14 year old geeky Alan he had last remembered, but the 39 year old – and still geeky – Alan.

Alan's eyes widened as he curiously gazed at the heavily breathing, toga-wrapped stranger on his doorstep.

"Alan? Alan! It's me, Alan… Your brother… Tommy. I'm alive!"

Alan's curiosity quickly changed to anger. "Is this some sort of sick joke?"

"No. It's really me," Tommy urged. "I know everyone thought I was dead, and I know my face looks different, and I know I have some love handles now, but it's me. Tommy! Apparently, they kidnapped my body."

Realizing this guy was simply a nut job, Alan's anger turned to amusement. "They?" Alan played along, "The aliens, you mean?"

Still breathing heavily, Tommy exclaimed, "No, not aliens. The guy calls himself Dr. Zimarchi, and he has a little sidekick. And by little, I mean little. Like Tattoo from "Fantasy Island." He calls him Taco or Paco or something. I've been in his basement-slash-laboratory for the past twenty-five years while they've been doing God-knows-wha…" Tommy cut himself off as he watched Alan pull some sort of device out of his back pocket. "What is that? What are you doing?"

Calmly, Alan answered, "I have a half-naked man wearing a toga, smelling like a Mexican brewery, and claiming to be my dead brother on my doorstep. What do you think I'm doing? I'm calling the police."

"With that?" Tommy laughed at Alan's strange device.

"It's called a cell phone. Us earthlings use them to communicate.

"But I'm telling you the truth," Tommy pleaded. "The doctor kidnapped my body! Maybe you should call the police. Then we can get the crazy doctor arrested and get this whole thing sorted out.

"Listen, buddy, Dr. Zimarchi is a well-respected doctor here in town, and he's been nothing but great to my family over the years. I don't know what kind of drugs you're on, but this is your last chance to leave before I call the cops." Alan raised his phone.

Tommy extended a hand out to him, "I can prove I'm your brother. My favorite band is Bon Jovi. Favorite movie is "This is Spinal Tap.' "

Alan looked up, pausing, "Anyone in town could have told you that about my brother."

Tommy continued, "Your favorite movie was "Revenge of the Nerds" and on the back of your bedroom door was a poster of," snickering, "Richard Marx."

"Any one of my friends could have told you that." Alan paused then defensively mumbled, "And for your information, Richard Marx was a very underrated singer songwriter." With that, Alan began tapping the phone.

"Wait!" Tommy yelled. "When I was 16 you walked in on me with my … you know … stuck in a vacuum hose. I told you if you ever told anyone I would kick your ass."

Alan stopped dialing and just stared at Tommy, shocked.

"Did you ever tell anyone?" Tommy asked. Alan slowly shook his head no. "Well, there ya go. How would I have known that?"

This time it was Tommy who paused then defensively mumbled, "And for your information, I was vacuuming crumbs off my lap and my ... you know ... got accidentally sucked into the hose."

Alan forgot all about his phone. "Uh huh. Vacuuming crumbs off of your lap? Naked? With Daisy Duke giving the General Lee a car wash on the TV in the background?"

"Shut up, Alan. I can still kick your ass, ya know." Tommy watched Alan continue to snicker. "Wait, so you believe me now, right?"

Alan's snickering immediately stopped when he realized he was actually starting to buy into this guy being his brother. "No. No, no, no. I was there. I watched them pull the plug. I watched them bury you."

"Oh for Christ's sake Alan, it's me! Go ahead, ask me something only I would know."

Alan thought long and hard. Then it hit him. "The tattoo. I want to see the tattoo." Tommy began to smile as Alan continued, "After one of the many drunken parties my brother went to in high school, he went and got a tattoo of a microphone ... on his penis. He thought it would be funny to walk up to a girl and ask her to"...

Tommy finished Alan's sentence with him, "Step up to the mic."

Hesitantly, Tommy removed the toga. "Keep in mind, it's a little chilly out this morning," Tommy warned as he slipped off his boxers.

When the tattoo was revealed, all Alan could do was stand there shocked with his mouth dropped open. "Oh my God. It really *is* you."

"See, I told you, bro," Tommy smiled.

Alan rushed forward and hugged his brother - his naked brother. A neighbor, who had been watching the exchange from his window, shook his head in disgust as the two men embraced each other. The cranky, old neighbor quickly closed the curtain and muttered, "I always knew he was a gay."

It wasn't long before both brothers realized what they were doing and quickly separated. Alan scanned to neighborhood for witnesses then ushered Tommy inside the house. As soon as Tommy entered the foyer it hit him - nostalgia overload. Besides the wall color being drastically different, everything else in the small foyer was the same; the 1960's style coat rack his mom bought at a yard sale, the creaky floor boards, and even the pictures on the wall were basically the same. What truly sent chills up his spine was the smell. Tommy closed his eyes and breathed it in. It was the smell of home.

Tommy opened his eyes to Alan giving him a strange look. "What? Ya still can't believe it's me, huh?"

Alan was still shell-shocked, but his strange look was more directed at Tommy's lower half - Tommy's toga-less lower half. When Tommy realized his junk was still hanging out, he quickly toga'd back up.

The two brothers headed into the kitchen. As familiar as the foyer was to Tommy, the kitchen was the exact opposite. *It looked nothing like it did yesterday*, thought Tommy. It would still take him a while to realize that yesterday was actually twenty-five years ago.

The old linoleum floor had been replaced with Pergo. The old laminated counter top was replaced with a black granite top, and the old shit-brown cabinets were now brand new bright white ones. The wallpaper was gone, and the walls were painted a pale yellow. He looked over in the corner, where his mother made him stand a lot. The paint made it look so … neat. The wallpaper had been peeling from the bottom-up. It was something that *might* have happened with age, but was really caused by the thumbnail of a certain 8-year-old who resented a 4-year-old for getting him into trouble. Where was anything familiar? Anything that proved he had ever been there? It wasn't until he spotted the one familiar remnant from childhood that a smile crept onto Tommy's face - The Rooster clock. It had been telling time on that wall for as long as he could remember.

"Nice. Still got the cock clock, huh?"

In unison, both brothers blurted out, "Tic Toc goes the cock clock." They chuckled, and Alan watched Tommy's attention curiously be drawn to the shiny new electric stove. *A coil-less electric stove.* Fascinated, he reached out to touch the flat burner surface, ready to jerk his hand back if it was hot. He then played with the knobs a bit and watched it turn on. Tommy lowered his hand to the now red circle. He smiled as he felt the heat.

"Holy shit, that's hot."

"No crap, Sherlock, it's a stove."

"Cut me a break, Alan! I've been in a brain-dead coma for twenty-five years!"

Alan immediately felt guilty and changed the subject. "You must be thirsty?"

Tommy nodded. Alan made his way over to a Poland Springs bubbler and carefully filled one of the paper snow- coned cups up. He turned around to hand it to his brother, but Tommy had already taken matters into his own hands. Alan cringed in disgust at the sight of Tommy's head under the sink faucet slurping up the water. Alan's face really cringed when Tommy's lips actually pressed onto the nozzle. When Tommy finally finished filling his gut with water, he let out a long, classic Tommy belch. Being out of practice, Tommy only made it to the letter "M" of the alphabet.

He then turned to see Alan standing there…repulsed…and holding his little paper-coned cup. Tommy took one look at the cup then matched Alan's repulsed look with a pathetic chuckle, "Oh God, Alan. You still have your Snoopy Sno Cone machine? It's bad enough you still live with Ma and Dad."

Alan paused, "I own the house now, Tommy."

"You do? Aw, lemme guess. They retired to Florida and left you the frickin' house? They were always giving you free shit. I know you were always their favorite and all, but I can't believe"…

Somberly, Alan interrupted, "Dad passed away five years ago, Tommy."

Tommy's jealousy quickly turned to shock. Alan motioned for Tommy to have a seat. Both brothers sat and Alan continued, "He had a heart attack at work."

Instantaneously, a tear formed in Tommy's eye. Alan couldn't remember the last time he saw a tear in his brother's eye. And for that very reason, a tear quickly formed in Alan's eye as well. Tommy swallowed hard andhesitantly asked, "What about…Mom?"

"About a year before Dad's heart attack, she began showing signs of early Alzheimer's. It's gotten progressively worse. I should have moved back here sooner. Maybe I could have taken some of the stress off of Dad. And maybe he wouldn't have"… A look of sympathy filled Tommy's face as he listened to his little brother. Even though Tommy's face was unrecognizable to Alan, he gladly welcomed the sympathetic look.

"After Dad passed, I moved back in and did my best to take care of her, but she started needing constant attention and couldn't really be left home alone. I was finally forced to put her over in Pine View's Assisted-Living Home." Tommy sighed and his shoulders sank. It was as if the gravity of the situation was weighted on them. "She's also developed a heart condition and is on all kinds of meds for it. I'm actually on my way over there now before work. The nurse called and told me that Ma had a rough night last night."

"I'll go with you," Tommy said.

"I don't think that's a good idea, Tommy. Most days she doesn't even know who *I* am. Between that and her heart condition, finding out that you're alive might push her over the edge."

"So what are you saying, Alan? We shouldn't go to the cops and have Dr. Zimarchi arrested? That we shouldn't tell the world I'm alive?"

No, I'm not saying that at all. I just think you should stay here and keep a low profile until I get back, then we can decide how to handle this." Alan paused, "And just so you know, Doctor Zimarchi is the one who's paying for Mom's home. I woulda never been able to afford it on my own. He said it was something that he wanted to do."

"I bet!" exclaimed Tommy. "He feels guilty for lying and kidnapping me and using me as a lab rat all these years."

"Look, Tommy, I know you're angry, but please promise me you won't leave here until I get back. I'm going to visit Mom, then I have an important meeting at school, then I'll"...

"School? You're still in school?" Tommy laughed.

"I guess I am, sort of. I'm the principal of York High.

"You're shitting me?"

"I actually started off as a science teacher. I did that for 12 years, but I was becoming more and more disenfranchised with the way the whole building was being run. I, like most of the other teachers, found ourselves bitching and moaning about the current regime."

"Principal Jenkins?" Tommy asked. Alan nodded. "That guy was a major dick."

Again, Alan nodded. "It was actually Dad who set me on my new path. I can't remember his exact cliché quote, but he told me I had no right complaining unless I planned on doing something about it."

Tommy smiled, "If you're not part of the solution then you're part of the problem."

"That's the one," Alan laughed. "Anyway, I went back to school and got my Administrative degree, and lo and behold, that following summer, Principal Jenkins resigned...like out of the blue. He only had a few more years left until retirement too. It was weird. What was even stranger was I was probably the most underqualified candidate, yet I got the job. But, like Dad always said, 'Don't kick a gift horse in the mouth.'"

"Wow. Principal Stevens, huh?"

Alan nodded then glanced at the cock clock. "Look, I'll be back as soon as I can, okay? I definitely need to get back before Richie gets home."

"Who?" Tommy curiously questioned.

"Richie. My son. My 17-year-old son,"

"You have a son? Holy shit! You know what that means, right?"

"Uh, yeah, that you're an Uncle."

"No," Tommy smiled, "It means my baby brother actually had sex with a girl!"

Slowly, Alan shook his head, "Different body, same sarcasm. Just don't leave the house, okay? Oh, and you might want to put some real clothes on. Feel free to raid my closet." Alan grabbed his keys and headed out. A second later, he reappeared and made his way to the sink. On the counter was a container of disinfectant wipes. Alan pulled one out and quickly, yet thoroughly disinfected the faucet nozzle. With that load off his back, Alan finally left.

Tommy stood there smiling. "Same body, same anal-retentive Alan." Tommy moved toward the countertop, touching each new, modern appliance. The microwave was a third of the size of their old one. "Magic bullet?" he pondered, "sounds more like a ..."

He stopped briefly, then rummaged through a few cabinets until he found exactly what he was looking for; a box of Chicken in a Biskit. "The classics remain," he said with satisfaction as he stuffed his face.

On his way out of the kitchen, he stopped at the wall near the doorway, puzzled at the calendar hanging there. He lifted it up, finding the old wall phone jack underneath. "No phone?" From there, Tommy headed upstairs to do a little more exploring.

Tommy headed up the old staircase. He once again noticed that the old floral wallpaper had been replaced with a fresh coat of light green paint. With all the modernizations, Tommy was happy to know that step #2 and step #4 still creaked (knowledge that had come in handy when sneaking out of the house). The nostalgia didn't end there, on the green walls were the same pictures as twenty-five years ago; the exact same pictures in the exact same spot.

Tommy paused on the stairs, and his walk down memory lane began. The first two pictures were Tommy and Alan as newborns (Tommy's was in black & white). Tommy's eyes then moved to a family picture of the four of them at York's Wild Kingdom. Tommy was 10, Alan 6.

In the picture, Tommy had a smug little smile. Little Alan forced a sad, brave face as he held in position the broken ear of the giant teddy bear he was so proud to have won in a balloon game. Tommy ripped off the ear moments before the picture was taken.

Sadness overcame Tommy as he scanned some more old pictures. He did let out a slight chuckle at the picture of him and Alan at York Beach (Short Sands). Alan was putting the finishing touches on a massive sand castle, and for all intents and purposes, the two brothers were playing nicely together. Tommy knew better. Moments after the picture was taken, Tommy turned into Godzilla, smashing poor Alan's architectural masterpiece. Tommy could have spent hours reminiscing at the wall of photos, but decided to move on to the upstairs bedrooms; in particular, his.

Once upstairs, the first room he entered was his parent's old bedroom. It didn't take long before Tommy realized that Alan had claimed it as his own. It was neat as a pin, exactly as Tommy would have expected. Framed degrees hung on the wall with a picture of Alan and his infant son on the dresser. In the closet, all of the clothing was neatly hung and arranged by color. Tommy looked back and forth from his toga to Alan's clothes. There was no way he could bring himself to wear something of Alan's. He promptly shut the closet door and moved on.

Next, he walked over to the bed. On the nightstand was an inhaler and a box of Breathe-Right strips. He studied the box then quizzically opened it. He pulled out one of the strips and placed it on his nose. When he didn't feel anything different, he simply shrugged and turned his attention to the bedside drawer.

He opened the drawer and smiled when he saw a pack of condoms. His smile turned into amazement when he saw the box had never been opened. Looking closely, he read out loud the words printed there, "Expiration date: July 2010. Poor bastard didn't even get to break the seal." Before Tommy left the room, he made it a point to look at the back of the bedroom door. It was j as he suspected, a Richard Marx poster.

The next room down the hall was Alan's old bedroom. The room was sparsely decorated with a bed, a computer, and little else. He walked in and touched the computer a little then looked around. "Richie's room," he surmised. There were posters on the wall of people he didn't recognize, and they were *all men*. Tommy's face scowled at the sight of a poster featuring a geeky looking man with the words *Microsoft* spread across the top.

"What the hell kinda crap does he listen to?" questioned Tommy."

The next poster he came across read *The Big Bang Theory*. Tommy didn't recognize a single poster or person with the exception of the one over Richie's bed: Einstein.

"Looks like the pocket protector doesn't fall far from the geek." Tommy shook his head in disapproval, but the real disapproval came when he couldn't find a stereo system…anywhere. "What kind of teenager doesn't own a stereo system?" Tommy mumbled and started to head out.

On a whim, he decided to check out the back of Richie's door. Hanging there in full color was a poster of … *who? …Gizell? …what?* He couldn't read the signature, but it didn't really matter. It was a *girl*. A hot girl. In a bathing suit.

"That's what I'm talking about! Maybe there's hope for you yet, little nephew!"

Tommy continued down the hall until he came face to face with his old bedroom door. His heart raced, and his hands clammed up.

Tommy took a deep breath then opened the door. It was the same as he'd last seen it, except the dust was newer or at least not the same kind of dust. It was like someone had wiped off the cigarette ash and then let it collect real dust, the kind that accumulates with time. And there were no fingerprints on the stereo door.

All of his posters were still in their proper places. Everything was just how he left it. He slowly opened his dresser drawers and saw all of his old clothes were still there. They were unfolded and shoved in, exactly how they were supposed to be. He wasted no time in putting on one of his old concert tees. It was a few sizes too small, but Tommy was determined to wear it. It was either that or one of Alan's Izod shirts.

It took some effort to get the tee on over his new husky body. The whole time he was cursing that stupid Mexican midget for feeding him so much. He then stared at his old ripped blue jeans. No matter how much he sucked it in, or how much he greased himself, Tommy knew there was no way in hell he was getting them on. Instead, he was forced to go with the stretchier sweatpants. They were stretchier, but still super snug and short. The whole outfit looked as though he had just turned into the hulk with those clothes on.

Craving more Chicken in a Biskits, Tommy decided to head back to the kitchen. He sprinted down the old staircase, and just as he was going to jump the final three steps, he stopped cold. Another photograph on the wall caught his eye. It was from December 1982. It was a family picture of them cutting down their Christmas tree together. Tommy's eyes were squarely fixed on his mother and father. As the memories began to get the best of him, Tommy angrily reached up and ripped off the nose strip and then proceeded to rush into the garage.

Once in the garage, he frantically searched until he spotted what he was looking for. *Jackpot! My old bike.* On the back wall, hidden by various lawn equipment, was Tommy's old blue Schwinn ten speed (Big Blue). A wide smile filled Tommy's face as he reunited with his old friend. *Double jackpot!* On Big Blue's seat was sat Tommy's old cycling cap. He knew what he must do. It was time to relive his *Quicksilver* days.

TRACK 12

You know that old saying: You don't forget…it's like riding a bike? Well, it wasn't so much that Tommy forgot how to ride a bike, but he definitely didn't take into consideration that his entire body had been non-mobile for twenty-five years. And he certainly didn't take into consideration the last time he rode this he was 50 pounds lighter. Now that he was fatter (huskier), he had the hardest time keeping balance.

By the time he returned to Dr. Zimarchi's house, he was huffing and puffing up an asthmatic storm. When he arrivedin the doctor's driveway, he jumped (fell) off of the bike, tripping over it as it crashed to the ground. When Tommy regained his balance, he turned back and kicked Big Blue twice. He headed towards the front door cursing his new physique, "Stupid … fat … fucking Taco!"

Tommy pounded his fist repeatedly on the front door. Finally, after 9 seconds of pounding, he stopped and attempted to calm himself, "When you feel it boiling up inside, count backward from ten, and it'll subside. When you feel it boiling up inside, count backward from ten, and it'll subside. Ten, nine, eight, seven, six, five, four, three (deep breath) …two (deeper breath)…one."

Not only was Tommy perplexed at where the hell that phrase came from, he was more perplexed at the fact that he said the whole thing in a deep southern accent. Either way, he was considerably calmer than just a few moments earlier. Before he could analyze this strange occurrence, the large door slowly opened, revealing Dr. Zimarchi.

The doctor looked at Tommy in his tight sweatpants, his super undersized Bon Jovi tee, and topped off with his cycling cap. The doctor then scanned the driveway and yard.

"Don't worry, Doc. I didn't bring the cops with me. Yet."

Doctor Zimarchi slowly opened the door wider, turned, and motioned for Tommy to follow him. They entered the living room, where Tommy caught his first glimpse of an awake, yet still hung-over Paco. He was sitting on the couch (feet dangling, not touching the floor) with a wide grin on his face. Tommy shook his head then plopped down onto a leather recliner. The doctor quietly sat next to Paco and awaited Tommy's words.

"I see that guilt has got the best of you, huh, Doc? Paying for my mom's medical care?"

Nonchalantly, without a hint of guilt, the doctor shrugged, "I see you told your brother?"

Out of the corner of his eye, Tommy could see that Paco was still smiling at him. "What are you smiling at, Taco?" snarled Tommy. "I hear that *you* were responsible for my diet – or lack thereof?"

Paco's smile turned into a look of confusion as he turned toward the doctor.

"I believe he's referring to you letting him get fat," clarified Dr. Zimarchi.

Tommy quickly interjected, "Hey! I'm not fat! I'm just a little husky."

"I know you must have a lot of questions," began Dr. Zimarchi, "and you're still probably a little upset."

"A little upset?" Tommy shouted. "Dude, you kidnapped my body! You faked my death! And you used me as your Guinea pig for the past twenty-five years! I'd say upset is an understatement." Tommy glared at the two culprits. "You two are gonna spend the rest of your lives in jail! And you know what they do to people who do stuff like this, right?" Paco and Dr. Zimarchi watched as Tommy continued to babble, getting it all out of his system. "They'll do bad, bad things to you. Like... like, drop the soap type of things, and some giant black dude named Zeus will make you his bitches! Especially YOU, you little burrito."

The doctor gave Paco's shoulder a pat, encouraging him that things would be okay. Tommy continued his rant, "So tell me, Doc, what would possibly possess a person to do what you did to me? Huh? I think you owe me that much. I think you owe my family that much."

138

The doctor stood up, making his way over to a large end table in the corner of the room. The table was adorned with many framed pictures. Carefully, he picked one up. It looked to be from the early 70's. In it was a 27-year-old Doctor Zimarchi sitting on a couch with a woman and a sweet looking seven-year-old boy.

After staring at it for the longest time, he finally spoke, "This picture was taken two weeks before my son's 7th birthday. The day this was taken was the last time I ever saw him." Tommy's anger softened as the doctor continued, "Regretfully, I was always away on business back then. I wasn't even there on his actual birthday. But I did what I always did - tried to buy his love. I had a present sent in hope of making up for my absence. That particular year was a new bike – dark blue, his favorite color."

Tommy looked over at Paco, who sat listening with his head hung low.

"I did find time to call him that night. He was so excited about his bike. It was the coolest most expensive bike on the market back then. He told me all his friends were jealous." The doctor paused, "I guess that was always my intention."

Doctor Zimarchi moved across the room and continued, "He kept asking me when I was coming home so I could see him ride it. I told him soon. I used that phrase a lot back then," he lamented. "With my wife, with my son, it was always *soon*."

The doctor turned his back, and Tommy used that moment to sit on the couch. "He was so excited that his bike came with a mini headlight," he continued, "but was disappointed because his mother wouldn't let him try it out that night." The doctor made his way back towards Tommy. "Of course, being the alpha male that I am, I told him to tell his mother that he had *my* permission to take it for a quick spin up the block and back. After we got off the phone, he did just that. But"...

The doctor slumped onto the couch, and Tommy noticed a tear form in the doctor's eye as he continued, "But he never came back. He never came back."

More tears followed down his cheek. Paco made his way over and sympathetically put his little hand on the doctor's shoulder. Tommy himself, was also fighting the urge to cry. The doctor appreciatively smiled at Paco then continued, "Apparently, Sam was riding down our street with his headlight lighting the way. Witnesses said he looked so happy...so excited." His voice slowed, "So excited that apparently he didn't see the stop sign...or the car turning onto our road. He hit the car and flew over the handlebars and slammed his head on the road." The doctor's gaze moved from the picture to Tommy's eyes. "I bought him the fanciest bike out there, but didn't bother getting him a God damn helmet."

Uncomfortable watching the tears fall from the doctor's eyes, Tommy forced himself to look away. The doctor wiped his eyes and continued, "The doctors told us he was brain dead and that there was nothing they could do. I was used to being in control of things, but with this, I was powerless. Absolutely powerless. The whole thing was my fault; for not being there, for overriding his mother's wishes. I wasn't there for his birthday, but I was there when they pulled the plug on my boy. On my beautiful, little 7 year old boy."

He closed his crying eyes and clutched the picture to his heart. The room was dead silent. Tommy felt a huge lump in his throat and even fought back his own tears.

Dr. Zimarchi placed the picture back on the table and continued, "Our lives were never the same. My wife never forgave me, and truth be told, I never forgave myself. We divorced soon after, and I haven't seen her since. It was at that point I dedicated my life to the medical field – brain trauma in particular."

Tommy was a little confused with the doctor's revelation. "Wait, you weren't already in that field?"

Dr. Zimarchi shook his head.,"No. Not at all."

"What business were you in?" Tommy asked.

The doctor glanced over at Paco then slowly answered, "Let's just say it was the family business." Tommy's suspicions grew. At this point, the doctor walked away from the picture table and stood face to face with Tommy. "I know you're confused and upset, but what I did was for the greater good. Because of this breakthrough, there's a chance no parent has to ever sit by and helplessly watch the plug being pulled on their child."

Tommy struggled between anger and sympathy. The anger came out first. "You're just trying to weasel out of me calling the cops on you guys, aren't you?"

"No Tommy," he answered, "I'm not trying to weasel out of anything. I'm telling you to just wait thirty days. Thirtydays for me to try and figure out what exactly cured you."

"Wait! Tommy exclaimed. "You don't know what cured me?"

"Not exactly," the doctor answered. "Let's just say, last night Paco gave you quite a few different...items.

Both the doctor and Tommy shot a look Paco's way. Paco widely and innocently smiled then shrugged.

"I just need some time to figure out what triggered your awakening. Give me thirty days. After that, call the police, if you feel you have to." Tommy's original anger wavered. "Just think how many lives could be saved ... lives *we* could save."

As Tommy stood there torn between anger and sympathy, he couldn't help but think that his own drunk driving could have killed someone. Someone's mother...someone's father...or heaven forbid, someone's child. He relented, "Thirty days. I'll give you thirty days."

Dr, Zimarchi graciously nodded then paused to point out, "Nobody can know your true identity over that time. I can get you a place to live if you'd like?"

"I'm fine. I'll stay at my house with Alan."

"Is he trustworthy?" the doctor inquired.

"Alan? Oh God yea. Trustworthy is like his middle name. Along with geek, and nerd, and fat ass...and, well, Michael. He's trustworthy. Besides, and he still hasn't told anyone about the vacuum cleaner incident."

Dr. Zimarchi and Paco shared a confused, yet amused smirk. Tommy made his way towards the front door, but before he opened it, he curiously turned back to the doctor, "By the way, how the hell did you pull this whole fake death thing off anyway? A lot of people must have been involved, no?"

"Let's just say, a lot of people owe me... favors. Luckily, due to your face being so damaged, your father convinced your mother to have a closed casket. That made it a little easier on us."

"So my casket was empty?"

The doctor looked over at Paco, who had a blank expression on his face, then he answered Tommy, "Something like that."

Unsure how to read into the doctor's cryptic response, Tommy slowly exited the house and climbed onto Big Blue. Through the window, Dr. Zimarchi watched Tommy pedal down the long driveway. When he was out of sight, the doctor turned to his trusty side-kick and spoke, "Well, my little friend, time to get back to work." Paco nodded, and the two headed down into the basement laboratory. They had thirty days to figure out what exactly triggered Tommy's miraculous recovery.

***

Tommy had the urge to pedal off and explore his old hometown to see what changes had occurred over the years, but he didn't. Partly because he promised Alan he wouldn't leave the house, but mostly because his legs felt like spaghetti, and at any moment he might cough up a lung. With his energy running low, Tommy thought it best to head back home.

Back at the house, Tommy put away Big Blue and went straight to the kitchen, where he once again buried his face under the faucet.

When his thirst was finally quenched, he grabbed the box of Chicken in a Biskits and slid into a kitchen chair. Just as he shoved a handful into his mouth, he heard the front door open and close.

"I hope you brought more Chicken in a Biskits, bro. I'm about to polish these little fuckers off!" Tommy yelled as crumbs spewed from his mouth. He leaned back in the chair and put his feet up on the table knowing full well this would send Alan into a disinfectant whirlwind.

The kitchen door slowly creaked open, but to Tommy's surprise, it wasn't Alan's disapproving mug that entered. Well, it was, and it wasn't. It was definitely Alan's mug, though much younger, and it wasn't disapproving as much as it was curious. *Richie*, Tommy guessed. Aside from the fact that he knew Alan was much older now, there was one blatant difference between younger Alan and this boy – the clothing. This kid actually looked normal. He wore a dark T-shirt, blue jeans (not too blue), and sneakers. Not a pocket protector in sight. And his hair – there were actually a few strands out of place and not smeared down with cream or a saliva-laden palm. Tommy smiled in pride.

"Who are you?" questioned Richie.

"Me? I'm...um"... Tommy removed his feet from the table as his mind raced for an answer. "I'm... I'm an old friend of your father's."

"Oh. Like an old college friend or something?" asked Richie.

"Yes. Exactly. We're old college buddies. Yup, I went to college with Alan."

For what seemed like an eternity (7 seconds), Richie stared at Tommy. *There's no way he's gonna buy it*, thought Tommy. But then, as the 7 second stare ended, Richie simply nodded then proceeded to get a drink of water from the Poland Spring's bubbler.

"Cool. How long you visiting for?" asked Richie.

"Um, I don't exactly know yet."

Richie finished his water, gave an approving nod then started to leave. "I'm gonna play a little X-Box if you want in." Before Tommy could ask what the hell an X-Box was, Richie continued, "Yea, I try to get my video game fix in before Dad gets home."

"Ohhh, video games. Yea, count me in!"

Richie motioned for Tommy to follow him into the other room.

"I have to warn you, though," commented Tommy, "I did own the high score on Galaga over at the Town House Pizza. And Tempest too."

Nonchalantly, Richie spoke, "Oh. Cool. What's *Galaga* and *Tempest?*"

"What's Galaga and Tempest?" exclaimed Tommy. "I'll tell you exactly what they are"… But before Tommy could school his nephew on the classics, they entered the living room. Tommy stopped mid-sentence and was taken aback by the completely different and updated living room. What was most obvious was how much bigger and brighter it looked with the paneling removed and the walls painted some shade of … beige? What the hell was that color? The couch … the couch was amazing. Tommy had fond memories of passing out on the old couch. It used to be worn and pilling, with the high back and the permanent dent three quarters of the way down from his ass spending so much time there. This couch was so much deeper and longer, inviting some serious napping. The solid color of it (almost the same color as the walls, but darker) made it look immense. If he had this couch years ago, it would have been dinners on the TV trays and video games non-stop. He would never have left it – not for school or anything (well, except maybe sex. *Holy shit! Sex on THAT couch?*)

Tommy probably would have continued in that same vein of thought if Richie hadn't moved, subverting his attention away from his teenage hornball-sex thoughts to the more manly arousal that happens at the sight of a video game system hooked up to a television that took up most of the wall space – right *on the wall! Like in a movie theater!* They were almost too much to take in.

When Richie handed him what looked to be a game controller, he turned it over in his hand a few times, trying to figure out how it was supposed to connect to the game. *Where were the wires*, he thought. Richie turned the TV on and all Tommy could do was just stare.

Richie asked him which game he wanted to play, but stopped when he saw Tommy's face, looking back and forth between the couch, the game controller, and the TV. It was like he'd never seen them before. Curiously, Richie watched as Tommy took the few steps towards the television and started touching it – or, rather, *fondling* it. At any second, Richie expected him to smell it or something.

Finally, after several *Ooo's* and *Ahh's*, Tommy spoke, "I don't get it. How can it be so thin, so flat, yet the picture be so…real?"

For a brief moment, Richie thought Tommy was just pulling his leg. "You're kidding, right? You've never seen an HD flat screen before?" Tommy didn't answer. He was too busy taking a whiff of the strange flat screen thingy. "Holy crap! You're serious. Have you been living under a rock the past ten years or what?"

Richie's question snapped Tommy out of his mesmerized trance, and without even thinking, he blurted out, "Twenty-five years, actually."

"What?" Richie had no clue whether to take this strange dude serious or not. "You're joking, right?"

Tommy's hands clammed up as he scrambled for a response. Trying his best not to make eye contact with Richie, he nervously scanned the room. He was panicked. It was only day one, and the truth was already going to come out. But then, with his eyes fixated on the stack of National Geographic's on the coffee table, an idea hit him. The wheels of Tommy's newly healed brain were quickly churning, concocting a master bullshit story.

"Um, yea, I kinda have been under a rock. More specifically, a jungle. I work for National Geographic, and for the last twenty-five years I've been in the jungles of Africa doing extensive research on a remote African tribe. Documentary kind of stuff. I've had absolutely zero communication with the outside world. No phones, no TV's, not even any electricity. Yup, we just lived off the land. On corn mostly."

"They grow corn in the jungle?" Richie skeptically asked.

Without hesitation, Tommy replied, "Well, yea, African corn."

Pausing for a moment, Richie stared blankly at Tommy then simply said, "Wow. Twenty-five years. That's like, more than my whole life. I hope they paid you well."

"Eh, no. It was more of a passion project."

"Hmm…cool." Richie offered a nod of approval then proceeded to turn on the X-Box. "Well, in that case, I really think you'll like this game. It's about survival, being creative, and living off the land."

"Alright, let's do this! What's it called?" Tommy asked.

"Minecraft. You're gonna love it."

Over the next hour, Tommy was introduced to the strange block-world of Minecraft. It was the longest hour of his life. It was also the longest hour of Richie's life as well. He lost track of how many times Tommy asked him things like: "When do we get to blow things up," or "How do I know if I'm winning?" And Richie definitely wasn't impressed with the giant block penis Tommy *erected*.

Richie was never so relieved when he heard his dad enter the front door. "We should probably shut this off. Dad's not big on video games on a school night."

Tommy couldn't agree fast enough, "Definitely. School nights should be about school work. That's what I've always said."

***

After dinner, Richie helped his dad with the dishes. Tommy had excused himself to, as he put it, "take a major dump." Richie joked with Tommy, asking him if he wanted him to gather some leaves to use to wipe with. Tommy thought the comment was hilarious. Alan, not so much. Not only was Alan uncomfortable with all the lying to his son, he was a nervous wreck knowing they might have thirty more days of this. Not surprisingly, Tommy was a natural at it, even if some of his stories were a bit ridiculous. Case in point:

"Mr. Neily is pretty cool, huh, Dad?" commented Richie while he loaded the dishwasher.

"Who?" Alan asked.

"Uh, hello…your friend from college, Vince Neily." Alan smirked and shook his head at his brother's lack of creativity. Richie continued, "Hard to believe someone would spend twenty-five years of their life in the African jungle studying the Mo-tah-lay-cru-ayy tribe, huh?"

Alan fought back laughter, ""Ah, yes, good ole Vince Neily and the Mo-tah-lay-cru-ayy tribe"

Just then, Tommy entered the kitchen asking, "If one was looking for a plunger, where would one look?"

"In the bathroom closet," laughed Richie.

"Good to know," said Tommy. "Hey, how about a little more video game action after? Maybe try out something other than that Minecrap game."

"Minecraft," corrected Richie.

"Ooo, you guys were playing Minecraft?" said Alan, a bit too excited.

Of course my brother would like that stupid game, thought Tommy.

"Um, maybe tomorrow, Vince. My girlfriend is picking me up in a few. We're going to study together at the library." Richie headed upstairs to get ready.

Tommy turned to Alan, "And by library, he actually means library, doesn't he?" Like father like son, I guess."

"Yea," Alan proudly nodded, "he's pretty great, isn't he?"

"Eh, he's ok," smiled Tommy. "Need some help cleaning up? Tommy asked.

Alan braced himself for the punchline, but there wasn't one. Tommy was actually helping clear the table. Alan was shocked and speechless. It was only when he saw Tommy throwing away the empty salad dressing bottle that he uttered, "Oh, that doesn't get thrown away. It gets rinsed out then thrown in the recycle bins." Alan pointed to the back wall of the kitchen. There were several green bins on the floor. It was Tommy's turn to be speechless.

Number 1 and 2 plastics go in the first bin, all other plastics in the second bin. Non-refundable cans go in the next one and cardboard in the last. Oh, there's also a bin just for paper in my office." By the look on Tommy's face, Alan could tell he was confused and overwhelmed.

"We pretty much recycle everything nowadays. It's the three R's -reuse, renew, recycle. It's all about keeping the earth green," Alan boasted.

What the fuck is my brother talking about, thought Tommy. "Is this because of that commercial when we were kids?" Tommy asked.

"What?"

"You know, the one with that Indian dude crying on the side of the road?"

Alan knew exactly what commercial he was talking about. "First of all, Tommy, you can't say Indian, it's not very PC."

"PC?" Tommy exclaimed clueless.

"Politically correct," Alan responded. There are a lot of phrases you can't use nowadays. The proper term is Native American."

Before Tommy could even try to wrap his mind around this whole PC thing, there was a knock at the front door.

"That must be Emma," Alan said. Tommy began to head towards the door. "What are you doing?" questioned Alan.

"I'm going to check out my nephew's taste in women. I bet she totally has braces, doesn't she?"

Alan's eyes widened in a panic as Tommy headed towards the front door. "Tommy, wait"…

It was too late. Tommy had already swung open the front door and was now face to face with … *Gina?*

The girl standing in the doorway could have been Gina the last time Tommy saw her; the same smile, the same green eyes, and even the same black hair, albeit with purple streaks in it. *This* was Richie's girlfriend, Emma? Tommy couldn't take his eyes off her. He was literally speechless.

"Um, hi, is Richie here? Emma said.

Tommy opened his mouth, but no words came out. Alan quickly stepped in to diffuse the awkward moment, "Hey Emma. Richie will be right down. This is my old college friend, Vince."

"Vince has been living with an African tribe the last twenty-five years," yelled Richie as he scampered down the stairs. "He's doing a documentary on them. He had no TV, no electricity, and he doesn't even know what a cell phone is! Isn't that right, Vince?" Without taking his eyes off Emma, Tommy nodded.

"Wow, that's cool," exclaimed Emma. "I can't go a day without my iPhone or else I start freaking out."

"I know, right," added Richie as he grabbed a light jacket. "I'll see you guys later."

"Goodnight, Mr. Stevens," Emma politely said on her way out. "Oh, nice meeting you, Vince."

It wasn't until the door had been shut for several seconds that Tommy uttered, "Nice meeting you too." Slowly, he turned to Alan. "Is it me or does she look exactly like"...

Alan nodded, "Emma is Gina's daughter."

Tommy moved to the window and watched Richie and Emma drive off. "So...Gina's married, huh?"

"Actually, she's not," Alan answered. "Emma's dad bolted as soon as he found out Gina was pregnant. She's had a few serious relationships since then but never married."

Alan sympathetically watched as Tommy sighed and leaned his face against the window pane. It was impossible for him to imagine what his brother was going through.

TRACK 13

For the next two days, Alan was adamant that Tommy not leave the house, and to Alan's surprise, Tommy actually followed orders. It didn't hurt there was torrential rain for two days, not to mention, Tommy's legs were still recovering from the bike ride days earlier – and, of course, the couch and TV were in the house.

By the time Saturday morning arrived, and there were no good cartoons to watch (as far as he was concerned), Tommy was bouncing off the walls. Literally. Richie had introduced Tommy to Red Bull.

"Come on," Tommy begged. "Can't we at least go out for a coffee or something?"

"I don't think that's a very smart idea," urged Alan.

"Come on, bro. Nobody's gonna recognize me. *You* didn't even know it was me."

"I'm not worried about people recognizing you. I'm worried about you opening your mouth with your stupid, unbelievable stories."

"What? I think I've been very creative."

"Vince Neily? Motley Crue tribe?"

"It's the Mo-tah-lay-cru-ayy tribe," corrected Tommy. Come on, Alan, just a coffee. Okay?"

"If you want a coffee, I can make you one in the Keurig."

Tommy stared blankly at his little brother. "I want to go out in a public place with real people around me and have a coffee made by a human being not by this Keurig thing you talk about. Preferably, a cute waitress, but at this point, I just wanna get the fuck outta the house!"

"Well," Alan smiled, "there is a new little café I fancy over in Kittery."

"Well, let's fancy our way over there then."

***

Lil's Café is located in the newly revitalized downtown Kittery area known as Wallingsford Square. It overlooks the Portsmouth Navy Yard. Due to the fact that Mr. Stevens worked his whole life here, this area was very familiar to the two brothers. Of course, back then the Square was nothing but vacant storefronts.

As Tommy's eyes took in the plethora of new businesses, Alan ushered him into the café. Immediately, Alan was greeted from behind the counter by Mia. Mia was in her mid-thirties with dark-rimmed glasses, and her brown hair pulled into a pony tail. Tommy could tell by the silly, smitten smile on Alan's face that this chick was the sole reason for him choosing this place. If his smile wasn't enough of a giveaway, the bumbling words that followed was.

"Morning, Alan. The usual?" smiled Mia.

"You know it. Actually, make it two. Mia, this is my br...my old friend Vince. Vince, this is Mia. Mia is the best barista in Maine. New England, for that matter. Heck, probably the best in the whole darn country," nervously babbled Alan.

Tommy knew this nervous look all too well. It was usually followed by a gaseous release from Alan's ass. Tommy used that moment to motion to Alan that he was going to grab them a table. Alan barely noticed Tommy walk away. He was too busy awkwardly flirting (and holding a fart in).

"Aw, thanks Alan," smiled Mia. "That means a lot, especially coming from probably the best principal in the country."

"Oh, I don't know about that," blushed Alan. "By the way, that shirt's a great color on you, Mia. Is it new?"

"Why thank you," she gushed. "Actually, it is. I bought it at the new boutique around the corner."

"Oh yeah. I've heard great things about that store (he's never heard of it).

"Hey, did you hear the latest rumors?" Mia questioned.

Alan's smile quickly faded. He looked panicked (and gassy). *She knew about Tommy! The cat was out of the....*

"Did you hear about that Zumba studio being a possible front for prostitution?" Mia giggled.

"Wait? What?" Alan was relieved and confused at the same time. "Which one?"

"The one on Main Street over in York."

Alan laughed, "No way! That's right around the corner from me. I guess my little town ain't so little anymore."

"I know, right?" Mia smiled as she handed Alan his two drinks. "Enjoy."

"Thanks Mia." Alan grabbed his drinks and headed over to Tommy.

Impatiently, Tommy snatched the drink from Alan. "About time." Tommy took one sip, nearly spitting it out on Alan. "What the fuck is this?"

"What? It's a mocha latte."

"More like a mocha crapé. I just wanted a normal coffee. And why'd you have to order for me. I mighta been dead for twenty-five years, but I'm not retarded."

Alan gazed around. "First of all, keep your voice down about that. Secondly, you can't use the "R" word. It's mentally challenged." Tommy didn't offer a comeback. He simply stared blankly into his brother's eyes.

When Alan wasn't gawking at Mia, he was staring at his brother. Self-consciously, Tommy tugged at his overly and embarrassingly tight Whitesnake tee shirt.

"I don't know why you just don't borrow some of my clothes," Alan asked.

"Duh! Because I don't wanna look like you, that's why!"

"I suppose I could take you clothes shopping or something. It is kind of embarrassing to be around you looking like that."

Alan, embarrassed to be around me? It was as if Tommy had entered the bizarro world. Alan continued to stare. "Dude, I get it! I need new clothes. Quit staring!" Tommy growled.

"No, it's just…I know it's you," Alan whispered, "but I'm still not used to your new face…or body."

Tommy turned red. "Pfft, tell me about it. I nearly shit a brick every time I walk by a mirror."

"And I really have a hard time believing Dr. Zimarchi kidnapped your body all these years," Alan whispered lower.

"Well, it's true," Tommy snapped.

"I would have expected that from Dr. Hargrove but not Dr. Zimarchi."

"Who's that?" Tommy asked.

He was the lead doctor assigned to you, and quite possibly the biggest asshole in medical history. Excuse my language," Alan apologized.

"Why, what was wrong with him?" Tommy asked.

He was cold, sarcastic, and extremely rude, especially to Mom and Dad. We all despised him. Dr. Zimarchi despised him too. They were constantly arguing over what was best for you. Dr. Zimarchi always made sure we were fully informed about everything. He was great to our family. He was the opposite of Dr. Hargrove. One time, Ma walked in on him feeling up one of the nurses in your room."

"Cool," Tommy said impressed. Alan just glared at him. "Whatever ever happened to him?" Tommy asked.

That's where the story gets interesting," Alan began. "Less than a day after he pulled the plug on you, he disappeared."

"Disappeared? Like moved away?"

"Nope. All of his stuff in his house remained untouched. He just disappeared. I guess it was all over the news, but we were all focused on...well, your funeral," Alan said somberly.

Tommy went on to ask Alan more about his funeral. *What was it like? Who showed up? Who said what?* Tommy was surprised and touched at some of the people who showed up.

Uncomfortable with the whole funeral conversation, Alan decided to change the subject, "So what do you want to do today?"

This caused Tommy to smile. "We should go see the old crew. I'm dying to see what Otto, Ricky and Pud are up to. And maybe pay a visit to Gina?"

Alan was quick to respond, "Oh no, no, no, no. You're supposed to be laying low, remember? I was thinking maybe a movie or a museum." The *yeah right* look Tommy gave Alan at the mention of a museum was so familiar it made Alan smile. "Besides," he continued, "you'd be pretty shocked to see them now."

"Dude, I just spent the last twenty-five years getting experimented on by a mad scientist. I don't think anything would shock me."

As the two brothers exited the café, Alan made it a point to wave good-bye to Mia.

"You guys leaving already?" Mia said.

"Yea, I don't wanna be late for my Zumba class," joked Alan. "I'm totally just kidding."

"Uh huh," laughed Mia. Tommy had no clue what was going on nor did he care.

***

They sat for the longest time in the parking lot just staring up at the building and its sign: Pine View Nursing Home.

"I really don't think this is a good idea, Tommy."

"Relax, Alan. It'll be fine. You didn't even recognize me until I showed you my tattoo. Besides, I wanna see Mom."

Once again, it was impossible for Alan to comprehend what his brother was going through, and because of that, he knew he had to respect Tommy's requests, but with extreme caution.

They made their way up the well-landscaped walkway and paused at the front door. Alan turned to his brother and softly spoke, "Remember, Tommy, she's not gonna know who you are. She barely remembers who I am half the time." Tommy nodded then followed Alan inside.

"Alan," said a female voice from behind the front desk. "How lovely to see you." A woman walked out around the desk and rushed to give Alan a tender hug.

"Hello, Barbara," Alan said warmly, then he turned and introduced her to Tommy. "Vince, this is Barbara, the woman who makes sure our—my mother is comfortable here." Alan caught his mistake fast. "Barbara, this is Vince. We went to, umm, college together, although he's been out of the country for a long, long time."

"Nice to meet you, Barbara," Tommy said, as he found himself pulled down into a warm embrace. Barbara couldn't have been taller than 4-foot-5 and almost equal in girth, but there was no mistaking sunshine in her eyes and her smile. *What a wonderful woman*, he thought, surprising himself with his choice of words – but it fit. Barbara just seemed *wonderful*.

"Oh! This is wonderful!" Barbara unknowingly echoed Tommy's words. "How nice of you to come visit, Vince. Most of our residents only get visits from family – when some of them deign to show up," her brow furrowed in consternation as she said that, "and having a family friend visit, well that's just wonderful!" She spied the flowers in Alan's hand. "Those flowers are lovely, Alan. Your mother's going to love them. Let me go get a vase."

Barbara continued to admire the flowers as she walked towards the back. Without turning around she spoke, "Your mom's in the sunroom."

The "sunroom," as they called it, was a small addition off to the back of the building. One wall consisted of six large windows that started just below the ceiling and stretched down to about two feet above the floor level. Taped to the lower level of the wall under the windows were faded construction-paper flowers. The room was longer than it was wide, and along the wall opposite the window were about ten patients lined up facing the windows. Some were in wheelchairs, some were not. Tommy looked outside but couldn't figure out what they were looking at. He wondered if any one of them was actually looking at anything. Even with the sun pouring into the room, everything felt *old*; from the faded paper flowers to the clouds of dust illuminated by the sun's rays to the people in it. He was depressed just being there.

Squinting through the visible dust towards the opposite end of the room, Tommy saw his mother. Her chair was the only one not facing the window. Instead, she faced a television on the opposite wall. Even though she faced away from him, he knew it was her because the television was off, and he could see her face in the reflection of the screen. Without even looking directly at her, he could see that time and sorrow had taken its toll on her. She looked so tiny and frail in the chair.

"Hey, Ma." Alan crossed his fingers and held his breath. Mrs. Stevens' eyes slowly moved from the blank TV to Alan's hopeful face.

"Alan," she beamed. "What a pleasant surprise."

Alan bent down and gave his mother a hug and a kiss on the cheek. As she returned the gesture, her gaze fell upon Tommy. She prematurely ended their embrace, so she could curiously take in this strange man standing next to Alan.

Alan took a deep breath then addressed his mother's curiosity, "Ma, this is"...

"I know who this is," she interrupted.

Tommy's hands clammed up. Alan felt a gaseous bubble forming. Their hearts raced as they simultaneously uttered, "You do?"

"Of course I do. It's about time you showed up." The two brothers looked over at one another as Mrs. Stevens continued, "Well, are you gonna fix it?" she questioned as she pointed to the blank TV.

"Um, fix it?" stammered Tommy.

Just then, Barbara entered and whispered into Tommy's ear, "She thinks you're the cable guy here to fix the TV."

Tommy had no clue what to do or say. He desperately looked over to Alan for help, but all Alan could do was shrug and motion towards the television set. Tommy put on a helpful smile and approached the TV. Slowly, he pressed his finger onto the power button. Nothing. Next, he made his way behind the television.

"Don't you need your tools?" Mrs. Stevens asked. Tommy didn't answer. He was too busy being overwhelmed by the amount of wires in the back of the set. Her impatience continued, "I don't know how you can expect to fix it without the proper tools."

Just as Tommy was going to give up and come clean, he spotted it – the TV power cord – it was unplugged. Discreetly, he plugged it back in and moved to the front and pressed the power button. And just like that, the picture came back on.

Mrs. Stevens' eyes lit up as she excitedly clapped her hands, "Great job! They should give you a raise, young man."

Tommy smiled at her then glanced over at the relieved look on Alan's face. Barbara carefully placed the vase of flowers on the table next to Mrs. Stevens.

"Oh, these are lovely," gushed Mrs. Stevens.

"They're from your son."

Alan warmly looked over at his mother while she admired the flowers. "From who?" questioned Mrs. Stevens.

"Your son. Alan," answered Barbara.

Mrs. Stevens' face glossed over in confusion. "I have a son?"

This wasn't the first time Alan had witnessed his mother's Alzheimer's, but nonetheless, his heart sank. This was Tommy's first go- around so he had no idea what to do or say. A thousand feelings ran through his mind; sadness - for his mom's condition, regret – for not being there over the past twenty-five years, but most of all, sympathy – for his little brother, Alan.

***

Not a word was spoken as the two brothers left the home and got back into Alan's car. It wasn't until a mile or so down the road when Tommy finally broke the silence, "Wow. That was really hard." Alan nodded. "I'm sorry, Alan. I'm sorry you've had to deal with this all on your own. Mom's condition…Dad's death."

"I'm not gonna lie, Tommy, the last five years have been hell.

Not to mention, dealing with the whole divorce thing. I tell you what, if it wasn't for Richie, I would have lost it years ago."

Again, it was another few miles before a word was uttered. Alan pulled the car alongside the York Village cemetery and stopped.

"What are we doing here?" asked Tommy.

"Thought you might want to visit Dad today too."

They exited the car but only made it as far as the gate. It was there that Tommy's legs and body froze up. Patiently, Alan stood beside his brother, waiting for him to take that first step. But Tommy never did. He just couldn't bring himself to enter. Alan put his arm on Tommy's shoulder and motioned back to the car.

"We'll come back when you're ready, okay?"

Tommy nodded, then he and Alan headed back to the car. As they drove through the small village, Tommy stared out the window and thoughtfully spoke (in a deep southern accent), "Although it's difficult today to see beyond the sorrow, may looking back in memory help comfort you tomorrow."

Completely dumbfounded, Alan turned to Tommy, "What's up with the profound quote? And what's up with the southern accent?"

Equally confused, Tommy pondered then shrugged, "I have no idea, but it's the second time I've done that."

Just then, the Prius' gas light came on and beeped. Up ahead, Alan spotted a small gas station with two full service pumps. Alan pulled his car alongside pump one. He smirked and turned to Tommy, "Well, looks like you're gonna get your wish." Before Tommy had a chance to question his brother, Alan motioned toward the approaching attendant.

Tommy did a double-take when he realized it was Otto Kringeman. In most every which way, he looked the same as Tommy remembered; long greasy hair, ripped jeans, a faded concert tee, and a jean jacket...it might even be the same jacket from high school. The two major differences were: Otto had added to his tattoo collection. Both arms and neck area were full of ink. The other major difference was: Otto looked old. There were obviously a lot of rough miles on those tires.

"Well, well, well, little Alan Stevens. Oh, excuse me, *Principal Alan Stevens.*"

"Hi, Otto. Fill it up please."

Otto shoved the nozzle into the tank, clicked it to automatic, and then just stood there scowling at Alan's Prius. Alan didn't really notice the scowl. He was more concerned with the cigarette dangling from Otto's mouth. He desperately wanted to ask Otto to put it out, but of course, he didn't. All he could manage was a meek request for Otto to give the windshield a swipe. Otto didn't even dignify the request, he was still preoccupied with Alan's Prius.

"I guess it's true what they say," sneered Otto, "people chose cars that match their personality. And it doesn't get more boring than a fuckin' Prius."

Innately, Tommy chuckled at Otto's put-down of Alan. His chuckle was short-lived, however, as Otto launched his next remark in Tommy's direction. "I guess it's also true what they say, faggots choose lovers who match their own body type."

With Otto's obnoxious laugh still hanging in the air, Tommy's smile quickly faded. Otto ended the pump at $35.00, twisted the gas cap back on, and proceeded to hock a loogie onto the ground. The chunky, neon green loogie was followed by a giant puff of smoke in the direction of Alan's open window.

"By the way, Mr. Principal, you need to tell that idiot English teacher Mrs. Thompson to quit giving Junior detention for no good reason."

"I'm sure she had a good reason," said Alan.

"Are you calling my boy a liar?" sneered Otto.

"Um…no, not at all. I'll look into it," Alan stammered as he handed Otto two twenties.

Otto snatched them from him and smirked as he stuffed them in his pocket. "Thanks for the tip, Principal Prius."

Realizing that he wasn't going to get his change back, Alan slowly rolled the window up and drove off. Tommy shook his head at his little brother. "Dude, why'd you let him take your money and talk to you like that?"

Alan shot Tommy a glare and responded, "I didn't see you saying anything when he called you my gay lover?"

Tommy realized he had no defense to this, so he changed the subject slightly, "So, he has a son in high school?"

"Yup," answered Alan. "Otto Jr. And he's a jerk and a bully just like his old man."

"So, did Otto end up marrying anyone I know?"

"Jill MacNamara," smiled Alan.

"No shit," Tommy laughed.

"Yea, but I don't think they're married anymore. They were having a running competition on who could cheat on each other the most. The last I heard, she's living in some trailer park in Florida with some dude who looks like Joe Dirt." Alan saw that Tommy had no clue who that was. "Looks like Kid Rock?" Tommy was still oblivious. "Umm...he looks like Axl Rose on a bad hair day?" Tommy gave a knowing look as the reference registers. "And just think," joked Alan, "you were on your way to end up just like that."

"Yea, right!" snapped Tommy.

"Seriously, Tommy, you used to worship the guy."

Tommy fought the urge to punch Alan in the face, but he knew Alan was right. That very well could have been him pumping gas today. Again, Tommy changed the subject, "So, what happened to Ricky and Pud? Lemme guess, a janitor and a garbage man?"

Alan pondered a second, shook his head at Tommy then said with a smile, "You really want to do this, huh?" Tommy returned the smile and nodded. "Okay then. Prepare to have your brain explode." Alan immediately regretted his poor choice of words. "Sorry."

***

Alan put on his blinker and pulled into a small shopping plaza. "What are we doing here?" asked Tommy. "Are we going grocery shopping? If so, we definitely need more Chicken in a Biskits." Before Alan could respond, Tommy noticed that the old grocery store was now something new. "Whoa, what happened to Dave's IGA?"

"It went out of business a while ago."

Tommy scanned all the store fronts. "Looks like everything that was here went out of business. So what are we doing here anyway?" Alan smiled and pointed to the storefront on the end. As they exited the car, Tommy read the sign out loud, "*Blendz & Bendz – A Smoothie and Yoga Experience.* Color me stupid, little bro, but I have no clue what that means."

"Oh, you will," Alan laughed as he held the door open for Tommy. Hesitantly, Tommy entered.

The first thing noticeable about the room was the fact that there were no chairs. Brightly colored cushions were spread out around the room on a huge oriental rug, arranged in groups of two, three and four, with one or two low tables between some of them. The lack of real furniture and the large windows on two sides made the room look bigger than it was. In each corner was a bamboo tree twisted into a spiral in a vase that was filled with small, colored rocks. Larger, uncolored rocks were placed strategically around each vase. The walls were a deep tan and bare, except for the wall where there was a bar – or kind of a bar. It had a façade that looked like rice paper, and on top of it was three blenders and three wooden bowls of fruit, all spaced about a foot from each other; blender, twelve inches, fruit bowl, twelve inches, blender, twelve inches, fruit bowl, twelve inches, blender, twelve inches, fruit bowl. Behind the bar, on the wall, was a large oriental symbol painted on in black. When Tommy squinted and turned his head sideways it looked like the number 35. While he was pondering the symbol, he heard an almost-familiar voice and turned around.

Ricky? Bald? Ricky was BALD? That was the first thing Tommy noticed about Ricky. His face momentarily contorted in horror when he took in the outfit below the shiny, clean-shaven head. *What the hell kind of shirt is that?* It was long-sleeved – or almost; there were about three inches between the end of the sleeve and Ricky's hand. It was loose with no buttons and flowed over his same-fabric pants. What kept the ensemble from looking like hospital scrubs was the oriental pattern on the pants that matched the walls – that and the beaded necklace above the V-shaped neckline. *Ricky! What the hell …?*

"Alan Stevens!" As Ricky approached, Alan stuck out his hand for a shake. Ignoring Alan's outreached hand, Ricky went straight in for a hug. "How are you, my friend?"

"I'm well, thank you. Wow, this place looks great, Ricky. I've been meaning to swing by and check it out. It's the talk of the town."

Ricky placed his hands together (as if praying) and gave Alan an appreciative nod. His attention then turned to Tommy.

"Oh, Ricky, this is an old friend from college"…

"Vince. Vince Neily," Tommy added as he stretched his hand out for a shake.

Again, Ricky ignored the hand and when in for a hug. "Nice to meet you Vince Neily. Great name, by the way. Very Motley Crue-esque."

Tommy shot Alan an 'I told you' glance. Alan rolled his eyes at

Tommy then scanned the room. When he finally found what he was looking for, he turned to Ricky and Tommy and said, "I'll be right back. I need to use the little boy's room."

As Alan headed to the bathroom, Ricky glided behind the counter and finished blending some sort of green smoothie concoction. He poured it into a cup and handed it to Tommy, giving him a 'What do you think' look.

Tommy took one look at the green creation and blurted out, "Looks like something that came out of Linda Blair." Tommy laughed. Ricky didn't.

"It's a wheat grass smoothie," corrected Ricky.

"Wheat grass? More like wheat ass," joked Tommy. Again, Tommy laughed out loud. And again, Ricky didn't. Ricky politely smiled then excused himself to go wait on a customer at the register. Tommy stared long and hard at the cupful of green then finally and reluctantly took a big swig. Just then, Ricky made eye contact with him, and with a mouthful of the green ooze, Tommy gave him an excited thumbs up. As soon as Ricky looked away, Tommy immediately spit it back into the cup. He desperately searched the counter for a napkin and began wiping the inside of his mouth out.

By the time Alan returned, Tommy's mouth was pretty much napkined out. Alan took one look at the smoothie and excitedly exclaimed, "Ooo, is that a wheat grass smoothie? May I?" Without hesitation, he handed Alan the cup and watched as he took a huge and highly enjoyable sip. Tommy shook his head and smirked as Ricky approached.

"Oh, congrats, by the way," Alan addressed Ricky. "Your son was amazing the other night." As Ricky proudly beamed, Alan filled Tommy in, "Ricky's son, Peter, is a super talented actor slash singer. I think he's gotten the lead in every one of our school's musicals." Tommy politely nodded as Alan continued, "Hey, listen, Ricky, we've been thinking of implementing a yoga program at school, and I was wondering if you were interested in helping out?"

"I would love that, Alan! You can never be too young to start exercising your mind, body, and spirit. Never too old either. You should come to one of our beginner classes. Both of you."

"Thanks, Ricky. Maybe we'll check it out."

Again, Tommy politely smiled. He had no clue what he was witnessing, nor did he have a clue what this whole yoga/smoothie experience was all about. What he did know, was wheat grass really does taste like wheat ass!

Ricky steepled his fingers together again, gave a slight bow and said, "Namaste."

"Nah-mah-what?" Tommy started to say, but Alan pulled him towards the door before he could say more.

***

They climbed back into the Prius. Tommy watched Alan continue to orgasmically enjoy the smoothie. Tommy stared blankly at his brother.

"What?" Alan asked. "Did you want more?"

171

Tommy slowly shook his head in disgust. "No, Alan, I do not. I'm still trying to wrap my mind around what the hell I just witnessed. A yoga instructor? A health nut? A shaved head? Are you kidding me? The dude used to eat pizza and Devil Dogs for breakfast."

"I warned you that you'd be shocked."

"And what's the deal with his son singing and dancing in musicals. Kinda queer, don't ya think?"

"Tommy! That's not very PC. You can't just throw around words like '*queer*'. This isn't the 80's anymore. Like I told you before, there are a lot of phrases and words you can't use anymore. And yes, for your information, Ricky's son is gay. Our society is quite different now, Tommy. It's much more about acceptance and tolerance."

Alan continued to drive down the road, and Tommy continued to ponder. Finally, out of the blue, Tommy blurted out (in southern accent), "What is tolerance? It is the consequence of humanity. We are all formed of frailty and error; let us pardon each other's folly – that is the first law of nature."

Alan looked over at Tommy, impressed. "Um…wow. Well said."

Tommy proudly smiled then spoke, "See, I have nothing against homos." And there went Alan's impressed look. "Alrighty then," urged Tommy, "next stop – Pud."

"The last I heard, he's married and works up in Portland at the C.S.I lab."

"C.S who?"

"C.S.I. Crime Scene Investigation. You know, the whole evidence gathering, examining fingerprints, blood samples, and DNA type stuff. There's quite a science to it."

"Science?" laughed Tommy. "The only science Pud was ever into was lighting his farts on fire with a Bunsen burner."

"Will you quit calling him that. It's Brett, not Pud."

"What are you talking about? He loved that nickname. Portland, here we come!"

"Tommy, we're not going to Portland."

"What? Do you have something better to do? Huh? Huh? C'mon, Alan. It'll be a fun road trip. Just like old times."

"We never took fun road trips together. I wasn't even allowed in your car, remember?"

Tommy pondered. "Well, this will be the start of a new tradition then. Please."

Alan sighed then relented, "Fine."

Tommy pumped his fist, "Yes!"

"But I'm drawing the line there, Tommy. Understand?"

"What does that mean? Tommy asked.

"It means Gina is still off limits," warned Alan.

Although Tommy was bursting at the seams to see Gina again, deep down, he knew Alan was probably right. For now, anyway, he would just focus on Pud.

"Do you know where the lab is?" Tommy asked. Alan shook his head no. "Well, let's go find a phone booth and look it up in the yellow pages then."

"Ha. Good luck finding one of those," laughed Alan.

"What? A phone booth or yellow pages?"

"Yup," smiled Alan as he picked up his I-Phone. "Let's ask Siri."

Alan pressed a button and was greeted by Siri's voice, "Hello, my Dungeon Master, how may I help you?" Alan blushed (& gushed) a bit at Siri's greeting.

"Siri, I need the address for the C.S.I. lab in Portland, Maine, please."

"Searching for address now," echoed Siri. "The address for the C.S.I. lab in Portland Maine is: 359 Prospect Street. Shall I map it for you, Dungeon Master?"

"No thanks," Alan answered, "I'll take it from here, Siri."

Tommy had no clue what was going on. He simply stared blankly from the I-Phone to his brother. After a few moments of silence, Tommy asked, "Are you banging her or what?"

Alan laughed. Partly at Tommy's cluelessness, but partly because it had crossed his mind once or twenty times what Siri might look like. Alan began typing the address into his car's GPS. "I'm running low on data on my phone, that's why I'm using the car's GPS," Alan pointed out.

"GP what?" questioned Tommy.

"GPS. It stands for Global Positioning System. It tracks where you are and where you want to go. It's all done with satellites," Alan said.

When Alan finished punching in the address, Tommy curiously looked up to the sky and mumbled, "Satellites?"

A moment later, the female voice on the GPS spoke, "In one quarter mile turn right onto Interstate 95 Northbound."

Before Tommy had a chance to open his mouth, Alan read his mind, "No, I'm not banging her either."

***

"You have reached your destination," the GPS stated.

Alan pulled his Prius into a parking space. The sign on the brick building in front of them read, *Maine State Police Crime Lab – Portland Division.* They exited the car and just stood there.

"Well, what now, genius? Am I just supposed to go I there and say, 'Hey Brett, remember me, Tommy's little brother? I just happened to be in the neighborhood and thought I'd stop in and introduce you to my old friend who's been in an African tribe the past twenty-five years?'"

Tommy pondered. He actually thought it sounded like a pretty good plan. Before he could relay this to Alan, they were greeted with a voice from behind, "Alan? Alan Stevens, is that you?"

The brothers turned around, and there, getting out of his Jeep Cherokee was Brett Cormier. His appearance was a far cry from the long, permed haired, head bangin' Pud. His hair was short, like really short. He wore a gray Maine State Police tee and navy blue gym shorts. And speaking of gym shorts, it looked as though he had just come from the gym. Actually, it looked as though he had been hitting the gym for some time now. His body was toned, buff even.

"Heyyy, Brett. How are you?" Alan said.

"I'm great," Brett answered as he extended a hand shake to Alan. "What are you doing here?"

"Me? What am I doing here? Well...ummm"... Alan froze up.

Sensing his brother's panic, Tommy jumped in, "We were just driving by this place, and Alan said he knew someone that worked here. I've always found this type of stuff fascinating, so I told him to see if you were here. I'm Vince, by the way. Vince Neily."

Brett smiled, "Cool name. Nice to meet you, Vince." Brett then reached out and gave Tommy a hand shake. Tommy was taken aback at how firm it was. Pud's handshakes were never that firm back in school. "Come on in. I'll show you guys around," Brett said. Alan didn't bother looking over at his brother. He knew Tommy was wearing a smug, *I told you so*, look.

Over the next hour, Brett led them on a tour of the lab. They were introduced to fancy machines with fancier names, microscopes, and gadgets galore. Both brothers found the tour fascinating, but Tommy still couldn't help be blown away with how Brett looked. On the way out of one of the rooms, Tommy noticed a blacklight-type wand. He picked it up and asked, "What's this?"

"Ahh," smiled Brett, "the *Wand*."

"The Wand?" Tommy asked.

"AKA, the *spew stick*," Brett said. "It's used to detect any traces of semen."

Tommy's eyes widened as he laughed, "That's awesome. It kind of looks like a mini light saber." Tommy picked it up and began waving it around. Brett added to his excitement by shutting off the light and motioning for Tommy to turn the wand on. The Jedi in him took over and in his best Darth Vader voice said, "Luke, I am your father."

Brett and Alan did their best to fight back laughter. It wasn't until their faces were bright red and about to burst that Tommy realized they weren't laughing at his Vader voice. Finally, Alan couldn't take it and pointed down to Tommy's shirt. Tommy looked down and nearly dropped the wand. There, on the lower half of his shirt, the blacklight revealed huge semen stains throughout. His thumb quickly shut the wand off. He placed it back on the table and left the room as if nothing happened.

TRACK 14

It was early evening when they returned to York. After listening to Tommy complain several (hundred) times how hungry he was, Alan decided to stop at the local favorite – Ruby's Bar & Grill. Ruby's was your typical small-town establishment. It consisted of a small dining room, a small front bar, and a much larger enclosed back deck. On any given night, you would see the same faces seated on the same bar stools, telling the same stories. Basically, it was a small-town version of Cheers – where everybody knows your name (and knows your personal business).

As soon as the waitress seated them in the back bar, Alan knew this might be a mistake. Most of the locals were either old classmates of Tommy's or of Alan's. Tommy recognized some of them right away, but others had to be clued in by Alan. The first five minutes consisted of a wide-eyed Tommy curiously pointing around and saying things like: *Oh my God, isn't that so & so,* or *holy shit, that's so &*

so!

"Hey, is that Ian Meigs?" Tommy asked as he pointed to a well-dressed man at the bar.

Alan nodded, "He's one of the biggest real estate moguls in town now."

"Really? Scoffed Tommy. "That dude used to be so in love with Prince. Every day in homeroom, he'd be singing and dancing some stupid Prince song."

Alan laughed, "That's funny considering the name of his company is Purple Reign Reality."

Tommy rolled his eyes and continued to scan the bar. "Hey, Alan," Tommy whispered, "Is that Tammy Dunn?"

"Where?"

"Sitting against the window with that black guy," Tommy answered.

Alan lowered his voice, "First of all, no, it's not her. Secondly, you can't say black person."

"Another PC thing?" Tommy sighed.

"Yup. The proper term is African American."

Tommy looked over to the man then back to Alan. He pondered a second then asked, "But what if he's from Canada? Would he be called an African Canadian?" Alan had no reply.

Tommy continued to look around the bar and pick out familiar faces. Alan did his best to curb Tommy's enthusiasm and constant finger pointing, not to mention his obnoxious comments. Comments like: *I knew she was gonna get fat when she was older*, or even *I aged better than he did, and I was brain dead,* and *what the fuck is up with that hair?* By the time the waitress came over to take their drink order, Alan was fed up with Tommy's rude (but slightly truthful) observations.

"Hi guys, how's it going? I'm Deren, and I'll be taking care of you tonight." She didn't look a day over twenty. She had wavy dirty blonde hair with the bluest of eyes. "Can I start you guys off with some drinks?"

"Just a water for me," Alan answered. "With a lemon please."

Deren turned her attention to Tommy. "And for you, sir?"

Tommy's flirtatious smile quickly fell from his face. *Sir?* It took him a moment to remember he was no longer 18, and to her, he was indeed a *sir.* Tommy let out a slight sigh, then turned his attention to doing something that was long overdue – ordering his first legal beer. "Hmm, do I want a Strohs or an Old Milwaukee?"

Deren's blank blue eyes said it all. Either she was a clueless idiot, or what he ordered was completely and embarrassingly outdated. By the look on Alan's face, Tommy assumed it was the latter. Needless to say, he settled for a Budweiser. After Deren walked off, Alan's glare continued.

"What? How was I to know they don't make Strohs anymore?"

Alan's look had nothing to do with Tommy's cluelessness. He couldn't believe Tommy would even consider drinking a beer again. Tommy was clueless about that as well. It wasn't until the beer sat in front of him, and he took his first sip that it hit him.

Within that one sip, his mind took him back to that day. The day of the prom. The day of the accident. He remembered pounding beer after beer with the boys. He remembered thinking about Gina heading across the country to go to college. He remembered thinking/knowing she would quickly forget about him and move on with someone more worthy, smarter. Someone with an actual future. He remembered the look of embarrassment and pain when he entered and then left the prom. He remembered all of that within that first sip of beer. It would be his last sip. He traded it in for a water…with a lemon.

Alan knew something happened to Tommy when he took that sip, but never asked him to talk about it. It wasn't long after Tommy's flashback that he went right back to making obnoxious comments about his former classmates scattered about the bar. Alan did his best to ignore his brother, until Tommy turned his sights on Alan.

"So what's the deal with that coffeehouse chick?" Tommy asked.

"Who? Mia?" Alan's face lit up as he spoke her name.

"Why don't you just ask her out instead of 'flirting'with her?" Tommy said as he put air quotes around flirting.

"I wasn't flirting with her."

"No shit. That's why I put it in quotes. Your game needs some serious improvement. Luckily, your big brother is here."

Alan bursted out laughing, "Ha. I would never come to you for advice on women – flirting or otherwise."

"Suit yourself, but I used to be a master flirter back in the day."

"Yea, well, this isn't back in the day. Real women nowadays wouldn't fall for your cheesy, worn-out lines."

"A hundred bucks says you're wrong," Tommy challenged.

"You don't have a hundred bucks."

"Your hundred bucks against anything you want. Anything!" Tommy confidently leaned back in his chair. The gauntlet was thrown down.

"Anything, huh?" Alan pondered. "You're on." Tommy leaned in and shook Alan's hand. "So, how do we do this?" Alan asked.

Tommy smiled. "I'll choose a random chick in here and go over and drop some cheesy, worn-out line on her, and within a few minutes I'll have her sucking face with me. Hell, give me ten minutes, and *I'll have her stepping up to the mic*, if you know what I mean?"

With that, Tommy set his sights on the drunkest woman in the bar. *Jackpot!* Corner booth. Three women. Three drunk women. One in particular, stumbled around the table before attempting to sit back down. Her ass missed her chair, and she fell to the floor laughing the whole way down. *Winner, winner chicken dinner*, thought Tommy.

Before Tommy stood up, Alan's voice halted him, "Not so fast, Tommy! I get to pick the woman." Tommy let out a tiny disappointed sigh, but was still cocky enough to allow Alan to take control.

"Fine. You pick. But you can't choose anyone who's already here with a guy. Ok?" Alan nodded in agreement with Tommy's stipulation and then began to scan the bar for a female he knew wouldn't succumb to Tommy's *charms*. If not, he would never ever hear the end of it. There was no way he would let Tommy win this bet...or would he?

"Dirty blonde at the end of the bar," Alan murmured. Inconspicuously, Tommy peered over to the bar then back to Alan. "How do you know she's dirty?" Tommy asked.

When Alan realized that Tommy wasn't joking, he slowly stated, "I was talking about her hair color."

"Oh. Ooooooh." Tommy winked at Alan then did another look-over.

At the end of the dimly lit bar sat a tall, well made up forty-something year old. The slit in her skirt revealed her long nylon clad legs. She sat alone nursing her Cosmo. She looked up as Tommy was checking her out and as their eyes met, she smiled. That's all Tommy needed. He was in. He pounded down his water, stood, then mumbled, "Watch and learn, little brother."

Not sure about the *learn* part, but Alan certainly watched, and he enjoyed every minute of it. He watched Tommy buy her another drink. He watched as they talked and laughed. He watched as Tommy slyly put his arm on her shoulder and whispered something in her ear. A second later, they both got up and headed across the bar. As Tommy walked by Alan, he patted him on his back and said, "I'll be right back." Alan watched them enter the bathroom together and immediately chuckled to himself.

Less than five minutes later, they returned to the bar. Tommy gave her a wink and a smile as she headed back to her seat. Arrogantly, Tommy returned to his seat across from Alan. His arrogance continued as he leaned his chair back on two legs and boasted to his brother, "What can I say, when you got it you got it!"

"So," asked Alan, "did you two *suck face?*" Tommy proudly nodded. "And did she *step up to the mic?*"

"She didn't exactly step up to it," Tommy explained, "but let's just say she knew how to *handle* a mic!" At this point, Alan couldn't contain his amusement. "I don't know what you're laughing at, Alan, but you're out a hundred bucks, dude!"

This time it was Alan's turn to lean back in his chair and address Tommy, "Do you remember Daniel Bagley from high school?" Tommy thought for a second then shook his head no. "You and Otto used to call him D-Bags."

Tommy's face lit up, "Oh yea! D-Bags. We duct taped him in his underwear to the goal post. Whatever happened to good ole D-Bags?"

Alan smiled and pointed to the dirty blonde at the bar.

"Oh my God," Tommy exclaimed. "Is that his sister? His wife?"

"Nope," Alan said. "Let's just say that Daniel Bagley is now Danielle Bagley."

"What? No. You're just fucking with me. You're just jealous I won the bet and you didn't."

"I'm being totally serious," laughed Alan. "You didn't notice an extra appendage down there?"

"I...I didn't get that far. Someone kept knocking on the bathroom door." Again, Tommy glanced over to her then back to Alan. "No way."

"Well, here's your chance to find out. She's coming over. Just remember, Adam's apples don't lie," Alan whispered.

As she walked by their table, she stopped and handed Tommy a piece of paper, smiled and left. Tommy never saw her smile. His eyes were firmly gazing at her large Adam's apple. On the paper was written her number followed by her name – Danielle. As soon as the door shut behind her, Tommy's pale face turned to Alan's smiling face, and he slowly spoke, "Oh...my...God. D-Bags is now...she-Bags?

Alan was nearly in tears he was laughing so hard. "Didn't you once shove his face in the toilet and make him bob for turds?" Alan asked. Tommy thought a second then nodded. "And here you are, twenty-five years later, kissing that same mouth. Talk about irony."

As Alan watched Tommy begin to dry heave, he started to feel a bit guilty for pranking his brother, especially after all Tommy had just been through.

"You're a major dick wad, Alan!"

And just like that, Alan's guilt faded. After all the shit Tommy had done to others (especially to Alan) over the years, it was nice to see the tables turned. Alan reached in his wallet and handed Tommy a crisp hundred dollar bill. "Best money I've ever spent."

Tommy's fist clenched around the hundred. His embarrassment transformed into anger. He might have a different face, but Alan immediately recognized the familiar rage in his eyes. At that moment, Tommy had every intention of punching Alan square in the nuts, but he hesitated as a familiar mantra entered his head. Under his breath, and in that same deep southern accent, Tommy mumbled to himself, "When you feel it boiling up inside, count backward from ten and it'll subside. When you feel it boiling up inside, count backward from ten and it'll subside. Ten, nine, eight, seven, six, five, four, three (deep breath) …two (deeper breath)…one." And just like that, his fist relaxed, and he slipped the money in his pocket and calmly addressed Alan, "You ready to go?" Alan had no idea what just happened, but whatever it was, his nuts were ever grateful.

As the brothers entered the parking lot, they came across two guys having a heated argument. They looked to be in their early twenties and were yelling at each other in Spanish. Alan immediately went into survival mode – *Mind your own business. Keep your head down. Don't make eye contact.* By the time Alan unlocked his door and was about to get in, he noticed that Tommy was lingering, still listening to the two boys argue. Not only was Tommy listening, he began to approach the two boys. Alan nearly shit his pants. He fumbled for his inhaler, took a puff then said a quick prayer. That was just like Tommy, sticking his nose where it didn't belong.

Alan couldn't hear exactly what was being said, but it sounded like Tommy was talking to them in Spanish. Alan watched Tommy put his arms on each of the boy's shoulders. With hostilities soothed, both boys hugged it out and all three laughed. Tommy shook their hands then walked to the Prius. Before getting in, he called back over to the boys, "Recuerda, vatos, los manos antés de putas!"

"What the hell was that all about?" Alan asked.

Tommy shrugged and answered, "They were fighting over the same chick."

"Oh," Alan said still stunned. "But what did you say to them?"

"Tommy smiled, "Bros before hoes.""

"Oh." Alan pulled out of the parking lot and less than a mile down the road he curiously turned back to Tommy and asked, "Since when do you speak Spanish?"

Tommy pondered a moment, then confusion washed over his face, "Yea, how *do* I know Spanish?"

***

Once back at home, Tommy sat in the living room and stared around at the unfamiliar, yet familiar surroundings. He remembered throwing his bean bag chair down on the orange shag carpet and watching Saturday morning cartoons (In particular, *Hong Kong Phooey*). He flashbacked to when he was ten and helped his dad remodel the living room, which basically consisted of renting a carpet shampoo machine and painting the brown paneling white.

Alan stood at the doorway and watched Tommy's mind race. He still couldn't fathom that his big brother was alive, and he definitely couldn't fathom just how different Tommy looked. "Overwhelming day, huh?" Alan said.

Tommy looked over at him and slowly nodded. "You weren't kidding about my mind being blown. I can't believe how different everything is…how different everyone is. I can't believe how old I am. I swear, there's part of me that still feels eighteen. It's like I'm that Rip Van Halen dude who fell asleep for 200 years then woke up."

Alan started to correct his clueless brother, but decided instead, to let Tommy's literary faux pas slide, for now. Alan entered the room and sat across from Tommy.

"I'll just say this one thing then drop it, okay? I really don't think it's very smart of you to let all these people get to know you as 'Vince'. What's gonna happen in thirty days when you reveal the truth?"

Tommy stood up and stretched. "Relax, little brother. You worry too much. You always did."

Alan was quick with a response, "And you don't worry enough. You *never* did."

Just like old times, Tommy paid no attention to Alan's babble. He was too busy gazing at his oversized stomach. Reaching down, Tommy grabbed hold of his love handles, "Man, I gotta get into shape."

"You should try Zumba," Alan joked.

"What the hell is Zumba?" Tommy asked. "It sounds like some sort of tribal dance."

"Right up your alley then," Alan said as Richie entered the room.

"What's right up his alley?" Richie asked.

"Nothing," Tommy said. "Your dad is just being a dork. Tommy continued towards the doorway. "Well, I'm hitting the sack. It was quite the day. Night guys."

"Night, Vince," Richie said.

"Hey, Vince, wait." Alan said grabbing a box of tissues. Just as Tommy reentered, Alan tossed him the box. "Now you don't have to use your shirt," Alan smirked. Tommy caught the tissue box, glared at Alan, then turned and headed upstairs.

"What's up with Vince?" Richie asked. "He sick or something?"

"Yeah," Alan smiled, "something like that."

***

The next morning, Tommy asked Alan to take him out for coffee. It really didn't take much convincing, considering Alan jumped at any chance to see Mia. This time, Tommy ordered for himself – a real coffee, not any of that *café shmafé crap*. Not only did Tommy thoroughly enjoy his coffee, he was highly entertained listening to Alan pathetically attempt to flirt with Mia.

When Alan finally pulled himself away from the counter and sat with his brother, Tommy was more than raring to go with the put-downs and jokes. But for Alan's sake, Tommy never even got a word out. Tommy's attention was focused on the front door. His mouth dropped open and his eyes widened.

Curiously, Alan turned to see the object of Tommy's silence. And there, walking through the door was Gina. Tommy froze mid sip. With his eyes fixated on Gina, he looked her over from head to toe. He took notice of all the ways she had changed, yet had stayed the same.

Softer, Tommy thought. Everything about her looked softer. Her hair was longer and fell in waves around her face and down to just below her shoulders. She still had bangs, but they were thinned out, longer, and were angled around her forehead and cheekbones – not straight across the brow anymore. It made her look older, but in a good way, in that girl-into-woman fantasy way. She was wearing faded blue jeans and a short-sleeved, button-down loose shirt of a deep fuchsia color that just made her green eyes stand out more. Tommy noticed she wasn't wearing a hint of black, except for the color of her hair, and even that shade had been toned-down ... *softer.*

Again, Alan became panicked as he looked from Tommy to Gina then back to Tommy. It was now Tommy, who wore the silly, smitten smile on his face. And then it happened: Gina spotted Alan and offered up a sweet smile and a wave.

Tommy whispered to Alan, "Introduce me."

Alan gave his brother a glare then sternly whispered back, "No way! I told you, she's off limits!"

And then it *really* happened: Gina paid for her coffee and headed straight towards Alan and Tommy.

"Shit, shit, shit," Alan nervously mumbled. Tommy just smiled.

"Hey, Alan," Gina said with arms outstretched. Alan stood and gave her a hug. Gina looked over at Tommy and politely smiled, "You must be Alan's old college friend"...

"Vince. Vince Neily." Tommy stood and offered up his hand. It was all he could do not to give her the biggest hug in the world.

"Ah yes, Vince. Richie and Emma have told me all about you. Have you really been living with that African tribe the last twenty-five years doing research?"

"Yes. Yes I have."

"Wow. That sounds fascinating. I'd love to hear more about that."

Without even thinking, Tommy blurted out, "We should have dinner sometime and I'll tell you all about it."

Gina was a bit taken back by his forwardness. Alan was practically shitting his pants.

Before Alan could diffuse the situation, Gina responded, "Um, sure. That'd be great. Just let me know."

Tommy's eyes widened in a pleasant shock. Alan actually shit his pants.

"Well, I should get going. I'm taking Emma last minute prom shopping. She's only changed her mind five times on the dress she wants."

"Luckily, Richie's tux is classic black and white. It should go well with anything," said Alan.

Gina nodded then started to head off. Before she got far, Tommy began making weird *clicking* noises with his mouth. Both, Gina and Alan turned to Tommy with confused looks.

Tommy proudly explained, "It's Mo-tah-lay-cru-ayy for, 'I'm looking forward to having dinner with such a pretty lady.'"

Gina couldn't help but smile at his strangeness as she headed out. Tommy pounded down his coffee then gave Alan a big, proud, goofy grin.

TRACK 15

With Alan and Richie back in school, Tommy was bored just sitting at home, and decided to take another ride out on the bike. It took him almost forty-five minutes to find some clothes that fit. Well, actually, none of them fit, but he needed something that would allow him movement enough to pedal a bicycle.

He was winded before he got as far as two blocks, but he huffed along, going past the beach, the basketball court, Fun-O-Rama, York's Wild Kingdom ... it was like riding through memories. Sand in his PB and J sandwiches at the beach (more sand in Alan's, he made sure of that), the bloody nose he got at the basketball court when he was too busy showing off for Gina to see the pole. He remembered how black his hands would get from handling cups full of quarters at the arcade, and the time he and Otto snuck into the zoo at night with the intent of giving beer to the monkeys (they got chased out by security before they got near the cages). A lot of memories. Too many.

Even though he was completely exhausted, sore, and sweaty, Tommy decided to pedal further into town. He rode by the plaza, studying all the new storefronts. Tommy paused in front of the Zumba studio (not by accident) and peered into the window. *Exercise class?*

Tommy checked out the ass of each participant until he caught the eye of the female instructor. Knowing he was caught staring (and knowing what he was caught staring at) he quickly looked away and pedaled in the direction of Ricky's shop.

Ricky saw him walk in and motioned that he'd come over to him shortly. Tommy watched him expertly tossing fruit in the blender for the customer in front of him. Tommy chuckled and thought, *Ricky should get one of Paco's Super Blenders.* As Tommy chuckled, he actually felt his flab jiggle beneath his extra tight shirt. The chuckling ceased. "Fuckin' Paco," he mumbled.

It was still awkward for him adjusting to this "new" Ricky. He couldn't picture the seventeen-year old Ricky knowing how to even use a blender; not without blowing its contents out the top. The thought made him smile again, and he was still smiling when Ricky joined him.

Ricky immediately offered him another wheat-ass smoothie, which Tommy politely, yet adamantly, declined. Ricky commented on Tommy's disheveled and winded appearance from riding the bike into town and insisted he have something to 'replenish his electrolytes' – whatever they were.

"Trust me," Ricky said, "we have something for everyone here. I guarantee it." He stared at Tommy for a moment, as if sizing him up, then snapped his fingers and spun toward the blenders. As he was adding ingredients, he suggested to Tommy to join him for his yoga class, saying, "It will make bike riding easier."

"Let me start with a smoothie, first. This is all new to me," Tommy answered.

Ricky placed a tall glass in front of Tommy. "This is the Nutty Banana. Banana, peanut butter, chocolate. I swear you'll love it." Not only did Tommy love it, he nearly had an orgasm it tasted so good. Tommy couldn't resist pointing out to Ricky that he should change the name to Chocolate Monkey Nuts, and even though Ricky had no intention of doing it, he did think it was quite funny. He actually laughed out loud. They both looked totally different than once upon a time, but having Ricky laugh at one of his stupid jokes made it feel like old times. It was exactly what Tommy needed. Tommy left with the promise to tell Ricky more about Africa next time.

From there, Tommy wandered by some of the other new storefronts in the plaza. He stood in front of a small clothing boutique. He really could use some new clothes, and Alan did give him a hundred bucks.

Tommy entered, but quickly exited when he saw the outrageous price tags of a pair of jeans and a shirt; *67 bucks? What the fuck!* Tommy was never the most frugal shopper, but he knew his money could be spent more wisely. That's why he took his hundred bucks to the next store over – "The CD Shack."

The "CD Shack" was a tiny music store stocked full of CDs (mostly pre-owned) and DVDs. A half-hour later, like the teenager he still was, he had blown all of his hundred dollars. He was excited to go home and crank up these shiny disc-like things, but his legs were not-so ready to start pedaling yet. While he rested his legs a bit more, he sat on a bench and opened up one of the CDs, staring at how unfamiliar they were.

He was reading through the liner notes on the changes of some of the band members when he was interrupted by a female voice, "So, did you like what you saw?"

Tommy turned to see the young, sexy Zumba instructor from earlier. He looked like a deer caught in headlights. "Um, excuse me?" he said.

"I saw you checking me out earlier. Did you like what you saw?" she asked.

"Oh, I wasn't checking you out. I was just checking out what you were doing. I've heard a lot about this Zumba thing."

"You have, have you? And what exactly have you heard?" she smiled.

"I heard you provide a good workout," he said.

Again, she smiled, "That's one way of putting it. So I was recommended to you?"

"My brother actually," Tommy said.

"Word of mouth is my best advertising," she winked. "You should give me a try."

"Me? Nooo. I'm more of a traditional kind of guy when it comes to this sort of thing. Besides, I don't know if this body could keep up with your moves, and I'd hate to embarrass myself."

"I think I can help you with your moves," she winked then reached into her bag. She pulled out a business card and handed it to Tommy. "I'm Amber. The studio is mine. Why don't you meet me here at midnight? I should be done with my other client by then," she said.

"Midnight?" he said a bit shocked. "Wow, you're dedicated." Tommy's gaze moved from her big brown eyes down to the card. "Zumba by Amber," he read aloud. "And it'll just be you and me? Like a private session?"

"Unless you wanna bring your brother," Amber smiled.

"Pfft, ya right," he laughed, "Midnight is past his bedtime."

"So, do we have a date?" Amber asked.

Tommy pondered a second. He looked at her card and then down at his love handles. "It's a date," he nodded.

"Excellent. I'll see you tonight," she smiled, tossed her chestnut brown hair back, then turned to walk away. "Oh, by the way," she added, "Amber only accepts cash."

After she left, Tommy grabbed his bag of new CD's and headed over to the bike rack. He felt satisfied with his day. Not only did he get another chance to visit his old friend, Ricky, he had an amazing Chocolate Monkey Nuts smoothie, and scored some new music as well. And the topper: He didn't have to go get a gym membership somewhere, for he had a cute chick personally offer up her services. Tommy felt good. So good, in fact, he decided to climb on Big Blue and ride along the beach again.

When he pedaled up Long Sands Road, he spotted the entrance to York high School. Tommy hit the brakes on Big Blue and sat there staring at the sign. After his huffing and puffing subsided, he decided to continue his trip down memory lane and take a stroll through the hallowed halls of York High.

One of the first things that caught his eye, was just how full the parking lot was. Not only did it seem like every kid had a car, but most were almost new. He coasted to the bike rack, which was absolutely empty. Other than that, the old school looked the same.

Tommy walked straight ahead to the cafeteria doors. Locked. He then tried the next set of doors. Locked. Every door he tried was locked. He was forced to walk around the building to the front entrance. Ironically, this was the first time he had ever entered through these doors. Completely frustrated with the front doors being locked as well, it took him another few minutes to realize he needed to be buzzed in.

Once inside, he was personally escorted by one of the secretaries to Principal Stevens' office. Alan was mid-bite into a large Italian sub when he saw Tommy. Alan's eyes widened, and as he wiped a glob of mayonnaise from his lip, he waved Tommy in, shutting the door behind him.

Tommy eyed the sub. "Ooo, that looks good. Got any more?"

"What the hell are you doing here?" Alan sternly whispered.

"What? I thought I'd check out the ole stomping grounds. Dude, what's the deal with all the doors being locked and having to get buzzed in? Kinda prison-like, don't you think?"

"A lot has changed over the years," Alan lamented. Tommy stepped further into Alan's office causing Alan to get a better look at his outfit. "What's up with those clothes? I thought you were going shopping for some new ones with that money I gave you?"

Tommy shrugged, "I kinda spent it on some other things." Tommy spied an old wooden chair in the corner of the office. He grabbed it and flipped it over. On the bottom was carved the words, *Bon Jovi Rules!* "Not everything has changed," he smiled. Tommy picked up the name plaque on the desk which said: Principal Stevens. He shook his head and laughed, "Well, Principal Stevens, how about a tour?"

Over the next thirty minutes, Alan gave his brother a personal tour around the school. Much of the school looked the same; the gym, the cafeteria, the hallways. Most of the teachers, however, were not the same. Tommy discovered this by sticking his head into every classroom they passed, despite Alan's disapproving glare. Many of the teachers had either moved on or retired.

Just when Tommy was feeling utterly out of place, the all-too familiar booming voice of Sue Thibodeau echoed across the school. She was yelling at somebody for not knowing what a perpendicular line was. Tommy wasn't sure, but he thought she actually just put the accent on the *dic* in perpendicular. That was something that he would have done. *Good for you, SuzyQ*, he smiled.

Tommy closed his eyes, attempting to take in the sounds and smells. The smells were similar to before, except, instead of Drakkar, the air was filled with another strong scent. He sniffed appreciatively and mentioned it to Alan.

"It's probably Axe Body Spray," Alan answered. He started to say, "half the boys use it instead of showering" just as Tommy was saying, "I gotta get me some of that shit."

Alan rolled his eyes and muttered, "Of course you do," and continued on down the hall. Tommy stayed where he was, awaiting the loud, chaotic sounds of students filing into the halls, but there was nothing. Well, not exactly nothing, there were voices and some laughter, but certainly not the noisy, zoo-like scene from when he went there. He looked around and almost every student was walking the halls with their heads down, firmly concentrating on their cell phones, thumbs tapping away furiously. It was like a herd of Axe-smelling-technologically-advanced-zombies making their way towards their next class. If Tommy had been able to hear what was being texted, he would have heard, "OMG-WTF-ROFLMAO-BRB," and he would have considered them to be more like aliens than zombies (but very nice-smelling aliens).

"Hey, Vince. What are you doing here?" Tommy and Alan turned around to see Richie and Emma standing there holding hands.

"Hey guys," Tommy said, "Just thought I'd check out where Alan worked."

"I heard you asked my mom out on a date?" smiled Emma.

Before Tommy could answer, Alan butted in, "I wouldn't call it a date, Emma. Just a friendly, non-romantic dinner."

Emma jumped in with excitement, "You should totally take her to that new Italian restaurant in downtown Portsmouth.

Again, Alan butted in, "They're probably just going to do Applebees or maybe even Longhorns or"…

Tommy cut his brother off, "What's the name of that Italian place?"

"It's *Ristorante Massimo*," she answered. "You should google it and check out the menu."

"Perfect. Thanks, guys," Tommy said.

Approaching the locker to their left was a slender, well-groomed boy. He gave Emma and Richie a big, animated smile and wave. "How's the cutest couple in school doing today?" the boy said.

"Hey Peter," Emma and Richie said at the same time.

Alan whispered to Tommy, "That's Ricky's son, Peter."

Tommy looked Peter over then whispered back to his brother, "Hmm, he doesn't look like a"… he paused as Alan glared at him, "a guy who does musicals?" Before Alan could chastise his brother, a teacher motioned for Alan to have a word with her. He momentarily excused himself and stepped into her classroom. Richie was about to introduce Peter to Tommy, but was interrupted by a commotion up the hall.

Strutting, sneering, and nudging their way down the hall were Otto Jr. and three of his sidekicks (Kenny, Kip, &Dale). Tommy stood shocked. It was as if he was staring at a mirror from years ago. Otto Jr. was a spitting image of his old man; right down to his ripped jeans, greasy hair, and tattooed arms. The one difference was Otto Jr. had a scraggly, angry looking goatee on his face. As Otto Jr. and his posse moved closer, Peter prepared himself for a confrontation. In his head he counted down, "Three, two, one"…

"Yo, Peter Pan, where's Tinkerbell?"" Otto Jr's filthy mitt crashed down on Peter's shoulder. Otto Jr. paused, looked at his posse, then smirked, "Or should I say, hey Tinkerbell, where's Peter Pan?"

Emma stepped in, "Knock it off, Otto."

"Oh yeah? You two geeks gonna make me?"

"You better watch out Otto," warned Kenny, "Richie might go tell his daddy on you."

Otto Jr. froze in fake horror and exclaimed, "Oh no! Not big, bad Principal Stevens!"

Tommy's blood boiled. It had been less than a minute, but he already had his fill of the spawn of Otto. Sensing his irritation, Otto Jr. turned his attention to Tommy. "What are you looking at, old man?"

Old man? There's no way he's talking to me, thought Tommy. In his head, he still felt 18…and in his head, he was about to open a can of whoop-ass on this punk. But he didn't. The words and actions escaped him. Tommy stood still, almost cowardly, as Otto Jr. laughed and began to walk off with his crew.

Before Tommy could process what just happened, Otto Jr's smug voice returned, "Hey, old man, phone call for you." Otto Jr. held out his cell phone.

Confusion washed over Tommy's face. "Phone call? For me?" Tommy stammered.

"Ya, the 1980's called and want their acid wash back!" Otto Jr. laughed.

"Burned!" yelled Kenny as they all high-fived Otto Jr.

"He kinda looks like that Chris Farley skit," added Dale, "Fat guy in a little coat, fat guy in a little coat."

Before any response was made, the bell rang. Otto Jr. and his crew hooted and hollered their way back down the hall. "Sorry about that, Vince," Richie said.

"Yea, don't mind them," Emma added. "They're all jerks."

Tommy was actually touched that the two of them thought to apologize for Otto Jr.'s actions. Emma looked just like her mother then, both in her disdain when she looked at Otto, Jr., and in her concern for his 'victim'.

"Believe it or not, I actually went to school with kids just like them," Tommy said.

"I bet they made high school hell for you, huh?" Richie was somber in his question, making Tommy wonder how much shit he got from them on a regular basis. Tommy then felt guilty, knowing that in high school, he had been one of them.

"I made it through," Tommy's answer was noncommittal. To a point, Otto *did* make his life hell, only not in the way Richie meant.

The students finished their texts, emoticons, and selfies, and then dispersed to their next class. Alan returned to Tommy's side just in time to watch Richie and Emma walk hand in hand down the hall. Tommy's face softened and he let out a sigh, "It seems like yesterday that was me and Gina. Of course, I never treated her as good as

Richie treats Emma."

"I wouldn't say never," Alan said. "Just towards the end maybe."

Tommy nodded in agreement and followed Alan up the hallway. They only made it a few steps before Tommy stopped dead in his tracks. He turned to his right and came face to face with locker #417. "My old locker," Tommy said. He knew exactly what he should find inside; the mirror shard, pictures of hair bands, hair spray … and the secret bag of weed shoved into the toe of the sneaker on the top shelf. He was brought back to the present when Alan cleared his throat.

Alan watched 1988 fade from Tommy's eyes as his mind returned him to present day. Slowly, Tommy slide his fist around the outside of the locker looking for its sweet spot. When he was satisfied, he gave it a swift, solid punch. Magically, the locker opened. Alan was beside himself with thoughts of: *Destruction of property? Invasion of privacy?* All he said was, "Way to go, Fonzie."

Tommy looked in the locker, disgusted; disgusted that it was neat and disgusted that he wasn't magically transported back to where he belonged, when the mess in the locker was *his.* He slammed it shut and turned to Alan.

"Well, I should probably let you get back to work," Tommy said. "I'm gonna head home and rest up. I've got an appointment later with a personal trainer."

"Are you serious?"

Tommy grabbed hold of his love handles. "Yup. I'll be back in shape in no time."

"Hmm. Good for you, Tommy. Good for you." Tommy gave him a thumbs up then headed home.

Alan strode back towards his office, he stopped in front of a locker and looked around to see if anyone was watching. When the coast was clear, Alan slide his fist on the locker feeling for the sweet spot. Solidly, he slammed his fist into the locker. Nothing. Again, his fist slammed. Still nothing. Frustrated with his lack of *Fonzie* - type skills, Alan proceeded to beat and kick the crap out of the poor metal locker and only stopped when he noticed three teachers were witnessing his actions.

He quickly composed himself and gave each of the teachers a thumbs up. When they finally returned to their classrooms, Alan straightened his tie, scolded himself, then started to walk away. Two steps later, the locker popped open spilling out books and various papers.

TRACK 16

Tommy pedaled past the church, and its clock struck midnight. "Shit," he cursed, "I'm gonna be late." He arrived at the village plaza at 12:04 AM. Still huffing and puffing from his ride, he leaned Big Blue against wall and rushed towards the front door. He pressed his face against the large picture window, but besides a faint light on in the back, the studio was dark. Maybe he got the time wrong. Maybe he got the day wrong. For the hell of it, he tried the door. It was open. He entered and crept towards the center of the room. "Hello? Amber?"

There was stirring in the back, then, out of the shadows appeared Amber. She wore bright pink yoga pants, with a matching sports bra. Like earlier, Tommy was awestruck by her exotic beauty. The same couldn't be said about her reaction to his attire; more amused than awestruck. Standing in front of her was a slightly husky, middle-aged man wearing super tight 80's shorts with sweatpants underneath. He was also sporting a Motley Crue Theatre of Pain concert tee with its sleeves cut off and a white head band.

Amber immediately burst into laughter. "I…I wasn't sure what to wear," Tommy said.

"Nah, you're fine," she said. "I love a guy with a sense of humor. So, are you ready for me?"

"I think so. Just so you know," Tommy added, "I haven't done anything this strenuous in a long, long time."

Amber looked him over again. "I assumed as much," she smiled. She gently took him by the hand and led him towards the back room.

"But just because I'm a little inexperienced at this type of thing, don't go easy on me. I have a lady to impress. Give me your most intense workout, okay?" Tommy said.

"I was hoping you'd say that," she said.

"Should I pay you now?"

Amber placed her hand on the door knob and answered, "When we go inside, you can place the money on the table. Understood?"

"Sure. How much was it again?" he asked.

"Two hundred," she answered.

"Two hundred?" Tommy exclaimed. "Wow, times really have changed." He pulled a wallet out of his shorts. "Luckily, I snagged my brother's wallet," he murmured.

As Tommy pulled out a wad of cash, Amber opened the door. The small 12x12 room was dimly lit by a single candle. All Tommy could make out was that there was a bed on the back wall with a tiny end table next to it. "Kinda small for what we're gonna be doing, isn't it?" Tommy asked.

Amber simply motioned towards the table then began lighting some more candles. Tommy grabbed his wad (of cash) and placed it on the table. When he turned back around, his eyes widened in surprise. In the corner of the room, the newly lit candles revealed a tripod, a video camera, and an older man. He was nicely dressed and was probably in his 60's. "What's with the old dude with the camera?" Tommy whispered.

"He's my...partner," Amber answered. "He likes to videotape my sessions. That okay?"

Tommy pondered then shrugged, "Sure, as long as he doesn't make fun of my moves."

Both Amber and the older man smiled. She led Tommy to the bed and motioned for him to lie down. "How about I loosen you up first?" she said. "I'd hate for you to pull a muscle right out of the gate."

As she pushed him face down onto the bed, Tommy answered, "Good idea." She straddled him, and as her hands begin to massage him, his eyes slowly closed and he let out a relaxed moan, "Wow, you have magical hands."

Meanwhile, as Amber continued her massage, the old man left his camera post and began removing his clothes. When he was down to just his tightie whities, he began to massage Tommy's legs.

With his eyes still closed, Tommy let out another relaxed moan, "Mmmmm. This Zumba thing is amazing. It feels like you have four hands and"… Amber licked Tommy's neck as the old man simultaneously licked his leg. In shock, Tommy's eyes opened as he finished his thought, "And two tongues? What the"…

Just then, the door was kicked open and members of the York Police Department busted in yelling, "Everybody freeze!"

Tommy had a shocked look on his face when he saw it was the police, and an even more shocked (and disgusted) look when he saw the old man in his tightie whities.

***

Tommy sat in the interrogation room of the YPD. His heart raced. Sweat flowed from every pore in his body. Finally, after what seemed like forever, two officers entered the room. Both were in their 40's. Tommy immediately recognized one to be an old classmate, Clark Goldsmith. Tommy was pretty sure that Clark was the victim of one of Tommy and Otto's atomic wedgies.

Before either officer had a chance to speak, Tommy blurted out, "I swear, officers, I absolutely wasn't paying to have sex with her…or him. I just thought I was getting a private Zumba lesson. I swear!"

Officers Goldsmith and D'Orsi had a seat in front of Tommy. Officer Goldsmith took the lead, "I see. And that private 'Zumba' lesson included a tongue bath from a 66-year-old pimp?" he said.

"Pimp?" Tommy exclaimed. "I know this looks bad, but I promise you this is just a big, comical misunderstanding. Not unlike a classic "Three's Company" episode."

Officer D'Orsi nearly choked on his coffee. "Ohhh, right. Was that the episode Jack got licked like a lollipop by Mr. Furley?"

Officer Goldsmith played along, "Oh yeah. It happened in the VIP room of the Regal Beagle." Both cops high-fived and continued to laugh at Tommy's expense. "Any reason you don't have an ID on you?" continued Officer Goldsmith.

"Ummm"…

"More importantly," interrupted Officer D'Orsi, "Any reason you have someone else's ID on you? You do realize the wallet you stole was from a well-respected member of our community?"

"I didn't steal it! Alan is my"… Tommy paused.

"Alan Stevens is your what?" asked Officer D'Orsi.

Tommy's hands clammed up, his face poured with sweat. You could probably get a cupful of sweat from his head band. The officers noticed Tommy's nervousness then turned to one another with a shocked look. "Oh my God," Officer Goldsmith said, "Alan Stevens is his lover. Principal Stevens is gay."

Frustrated with the whole misunderstanding, Tommy stood up. "No! I'm telling you"…

"We've heard enough!" Officer Goldsmith said as he motioned to his partner, "Fingerprint him."

Tommy's mind raced. His fingerprints were in the system from a vandalism incident back in his senior year. Tommy's secret was over. The truth was going to come out. Without thinking, Tommy blurted out, "No! You can't do that."

"Oh really?" Officer D'Orsi said. "What other crimes are you wanted for?" With that, he grabbed Tommy and started to haul him out of the room. Just then, Sergeant Walsh entered the room, pulling his officers aside for a quick conference. As Tommy watched, he sensed anger and disappointment on their faces.

Reluctantly, Officer Goldsmith turned to Tommy, "Looks like this is your lucky day, ya perv. Apparently, someone called in a favor for you. You're free to go." Tommy stood dumbfounded.

"You heard my partner, get outta here!" Officer D'Orsi yelled. "Before we accidently Taser you." Tommy hurried out of the station. All three officers shook their heads in disgust

***

Alan's hands were at the proper 10 and 2 on the wheel. His eyes focused on the road ahead. His lips moved as he mumbled to himself, and every so often he would shoot Tommy a quick disappointed glare. It felt as though Tommy was a little kid driving with his dad. The silence of disappointment was always the worse punishment.

"If you think about it, it's kinda your fault, Alan. You're the one who recommended Zumba."

Alan looked blankly at Tommy then spoke, "You didn't think it was weird to have a two hundred dollar Zumba lesson? At midnight? With a strange man videotaping it?"

Tommy shrugged, "I just thought she was dedicated. And how am I supposed to know what things cost nowadays? I've been brain dead for the last twenty-five years, remember?" He paused a second then continued, "And as far as the old man is concerned, I thought we were gonna review the tape later to see what I could improve upon. You know, like a football film session?"

Again, Alan stared blankly at his brother. "That is the most ridiculous thing I've ever heard." Alan returned his attention back to the road, and muttered, "And speaking of ridiculous, you really need to go buy a new wardrobe."

Tommy glanced down at his under-sized and out of date attire and nodded in agreement. "Yea, you're right," he said. "Especially for my date with Gina later tonight."

Alan pulled into his driveway and put the car in park. "For the record, Tommy, I really think this whole Gina thing is a train wreck waiting to happen."

"Don't worry, little brother, Vince Neily has everything under control."

Alan rolled his eyes and exited the car. As they headed up the walkway, Alan inquired, "Hey, who do you think pulled the strings to get you off tonight?"

"Duh. Who do ya think?"

"Oh yeaaa," Alan joked, "Dr. Zimarchi Corleone, the Godfather doctor of Maine."

"Make fun all you want, Alan, but I know what I know." Tommy's mind went directly to the conversation he had with the doctor earlier in the week:

"Let's just say a lot of people owe me favors."

... *"So my casket was empty?"*

... *"Something like that."*

It was all starting to make sense to Tommy, Dr. Z must be in the mafia; the kidnapping, the connections, people owing him favors? The not-so-ironic disappearance of his arch enemy, Dr. Hargrove? Yup, it was all making sense.

Alan inserted the key in the door, "You've been watching way too much television if you think the mafia is here in Maine," he laughed.

"Oh yeah," Tommy countered, "What about the 'out of the blue' retirement of Principal Jenkins? And you yourself said you were the most underqualified candidate for his replacement. And you also said Dr. Z was always good to our family."

"I take offense to that," huffed Alan. I might not have been as qualified as some others, but I totally nailed the interview! And despite what you may think, I'm a darn good principal, and I don't need a mafia boss to pulling strings for me!"

Tommy knew his suspicions about the doctor were right, but he also knew on this occasion he needed *not* to be right. He hurt his brother's feelings so many times in the past, so he decided to let this one go. "You know, Alan, you're probably right. Maybe I have been watching too much TV since I've been back. Sorry."

Did my big brother just say sorry to me? Alan's mood quickly lightened as he graciously accepted Tommy's apology, "It's okay. I shouldn't have snapped at you. You've been through a lot." Tommy nodded at Alan. "Oh, and just so you know, Tommy," Alan added, "the Amish mafia isn't real either. Just more fake reality junk to get ratings."

They entered the darkened house and Tommy decided to change the subject. "Does Richie know about 'the Zumba incident?'" he whispered.

"No. He's at his mother's house tonight."

"Ah, good," Tommy said as he started up the stairs. "Well, I'm hitting the sack. I'm exhausted.

Before he headed upstairs, Alan said, "I think we need to have a talk first."

"Jesus, Alan! Give it a rest! I told you, I didn't know she was a hooker, and I don't really believe in the whole mafia thing!"

"No, not about that," Alan said clutching the bag of CD's Tommy bought earlier in the day. "About these."

"Oh, yeah, those. I know I was supposed to buy clothes, but"…

Alan didn't care that Tommy blew the money on CDs. He was more curious about Tommy's selections. One by one Alan pulled them from the bag.

"The Bon Jovi ones I get," Alan began, "and the Best of 90's Hair Bands is totally understandable. You wanted to see what you had missed. But, what's the deal with these?" He held up three CDs. "Gloria Estefan? Ricky Martin? The Best of Menudo?"

Tommy stammered, "Umm, umm, the idiot cashier must have slipped them in…you know, promotional-type stuff." Alan wasn't buying his brother's story. He laughed and shook his head at Tommy.

"Shut up, Alan!" snapped Tommy. He snatched the CDs

from Alan and stormed up the stairs. With Alan still cracking up, Tommy stopped on the top step and turned and tossed Alan his wallet back.

Alan caught it (totally didn't catch it), and shot Tommy a quizzical look. "I used it to pay for my 'Zumba' lesson." Alan's laughter stopped.

"And what was the PC word again for being queer?" Tommy asked.

"Um... gay," Alan answered. "Why?"

"Well, the police may or may not think you're gay then."

TRACK 17

Tommy stood by the window in the foyer nervously waiting for Gina to pick him up. *What kind of dude asks a chick out and has to have them pick you up?* It reminded him when he asked Gina out for the first time back in 7th grade. It wasn't much of a date. They just went to a movie then hung out at the mall and shared an Orange Julius. He asked her out then immediately asked if her parents could drive them. Embarrassing yes, but the alternative was to be in the same car with *his* parents. That would have taken embarrassment to a whole new level.

Alan actually volunteered to drive and pick him up, but Tommy would rather play with himself with a handful of tacks than be escorted to and from a date by Alan. It was bad enough that he turned to his brother for his outfit. Khakis and a sweater? He supposed he looked neat, but he also thought he looked *old*. At least Alan didn't choose the sweater; v-necks and prints? Was he expecting him to wear *a tie* underneath? The mental picture he came up with of him wearing a tie and sweater vest made him laugh to himself, but his expression sobered up fast when it made him think of his father. *Oh, Dad, I'm sorry.*

When Gina pulled in the driveway, Tommy didn't want to seem over-excited, so he waited until she (almost) put the car in park before exiting the house.

Tommy left it up to her to pick where they went. Gina chose to cross over the bridge and hit the downtown area of historic Portsmouth, New Hampshire. Considering this was *Vince's* first time in this area, Tommy prepared himself to pretend to be seeing it for the first time. He quickly realized there was no pretending necessary. He didn't recognize any of the names of the stores, restaurants, or bars. It was as if he was seeing it for the first time. There was no Café Brioche on the corner. There was no Eagle Photo next to the church, and there was no Sessions music store. Tommy's heart sank. Sessions was where he used to buy all his tapes.

Gina chose a bar called the Thirsty Moose. They boasted to have the largest beer selection in the area. They weren't kidding. Tommy was blown away with their selection, even if he only recognized 4% of the names. As he read through the beer menu, his first thought was *Oh man, Otto, Ricky and Pud would love this place!* His second thought was *Fuck Otto! Ricky and P...Brett would love this place.*

He was actually surprised she chose a bar for their first 'date'. But then again, why wouldn't she, he thought? A bar is a good, casual place for a first date. And besides, she was sitting across from Vince, not Tommy. Gina watched him stare around the bar in wonderment.

"You okay?" she said.

Tommy snapped back to the present immediately and smiled at Gina. "Yea, I'm fine, thank you. I'm just confused by all that's going on around here." He waved his arm around in a gesture that encompassed the whole room. "All the televisions, the computer things on the tables – is that a jukebox? And how many beers do they make nowadays?"

Gina looked around. "I guess I take all of this for granted. I can't even imagine what it would be like to have just 'dropped back in' after twenty-five years of being out of circulation. Maybe I should have suggested a coffee shop?"

"No, this is fine. I have to make my way back into society, anyway," Tommy answered. "I'm just glad you agreed to go out with me."

While he waited for her to speak, Tommy took in just the look of her. Jeans and a sweater. He mentally thanked Alan (not that he would directly) for helping him with his clothes. The pale pink emphasized the green in her eyes, and he wondered if it was as soft to the touch as it made her look. Her jeans loved her, too, he could tell. They seemed to hug her all the way down.

She began to speak, and somehow, he managed to bring his eyes back up to her face, "I'll be honest, I'm kind of surprised myself. I don't usually accept invitations from guys I just meet."

"Then why did you?" Tommy was actually curious. He had no real idea other than thinking that maybe he had magical powers to hypnotize her – he knew what he'd looked like (especially in the clothing he'd been wearing).

"I'm not entirely sure. This may sound a little bizarre, but, there was something about you … something" …

"It was my clothes, wasn't it?" Tommy joked, proud of himself and surprised that so far he hadn't said something *high school.*

"Well, the outfit was … uh … unusual, but I understood that you just got back. No, it was … I don't know … something … familiar?"

Tommy's heart jumped at that, but he tried to sound cool when he answered, "Familiar like a brother?" *Please say no, please say no, please say no.*

"No." (*Whew!*) "I can't quite put my finger on it. There was something about. Besides, you're friends with Alan, and I know he wouldn't be hanging out with a psychopathic moron. I've known him for a long, long time.

Before Gina could expound on that, the waitress approached for their drink order. Gina ordered a red wine, and when it was Tommy's turn to order he glanced at the row of taps on the bar. He was going to ask the waitress what was good, but his glance passed Gina first, and he immediately remembered what she looked like … how she looked at him … *that night.* And he remembered that he didn't remember much after that.

"Just a water for me," he said to the waitress.

The waitress headed towards the bar. Gina gave him a quizzical look. "You don't drink?"

"Um, I kinda had a bad experience with alcohol," he said. "Besides, it's really hot in Africa. I found out very fast that my tolerance for alcohol was low. So low that I'd forget what I was doing."

When the waitress returned with their drinks, Tommy watched Gina sipping her glass of wine. *Red wine?* She looked so sophisticated…so adult. He supposed it was the natural progression, seeing as her drink of choice used to be strawberry daiquiri wine coolers. Well, that and tequila. A few shots of that and she'd be laughing and dancing on tables. The eighteen-year-old Tommy would have immediately ordered several tequila shots for her just now, but the new Tommy/Vince-guy kind of liked watching the adult Gina sipping her wine.

Gina looked at his glass of water. "If I knew you didn't drink, I really would have suggested a coffee shop. I'm sorry."

"Oh no, this place is great," he reassured. "I can enjoy myself without alcohol. Besides, it's not about the place you're at, it's about the company you're with. That's what my…dad always used to say."

"Aww," she gushed, "that's sweet. To be honest, I'm not much of a drinker either. Usually only when I'm nervous or when I have a bad day at work."

Tommy gazed at her wine. "Which reason is that?"

"A little of both," she smiled. "Mostly the second reason though."

Tommy returned her smile and said, "Do you have a stressful job?"

She shrugged embarrassingly, "A nightly two glass of wine kind of job?"

"Ahh, what do you do?" he asked.

"I'm a therapist."

Tommy was taken aback. *A therapist*, he thought? Gina never mentioned wanting to be a therapist. A writer. A writer was her dream. She was accepted into that writing school and everything.

"I actually specialize more in grief counseling," she said. "I was on the other side of the couch for so many years, I guess that's when I found it to be my calling."

Gina isn't a writer? Gina was in therapy? (and they really sit on couches?)

Before Tommy could utter a word, Gina explained further, "You knew that Alan's brother was killed in a car accident, right?"

As the word *killed* rattled around his head, he simply nodded his head yes. Without thinking better of it, he spoke, "You two dated, right?"

Sadly, Gina nodded. "When it first happened, I just shut down – went into a dark depression. It wasn't until months later, after constant badgering from my mom that I went to see somebody. It ended up being the best thing that happened to me. Not only did I work through my pain and regret"... Tommy lost his concentration on what she was saying. *Regret? Did she blame herself for what happened?* Tommy's stomach churned, and his heart actually ached. He wanted to stand up and blurt out that none of what happened was her fault. None of it.

Tommy found out later from his brother that not only did Gina sink into a huge depression after the funeral, but she postponed and eventually ended her dream of attending the writing college in California. He was absolutely responsible for the death of her dream of being a writer. He literally wanted to throw up.

He fought back the single tear that was attempting to escape from his eye and tried to refocus on what she was saying. "Anyway, that's how I found my calling," she said as she took a giant sip of wine. Thankfully, for Tommy's sake, her next comment lightened the mood a bit, "Okay, enough about me, I really want to hear more about this tribe you were living with. What was their name again?"

"The Mo-tah-ley-cru-ayy tribe," he answered.

Gina giggled. "Every time I hear you say that, I can't help but think of the band Motley Crue. I wonder if they named themselves after them?"

"Hmm, I bet they did," Tommy said. The tribe is pretty bad ass."

"So what part of Africa were you in?" Gina asked.

"Um, the jungley part," Tommy replied. He knew he'd be lucky if he could identify Africa on a map.

Gina laughed at his silliness. "So the rainforest then?"

"Yea, the jungley part."

"You must have some great stories," she smiled.

Even before the accident, Tommy was a great storyteller. He was the guy who would hold court at parties and have everyone cracking up at his crazy, animated stories. He was also the type of guy who could make any joke funny just by the way he told it. Over the next hour, he told story after made-up story. Gina was in stitches she was laughing so hard. God, he missed and loved her laugh. She especially loved hearing about his friend.

"Your friend sounds like quite the character," she said. "How do you pronounce his name again?"

"Malahkahnunu," he said, "but I just called him Bob. Wait until I tell you about the time Bob and I were out hunting kangaroos."

Gina's laughter paused with a curious look, "Kangaroos? In the rainforest?"

Without missing a beat, he replied, "Yeah, the African rainforest kangaroo. The elusive and dangerous African rainforest kangaroo, I might add. Gina was skeptical to say the least, but it didn't matter if he was telling the truth or not, she was enjoying his many fantastical stories. Tommy took a break from his storytelling and turned his attention to the Sox game on one of the many flat-screen TVs. He was still shocked they had put seats on top of the green monster.

Finally, Gina broke his trance. "You do realize, I don't believe you, right?"

Oh shit, he thought. *I'm busted.* "You don't?"

"There's no way a twenty-something year old would choose to leave the real world and live with a remote African tribe. Especially for twenty-five years! I mean, what kind of documentary takes that long to film?"

His mind raced. He quickly reached into his bag of tricks (creative imagination) (lies) and tried to pull out a new and improved story. "Um, yeah. You got me there...I wasn't really doing a documentary the whole time…I was…umm"…

"Do you wanna hear what I think?" she interrupted. "I think you originally went over there to film a documentary on this tribe, but by the time you were finished with it, you found yourself more affected than you thought you'd be. Just like I found my calling while in therapy, I think you found your calling while filming that documentary."

"My calling?" Tommy hesitated.

"Yup. You decided to dedicate your life on helping the less fortunate. I bet you went from poor village to poor village trying to help in any way you could. And I'm also thinking that you're just too modest of a person to tell people that."

Tommy lowered his head and slowly nodded in agreement, "You caught me. I guess I was uncomfortable telling everyone I spent half my life helping the less fortunate."

Gina's eyes beamed at him in pride and admiration. He felt like shit, but he knew his guilty feelings would have to wait – he needed to put a bow on this tale that Gina had laid out for him.

"Now that the cat's out of the bag," he began, "when I joined the Peace Corps, I honestly figured it would be a quick stint. You know, a cool way to see different parts of the world. But the more I saw the conditions these tribes and villages were living in, I knew I had to do more. I needed to become one with them."

Gina sat still and said nothing. Tommy worried he might have laid it on too thick. After several minutes of her just staring at him, he said, "What? What are you thinking, Gina?"

"I'm thinking, I've never met anyone as selfless and as dedicated as you. I'm truly in awe, Vince.

Tommy knew he was the furthest thing from selfless and dedicated. He was overcome with guilt, but he had to admit, he loved the way she was looking at him. Pride, adoration – it wasn't a look he was used to with her or anyone for that matter. But it was a look he could get used to.

After they left the Thirsty Moose, they walked down to Prescott Park. Prescott Park is a beautifully landscaped park directly overlooking the Piscataqua River. Tommy's parents used to bring him there for Sunday picnics when he was young. He hated it. He was always bored, and he especially hated when they forced him to play Frisbee with Alan. Alan was probably four or five and couldn't catch or throw very well; definitely not up to Tommy's standards. Tommy would purposefully throw it over Alan's head as close to the riverbank as possible. His intentions, of course, was Alan would slip and fall in. Unfortunately, he never fell in, but that didn't stop his parents from scolding him in public. Yup, he fucking hated the park, but he would give anything to have both his parents there with him now (yes, even Alan).

As they walked through the park, they continued to laugh and share small talk. He was surprised at how much he missed Gina's laugh. The whole evening surprised him actually. He began to see Gina all over again, and it wasn't sexual (well, not all of it). She was smart and funny … and *deep*. He laughed at himself using that word, but he also began to understand why Gina used to be interested in that guy, Adam. It also made him question why she had even been interested in *him*. He'd been very lucky. And he blew it.

Inevitably, like most first dates, the conversation turned to Exes - in particular, Emma's father, Nick. Gina was honest and matter of fact about him. She admitted that she was into him way more than he was into her. She also admitted that he was a major jerk to her, which sadly caused her to be into him even more. It's the age-old story; girl likes guy, guy treats girl like shit, girl likes guy even more.

Listening to her talk about this A-hole made Tommy's blood boil. *How could someone treat this beautiful girl, woman, like shit?* As he thought deeper on this, the irony certainly wasn't lost on him.

After leaving the park, they walked along the sidewalks back toward Gina's car. They passed by a yoga studio which also was advertising Zumba classes. This caused Gina to smile and say, "Did you hear about that Zumba instructor that was busted for prostitution?" Tommy simply shook his head and shrugged.

On the ride home, Gina asked him why, after twenty-five years, did he decide to leave Africa and rejoin the 'real world'? Tommy thought for a second, then slowly responded, "Because it was time."

His answer seemed to satisfy her. A few minutes later, she decided to push the envelope a bit. "Can I ask you a personal question?"

"Yeah, sure," he answered.

"I'm assuming over all those years that you never were married?"

Tommy laughed, "Nooooo."

"How about a girlfriend?"

He hesitated for a moment then answered, "I did have one before I went away, but...but I screwed it up."

"I'm sorry."

"Don't be. It was totally my own fault." Tommy paused then added, "Tonight was actually my first date since I left all those years ago. Not that this is date," he quickly corrected.

Gina giggled and blushed, "I kind of thought it was a date."

"Yea? So how did I do?" he grinned.

"Let's just say more guys should go away for twenty-five years before going on a date."

Her response rattled around his head. "So I was a good date then?"

Again, she giggled. "Yes, Vince, you were a good date."

He spent the next few minutes gloating to himself – *See, I still got it! Tommy Stevens is a good date...a damn good date!* When he was finished self-congratulating himself, he noticed Gina smirking. He worried that she had somehow heard his internal thoughts. "What? What are you smirking at?" he asked.

"If this is your first date in twenty-five years, what about"... she hesitated, "you know what, forget it. It's totally none of my business."

"No, no, it's okay." Tommy knew exactly where she was going with this. "You're curious if I've sex in the last twenty-five years, aren't you? Or as the Mo-tah-ley-cru-ayy say"... Tommy proceeded to make random and strange clicking sounds with his mouth. Gina bursted out laughing, which is exactly what he was going for.

"I'm sorry. That question totally crossed the line," she said.

"Nah, no lines with me," he insisted. "The answer to answer your question is no. I haven't had sex in twenty-five years."

Gina let that sink in. "Wow. And here I thought my ten-month drought was bad." She paused a second then continued to pry, "So, not even with any of the female tribe members?"

Tommy shook his head no. "There's something about a huge bone through the nose that's a big turn off." They both laughed and continued laughing as Gina pulled into Alan's driveway.

"Thanks again for driving. I guess I gotta get my license. I didn't really need one to drive the camels."

"Camels? Didn't you say you were mostly in the rainforests?"

"Um, yeah…the African rainforest camels."

"You crack me up, Vince. I really did have a great time tonight," she said.

"Me too," he admitted. "But next time will be more about you and less about me."

"Ha! I'm afraid my stories would bore you to tears. Wait? Is that your way of asking me out again?"

"Maybe," he said. "Would you say yes if I did?"

"Maybe," she laughed.

With Gina warmly smiling at him, it was a perfect moment for a kiss, but Tommy thought better of it. Quickly and awkwardly, he exited the car.

"Night, Gina."

"Um, night, Vince." She was disappointed yet refreshed with his choice of no goodnight kiss. Tommy waved as he watched her back out of the driveway. When her taillights finally faded, he entered the house.

***

Alan and Richie were waiting for him when he got back. Alan was very curious about how the evening went, and he asked if Tommy had a nice time. Tommy said he did, but said little else. Normally, Alan would have pressed for more, but there was something about Tommy that made him hold back. He *did* seem like he had fun, but there was also an aura of ... something about him. Sadness? Reflection? Going out with Gina after losing twenty-five years of his life had to impact him. Alan decided to give him a little space ... for now. Plus, he knew that he and Richie were about to give him more to think about.

"We made you a video," Richie told Tommy. "Some of the highlights of the past twenty-five years. To help you catch up a bit."

The video started with Ronald Reagan, George Bush, Bill Clinton, and George W. Bush, and Barak Obama. Richie and Alan gave a running commentary to explain what he was watching. "Our presidents since 1988," said Richie.

"Given the age you were at when you ... left," Alan began, "there are many world events left out that you wouldn't find relevant right now ... Tiananmen Square, the dissolution of the U.S.S.R. and end of the Cold War, Rwanda ..."

Tommy understood nothing about what Alan was saying. *Pee Wee Herman arrested for public masturbation?* "I didn't even know he had a dick." The video quickly moved to 'the white Bronco'. *What? Not OJ! Whoa, Lady Diana? MICHAEL JACKSON?*

News clippings of military fighting ran in succession: The Gulf War, Kosovo, Bosnia …Tommy's head began to spin. Then images of the World Trade Center towers falling splashed across the screen, and he had trouble believing what he was seeing. It was like watching Creature Double Feature on a Saturday afternoon, only instead of large buildings in Tokyo being destroyed by Godzilla, he was seeing familiar American landmarks being blown up … by planes. He looked up at Alan and Richie in question and saw the serious looks on both of their faces and knew none of this was a joke. He turned his head away from the television during the recap of the ensuing war clips and took that time to ask Alan, "We got the people that did that?"

Alan shrugged, "Kinda."

From there, the video thankfully lightened quite a bit. Tommy was introduced to some of the music trends he missed; from grunge to hip hop to boy/girl bands. *What the hell is a Spice Girl?*

Next, was popular movies of the last twenty-five years. This was highlighted with the classic scene from Titanic (DiCaprio and Winslet on the bow of the ship). It was obvious by Richie's expression that this was all his dad's doing. Tommy and Richie looked over at Alan. He had a tear in his eye as he watched mesmerized.

"What's this? A commercial? You made me a video with

commercials? Wait! Is that Bon Jovi? Where's his hair? A HEADACHE commercial?" Tommy began to feel like a 17-year-old old man.

"Hey, you picked someone who actually stuck around. At least he's still making music." That was the only thing Alan could think of. Just then a clip of "The Osbournes" showed, and Tommy looked up at him.

"What the *hell?*"

"A lot has changed," was all Alan said.

"I'll say." Tommy watched a news clip announcing the legalization of gay marriage in Massachusetts. He perked up considerably with the clips of the four Boston sports teams winning their respected championships highlighted with the 2004 World Series. "The Sox won? The curse is over?"

The final clip on the video was of a guy in full astronaut gear, holding his helmet in front of the York High School road sign. Tommy seemed to recognize him, but before he or even Alan could say a word, Richie spoke up, "That's Chris Casey. He graduated with my uncle Tommy. He was a Navy Seal and then became an astronaut."

Tommy did his best not to reveal to Richie that he knew exactly who Chris Casey was. He was in a handful of Tommy's classes in high school and was also the captain of the football team...but a Navy Seal? An ASTONAUT? "Wow," Tommy said. Like an astronaut astronaut?" Alan and Richie nodded. "Like in space? Outer space? Like Star Wars space?"

"Yea, Vince, they let him use the Millennium Falcon and everything," joked Richie.

"Really?"

"No, you fool!" snapped Alan. "He took a space shuttle! Geesh." Richie chuckled at the banter between the two brothers (college buddies).

As the video on the laptop faded to black, the enormity of how much time had passed, and how much he'd missed was really beginning to sink in. It felt … heavy. The heaviness was about to lighten, however. The video faded back in. Richie smirked.

"What's this?" questioned Alan.

"I added a little eye candy montage for Vince," smiled Richie. Alan shot his son a disconcerting look. "Aw, come on, Dad, the guy spent twenty-five years studying and helping out others. The least we can do is show the poor guy the hot chicks he missed out on."

Tommy beamed, "I love this kid! Are you sure he's your son?"

"Richard!" scolded Alan, "We don't refer to females as"…

"Hush Alan," interrupted Tommy, "Do you have to suck the fun out of everything?"

On the screen, quick shots of Cindy Crawford, Heidi Klum, Gisele Bundchen...and on and on. Even Alan couldn't help be mesmerized. But when Jenna Jamison popped on the screen, Alan nearly choked on his seltzer water. *How the heck does Richie know about her? OMG, did he raid my under-the-mattress video collection?*

Richie ended the video with the opening intro to *Baywatch*. Tommy's eyes widened, "Whoa, who is that?"

"Pamela Anderson," Richie answered.

Alan added, "AKA, the mother of Tommy Lee's kids."

"I knew he was the man!" Tommy boasted. His excitement turned a bit curious when he saw David Hasselhoff. "Whoaa, Nightrider is a lifeguard? Hot chicks in bikinis? This must have been the best show ever!"

When the video officially ended, all Tommy could say was, "Wow, what a world." Both Richie and Alan nodded.

"Well, I'm gonna go pick Emma up for breakfast. You guys wanna come?" Richie asked.

Both Alan and Tommy shook their heads no. Before he headed off, Tommy gave him a fist bump and said, "Thanks again for making this for me."

"Hey," Alan interrupted, "I had a hand in it too."

"Yea, but Richie provided the best parts," Tommy smiled and gave Richie another fist bump.

After Richie left, Tommy turned to Alan and said, "I was just kidding, I really do appreciate you making this for me. It's a lot to take in." Alan nodded, patted his brother on the back. "Oh, by the way," Tommy continued, "I set up a little get together with Ricky and Pud…um, Brett."

Alan shot him a disapproving look. "Tommy, don't you think it's weird that someone they just met would invite them to hang out?"

"That's why I told them it was your idea," smiled Tommy. "We're meeting them at that Ruby's bar & grill place at six tonight."

"Six? Tonight? What if I had plans already?" Alan regretted the words even before they fell out of his mouth.

TRACK 18

Tommy sat across from Ricky and Brett. He still couldn't get over their drastic makeovers. Brett's now-short hair was way too neat, and even though he was wearing jeans (that looked brand new) and a turtleneck (tucked in), he still looked like he was dressing up to go somewhere special.

Ricky on the other hand, had all of the 'B's' covered - bald, bedsheets, beads and Birkenstocks. Tommy also couldn't get over how it felt like just last week they were jamming in Otto's garage, yet, it also felt like a lifetime ago.

After the four were seated, Deren made her way over to them.

"Hi guys, my name is Deren, and I'll be taking care of you tonight."

"Hey, I know you!" Tommy blurted out. "You were our waitress the other night."

Deren acknowledged him with a nod and wide smile. "Can I start you guys off with some drinks?" Her piercing blue eyes met Alan's first.

"Just a water for me, please," Alan answered, but quickly changed his mind. "You know what, I feel like living on the edge tonight. How about a… Diet Coke, please."

Whoa. You sure you can handle that, big guy? Deren thought as she turned her attention to Brett.

Brett pondered, "A large Iced Tea, please. Oh, raspberry tea, if you have it?"

Again, Deren smiled and nodded and thought, *Jesus! Could these fucknuts be any more lame?* Her question would quickly be answered. After extensively studying the drink menu, Ricky asked, "Do you have any smoothies?" *For the love of God, shoot me now*, she thought.

Deren fought through it and offered her best fake cheerleader-esque smile and pointed out, "We have frozen alcoholic type drinks, if you want?"

Ricky gave an unsatisfied shrug then continued to ponder. Finally, he sighed and answered, "Just a water with a lemon, please."

Externally, Deren's face remained pleasant, almost angelic. Internally, however – her mind just exploded. Every server knows that alcohol drives the bill up, which in turn, usually drives the tip way up too. Tommy was her last salvation. It was time to turn on the charm.

"And last but certainly not least… what can I get you, Hun? And no, we still don't have your Strohs." With her hand on his shoulder, she winked and giggled. *Hun? Physical contact? Giggles?* Tommy was hooked. All she needed to do now was reel him in. "You look like a Captain Morgan's kind of guy," she smiled. Her smile was a combination of flirting mixed with *please buy a friggin expensive drink, dude!* Her adorable dimples nearly sealed the deal, but unfortunately, Tommy didn't cooperate.

"Ummm, I'll just have a Coke," he said. He immediately felt Alan's motherly glare, and changed his answer. "Actually, make it a Diet Coke."

FML! she thought. As she walked off, Tommy found himself staring at her black leggings underneath her black skirt. So basically, he was ogling her ass. When she finally disappeared into the kitchen, Tommy turned to read his friends thoughts regarding her award-winning posterior, but to his surprise, all six of their eyes were fixated on the menus. *Yup, times have a changed.*

The next couple of hours were eerily similar to his 'get together' with Gina the night before. The adult nature of their conversations were extremely foreign to Tommy. Between Gina talking about her seventeen-year-old daughter, and Ricky preaching healthy living, and Brett babbling about scientific CSI-type shit, Tommy's head was spinning in middle-aged wonderment. He was blown away that Alan and Ricky spent twenty-four fucking minutes gushing over the rumor of a *Whole Foods Market* coming to the area.

What made the two get-togethers completely worth it was the many familiarities of his old friends: Brett's machine-gun-esque type laugh, or the way Ricky still used his hands to speak when he was excited, or how Tommy could read Gina's mood just by looking into her eyes. Despite Otto's rude and obnoxious comments earlier in the week, it felt a bit strange not having him present at their get-together tonight. Tommy wanted to ask Ricky and Brett if they were still in touch with Otto, but considering they hadn't even been in touch with each other, Tommy assumed not. Tommy and Otto were pretty much inseparable back in high school, so it was only normal that he felt sad for Otto's absence. That sad feeling would soon drastically change.

They ate. They drank (if you could call it that). They laughed. Tommy repeated some of his African tribe stories from the night before and got a warm feeling every time he heard Brett's staccato laugh rip through the bar. It was also nice to see his little brother having a good time as well.

Just then, over the bar's speakers, a Taylor Swift song blared out, which caused Tommy to laugh and ask, "Who's this chick?"

All at once, Alan, Ricky, and Brett answered, "Taylor Swift."

Before Tommy could offer his thoughts on this silly bubblegum-pop crap, something strange happened. He noticed all three guys be-bopping and mouthing the words to her song. Yup, Tommy was now positive he had entered the bizarro world.

"You guys actually listen to this stuff?" Tommy gently questioned.

"You can't *not* listen to TS when she comes on," Ricky said. "Her catchy melodies and lyrics are very addictive."

"I know, right," agreed Brett. I took my niece to see her last winter. She's so amazing in concert!"

"No way!" Ricky exclaimed, "I would love to have gone." Tommy watched Alan nod in excitement.

The fact that Alan was digging this crap didn't really surprise him, but Ricky and Brett? If this was twenty-five years ago, this would be the equivalent of them singing along to a Debbie-fuckin'-Gibson song. Or worse – a Tiffany song. It would certainly be punishable by death (or at least an atomic wedgie).

After what seemed like forever, their *pop princess-cute-as-a-button* comments finally and mercifully subsided. Of course, the next topic of discussion wasn't exactly music to Tommy's ears either.

"Hey, what do you guys think about that Zumba-prostitution ring?" Brett laughed.

Tommy nearly choked on his buffalo wings. He felt Alan's judgmental eyes burning into his forehead. "So," interrupted Tommy, "tell me more about this Whole Foods Store." Tommy's comment led to another eleven minutes of Whole Foods discussion; a welcomed distraction from Zumba.

When the conversation once again faded, Tommy decided to do what the average person couldn't do: To find out what others really think of you without them knowing it's you. He briefly experimented with this last night and decided to give it a go with the guys.

"Sooo, you guys were friends with Alan's older brother, huh? What was he like?" As Tommy posed his question, Alan shot him a *What the hell are you doing* look.

"Tommy? Brett sipped at his tea. "Tommy was…loud."

"A little arrogant," added Ricky. "But in a good way," Ricky said as he and Brett looked over at Alan.

Is there really a good way to be loud and arrogant, thought Tommy?

"Ironically," said Brett, "he was a pretty normal, semi-quiet guy until freshman year.

"When Otto moved to York," Alan interrupted.

"Yea," Ricky nodded, "Otto definitely brought Tommy out of his shell...all of us actually.

"So you four were pretty tight?" asked Tommy.

"We all hung out, but I'm not sure I'd say we were tight," Ricky said as he looked over at Brett. "Tommy and Otto were definitely tight, but we were - just kind of there."

And just like that, Tommy's mind transported him back to high school. A mini montage played in his head of all the times either he ignored Ricky and Brett or followed Otto's lead and poked fun at them. The montage ended with Otto making fun of Brett's new song, and with Tommy not coming to his friend's defense.

"Hey Brett, do you remember how much you hated them constantly calling you Pud?" Ricky asked.

"Oh God," Brett said, "don't remind me. It took me forever to shake that stupid nickname."

Alan looked over at Tommy. His face was oozing with disappointment and regret. Brett and Ricky noticed Alan's look and were quick to set the record straight.

Ricky spoke first, "Don't get us wrong, we were all loud, arrogant punks back then."

Brett added, "Yea, we gladly joined in on all the bullying and crazy antics, and Tommy was always supportive of my music, even if he didn't say as much to his so-called best friend Otto."

"Why do you say so-called?" Tommy asked.

Brett looked at Ricky and continued, "He was always talking crap behind his back."

"Not to mention, what he did with Tommy's girlfriend," Ricky added.

Without thinking, Tommy blurted out, "With Gina?"

Before Tommy's blood had a chance to boil over, Ricky specified, "No, not Gina. Joni Parker."

When Tommy first met Otto, he was still pining (and whining) over the Gina breakup. Not only did Otto provide Tommy with a welcomed distraction from Gina and Adam, he did one better: He introduced him to Joni Parker. Joni and Jill MacNamara were best friends. They were also some of Otto's new-found groupies. He wasted no time bragging about being the lead singer of a band (that he founded). His lead singer status and the fact he could get alcohol or any type of drugs made him well liked among a certain female clientele. Jill and Joni were part of that clientele.

Tommy and Joni hit it off immediately, and it wasn't long before they were dating...and having sex (not in that order). Needless to say, Tommy's pining and whining over Gina and Adam was a thing of the past. He now had his very own *new-car smell* – even it was more like Camel Lights, bubblegum, and Obsession perfume.

New self-confidence, free beer and pot, a new girlfriend, and finally losing his virginity – Tommy had Otto to thank for all of these.

Alan sensed Vince turning into Tommy and quickly tried to reel his brother back in, "That's right, VINCE, my brother dated Joni after he and Gina broke up.

Ignoring Alan's attempt, Tommy persisted, "So this Otto guy fooled around with my...with Tommy's girlfriend?" Ricky and Brett both nodded. "Why didn't you guys tell me...um, Tommy?"

Ever since Tommy became friends with Otto," began Brett, "he pretty much stopped listening to us. He never would have believed us over Otto."

Ricky nodded and added, "Besides, Joni ended up dumping Tommy a week later. He was devastated enough by the breakup, we didn't want to pour salt in his wounds."

The fact that Ricky and Brett were considerate enough of his heartbreak, made Tommy temporarily forget his anger towards Otto. When it came to friendship, Ricky and Brett were the real deal, and he had treated them like shit.

This was the first time Alan heard of this Otto/Joni thing, and even though it didn't shock him, he did feel bad for his brother. Alan had the same thing happen with his ex-wife, and he didn't wish that feeling on anyone.

Brett tried to lighten the mood, "I will say this, Alan, your brother was definitely the life of the party." Brett turned his attention to Ricky and smirked, "Remember that time Tommy got shit-faced outta his mind and made us take him to get a tattoo?"

Ricky's grin turned into a full-on laugh, as he looked over at Tommy. "Did Alan ever tell you that story, Vince?" Tommy played along and shook his head no. Excitedly, Ricky continued, "We ended up at this little hole in the wall that one of Otto's bimbo's worked at. Without even hesitating, Tommy told her to tattoo a microphone on his junk with the phrase, *Step up to the Mic* written above it. It was classic Tommy." Between Ricky's enthusiasm and his animated hand gestures, Alan, Tommy, and Brett couldn't stop laughing.

"You left the best part out," Brett interjected. "The only way she could do the tattoo was if Tommy was…you know…hard."

Ricky covered his face and laughed, "I totally forgot about that! The woman had to take Tommy into a private room and put a porno on while she did the tattoo."

Due to Tommy's alcohol level on the tattoo night, details of what actually happened were always fuzzy at best, but thanks to his friends, he heard that story recounted a hundred times, and found himself laughing every time – none harder than tonight.

Before Vince could ask for more Tommy stories, Ricky looked at his watch and exclaimed, "Whoa, I should get going. *The Voice* is on at nine.

"Yea, I should head home too," added Brett. "There's a new CSI episode on tonight. This was fun though, we should do it again."

***

The next day, Tommy paid Dr. Zimarchi a surprise visit to check on the progress of the miracle cure. Dr. Zimarchi ran a battery of tests on Tommy, all of which, he passed with flying colors. Tommy also informed him that his memories from the week leading up to the accident were slowly coming back to him. The doctor urged Tommy to have patience – that his full memory would probably return in due time. After losing twenty-five years of his life, patience wasn't a word Tommy liked to hear. He wanted nothing more than to put this whole crazy nightmare behind him and start his future – which he hoped included Gina.

Tommy made it a point not to mention that not only did he hang out with his old friends, but that he (Vince) even had a semi-date with Gina. Technically, he didn't break his promise. Alan was still the only one who knew the truth on the whole Tommy/Vince charade.

"So, Doc, any luck figuring out what fixed me?" Tommy asked as he sat on the large black leather couch.

Doctor Zimarchi sat across from him in his arm chair and slowly shook his head, "No, son. Not yet. We're getting close…I think." The doctor curiously looked Tommy over. "Are you sure you've been feeling okay?"

"Yea, fine. I'm not gonna lie, I'm still having a hard time adjusting to just how much everything has changed. And don't even get me started about looking in the mirror at... this."

"I can only imagine how strange it must be. The adjustment will come in time, but the important thing is you're better."

Actually, Doc, in some ways I'm better than better."

The doctor raised his eyebrow, "What do you mean?"

"I mean, how is it I know things…things I didn't before the accident?"

"What kind of things?"

"For starters, I can speak and understand Spanish."

"And you couldn't before?" asked the doctor.

"I barely had a grasp of the English language, Doc. And how is it I did horribly in school, and yet, I knew almost every answer on Jeopardy the other day? My nephew thinks I'm a freakin' genius." Doctor Zimarchi leaned in closer, stumped. "And how come whenever I start to get angry about something, I do this count backwards from ten thing? Which actually works, by the way." Before the doctor could say anything, Tommy continued, "And…why is it that I've been blurting out weird, random phrases?"

"Phrases?" questioned Doctor Zimarchi.

Tommy began spewing phrases in a deep southern accent, "Are you doing what you're doing today because you want to or because you were doing it yesterday? Or how about this one - It's better to be healthy alone than to be sick with someone else."

"Very interesting." The doctor rubbed his chin and pondered. "But what's with the southern accent?"

"You tell me, Doc. And don't even get me started about my strange love of Latin music. Whenever I used to hear Gloria Estefan, I wanted to punch her in the throat. But now, whenever I hear her, I can't help but shake my body and do the Conga, and"…

"You can't control yourself any longer?" the doctor asked.

Sadly, Tommy nodded in agreement. "I should be bangin' my head to Motley Crue or Twisted Sister, but instead, I'm running around the house shakin' my bon bon. And I don't even know what the hell a bon bon is!!"

The doctor started to laugh, but then it hit him. "Ahhh."

"What?" asked Tommy.

The doctor stood and headed towards the basement door. "Follow me," he ordered. Slowly, the two men crept down the stairs into the make-shift laboratory. Before Tommy could ask what they were doing, the doctor pressed his finger to his lips and pointed across the room. In the back left corner was the bed where Tommy had slumbered the past twenty-five years. On the opposite side was a leather recliner facing a large flat-screen TV. The television was not only on, but the channels were constantly being changed.

The doctor focused his attention on the actual channels. Tommy's attention, on the other hand, was trying to figure out how the channels were being changed. There was nobody in the room...or was there? From the side of the recliner appeared a tiny hand engulfed by a giant remote. Paco. Tommy chuckled, but he still had no idea what this had to do with anything. It wasn't until the doctor pointed to the TV that Tommy finally started to put the pieces together.

Tommy didn't recognize the visual, but he certainly recognized the audio. It was the Spanish channel – *Telemundo*. Before Tommy had a chance to process this, Paco switched the channel to *Jeopardy*. Doctor Zimarchi watched as Tommy mouthed along with the contestant the correct answer (question). When the show went to commercial, Paco switched the channel to the Dr. Phil show. Tommy's ears perked up when he heard the familiar, booming southern drawl of Dr. Phil, spouting off one of his classic sayings.

Paco's channel changing didn't stop there, he quickly moved from Dr. Phil to the music channels. In particular, the Latin channel. As Shakira belted out something about her hips not lying, Dr. Zimarchi smiled in amazement and motioned Tommy to follow him back upstairs. When they returned to the living room, Dr. Zimarchi attempted to explain his theory on the matter.

"Let me get this straight, Doc, whatever Paco has been watching the past twenty-five years has somehow sunk into my brain?"

Dr. Zimarchi shrugged and nodded, "It's as if you benefited from some sort of subliminal learning. Amazing."

Tommy made his way towards the front door. "What's amazing about it? First, I was brain dead, and now I'm brainwashed? I'm just a giant lab rat, aren't I?" Tommy didn't wait for a response. He opened the door and started to leave. "I'll talk to you later, Doc."

The doctor called to him as he headed down the walkway, "Hey, Tommy?" Tommy turned around. "You may want to hang out with your old friends and ex-girlfriend a little less. It might be more prudent to wait until you can tell them the truth."

"You just concentrate on finding out what cured…wait…how did you know I've been hanging out with them?"

"I told you, I have my connections."

Tommy again started to walk away, but curiously turned back

around. "Speaking of which, did you have anything to do with me getting bailed out the other night?"

The doctor shrugged, "I have no idea what you're talking about. I'll see you soon, my friend." With that, he shut the door and chuckled to himself, "*Zumba.*"

TRACK 19

The next couple of weeks were a revelation to Tommy. There was so much more to Gina than he had ever realized. He knew she was smart, funny, but she had a way of looking at him, like she really *saw* him (and liked him anyway). There was a certain *depth* to her. That was the word. While time and experience may have enhanced it, it was always there, even if he wouldn't have been able to describe it years ago.

He looked over at her. She was leaning back on her elbows on the blanket they had laid out on the beach. Her eyes were closed, and her face turned up to the sun. She looked calm, like she hadn't a care in the world. He knew better. She was raising a child alone, and she had a job that involved her taking on the problems of everyone else - and that was *his* fault, in a way. But through it all, she still managed to just *be*, here, now. He was really beginning to admire that about her.

When she laughed, she *laughed...* she never pretended anything. She was *real...* and she was still *his* Gina... and he had treated her terribly.

He was going to make it up to her, somehow. "Awareness without action is worthless," he said in a southern drawl. *Where did that come from?* "Pfft, Dr. Phil." Tommy said shaking his head, not realizing he said it aloud until Gina opened her eyes and turned her head to look at him.

"What?" she asked.

At first Tommy was going to evade the question, but he decided to be honest. "I was just thinking about something Dr. Phil said, about surrounding yourself with 'good and authentic' people. That's you, Gina. You're good. You're real."

Gina smiled softly. "Thank you, that's a very kind thing to say."

"I mean it. Life certainly hasn't been easy for you, yet you're just so... so... nice." Tommy was flailing for the right word as his voice trailed off.

"I'm just trying to do the best I can with what I have. My life hasn't been terrible; so many others have had and still have it worse. I've been loved, and I have loved. I have Emma. I have so much more than so many others. I'm not perfect, not by a long-shot. And, believe me, I have my moments. You're just lucky that right now isn't one of them," she joked at the end, not wanting to be too serious.

"Should I be afraid?" Tommy joked back.

"Just wait and see."

The more time he spent with Gina, the more time he wanted to spend with her. They didn't do anything overly fantastic, either.

They'd ride their bikes around town, and Gina would be a full-on tour guide, pointing out places of interest and telling him what it used to be like. It was nice hearing how she looked at things, past and present.

If her workday wasn't too hectic, they'd share an occasional walk along the beach or stop for lunch at Flo's for a dog or three. On one of their walks, he asked her if she still did any writing. He quickly quelled her shock by telling her that Alan had mentioned she used to be a writer. She was hesitant at first, saying that it was a lifetime ago, but the more she talked about it, the more she lit up. Tommy insisted she dig up her old stories and let him read them. She was tentative, but after much prodding from Tommy, she dug them up. And like all true writers, she prefaced it by saying, *these are just rough drafts and don't read them for grammar because they're not edited*, and, *I was only a teenager when I wrote these, so I'm sure they're horrible.*

Tommy stayed up until four in the morning that night reading every last amazing word. He was blown away at how talented a storyteller Gina was. He was also extremely pissed at himself. These were the same fucking stories Gina had given him to read back in high school; the same stories he never bothered to read. He would lie to her and tell her he'd read them and they were pretty good. Of course, she knew he hadn't, but she never pushed the issue.

What a fucking idiot I was. Since his 'awakening,' Tommy began to think that quite a bit. Tommy did his best to make up for it by urging Gina to start writing again.

As good of a time Tommy was having with Gina, he felt an

immense amount of stress and guilt. He hated that he was lying to her, not to mention, the stress of trying to keep track of his fake back stories. He'd spend hours before each date memorizing these details. *I'm Vince Neily from Sayreville, NJ. Capricorn. Attended college in Boston. I have one younger brother and two older sisters. My favorite color is blue...* and countless other fake details he'd made up. Tommy spent more time studying and memorizing these fake facts more than he ever did for a test back in school.

Not only was Tommy spending a lot of time with Gina, he had Alan line up numerous playdates with Brett and Ricky. While Alan was still certain that Tommy hanging out with Gina and the guys was a horrible idea, he didn't try too hard to discourage it. Actually, after only a couple of half-hearted attempts to interfere, he stopped completely. The truth was, he was having too much *fun*. He was living the best of both worlds. He had his brother back, *and* he got to hang out with him. That never would have happened twenty-five years ago, at least not without public humiliation and/or severe bruising.

At one point, Tommy considered trying to get Ricky and Brett to jam with him, but realized he'd probably have a tougher time pretending he wasn't Tommy. When moments like that happened, when he almost forgot who he was supposed to be, he'd turn the subject around to them and their lives. By doing that he was able to learn so much more about them, and he began to appreciate not just who they were now, but who they were back then. He kind of owed them, too. They were good guys. Even Alan, who always had to do everything *right*, was a good guy, and actually fun to be around.

It was also nice having Tommy with him when they visited their mother. There were brief moments when things almost seemed normal. Tommy would make a joke at Alan's expense, though not as crudely as years earlier, and he'd get reprimanded by their mother. Sometimes, he thought she was able to sense it, too. Most of the time she seemed happy that Alan brought a 'little friend', even if he was the cable guy.

Throughout this time, Tommy was also becoming closer with his nephew. Richie introduced him to one new video game after another, all of which blew Tommy's mind. He also introduced him to Netflix. This came in useful during the days when everyone was either at school or at work. There were two favorite shows he watched over and over (for different reasons). The first was Beavis and Butthead. He never laughed harder. They were so relatable. He swore they were based on Ricky and Pud back in high school. The second was Baywatch.

More and more, Tommy was getting quite used to his whole Vince persona – maybe too used to it. With a little help from Alan, he was also getting good at making up stories about his African experience. Alan introduced him to a wondrous website called *Google*. Any funny story could have happened in Africa, if you know what the clothing is called and what the weather is like. Google even told you how to pronounce stuff. Alan would leave his laptop (open to the Google page) on the kitchen table for Tommy. If Tommy had a question about anything, he googled it – and he'd get about 587,000,000 answers in 0.60 seconds. It took him longer than that to type in his questions.

Alan also gave Tommy a quick lesson on being more PC. He used a whiteboard to write down some common PC terms. This left Tommy's head spinning. *Not handicapped – disabled? Not retarded – mentally challenged? What? I can't fucking say Merry Christmas anymore?*

***

One day, while rummaging through his old room, Tommy came across a pair of his drum sticks. It was strange. In his head he knew it had been twenty-five years since he held sticks, but as he clutched them in his hands, it felt like yesterday. He wondered if he could still play. He started to rush towards the garage, where he kept his kit, but then it hit him; the last time he saw his drums were in Otto's garage. He'd bet his left nut that Otto probably hocked them the next day after the accident.

As he stood there holding the drum sticks, pieces of that night came flooding back; drinking beers, smoking pot, jamming with the guys, Pud's new song, not standing up for his real friends with Otto, and drinking more beers. Tommy stopped short of trying to recall the rest of that night. He was too confused, too upset. The more he thought about that night, the more his confusion turned to anger.

The next thing he knew, he was downstairs with an assortment of pots and pans lined up on the kitchen table. He channeled his inner Tommy Lee and began banging away to the Crue's "Looks That Kill."

With sweat pouring off of him, he finished the song then slammed the sticks to the floor. He'd forgotten just how cathartic drumming could be. Mentally and physically exhausted, he headed into the bathroom for a shower. He was tired, but overall he was happy that he hadn't forgotten how to play. *I still got it*, he thought. He closed his eyes and smiled as he pictured the long haired, skinny eighteen- year-old who was the king of the drums. His smile faded when he opened his eyes and looked into the mirror. He knew, even if he had his hair back, he still would have looked ridiculous. And fat. And *old*.

When he finished his shower, he decided to do something that he'd been putting off from day one. No, not going to cemetery to visit his Dad, he still wasn't ready for that one yet. Instead, he decided to return to the scene of his demise – thrill hill. He could have asked Alan to take him, but he knew he needed to do this on his own. Tommy jumped on Big Blue and headed for thrill hill.

He pedaled past the small cemetery which was directly before the hill. Again, the irony wasn't lost on him. His entire body tensed up. He had never ridden over thrill hill on a bike before, but as he approached the crest, his heart surged with an eerie familiarity. He was no longer on Big Blue, he was in his rusted out GTO with his foot weighing down on the gas pedal.

Piece by tragic piece, it was all coming back to him. All the stupid, angry, drunken thoughts he had twenty-five years ago began to dance around his head; dancing to Bon Jovi's "You Give Love a Bad Name." Even the garbled sound of the cassette being eaten was as clear as a bell to Tommy. He remembered everything – hitting the hill, landing, trying to regain control, a large oak tree, then…nothing. That was his last memory of that night.

When night turned back to day, and his GTO turned back to Big Blue, he found himself face to face with the giant oak. Twenty-five years had passed but the chunk he had taken out of the tree was still visible. It took him a few seconds to realize his hands were shaking uncontrollably, and even longer to notice that there were tears falling from his eyes. His trembling hands did their best to wipe away the tears.

What finally snapped Tommy out of his trance was a voice, "Nice ride, dude." From behind the tree, two sixteen-year-old boys poked their heads out. It took a moment to realize they were referring to Big Blue. The boy was clutching a bottle of beer while the other one finished up rolling a joint. He motioned as if to offer it to Tommy. Tommy shook his head no.

"Shouldn't you two be in school?" Tommy asked then immediately felt like his father.

"What are you, a bike cop?" scoffed the first kid.

Before Tommy could answer, the second kid chimed in, "Just like York PD to have bikes from the 70's.

Both kids laughed. It was now Tommy's turn to retort. He opened his mouth, but nothing came out. He had nothing to come back with. *What the fuck*, he thought, *I used to live for these moments*. He almost blurted out, *If I was twenty-five years younger, I'd wipe the floor with you two dick wads,* but realized that just sounded stupid, and old.

Instead, he chose to leave well alone and head back home.

"Good luck getting any air off of kill hill on that thing," joked one of the boys.

"You mean thrill hill," Tommy corrected.

"Uh, no. This is called kill hill, dude. Named after the kid who bit it here." Tommy's stomach lurched.

"I heard he hit it doing 80," added the other kid.

91, Tommy corrected to himself then proceeded to pedal home.

***

When Tommy returned home, he entered the kitchen to see Richie's face planted in a text book. It was as if he was walking in on Alan twenty-five years earlier. The one striking difference was all the technological accessories Richie had surrounding him. He seemed to be doing his homework on a laptop, while listening to his iPod, while watching TV on his iPad. Oh, and of course while he texted on his iPhone. Tommy made his way over to the bubbler,and as he pounded down cup after tiny cup, he continued to curiously stare at all of Richie's *stuff.*

"Still getting used to how much things have changed, huh, Vince?" Richie asked. Tommy nodded. "I still can't believe you were out of the real world for that long. I hope National Geographic paid you well." Tommy smiled and shook his head no. "Well, as my Grampa Ernie used to say, 'You can't put a price on life experience."

Sadly, Tommy smiled. He heard his dad say that phrase dozens of times, and probably had made fun of him a dozen times as well.

"Did you know my Grampa Ernie?" Richie asked.

Tommy thought for a second before responding, "Not as well as I would have like to, but yea, I knew him."

"Grampa always simplified every situation with a cheesy"...

"Cliché," Tommy and Richie simultaneously said.

Richie did his best Grampa Ernie voice, "Just remember, Richie, when the going gets tough, the tough get going."

Tommy added, "If you build a better mousetrap..." Richie joined in, "The world will beat a path to your door." They both laughed as Tommy took a seat next to Richie. "I still haven't figured that one out yet."

"Yea, me neither," Richie said. "The sad thing is, when I was younger, all of his little sayings and clichés used to drive me nuts, but now... I kinda miss them." Right at that moment, Tommy felt the exact same way. Richie continued, "It's funny, I sometimes catch Dad sounding just like Grampa."

Tommy noticed the same thing the past week. "Speaking of which," Tommy said, "where is Alan?"

"I think he's at a SADD fundraiser or something."

"What's so sad about it," Tommy asked.

Richie chuckled, "Not sad, SADD. Students against Drunk Driving. I guess he's been involved with them ever since my Uncle Tommy's accident."

Tommy's heart sank, and a lump formed in his throat. When he felt his eyes were about to give birth to a tear or two, he quickly stood and walked around the room. The fact that Alan had been championing this cause all these years made Tommy sick to his stomach. It was becoming painfully obvious that not only didn't he deserve friends like Ricky and Brett, but he sure as hell didn't deserve a brother like Alan.

From across the room, Tommy asked Richie, "Alan is a pretty good Dad, huh?"

Richie paused a moment then nodded. "Yea, he is." Tommy smiled at his answer as he returned to his seat next to Richie.

"Hey, Vince, let me ask you a question. When you and my dad were in college, did he ever do anything wild or crazy?"

"Why do you ask?"

"As long as I've known him, he's always been a *by the book* type of person. Not that that's bad, I was just curious if he was different when he was younger."

Tommy smiled. "Alan has pretty much always been a *by the book* kinda guy. Wild and crazy were never your dad's style."

"That's what I figured," Richie said. "I guess it's true what everyone says, Uncle Tommy got all the wild and crazy genes."

"Wild and crazy ain't all it's cracked up to be," Tommy said.

"Do you know what I find kind of strange, Vince? Until a couple of weeks ago, I never heard my dad talk about you…not once."

Tommy scrambled, "Um, well, I guess being gone for so long, I became forgettable."

"I didn't mean it that way," Richie said. "Besides, now that you're here, it's obvious how close you two are."

"Why do you say that?" Tommy asked.

"Because he's letting you stay in his brother's old room. Nobody's allowed to even open Uncle Tommy's door, never mind sleep in his bed. He's a different guy when you're around too."

"How so?"

"He's a little more laid back, less uptight."

Tommy laughed. "Yea, Alan was always the king of uptight."

"I've even noticed him crack a few jokes that were actually funny," both of them smiled in agreement. "Well anyway, I'm glad you're here, Vince."

"Yea, so am I," Tommy thoughtfully said. "And I'm glad I got the chance to get to know you too."

On Richie's screen saver, Tommy noticed a cute picture of Richie and Emma. It reminded him of a picture of Gina and him that she had in her locker. "You two are pretty close, huh?" Tommy asked. Richie nodded as Tommy continued, "Don't ever take her for granted, okay?"

Richie looked at him like he had three heads. "Why would I do that? She's the best thing that's ever happened to me."

Right then and there, he couldn't have been more proud of his nephew, and of his brother for raising such a great kid. Tommy pushed the chair back, stood up, and started to head out. He stopped at the doorway and turned back to Richie and said, "Hey, you know that PMS thingy your dad has in his car?"

Again, Richie looked at him as if he had three heads. "PMS thingy?"

"You know, the satellite direction thingy?" Tommy said.

A wide smile crept across Richie's face. "You mean GPS?" he said.

"Yea, whatever," Tommy shrugged. "He said they have different voices you can choose?"

"They have tons and tons of different voices you can download. Why?" Richie asked.

"We should get a funny one and surprise him with it."

"I don't know," hesitated Richie, "Dad doesn't like change."

"That's exactly why we need to do it!"

Richie pondered a second then started typing on his laptop. Tommy watched Richie's eyes scroll down the page. Finally, Richie's fingers stopped typing and a sly smirk appeared on his face.

"What? Did you find a good one, Richie?" asked Tommy.

"I didn't realize this, but they actually have X rated ones."

Tommy's eyes widened. "What do you mean by X rated?" Tommy asked.

Richie was practically blushing as he handed his headphones to Tommy. "This one is called *Seductive Sarah.*" Within seconds of putting them on, Tommy's face lit up like a Christmas tree.

TRACK 20

On most days, when the final bell rings, the students can't leave school fast enough. They are one body united in one mission - mass exodus. The charge out of the building was usually led by whichever student reached the doors first. Today, they had a new leader - Principal Stevens. He was on a mission of his own – to head over to Lil's Café and ask Mia out! Tommy was right, he needed to just grow a pair and do it. Alan spent the entire day in his office giving himself one motivational speech after another. He went through his dad's entire repertoire of motivational clichés (You never know until you try…What's the worst that can happen...etc).

Alan continued repeating these to himself as he circled around Lil's three or seven times. Finally, after much hesitation, he parked and headed towards the front door. With each step, his heart raced faster and louder (embarrassingly, not as loud as the gastric sounds from within).

He paused at the door, pulled himself together, and entered. Alan was immediately greeted by... Margaret. Sixty-five-year-old Margaret. He had nothing against Margaret. She was a nice, sweet lady, but he had counted on Mia being there to greet him. He even had several clever (lame) ice breakers rehearsed.

"Alan Stevens!" Margaret loudly announced. "Am I getting older or are you just getting younger... and more handsome?" she said.

Obviously, Margaret had been rehearsing her ice breakers as well. Alan politely smiled and made his way over to a stool at the counter and sat.

"The usual?" she asked (loudly).

"Yes, please," he answered as he scanned the small café for any signs of Mia.

"Cappuccino, right?" she asked. "No, wait - Café Americano?"

Before Alan could correct the poor woman, a familiar voice echoed from the back room, "Mocha Latte." Alan's heart literally skipped a beat as he turned to see Mia exit the kitchen area. "Didn't I see you once already today?" she said. Alan was relieved to see her, but it also got his stomach in knots, for he knew it was *game on*. "How was school today?' she asked.

Words seemed to escape Alan's lips. Not certain words, but any words. He simply smiled and nodded okay. Before he could scold himself for being an idiot, he watched Mia put on a light jacket and grab her purse.

This wasn't part of the master plan, he thought. "Are you leaving?" he blurted out.

"Yea, I have to drive down to Boston to pick my sister up at the airport." Mia grabbed her keys, waved to Margaret then rushed towards the door. "I'll see you tomorrow, Alan." The word *Alan* still hung in the air as the door closed behind her.

A whole day of motivational speeches and pep talks to himself was all for naught. He was left high and dry - just himself, Margaret, and his Mocha latte. "Here's your decaf coffee, sweetie," Margaret said loudly. Scratch that – just himself, Margaret, and his decaf coffee.

"If it wasn't for bad luck, I wouldn't have any luck at all," Alan mumbled as he politely accepted his decaf coffee. That wasn't one of his dad's sayings, but it probably should have been.

Just when he decided to resign himself in drowning his disappointment in a cup of decaf Joe – it happened. A minor miracle. A sign from God. Well, maybe it was just dumb luck, but he'd gladly take it. Mia reentered the café frustrated and upset.

"Everything okay?" Margaret asked (loudly).

"My car is dead."

Needless to say, Alan jumped at the chance to help her. Alan dug into his self-made emergency kit in search of jumper cables. Considering his kit was the size of his trunk, it took him a few minutes to find them. As you might guess, Alan was well-prepared for anything from a blizzard to a tornado and even for a possible zombie apocalypse. What he wasn't prepared for was the battery being jumped and still not starting. This was a job for AAA. Unfortunately for Mia, they couldn't get there for at least 45 minutes.

When Alan heard this, he knew what he had to do.

"That's very sweet of you," smiled Mia, "but you don't have to give me a ride into Boston, Alan. I'll just call my sister and tell her I'll be late. I'm sure you have more important things to do tonig —"

"No, not at all." Alan cringed at his quick, pathetic-sounding response. "I mean, I can probably rearrange some things for you."

Mia gave him the warmest, most appreciative smile. "Really?" she said.

"Really," Alan said as he led her to his car. Her smile doubled, and she blushed when Alan chivalrously opened her door for her.

"Aww, what a gentleman. Thanks, Alan."

Alan shut her door then floated his way around to his side. He actually felt as though he was on a cloud. This was the closest thing to a date he had in years, and he was going to make sure to take advantage of every minute of it. And when the moment was right, he'd ask her out on a real date. *This will be perfect*, Alan thought as he shut his door and buckled up.

He threw a sweet smile her way then proceeded to start his car. Within a second of turning the key, his sweet smile and positive thoughts were quickly drowned out by the blaring (yet soothing) sounds of Richard Marx singing "Hold on to the Nights." Alan's heart stopped, his smile disappeared, and a gaseous bubble rumbled as he hastily turned the volume down.

Before he could offer up an apology to Mia, she giggled and continued to smile her adorable smile. What came out of her mouth next completely changed Alan's feelings about her. He went from wanted to go on a date with her to wanting to marry her.

"Why'd you turn it down?" she said. "I love Richard Marx! (Wait for it...) I've always thought he was one of the most underrated singer songwriters ever." BOOM!

The next thirty minutes were not only spent listening to the dulcet tones of Richard Marx, but were spent discovering all the other favorite bands they had in common. REO Speedwagon, Chicago, Styx, Journey, Queen, and The Doobie Brothers were each of their top six favorites, but in different order. They had lively debates about whether or not Chicago was better pre-Peter Cetera and if Journey made the right decision to go with a Steve Perry sound-a-like after he left the band.

On more than one occasion, Mia mentioned how much she liked his new Prius. She also lamented about the most certain death of her ten-year-old Chevy Malibu. She was amazed at all the cool features of Alan's Prius; Bluetooth, XM radio, voice controls. She was also impressed with the built-in GPS.

"I really need one of these," she said. I hate using my phone for directions. I like that there's a big screen in front of you so you don't have to constantly look down at your phone. Are they easy to use?" she asked.

"Oh yeah," Alan nodded. "Go ahead," he urged. He then talked her through punching in Logan Airport as their destination. As she punched in the location, Alan thought, *Damn, even her fingers are adorable.*

"Is that it?" she asked.

"Yup, now just hit *Start navigation* and sit back and enjoy."

What happened next nearly caused Alan to shit in his pants, literally. The voice which emitted from the GPS wasn't the normal woman, instead, they were greeted by Seductive Sarah. "Hey sexy, in 250 feet you're going to BANG a right...a HARD, HARD right,"

Alan's face immediately turned bright red. He was pretty sure he would have a panic attack. His knuckles whitened as his 10 & 2 grip tightened. Not wanting to see Mia's expression, Alan's eyes focused straight ahead. Sarah's instructions continued, "It's coming...it's coming...a hard right! Harder...HARDER, baby!"

As Alan turned (hard) around the corner, Seductive Sarah continued her moaning, "YES...YES...YES!!!" Finally, after the orgasmic turn was over, Alan casually shut the GPS off.

Alan knew Tommy was the mastermind behind this, and he assumed his own son was Tommy's accomplice. He would deal with those two clowns later, right now he had to find the words to explain this to Mia.

She didn't give him a chance as she said, "Well, I'm sold! A new car it is." The red hues of his face lightened a few shades as he looked over to see a wide-grinning Mia. "I don't know about you," she continued, "but I could use a cigarette now." At that point, Alan almost told her that he didn't smoke (then he caught on).

***

Back in York, Emma soaked in the warm, late afternoon sun as she did her daily run along the beach. Her running attire consisted of black yoga pants, a grey tank with a black sports bra underneath. Her hair was scrunchied up in a ponytail with ear buds blasting her favorite tunes. From anyone from Paramore to the Foo Fighters and with plenty of 80's alternative bands thrown in. Emma was definitely her mother's daughter.

She jogged up Long Sands beach, and as she approached the halfway point, she decided to head up to the Oceanside Store for a bottled water. She stopped her jog at the bathhouse and began to walk up the ramp towards the crosswalk. As she walked up the sand covered ramp, she was greeted by a haze of cigarette smoke and the sounds of obnoxious laughter. Her head lowered, and she let out a sigh in preparation for the inevitable: A creepy confrontation with Otto Jr. and his equally creepy crew.

"Well lookie here, guys, it's Emma Cassidy. Sweaty Emma Cassidy." Otto Jr. gave her body a lecherous look-over then continued, "Did you know that sweat is an aphrodisiac, babe?"

Emma's skin crawled as she uncomfortably crossed her arms in hope of deflected their perverted breast stare. "You're a disgusting pig, Otto," she said. "All of you are." Emma attempted to get to the crosswalk, but was rudely blocked by Otto Jr's greasy, BO ridden body.

"Move it, Otto!" she ordered.

"Nice manners, babe! How about a pretty please?" Otto Jr. gave his minions a smirk then looked back to Emma. "Maybe a pretty please on your knees?"

"Fucking loser!" she snapped as she pushed her way by Otto Jr.

"When are you gonna drop that geek of a boyfriend and get with a real man?" Otto Jr. said.

Emma stopped in the crosswalk and turned back around. "Richie is ten times the man you'll ever be."

"I bet his little pencil dick doesn't even get her off," yelled Kip.

"Aww, is that true, Emma?" Otto Jr. asked. "Even more of a reason to get with me. Where his ends, mine bends. They don't call me Otto-matic-orgasm for nothing."

Emma shot back, "Who calls you that? Your hand?" Emma then turned her attention to Kenny, Kip, and Dale, who were snickering behind Otto Jr's back. "Or their hands?" Their snickering stopped immediately. Before they could think of a clever comeback, Emma was already across the street with her middle finger raised over her shoulder at the four knuckleheads. Yup, she was certainly Gina's daughter.

After she entered the store, Otto Jr. turned to his friends, Dale in particular, "Yo, isn't your little brother a computer wiz? Like Photoshop type shit?"

"Yeah, why?" asked Dale.

"Cuz I have an idea, that's why," Otto Jr. snarled. "They don't call me Otto-matic genius for nothing!"

Nobody touched that one.

***

At the same time across town, Tommy and Gina entered Blendz and Bendz. Ricky's eyes lit up when he saw Gina. He approached her with arms outstretched. He gave her a big hug then did the same to Tommy. Tommy still hadn't gotten used to this whole Ricky being a hugger thing, but he did like hanging around him, and he definitely liked him some of that chocolate monkey nut smoothies.

Gina looked around at the colorful interior, "This place looks great, Ricky," she said. "I've been meaning to come in. My daughter raves about this place."

"Emma, right?" Ricky asked.

"Yea. She can't get enough of your smoothies, and she also says you're a great yoga instructor."

Ricky put his hands together and gave Gina a modest, appreciative bow. "You should totally come to one of my classes, Gina." Ricky looked over at Tommy. "Both of you," he said.

"Oh, I don't know," Gina hesitated, "my body might be a little too old for that."

Ricky smiled and placed his hand on her shoulder and said, "Yoga isn't about the age of the body, it's about the age of the mind… and our minds are ageless. Besides, Gina, your body still looks amazing."

Coming out of anyone else's mouth, that would be creepy, but somehow, when Ricky said it, it was sweetly innocent, not to mention, Tommy couldn't agree more. Gina truly was amazing looking still. Without even thinking, Tommy blurted out, "We'd love to do one of your classes, Ricky."

"That's the spirit, Vince," smiled Ricky. "My next class is at seven tonight. I expect to see you there. Now, let's get you two some smoothies."

Tommy had no idea what he had just gotten himself into, but by the happy look on Gina's face, he knew it would be worth it.

***

Unfortunately for Tommy, his shopping spree with Alan didn't include any yoga-type clothing. Then again, Tommy hadn't the foggiest idea what the hell yoga-type clothing was. He assumed it must be similar to his Zumba attire... hopefully without the Zumba experience. Tommy dug up an old Celtics tank from his drawer and matched it with an old pair of sweatpants. Luckily, the jersey was always a bit on the larger size, so it fit him like a glove now. The sweatpants were a different story. Tommy figured they were just too tight-fitting for yoga, so he was reluctantly forced to borrow a (freshly ironed) pair from Alan's drawer.

Gina's attire, on the other hand, was in a word - *Wow*. Tommy took one look at her and thanked his lucky stars that he didn't go with the tight-fitting (erection revealing) sweats. She wore black yoga pants, a white tank, and her hair was pulled up with the sexiest strand of hair dangling on her forehead.

Gina handed Tommy a mat as they entered the studio. When Ricky spotted them, he smiled and gave them another one of his praying-hands-bow. There was about a dozen people in the class, ranging in age from nineteen to fifty-seven. Besides Ricky and one other man, Tommy was the only guy there. That was the least of his self-conscious worries, though. Compared to everyone else, he looked like an idiot. He was shocked that no one else wore a sweatband on their heads (or wristbands).

Everyone was staring at him. *What, doesn't anyone like Larry Bird anymore?* The one accessory he did feel hip in, were his brand-spanking new Nikes, but that pride quickly faded when he looked around the room. *Why the hell was everyone barefoot?* Strange looks or not, Tommy loved his new kicks. The sneakers were staying on!

Gina noticed his nervous, uncomfortable look, so she chose a spot in the back row by themselves. Tommy welcomed her choice. While Gina spread out her mat, Tommy began to loosen up. This basically consisted of him running in place for ten seconds, followed by seven jumping jacks, and was topped off with a crack of his back and neck. He was ready for this thing called yoga. It was obvious that he was a fish out of water and that the only reason he came was because of Gina. "I know this isn't really your thing," she whispered, "but I appreciate you coming with me."

Before Tommy could respond, Ricky's voice filled the room. The class had started. He began with some basic breathing. Inhale, exhale. Inhale, exhale. This was followed by some simple side stretches. Tommy's nerves lessened, and his confidence grew. *Pfft, I got this whole yoga thing!* In between side stretches, he shot Gina a wink and thumbs up.

Next, Ricky had them do deep knee bends. This is where it went downhill for Tommy. On his second, third and fifth bend, a squeaky fart escaped from his butt cheeks. On his second, third, and fifth bend, everyone's eyes turned to look at him.

Tommy's first thought was: *Maybe I shouldn't have eaten those frozen burritos before I came.* Ever the quick thinker, Tommy looked down at his Nikes and said, "Ya gotta love new sneakers. They should probably be called squeakers, huh?" With the exception of the smirking Gina and the ever-patient Ricky, no one else was amused.

The snooty soccer Mom directly in front of Tommy was definitely not amused as she gave Tommy a condescending glare and murmured, "Pfft, who wears sneakers to yoga anyway? This isn't Zumba, you know?" That last comment alone made Tommy want to put his size 10 ½ sneaker right up her ass. Of course, he'd have to remove the stick from it first.

As Ricky continued his instructions, Tommy finally fell to the peer pressure and took off his sneakers. He thanked God that he had showered earlier and that his feet actually smelled not-so-bad. Now barefoot and on his mat, Tommy attempted to follow along with Ricky's movements. He was continually amazed at just how limber Ricky was. At one point, Tommy's mind debated whether Ricky could suck his own dick. Just then, Tommy's internal debate was interrupted by an ever squeakier fart from his ass. Again, all eyes fell upon him. "That was the mat!" he defensively explained.

Without turning around, the snooty lady announced, "Is that rancid smell the mat too?" Tommy's face was red with embarrassment. Gina's face was red as well – red from trying to hold back her laughter.

Tommy made it three minutes before ripping another one. This time the snooty lady turned and shot Tommy the most disgustedly pissed-off look ever. Tommy not-so-subtly pointed the blame towards Gina. Seeing this, Gina playfully gave him a smack. The lady was not impressed - with either of them.

By the time the class approached minute nine, Tommy was not only out of excuses, but was out of any and all control of his sphincter. Ricky's next simple instruction was what finally did Tommy (and the class) in. "And now, for the Downward Dog," said Ricky.

In three... two... one... Tommy ripped the loudest and longest fart ever recorded (at least in a yoga studio). And for the final time, everyone's eyes went directly to the culprit. "That time it was me," Tommy confessed. He then grabbed his mat and sneakers and nonchalantly exited the class.

With tears streaming down her cheeks, Gina finally let out the laugh she had been holding in. As she gathered her things to follow Tommy, she was met with a disapproving stare-down from the snooty lady. "Oh relax, lady," laughed Gina. "Don't you have kids to pick up at soccer practice or some wine to buy or a book club to go to?" Gina mouthed the words *sorry* to a smirking Ricky, then she left.

TRACK 21

The next morning, Richie and Emma entered the school together. As they walked down the hallway, they couldn't help notice everyone pointing and snickering. Self-consciously, they continued towards their lockers. As they neared, Emma stopped dead in her tracks. Taped to her locker was what looked like the school newspaper. Both their mouths fell open when they read the headline – "EMMA CASSI-DICK! The truth revealed – Emma Cassidy is a HERMAPHRODITE!"

Underneath the headline was a giant picture of Emma. The upper half was actually Emma, but the bottom half, not so much. It was graphic, disgusting, and obviously photoshopped, but it served its purpose; it caused Emma to shriek in embarrassment. It didn't matter that most of the students knew it wasn't true, Emma felt violated and sick to her stomach. There were a few (mostly freshmen) who wondered if it was actually true; was Emma Cassidy actually a chick with a dick? There was also a few (also freshmen) who needed to google hermaphrodite.

Richie quickly took action by ripping it down off the locker. He took his girlfriend's hand and angrily marched up the hall. He stormed past the secretary and barged into his dad's office, slamming the newspaper on his desk.

"What are you going to do about this?" Richie said.

Before Alan could ask what was going on, he took one look at the front page and cringed. His face turned fifty shades of red. He was literally speechless. Uncomfortably, he took a quick glance at some of the other pages, which had more ugly headlines, including one about Ricky's son, Peter.

Finally, Alan put the paper down and stammered, "Where did you get this?"

"It was on Emma's locker, and by the looks of it, there's plenty more circulating around the school."

What the heck, Alan thought. He'd only been out of the hallways for twenty minutes.

"I'll ask you again, Dad, what are you gonna do about this? It's obvious that Otto is behind this."

Alan knew his son was right. This had Otto Jr. written all over it. Hell, Otto Sr. probably had a hand in this too. There was nothing Alan would have loved more than to punish them to the full extent. Unfortunately, he was the principal and had to handle this situation not only prudently, but responsibly. With that in mind, Alan knew his next statement wouldn't go over so well with his son, "Do you have proof that he did this?"

"Proof? They're assholes! What other proof do you need?"

Richard! Watch your language, Alan was tempted to scold, but he didn't. Again, he knew Richie spoke the truth. This was definitely Otto Jr's handy work. Although, considering the Photoshop skills that were used, and the fact that hermaphrodite was spelled correctly, this was more than likely the work of someone under his direct orders. Either way, he couldn't punish anyone without solid proof.

"I promise this matter will get my full attention. This sort of slander and hijinks will not be tolerated in my school!" Alan's stern tone did nothing to satisfy Richie or Emma. The use of the word hijinks didn't help matters either.

Before Alan could respond to their disappointment, Richie grabbed Emma's hand and marched out of his office. They were immediately greeted by Otto Jr's smiling mug. Richie started to make his way over to where Otto was standing, but Emma tightened her grip on his hand. "It's not worth it, Richie. Let your dad handle it," Emma urged. Richie relented, but heeded his girlfriend's advice and walked away with her in the other direction.

They hadn't taken two steps, when Otto Jr's voice boomed out, "Hey Emma, how's it hanging?"

Richie stopped dead. Usually, he was quiet, reserved, and most definitely non-violent, but when he heard Otto's wise-ass comment, he lost it. With his face flushed red, he released Emma's hand, turned, and sprinted at Otto Jr, clocking him dead in the face. It would be the only punch Richie would land. Otto Jr. stood up and quickly wrestled him to the ground. Before he could do any damage to Richie, Alan sprinted out of his office and broke it up.

With his nose bleeding, Otto Jr. glanced around at the secretaries. "He threw the first punch!" yelled Otto Jr. "I have witnesses."

By the look on the secretaries' faces, Alan could tell that Richie was guilty, and he had no choice but to order him back into his office. For Alan, this was the classic case of *this will hurt me more than you* (another one of Alan's father's favorite clichés). But in this case, it was true, the look of betrayal on Richie's face cut Alan to the core.

TRACK 22

The morning of Gina's birthday couldn't have been a more beautiful spring day. By 8 AM, it was already 70 degrees. As instructed, Gina picked Tommy up at 8:15 AM sharp. Tommy was dressed in a tan short-sleeved button down and army green cargo shorts. His face lit up when he saw her pull in.

"You look nice. New clothes?" she asked as Tommy climbed into her car.

"Yea. Alan took me shopping. I mean, he didn't pick out my clothes. He just drove me. I picked them out myself."

"You did a good job," she giggled.

"We went to a place called Kohls. It's no Bradlees, but it was cool."

Gina laughed. "Bradlees. Now there's a blast from the past."

"I hope you're ready for the best birthday date of your life," Tommy said.

"Of my life, huh?" She put the car in reverse and began backing out of the driveway. "Where to?"

"Phase one – coffee," he answered.

"Ahh, so this is a phase type of date, huh?" she said. Tommy didn't answer. In he simply gave her a mysterious shrug.

They made their way to a little bakery overlooking the Piscataqua River. It was directly next to the bridge which connects Maine and New Hampshire. While they drank coffee, Gina did her best to get any sort of clues about what Tommy had up his sleeve for her birthday date. Tommy held firm, despite Gina pulling out her puppy-dog look. When he started to waver from her eyes, he quickly stood and said, "Let's go. Phase two awaits."

He directed her to the backside of York and headed up Mountain Road. About ¾ up the road, he motioned her to pull into Chapman Stables. Immediately, her eyes and smile widened.

"Oh my God! Are we going horseback riding?"

It had been years since Gina was on a horse. It was much, much longer for Tommy. Besides a carousel, the only real horse (pony) he'd been on was when he was six at Benson's Animal Farm in New Hampshire.

While the trail guide went over some safety precautions, Gina couldn't control her excitement as she anxiously bounced around. Tommy didn't bounce. His attention was focused on the safety precaution speech. With a little help from the guide, Gina gracefully mounted her horse. With a lot of help from the guide, Tommy attempted to mount his horse. After three failed attempts, he finally got his leg over and was good to go. After the guide instructed Tommy to loosen up his white-knuckled grip on the reigns, they began their ride through the woods and up the mountain.

It took him awhile, but Tommy slowly gained confidence. So confident in fact, he even released one hand from the reigns to scratch his nose (2.1 secs). His confidence really grew when he started fantasizing that he was John Wayne leading the Calvary towards an Indian camp – um, Native American camp. Every few minutes Gina would turn around to snap pictures of Tommy and ask if he was okay. Of course he was okay! He'd just successfully raided three Redskin villages – um, Native American villages.

When they arrived at the top, the guide tied off their horses and helped them (mostly Tommy) dismount. He told them to take as much time as they needed to explore. Tommy had been up here dozens of times, but as he stood there looking around at the scattered picnic tables, one particular occasion came to mind - end of the year 8th grade picnic. He even spotted the giant boulder he and Gina snuck behind to make out. That was back when life was simpler. They were just a happy couple without a care in the world. It was back before their big breakup… back before Tommy stopped giving a shit about things.

The more he stared at the boulder, the more the memories came flooding back. He even remembered exactly what they were wearing that day. He had on his favorite pair of Levi's and a brand new, hip shirt from Chess King. Gina wore a plain black tank top over black bullethole jeans, which were adorned with safety pins (on one leg only – he was careful to keep his hands on the other side, not wanting to be stabbed by accident), and she had on those black lace-up creeper shoes, which he'd tease her about regularly.

All black. No … not all, he remembered; she had a roach clip in her hair that had a deep blue feather hanging from the end of a long chain, and a second one hanging from her belt loop. See? He *did* remember.

He remembered how nervous she was that they were going to get caught. He also remembered how many times (5) she successfully thwarted his under-her-shirt advances. She did allow two quick over-the-shirt gropes which Tommy chalked up as getting to second base.

By the time he snapped out of his trip down memory lane, Gina was across the field zooming in on a hawk perched in a tree. He made his way towards her and couldn't help but wonder if she also remembered the picnic... the boulder... the good times in general.

They made their way to the edge and looked down at the little town they had grown up in. Despite having the perfect date so far, there were many occasions where Tommy felt overwhelmed with guilt. Most were triggered by Gina addressing him as Vince. Over the past couple weeks, there was definitely a part of him that liked being Vince. There were times when being someone else had its advantages, and at times, it was even fun. He loved that she seemed to be falling for him again, but hated that he was lying to her. With each date, and with each beautiful moment together, he knew he was only digging himself a deeper and deeper hole, but he decided to do what he did best; ignore possible future consequences and just live in the moment.

They stood near the edge and held hands. Gina pointed out various spots in the town, talking about what it looked like when she was younger. Even though he knew most of the history, he listened intently.

Before they headed back, Tommy insisted on taking a picture of Gina on her horse. Despite her modest attempts at not having her picture taken, he snatched her camera and began focusing in on, as he put it, *his little cowgirl.* It took him a while to figure out which buttons did what, and an even longer time trying to get the perfect angle.

"Come on, Vince. Just get on your horse. I really don't need my picture taken."

He ignored her pleas. From high on her horse, Gina watched Tommy attempt to focus the camera for the perfect shot. In search of the best angle, he began taking a few steps backwards.

"Vince, stop!" yelled Gina. Tommy didn't listen. He thought she was just playing hard to get. Not to mention, he was too busy channeling his inner photographer. "Seriously, Vince, stop! You're gonna"... she didn't get a chance to finish her sentence, which would have been, "step off the edge."

And step off the edge is exactly what he did. He tumbled head over ass down the mountain side. Luckily, he didn't tumble far. The giant pricker bush broke his fall.

By the time they got back to the car, it was late afternoon. "Thanks again, Vince. That was so fun," she said as they climbed into her car. She watched Tommy continue to pull the little nettles from the ass of his pants. "Fun and entertaining," she added.

"Ha, ha, ha," he said in a playful tone. "Just drive. The next adventure awaits."

He directed her over the bridge into Portsmouth, NH. They drove along the waterfront, and when he told her to turn in by the giant salt piles, she knew exactly what they were doing. That particular area along the waterfront was designated for boat cruises out to the Isles of Shoals. Her face beamed. It had been awhile since she had been here; Mother's Day with Emma - five years ago.

"Aw, Vince, this is perfect. I love these cruises. Not being from here, I'm assuming you've never been?"

He shook his head no. In his eighteen years growing up around here, Tommy had never been, nor did he ever have a desire to. As Gina parked the car, Tommy's mind took him back to twenty-five years ago; to when Gina requested this cruise for her birthday. The exact conversation came flooding back to him as if it was yesterday.

"I was thinking we could go on one of those harbor cruises out by the Isles of Shoals. They even have one that'll take us out to Star Island and we can have a picnic. I've always wanted to go out there, and I heard it's very romantic. Or, we could go out to the Chapman Stables up on the mountain and go horseback riding...also very romantic I'm told."

Tommy cringed when he remembered his wise-ass reply, *"So my choices are seasick or sore ass?" What a fuckin' asshole*, he thought. All Gina wanted was a nice, romantic day doing things that she enjoyed. Instead, he presented her with concert tickets to a band she didn't even like. Whitesnake tickets? *What the fuck was I thinking?*

"Hello? Vince? You okay?" she snapped her fingers in front of his face causing him to return from his flashback.

"Um, yea, I'm fine," he said. "Let's do this!" Gina smiled, grabbed his arm, and they headed towards the ticket booth.

"Good Morning. How can I help you?" asked the sweet looking older woman from behind the counter.

"Good morning," Tommy said. "I have two tickets reserved."

"Your name?" she politely said.

He started to say Tommy, but quickly caught himself. "Vince Neily."

A wide smile appeared on her face. "Ah, yes. Mr. Neily. We've been expecting you."

Tommy pulled out a handful of crumpled money from his pocket. "How much?" he asked.

She continued to smile as she spoke, "They're already paid for."

"They are?" he questioned.

"Yup. And as a matter of fact, you've been upgraded to the VIP package." Before Tommy could open his mouth, she handed him the tickets and pointed to a ramp leading onto a boat named 'The Thomas Laighton'. "Have a great time you two."

Tommy hesitated, but took the tickets and headed towards the ramp with Gina. She gave him a nudge, "Aw, Alan must have done that, huh?"

Tommy politely nodded, but knew full well this had Dr. Zimarchi written all over it. *What the fuck*, he thought, *I never even told him about the cruise.* It was becoming clearer and clearer that Dr. Zimarchi was very well-informed ... and connected. Either way, Tommy was beginning to see what a benefit it was to him.

"What do you think VIP means?" Gina asked. Tommy shrugged.

Once on board, she grabbed his arm and excitedly dragged him around every inch of the boat. They entered the empty interior cabin where a bartender attentively stood behind the bar. She then dragged him through each of the three exterior decks - also empty. By the time they hit the top deck, it was obvious that VIP meant they were the *only* passengers. They had the boat to themselves.

As the boat's horn sounded, and it pulled out of the dock, Gina made her way around to every available area of the boat, snapping pictures the whole time.

Tommy was blown away. This was the first time had had ever seen a real whale in person. Together, they were like two kids in a candy store. When they finally took a break from sightseeing, they decided to head inside for some refreshments. Not only did the bartender serve them free of charge, but he informed them the captain would like to see them. Initially, the words *Oh shit, what did I do wrong* ran through Tommy's mind.

They reported immediately, and to Tommy's surprise, he hadn't done anything wrong. In fact, the captain just wanted to personally welcome them aboard. He even let Gina steer the boat. Tommy took her camera and took pictures of her behind the wheel. She was in heaven.

After a few minutes, Gina looked at Tommy and said, "Your turn to drive, Vince." He casually shook off her request. "Oh come on, Vince, you know you want to."

Tommy absolutely wanted to! He played it cool, but inside, he was bursting at the seams to get his hands on the captain's wheel. Gina released the wheel and motioned for him to take over. He did. With both hands firmly on the wheel, it was now his turn to be in heaven. His excitement level went up a notch when the captain let him wear his hat. Tommy beamed. He was now an official sea captain in the same vein as some of his nautical heroes – Captain Stubing from the *Loveboat,* and of course, the Skipper of the S.S. Minnow fame. It wasn't long before he was whistling the theme songs from each show.

The captain and Gina were highly amused. Gina switched her camera to video and began capturing Tommy's antics. The more they laughed, the more animated Tommy became. He steered with both hands, with one hand, and the famous *Look Ma, no hands.* He even turned around and steered with his butt.

Of course, in true Tommy fashion, he took things too far when he pretended to be a contestant on the *Wheel of Fortune.* After exclaiming, "Big money, big money," Tommy gave the wheel a big spin.

Abruptly, the boat veered hard right, knocking all three off balance. What actually sent them to the floor was the loud thud as the boat slammed into something large. When they all regained their sea-legs and stood back up, Tommy slowly stepped away from the wheel. The captain glared at him then promptly snatched his hat back. Tommy and Gina quickly scuttled back out onto the deck and watched the island approach.

Star Island, named for its star shape, was the second largest island of the Isles of Shoals that border Maine and New Hampshire. And, like pretty much any spot in New England, it has a cool history whichdates back to 1914 and Captain John Smith. A popular spot for conferences and retreats, it is also known to be a great place for spectacularly romantic sunsets and beach walks. (That last part was all Tommy had been interested in when he Googled it.)

As they exited the boat onto the dock, the captain handed Tommy a large picnic basket. Tommy looked up at him in question, and the captain said with a wink, "Now, you don't want to be forgetting this!"

Gina squealed with delight, "A picnic! Vince, you thought of everything! What'd you bring?"

Good question, Tommy thought, mentally thanking Dr. Zimarchi. "You'll see, later!" he answered. *And so will I!*

They spent a good part of the afternoon walking around the island. Gina was impressed by the majesty of the Oceanic Hotel and the view from its front porch. Tommy even thought the Gosport Chapel was pretty cool, with all its stone. Gina laughed when Tommy questioned when she was going to run out of 'film' in her camera.

They walked along the small beach hand in hand. Tommy was surprised how much he was enjoying himself, even when they weren't talking. It was always like that with Gina, just being near her was fun. There were a few moments when he wished he'd done this with her sooner, like when she knew she was with Tommy instead of Vince, but he was still grateful that he had this time with her at all.

They found a nice spot on the small beach and tossed the blanket down on the sand. While Tommy relaxed, Gina headed off to take some more pictures. He set the picnic basket aside and laid down on the blanket. Less than a minute later, his eyes were closed and he was sound asleep.

Off to his right, under a small pile of seaweed, emerged two crabs. It was as if Tommy was the Pied Piper and his snoring was the flute. The crabs exited the seaweed and made a B-line directly towards Tommy.

Upon returning towards the blanket, Gina's eyes widened when she saw the two crabs climbing onto him. They seemed to be dancing around on his chest. *How could he not wake up*, she thought. *Hey Vince,* she warned, *don't panic, but you have two crabs on your chest.* Well, that's what she intended on saying. Instead, she decided this would be a great photo opportunity for some amusing shots.

Little did she know, apparently crabs hate having their pictures taken. As soon as she started to click away, they stopped dancing, clutched hold of his nipples, and did what crabs do best – pinch. Hard. Tommy jumped up, flailing wildly around the sand. His voice shrilled higher than it ever had. Skid Row's Sebastian Bach would have been proud. None of the people near him offered to help. Instead, they did what humans do best: They pulled out their phones and Instagramed and You Tubed the shit out of the moment. Little did he know, he'd be the next viral sensation.

Mercifully, Gina put down her camera and helped him detach the crabs. Out of breath and nearly in tears, Tommy snatched up the blanket and moved as far away from beach as possible. Gina felt bad, she really did, but as she looked at his giant black and blue nipples, she couldn't help but laugh. It was as if he had just got a purple nurple from King Kong.

Gina thought it best that they move their little picnic from the beach to an actual picnic table, far away from the water, the sand, and any sort of crustaceans. They dined on finger sandwiches (he was happy to recognize the tuna), cubed cheeses, grapes, strawberries, and other small pieces of fruits? Vegetables? Some of them were pretty good, too, although Tommy did duck away from Gina once to spit something out into his napkin.

Just before sunset, they came upon the Summerhouse, which to Tommy was just a gazebo-thingy with a title (Google said this spot was famous for sunsets). He was happy to see they had it mostly to themselves. They toasted the beginning of sunset with some sparkling cider in red Solo cups.

Even Tommy was impressed, watching the sun drop in vibrant color over the ocean. He admitted to himself that the spectacle would have been wasted on him if he'd seen it twenty-five years earlier, and that sometimes getting older wasn't necessarily a bad thing.

After the sun set, they packed up the basket together and headed back to the boat. As they were boarding, the captain asked them if they had a nice time. Gina gushed on and on about how beautiful the island was and talked even more about the romantic picnic. She spared Tommy further embarrassment by leaving out the crab incident.

The boat ride back was quiet. With his arm around her, they stood on the deck close together. For an uneventful ride, it was something that Tommy knew would be a permanently good memory later; Gina under his arm, leaning against him, the wind whipping her hair into his face, and that feeling that they had the world to themselves.

Well, there was *one* moment when they passed by the spot where Tommy got to steer the boat earlier. They saw a few Green Peace boats attending to a whale with some kind of injury, as if a boat bumped into it (on accident of course). Tommy could feel the pointed looks he received from both the captain and Gina, but just shrugged innocently.

They got back just in time for a late dinner. The picnic food was filling enough at the time, but light, and now they were both ready for a real meal. Sea air can really increase the appetite.

The Beach Cove Restaurant was the next phase of Gina's birthday date. The *Cove* was a casual place overlooking the Atlantic Ocean. The waiter sat them on the more intimate second floor. It was more intimate mostly because they were the only ones up there. You guessed it. Someone had connections. Their table was candlelit and was next to a large picture window. They had a perfect nighttime view of York Beach.

Gingerly, Tommy sat in his chair. Between horseback riding and the pricker bush, his ass took a pounding that day. To add insult to injury, on the front cover of the menu was a cartoon picture of two crabs. The pain he felt in his ass quickly transferred upwards as his hands delicately rubbed his nipples. Despite her uncontrollable giggling, she felt bad for the poor guy. Thankfully for Tommy, he made it the entire dinner without an incident or accident.

As they were leaving the restaurant, Gina received a text.

"Everything okay?" Tommy asked.

"Yea. It was Emma checking up on me. I guess tonight is her night to play the worried Mom."

"She seems like a great kid."

"She's the best thing that's ever happened to me," Gina smiled.

He watched Gina text Emma back then asked, "How is she doing? I heard about what happened at school the other day."

Gina rolled her eyes in disgust, "She's okay. She's a tough cookie."

"Just like her mother," Tommy said.

"Ha, I don't know about that," she said modestly. "Anyway, I just hope Alan is able to nail Otto Jr. for this."

"So you think it was him, huh?"

"Of course!" If you knew his father, you'd agree too."

"Yea, Alan said Otto is kind of a jerk."

"That's being polite. Otto is the biggest asshole I have ever met."

If the 'Joni Parker' incident wasn't bad enough, Gina was about to reveal something that would totally seal the deal with Tommy's new-found hatred of his former best friend.

"Can I tell you something that I haven't told anyone before?" Gina said. Tommy slowly nodded. "The night of Alan's brother's funeral, I ran into Otto. I was in rough shape, and he totally tried to take advantage of that."

With clenched fists, Tommy raised his voice, "What did he do?"

"It's not what he did, it's what he wanted to do. He flat out asked me to have sex with him. Or to use his exact words, 'We should go back to my place and bone.' Get this, he told me Tommy would *want* us to do it."

Tommy cringed in anger. His blood boiled, picturing Otto trying to get with Gina…his Gina. He tried to compose himself and hesitantly asked, "So, what did you say to him?"

"I kicked him in the nuts and told him to go fuck himself!"

A relieved smirk came over Tommy's face as he thought, *That's my girl*. Gina didn't offer any more thoughts on Otto Kringeman, and Tommy didn't bother pushing it. The last thing he wanted was for Otto to bring down Gina's special night. Besides, he still had one more phase of the date left – the Nubble Lighthouse.

Without a doubt, the Nubble is York's most iconic and most photographed tourist attraction. For those old enough to remember the show *Happy Days*, the Nubble at night was *Happy Days* version of Inspiration Point. Tommy and Gina experienced their share of 'Nubble Light sessions' in high school, but that wasn't why he brought her here tonight. He just wanted to go to a familiar place and sit next to her and talk. No, seriously, that was his only intention. And talk they did – for hours. They talked about everything under the sun, or moon in this case.

As luck would have it, the radio station was having their weekly 80's night. It was a perfect complement to the already perfect atmosphere. With each song played, Tommy's mind took him back to when and where he and Gina had first heard that song. Music was a powerful trigger he realized. Each song brought back very specific memories of things they had done together, what they were eating at the time, things they talked about – in detail.

With each memory, Tommy fought the urge to blurt out, *Hey, do you remember when we danced to this at Happy Wheels?* Being Vince Neily was definitely taking a toll on him.

It was well after midnight when they hit their first lull in conversation. It was also about that time, Gina began getting touchy-feely. She slid her body closer. Her fingernails began running through his hair. The look she had in her eyes was a look he remembered all too well. Usually, though, that look came after Tommy had worked his charms to seduce her. Strangely, he hadn't even attempted to charm or seduce her tonight, and yet, there was that look in her eyes.

His heart beat faster. His blood pressure began to rise (as well as other areas). He couldn't do this... not as Vince. Because of this, he did the unthinkable: He turned down the opportunity to have sex with Gina Cassidy.

"It's really stuffy in here," he nervously said. "Wanna get some fresh air?"

Gina was taken aback. Usually when she ran her nails through a man's hair (or woman's…one time in college) sex would soon follow or at least heavy petting. But no one ever, EVER requested to get some fresh air. This guy was an enigma. Luckily for her, she was a therapist, and she specialized in enigmas.

She slowly extracted her nails from his hair and joined him in the whole fresh air thing. They made their way over to a bench overlooking the lighthouse. By now, the moon was high above casting a silvery glimmer across the ocean. Without saying a word, they sat and watched the waves crash into the rocks. The cool night air mixed with the wind whipping off the ocean caused Gina to shiver.

"Let me go get your sweatshirt," Tommy offered.

"Aw, thanks," she gushed. Despite having her sexual advances denied, Gina couldn't have been happier. Sitting here with this amazing guy was the perfect end to a perfect birthday.

Any concerns Gina may have felt about Vince's rebuff of her advances were laughed off when she saw how gingerly and stiffly he walked when he went to the car to get her sweatshirt. He *was* affected by her, he was just being a gentleman. She was okay with that, *for now*. She smiled as she turned back to look at the ocean.

Tommy grabbed her sweatshirt and a bottle of water from the back seat. Before he closed the car door, he leaned a hand on the top of the window and looked over at Gina. She wasn't looking at him. She was busy staring at the waves, so she couldn't see the love he hid in his eyes. He closed the door with a good slam, bringing himself back. Gina still didn't turn around.

The sound of seagulls flying overhead caused him to look up. They all seemed to be on a mission. Their playful squawking, the salty air, the sound of the waves, and Gina waiting for him were enough to make him realize how content he was. With his face still towards the sky, he stretched his arms out, closed his eyes, and offered a mental *thank to the big guy above. He* took a deep breath of the ocean air, but got more than he bargained for – a giant mouthful of seagull shit.

Immediately he started spitting and wiping his mouth. He couldn't open the water bottle fast enough to rinse, spit, then rinse and spit again. Frantically he opened the car door and began rummaging through the glove compartment and found a napkin. He began scrubbing his tongue and the inside of his mouth.

"Is everything okay over there?" she called out.

Tommy spit again. "Yeah. Fine. Do you mind if I use some of the breath freshener spray from your glove box?"

Without thinking, Gina answered, "Sure." Then she thought for a moment. "Wait! Breath spray? That's not breath spray! It's pep..." Tommy's howl stopped her before she could even finish what she was saying. She jumped up and ran to the car to find Tommy red-faced, clutching his throat in pain, and gagging on the water he was pouring down his throat.

Twenty minutes later, they were sitting together on the bench outside of the lighthouse. Neither looked at each other. There was no touching and no talking (not that Tommy was fully able to, yet).

Finally, with a slight smirk, Gina said, "Sorry about the whole pepper spray thing."

When Tommy answered, his voice sounded like sandpaper wiped over a stone, "Nope. My bad."

"Are you sure you're okay?"

They looked at each other and smiled. Gina's smile was more sympathetic and Tommy's more sheepish. He shook his head at her.

"What?"

"Why are you single? There has to be at least a dozen guys around who'd love to date you."

Gina laughed. "You think you're the first guy I got to pepper spray himself? No. You're just the first one to stick around afterwards!"

"I'm serious," Tommy said.

"So am I." She laughed again, then spoke soberly, "Most of my date offers are either jerks, stalkers, or creepy married guys." This time it was Tommy's turn to laugh sympathetically. Gina went on, "It's not like I'm overly picky or anything like that. I just have two rules when it comes to guys I date - they have to make me laugh, *really* laugh, and they have to be 100 percent honest. I hate liars!"

Tommy looked away, grateful for the darker sky helping him to hide the guilt he was feeling. Fortunately, Gina didn't notice.

"Of course, I have to be attracted to them, too. No one wants to date a funny, honest, ugly dude," she laughed. "I could write a book about all of my dating disasters. I'd call it 'Loser Magnet'.

Tommy seized the opportunity and said, "All starting with

Alan's brother, Tommy?"

Gina whipped her head around fast. "What? Why would you say that?"

"I just heard he was kind of a jerk to you."

She looked away. "Our last year of high school, things started getting bad. His so-called best friend Otto was the biggest loser, and it was like Tommy couldn't get enough of him. All they wanted to do was get drunk and high."

Tommy looked ashamed. Gina misread the look on his face. "Don't get me wrong. In high school, all of us were little shits in some way. I had my own wild streak, too, but I was able to keep my grades up and get accepted into the college I wanted. Tommy barely had the grades to graduate. Outside of hanging with Otto and the guys, I don't think he really knew what he wanted to do, or even what he was able to do. I think it was just easier for him to act like he didn't give a shit, you know what I mean? But it bothered him. I could tell."

Tommy looked down at his hands. She was right.

"So, yeah," she continued, "he was a big jerk to me that last year, and that last night, but...but Tommy Stevens was not a loser, and certainly not a regret." She smiled, "He was the best guy I ever dated."

Her comment caught him off guard. "Really? From what I heard, you two were so different," he said.

Gina was too caught up in her memories to notice that *Vince* seemed to be fishing for information. "We listened to different music, therefore we dressed differently – it was the 80's. I listened to alternative bands and dressed in black, and he listened to hair bands and wore acid-wash. On the outside, especially at that age, those are big differences. But we were alike in all the ways that counted. No one could make me laugh as hard as Tommy could. Although"…

"Although what?" he asked.

"Although you came pretty close today. When that crab grabbed your nipple, I nearly peed my pants!" She was smiling when she looked at him, but it faded when she looked towards the water again. "My friends gave me all kinds of shit, telling me I should break up with him – especially that last year. They called him Jon Bon Burnout, or Jon Bon Bonehead. But every single time they asked me why I was still with him, one thing would always come to mind"…

Her voice trailed off. A moment later, she shook her head and looked at him in apology. "What am I doing? I'm sorry. You totally don't want to hear about my teenage angst and my old high school boyfriend."

"No, go on." Tommy desperately wanted to hear what she had to say.

She gave him a look that said, *really?* "We all have our little things that we keep inside. Every so often, it's nice to air them out." he said.

Gina was well enough into her reverie that it didn't take any more to get her talking. "Sixth grade. Mrs. Conlon's class," she continued. "My mom and I moved here halfway through the school year. I was the 'new kid' – the weird new kid."

"I'll bet you were adorable in sixth grade," Tommy said.

"Not by a long shot. I was a big, giant Dork!"

Tommy answered doubtfully, "I don't believe that."

"No, it's true. Braces, a bad (even for that time period) haircut, and the most un-hip clothes. Being a single mother, my mom couldn't afford the cool clothes. I was the queen of thrift store shopping - the more eclectic the better. The kids used to call me Punky Brewster. I totally didn't fit in, and everyone was happy to let me know it. One day, as usual, I was hanging out at recess by myself, and Shawn Geiger thought it would be funny to peg me in the face with a kickball. The ball hit my lip, my lip hit my braces, and the next thing I knew, I was lying on the ground in tears with a big, fat, bloody lip. Everyone was laughing at me."

Tommy remembered that day. He remembered that strange feeling that seemed to grab at his insides when he saw her get hit by the ball. And he remembered how much more intense it got when he saw her on the ground, bleeding and crying. He remembered feeling that he *had to* do something.

He nodded sympathetically while she finished her story.

"Everyone was laughing and pointing at me, calling me names. Everyone except Tommy Stevens. He came over to me, reached his hand to help me up, and then walked me to the nurse's office. On the way, he was trying to comfort me, saying things like 'Everything is gonna be all right.'"

She looked at Tommy – *Vince*, Tommy corrected himself. He had to remind himself that she thought she was talking to Vince.

"And it was. It was gonna be all right. Tommy made sure of that.

I don't know exactly what he did or what he said to everyone, but after that, things were very different. When I walked into class the next day, the other kids were polite, almost friendly, and they never harassed me again. So, even though we didn't actually start dating until much later, that sixth-grade moment was when I fell in love with him." She grinned, sheepishly. "I know. Corny."

"No, not corny. *Sweet*," Tommy answered, thinking at the same time how odd it was talking about himself like that, as if he were a different person. *Sweet?* Never in a million years would he have expected to hear that word used to describe him, especially not from his own mouth.

Back then, his sixth-grade self didn't think about what caused him to react so strongly to her, to seeing her in distress. He just went with it. Now, with the seven added years of practical experience combined with twenty-five years of 'sleep-learning' from the combined mastermind set of Gloria Estefan, Alex Trebek and Dr. Phil, he understood that feeling to be one of wanting to protect her, to keep her safe and close and happy …like he did right now. He wanted to see her happy and smiling again.

"I have to tell you something," he said. "Earlier today - the crabs…the nipples? I'll have you know that was a carefully executed plan between me and the crabs. Mainly the one on my right nipple. It was his idea, though, I never thought it would work. I guess he was right. Now I owe him five bucks! Pfft! I'd like to see him try to collect!" Gina's wide, appreciative smile and accompanying laughter were exactly what he hoped to achieve with his silly joke.

When the sun came up, they were still laughing.

***

Gina pulled into Tommy's driveway and turned to him, "I can't believe we stayed out all night. I haven't stayed out 'til the sun came up since… since forever." Tommy just smiled warmly at her. "Thanks again for a wonderful day, and night. It was really fun." She leaned in a little closer … and closer still. Tommy could feel everything building up in him all over again. He wanted to grab her and kiss her until he couldn't anymore. When she took the initiative and put her face right in front of his in that *kiss me* demand sort of way he almost gave in. He moved his head a fraction closer to hers, then abruptly pulled back and kissed her on the forehead and got out of the car fast.

Extremely disappointed and frustrated, Gina put the car in reverse, only to suddenly slam on the brakes as *Vince* reappeared and knocked on her window. When she rolled the window down, he swooped his head in and planted a swift kiss on her lips.

"Happy Birthday, Gina."

The look he gave her … the kiss … was so *sweet*. Gina smiled and said nothing, then she continued to back out of the driveway. Tommy stood there, watching her drive away until he couldn't see her car anymore.

TRACK 23

Alan was in the kitchen reading the newspaper when he heard the front door open and close. Before Tommy could head upstairs, he was greeted by Alan standing in the kitchen doorway.

"I'd ask how your date went, but seeing as it's nearly 7:00 AM, I'm assuming you two, you know, engaged in adult activities?"

Tommy turned to his brother, gave him a blank look, then spoke, "If by adult activities you mean SEX, then no, no we didn't."

Alan shook his head in disbelief, "Yeah, right."

"Trust me, Alan, we didn't! As a matter of fact, I barely gave her a good-night kiss. And on that note. I need to go take care of a few things. Night."

Tommy rushed upstairs and Alan returned to the kitchen, not believing for a second that Tommy was telling the truth.

***

When Gina arrived back at home, she was greeted with a similar response from Emma. "I'd ask how your birthday date went, but seeing as it's nearly seven in the morning, I'm assuming it went well, as in really well?"

"If you're hinting at S E X, Emma, then no, it didn't go that well," Gina said.

Emma looked at her mother's beaming face. "Well, either you're lying to me, or it was an amazing, sexless date."

Trust me, kiddo, I'm not lying. He barely kissed me good night. But that being said, it might have been my best date ever."

"Ever?" Emma echoed.

"Ever," Gina beamed. "It was fun and romantic and Vince was so sweet and patient. Too patient, actually. Way too patient."

Emma made room for her mom to sit next to her. "You're telling the truth, aren't you? Emma asked. "You two still haven't done it yet?"

"Not even a real kiss," Gina sighed.

"He's obviously into you, Mom." Maybe he's worried if he moves too fast he'll screw things up. That's how Richie was when we started dating. It was like he was too scared to make a move. That's why I jumped him first." Gina shook her head at her daughter with a look that said two things simultaneously: *I appreciate your openness with me*, and *I don't need to hear the details*.

"You should be thankful," Emma continued, "especially considering the type of guys you usually date."

Sadly, Gina knew that Emma spoke the truth. "I suppose you're right. It is kind of refreshing - in a sexually frustrated sort of way."

They both grinned as Gina put her head on Emma's shoulder. "Aw, it'll be okay Mom. Besides, just think how frustrated this must be for Vince. Didn't you say he hasn't been with a woman in twenty-five years? I'm sure he's just nervous. The poor guy, he's probably ready to explode." Both girls burst out laughing.

***

After Tommy headed upstairs, Alan remained in the kitchen, sipping his green tea while working on the newspaper's crossword puzzle. "13 Down – *to excite*. Nine letters."

Alan's train of thought was immediately interrupted by a strange, yet familiar sound from upstairs. It was the theme song from *Baywatch*. Slowly and curiously, Alan gazed up at the ceiling. About halfway through, the theme song was drowned out by another familiar sound – the new vacuum cleaner. The next sound that was heard was a blood curdling scream from Tommy.

Without missing a beat, Alan turned his attention back to the crossword puzzle. "13 Down – S T I M U L A T E." With that, he placed his pen on the table and headed upstairs.

Unsure of what he might find, Alan carefully pushed open Tommy's door. On the nightstand sat Alan's old laptop with a YouTube video of the Baywatch theme playing on repeat. The vacuum continued to blare, but there was no sign of Tommy. Just then, from behind the bed, Alan spotted Tommy's hands feverishly attempting to pull the hose off. Nonchalantly, Alan walked over and pulled the plug. Alan still couldn't see Tommy, but he heard him release a huge sigh of relief. Alan stood in the doorway smirking and shaking his head.

From on his back, and still hidden behind the bed, Tommy yelled out, "Not a fuckin' word!"

Alan couldn't resist, "Let me guess, you were just vacuuming crumbs off?" Tommy responded by blindly whipping a sneaker at his brother. It missed by a mile. By the time Tommy finally sat up, Alan was already back in the kitchen smiling to himself, "Ah, the power of a Dyson."

About an hour later, Alan was joined in the kitchen by his son. Richie grabbed a yogurt and sat across from Alan, who was just finishing up with the crossword.

"What was all that noise coming from Vince's room earlier?" Richie asked.

"He was having some vacuum issues," smiled Alan.

"So what's the deal with Otto Jr? Are you going to expel him and his crew?"

Alan hesitated. He knew his answer wasn't going to go over well with Richie. "I'm sorry, son, but we don't have any concrete proof that it was them. As of now, there's nothing I can do."

"Yeah right!" snapped Richie. "There's never anything you can do when it comes to them. Face it, Dad, you're afraid of him and his loser father."

Before Alan could respond, Richie angrily slid the chair back and got up to leave. "Richie, where are you going?"

"I'm gonna spend the weekend at Mom's."

As Richie stormed out, he passed Tommy, who had been eavesdropping outside the door. Tommy entered the kitchen to find his brother with a sad and helpless look on his face.

"Do you think they did it?" Tommy asked.

"Otto Jr. and his crew? Of course they did it, but how can I prove it? I can't do anything – my hands are tied! I'm the God-damned principal!"

Tommy nodded, beginning to understand that what Alan said was true. Things were different now. Even with his eighteen-year-old brain, he was beginning to see that Alan could only do so much. He *was* the principal.

"But I'm not," Tommy declared, and with fists clenched, he turned to head out.

"Where are you going?" Alan asked.

"No one messes with my nephew and his girlfriend. Especially the spawn of Otto!"

"What are you going to do? Gather up Brett and Ricky and go kick some ass?" Alan joked.

Tommy pondered for a second then smiled and nodded, "That's a great idea, Alan. I'll talk to you later."

Before Alan could tell him he was only joking, Tommy was gone.

***

By the time Brett rushed through the doors of Blendz & Bendz, it was already late afternoon. He headed towards the counter where Ricky was blending one of his famous concoctions.

"Hey, man, I would have been here sooner, but I was in the middle of work. Your message sounded urgent. What's up? Brett asked. Ricky shrugged then pointed over to Tommy, who was nestled in a corner booth. The two old friends curiously made their way over and took a seat.

"Thanks for coming," Tommy said with a sullen look on his face.

"Yea, of course, Vince," Brett said. "What's the emergency? Did something happen to Alan?"

Brett and Ricky braced themselves for bad news. Tommy quickly eased their minds regarding Alan, but spent the next twenty minutes informing them about the latest antics of Otto Jr.

When Tommy was finished, Brett spoke first, "I can't say it's a shock considering who his father is. Look, Vince, I completely respect your concern for Alan's son and girlfriend, but I'm not quite sure what you want us to do about it."

Ricky nodded then added, "Agreed. Otto Jr. and his friends have been a pain in my son's butt for years, but we just have to trust that karma will take care of it."

"Karma?" Tommy chuckled. "Does karma know that Otto Jr.

calls your son a homo? A queerbait? A gaylord? And even the F word that rhymes with hag? As in every day."

Ricky was taken aback. "Every day? Peter never told me that."

"You *did* see the fake newspaper that was passed around school, didn't you?" Tommy asked.

"Um, not exactly. Peter just said there were a bunch of obnoxious, fake photoshopped pictures and that Otto Jr. was obviously behind it."

Tommy slowly pulled out the paper and handed it to him. Both Ricky and Brett looked on in disgust at the front page pictures of Emma.

"Page 2," Tommy quietly spoke.

Ricky flipped to the next page. His mouth dropped open when he saw the doctored pictures of his son *with* random male students. His shock quickly turned to anger as he read the headline – "PETER MARTELL RECRUITING PLAYERS FOR HIS TEAM."

This was the first time since Tommy's return that he had seen a chink in Ricky's love, peace, and harmony attitude.

"Peter never told me that…any of that," Ricky said.

"Maybe he thinks you'll just tell him that karma will take care of it?" Tommy was still the master of pushing the right buttons. Ricky was hooked. It was now time to work on Brett. Tommy knew he'd have to dig deep to pull this one off. He turned to Brett and cast out a slight, yet believable white lie, "And does karma know that back in high school Otto Sr. did the deed with your sister?"

"What?" snapped Brett. "Who told you that?"

"Alan did," Tommy fibbed. "He said his brother once told him that." Brett looked over to Ricky to see if this was true. Ricky looked equally surprised and motioned that he had no clue about this.

"My little sister would never have been with Otto. He would have had to get her drunk or something."

"As in two 4-packs of Bartles & James Fuzzy Navel? From what I heard, the poor girl never stood a chance," Tommy said.

Three...two...one...and there it was, the bulging vein on Brett's forehead. He too was now hooked. It was time for Tommy to reel them in. Tommy pulled his chair in closer and spoke, "Look, Alan also told me that you and his brother used to be quite the bullies in high school." A bit ashamed, Ricky and Brett slowly nodded as Tommy continued, "I was kind of a bully too. I definitely said and did things I wasn't proud of. We should look at this as our chance at a little redemption."

"But what do you have in mind," Ricky asked.

"I'm not talking about any violence," Tommy answered, "just some humility...of the highest level."

"Part of me thinks we really should leave this up to karma," Ricky said, "but," he paused and looked over at Brett and smiled, "but some innocent shenanigans could be fun." Brett and Tommy smiled and nodded in agreement.

"I want in!" boomed a voice from behind them. They turned to see Alan standing there. With his 'game face' on – or, rather, Alan's best imitation of a game face.

It was as if Tommy was eighteen again, and his little brother was attempting to hang with the big boys. "I think you need to let us handle this," Tommy said.

"I want in!" Alan demanded. Proof again, that it was no longer 1988, and that Alan had actually grown some balls over the years. Ricky and Brett were equally impressed with Alan's new-found moxie for adult shenanigans. Tommy smiled and motioned for Alan to join them. Ricky flipped the OPEN sign to CLOSED and for the next hour, the four of them planned the attack.

When "Operation Otto Jr." was finally planned, the four of them split up. Ricky and Brett left together, and Tommy headed out with Alan. Tommy climbed into the passenger side of Alan's car and cringed as he watched Alan carefully place a CD in the player. *There was no way they were getting motivated for this mission with Richard Marx*, thought Tommy. He immediately regretted bringing Alan on board, but before he could say a negative word, the familiar beat of Motely Crue's "Wild Side" blared out.

Tommy looked at him in shock. Alan said nothing, just smiled. His smile got even wider when Tommy uncharacteristically reached out and ruffled his hair in approval and then gave him a fist bump.

As they drove down the road, Tommy looked out the window and said, shaking his head, "Motley Crue in a fucking Prius!"

TRACK 24

The first phase of their plan involved leaving Alan's Prius at home. Tommy knew how much Alan had to lose and was adamant about Alan not getting noticed at all. Phase two involved placing a pizza delivery to Otto Jr's house. Before the driver got out of his car, he was approached by Tommy – and only Tommy. He was also very conscious of Ricky and Brett's stature and made sure no one knew they were a part of this.

Tommy took the pizza box from the delivery boy and told him to wait a second. Then, with his back turned from the pimply-faced driver, he opened the box and carefully placed two types of finely crushed pills under the cheese. He rearranged some of the toppings to make sure everything was concealed and then handed it back to the kid with a fifty-dollar bill. The kid gladly took the money, but if truth be told, he would have done this for free. He didn't know exactly what the pills were, but he didn't need to. All he cared about was it was for the Kringeman residence. The kid was obviously a previous victim of Otto Jr. and his crew.

With the delivery driver on board, Tommy joined the others behind a bush in the shadows of the house. "Operation Otto Jr. is now in motion," whispered Tommy.

They eagerly watched the kid head up the walkway, but before he reached the door, a loud pickup truck barreled into the driveway. It ws Otto Sr. With a case of Pabst in hand, he headed to the front door.

"Nice! Junior ordered some pizza," Otto meanly smiled. He snatched the box from the kid's hand. "Is this paid for or what?"

Nervously, the kid nodded.

"Suppose you want a fuckin' tip, huh?" Otto scoffed. He set the beer down and reached into his greasy jeans pocket, but pulled out nothing but his middle finger. He then made a fist and swung it back as if to hit him, laughing as the poor delivery driver ran off.

From the bushes, Brett chuckled, "Looks like "Operation Otto Jr. *and* Senior" is now in motion."

"Now we wait," Tommy smiled, holding up the two pill bottles. Each were marked clearly: Ambien and Viagra.

Alan actually giggled as he spoke, "Where did you get those Tom…um, Vince?"

Tommy answered matter of fact, "Rite Aid…and your nightstand drawer."

Alan's giggles stopped.

Brett crept out from behind the bushes and peeked into the

windows of the house. When he returned from his recon, he reported, "Pete, Re-pete, and the two stooges have their asses planted in front of the television playing video games and drinking, and the pizza is almost gone. I'd say another fifteen minutes should do it."

Tommy nodded, "We should get ready." He motioned to the backpack at Brett's feet. Brett reached in and pulled out four Halloween costume wigs labeled "80s Rocker" and passed them out. Tommy, Brett, and Ricky put theirs on then looked over at Alan, who was still staring dismally at the package.

"Why do I get the mullet?" he whined.

"These were all they had. Shut up and just put it on," said Tommy, hiding a grin. He told Brett ahead of time to make sure Alan got that one. Tommy looked at his two old friends – their long headbangin' hair flowing in the breeze. It was as if it was 1988 again. Tommy almost exclaimed, "Ah, just like old times," but he smartly held back.

Ricky nudged Brett, "Give me your cell phone. We need a picture of this, and yours is probably the safest one to use!"

They stood together, with the cheesiest grins on their faces as Brett took their group selfie. He was careful to focus in on their faces only, making sure there was nothing in the background to see. With Alan's mullet free-flowing behind him, it looked as though Billy Ray Cyrus had joined Bon Jovi.

Tommy was elated at how he felt hanging with the guys again. It was even nice with Alan there. Alan was also enjoying himself; the little kid finally getting to hang out with his big brother and his friends. It was a moment that managed to erase so many not-so-nice memories.

It was twenty minutes before they made their move towards the house. All wigged out and with backpacks in tow, they reached the front door. Brett reached into his back pocket and pulled out a small wrapped kit of tools preparing to pick the lock. Tommy gave him an '*are you serious?*' look and reached his hand out to the doorknob and gave it a turn. Unlocked.

They found the Ottos and the two minions passed out cold; one on the Barcalounger, one spread out on the couch, two on the floor – and all of them with 'excited activity' in their pants.

"There's nothing like a pepperoni pizza with Viagra and Ambien to make the night special!" Tommy joked. "Hey, Ricky, I'm getting an idea for a new smoothie recipe!"

Alan was quick with, "Yeah, you could call it the 'Vince Nealy Made It'!" Ricky, Brett, and Tommy looked over at Alan with surprised admiration, and he knew he was beaming like a child.

"Nice one, little broth-- ... er, bro!" Tommy caught himself at the last minute.

"Time to rock!" Tommy announced. "I want Otto!"

"I'll take Junior," Alan chimed in.

The four of them opened their backpacks and pulled out little makeup cases. Then they each went over to an unconscious body and got to work, putting eyeshadow, blushes and lipsticks on the thug's faces.

"Remember," Ricky warned, "Less Alice Cooper and more Boy

George!"

When they were done with the makeup, Alan pulled a camera out of his backpack while the others pulled out various 'props'. They started positioning Otto and the boys for the camera.

Otto Sr. was bedecked in 'Pretty Please' pink lipstick with a matching feather boa, laying back on the lounger, mouth open, hand on his crotch. *Click!*

Alan moved in for a closer shot to ensure that the lotion and tissue box next to Otto were in view – *Click!* Just then, Alan noticed what was near Otto's other hand: a Playgirl magazine and an old Richard Marx album. He immediately put the camera down and snatched up the album. He could hear Tommy laughing at him when he carefully put the album away in his own backpack.

After mumbling something about being an under-rated, under-appreciated singer songwriter, Alan continued around the room snapping pictures. Next up was Otto Jr. His shirt was off, and he was wearing a cowboy hat. He was sitting casually on end of the couch with Kenny laying with his head in Otto Jr.'s lap and his hand on Jr.'s knee. *Click!*

On the other couch, Dale was bent over the arm rest with a bottle of KY Jelly and various sex toys strewn about around him. *Click!*

The four of them had a grand time for the next half hour. "Move his hand there!" and "Put this on him!" and other variations on the same instructional theme were the only words said above the *Click* of the camera.

315

The four of them looked down at their handiwork, then beamed at each other with pride. Alan leaned forward with the camera for the final shot.

Click!

Click!

***

As the clock struck midnight at Gina's house, Gina was still wide awake, feverishly typing a new short story idea on her laptop. Yup, Gina was writing again, and it felt great! She had even dug up some old story ideas she started years ago, but never finished. She knew she had Vince to thank for the rediscovery of her original passion – writing.

Across the hall, Emma was lying on her bed texting with Richie…while playing Candy Crush with two other friends…while listening to I-Tunes, while checking her Facebook page, and of course, while binging on Netflix. Then, in the 3 minutes and 17 seconds between checking Facebook - it happened. *It* being: dozens of the photoshopped photos of Otto and Otto Jr. and his crew, appeared on Emma's news feed. Emma's fingers quickly texted Richie to see if he was seeing this too.

Within minutes, not only did Richie see them, but half the school had as well. As Emma scrolled through the many, many comical poses, she literally LOL'd. So loud, in fact, that Gina was forced to stop writing and come see what the commotion was.

Gina's eyes widened as she saw the first picture. It was of Otto, Otto Jr., Kenny, and Dale made up like prostitutes and spooning each other in a row on a large bed. And there were more pictures, with the guys in various poses all mimicking sexual acts. The caption on the first picture read "Spoonfellas" and each picture had its own uniquely clever and dirty title.

"Where did these come from?" Gina was trying so hard not to laugh.

"I don't know!" Emma was wiping tears from her eyes. She checked her phone for Richie's latest text. "Richie says the link is inactive. It doesn't open to the page it came from."

"What does that mean?" Gina asked.

"I'm pretty sure it means there's no way to find out where they came from or who took them," answered Emma.

Gina and Emma spent the next half hour scrolling and rescrolling through the pictures - LOL'ing the whole time.

***

Back at Alan's house, the four guys high-fived in celebration of their highly successful mission. "Yes!" yelled Brett. "Great plan, Vince."

"Thanks," Tommy said, "but Alan deserves a lot of the credit. It was his computer mastery that really brought it all to life."

Brett and Ricky exchanged more high-fives and fist bumps with Alan. Alan beamed. Deep down, he knew what he did tonight was wrong, and he knew if anyone ever found out, his career would be ruined, but getting his first ever fist bumps from his brother and friends made it all worth it.

Ricky's calm and laid-back manner turned into more of a hyper-active enthusiasm. That was the Ricky Tommy remembered. "Oh man!" shouted Ricky, "I haven't felt that kind of adrenaline in years."

"Not even from a wheat grass smoothie?" joked Tommy. Ricky stared at Tommy, deadpan, before cracking up laughing.

Brett laughed as well, then looked over at his friends and spoke, "Too bad Tommy wasn't here. He would have loved tonight."

"Don't worry, Brett," spoke Ricky, "he's here." Nervously, Tommy and Alan looked over at one another then back to Ricky. The old Ricky's hyper-activeness had transformed back into the new, enlightened Ricky as he closed his eyes and spiritually gazed around the room. "Yup, he's here with us. I can feel it."

***

The next morning, well before school had even started, Otto and Junior were sitting in Alan's office. It was the earliest either one of them had ever arrived. Ever. Alan patiently sat and listened to Otto as he ranted, raved, and swore up a storm. When Otto opened up his phone to show Alan the pictures in question, Alan did his best not to laugh. He put on his best *concerned principal* face, and assured Otto that he would look into it. This didn't set well with Otto.

"Look into it?" yelled Otto. "You better do more than that! "It's obvious that your son is behind this. Either you expel him or I'll make sure they fire your fat ass!"

Normally, this would be the point where Alan would kowtow to Otto, but he didn't. Maybe it was the confidence he gained from being a part of the shenanigans, or maybe he was just sick to death of not standing up for himself, but either way, Alan stood his ground. He examined the pictures on Otto's phone again.

"As far as I can tell, these pictures were posted from your son's account."

"Obviously he was hacked, dipshit!! This is the part where you get off your fat ass and do something about it!" Otto leaned closer to Alan, sneering the famous Otto sneer.

Alan was forced to slide back in his chair. It wasn't the Otto sneer that caused this. It was the Otto bad breath – a combination of cigarettes, cheap beer, pizza, and Funyuns. Alan stood and once again looked at the pictures on Otto's phone.

"Well, if indeed your son's profile was hacked, then it looks like a job for the local authorities."

Otto turned and shared a smirk with his son, "Now we're talking! Let's see Richie get into a big, fancy college with a criminal record," laughed Otto.

"Speaking of records," began Alan, "I noticed an awful lot of drug paraphernalia in those pics."

"Yea, what's your point?" Otto snapped.

"I would assume someone who's already on probation, wouldn't want the authorities to see that, but I could be wrong." The smirks immediately fell from the Kringeman's faces.

Who's your daddy now, bitch! Alan yelled. Well, he yelled it in his head. Baby steps. Needless to say, Otto snatched back his phone and stormed out of the office and with Junior close behind him, they headed up the hallway with all eyes on them – snickering and pointing.

Before Alan had a chance to lean back in his chair and gloat, his office door opened. It was Richie. It was the first time Alan had seen him since their argument the other morning.

"Hey son, what's up?"

"Um, I just wanted to apologize about the other morning and to say thanks."

Alan looked confused. "Thanks for what?" he asked.

"Come on, Dad, Vince told me."

"Vince told you what exactly?"

Richie made sure the door was shut then lowered his voice, "That you were the mastermind behind this." Alan was taken aback. "I guess I totally underestimated you. Don't worry, Dad, I won't tell anyone."

Richie gave his father a proud smile and left. The only thing better than having Richie admire him was having Tommy shy away from the spotlight and giving Alan all the credit.

***

Taking a break from her newest writing idea, Gina headed

downstairs to get a much needed wine refill. As she walked by the living room, she saw Emma lounging on the couch giggling at her phone. Upon further inspection, Gina saw that she was still flipping through the now-famous pictures of Otto.

"You still looking at those?"

"Well yea," Emma answered. "These might be the funniest things I've ever seen."

"They are pretty hilarious," laughed Gina. "Any word on who actually did this?"

"Nope. It's like a big mystery. Whoever it was might be my new hero."

Gina rolled her eyes at her daughter and continued into the kitchen for her wine. On her way back, she again stopped in the living room. "Hey Emma, what do you think of me cooking my famous lasagna for Vince? You know, to thank him for such a great birthday date?"

Emma pulled her attention away from her phone and looked at her mother. "Personally, Mom, I think you need to step your game up - big time."

"Oh really? And what do you suggest?"

Deviously, Emma shrugged, "I did hear that Victoria Secret is having their big spring sale. Not to mention, I'm spending the night at Melissa's on Friday night, so you'll have the whole house to yourself."

"Why Emma Cassidy, what are you suggesting?"

"I think it's obvious, Mom. You totally need to seduce him.

Guys love that...so I've heard."

A bit embarrassed by her own daughter giving her sex advice, Gina shook her head and made her way back up to her desk. As she stared at the blank screen, she giggled and spoke to herself, "Seduce him, huh?"

***

Ten minutes later, Tommy hung up the phone and joined Alan on the couch. It was obvious by Tommy's sullen look that something was on his mind.

"What was that about?" Alan asked.

"It was Gina. She wants to cook me dinner Friday night."

"And that's a bad thing?"

Tommy sighed and spoke, "You were right, Alan. You were totally right. I should never have gotten this close to her. Or Ricky and Brett, for that matter. At least not until the truth came out. They're all gonna hate me for lying to them. Especially Gina. Do you know what she told me the other night? She said the one trait she absolutely needs in a guy is honesty."

Alan knew he had warned Tommy about this happening, but he also knew this wasn't the time to say I told you so. He chose a more sympathetic route, "What are you going to do?"

"What am I going to do, or what do I want to do? Because part of me wants to keep Tommy dead and just continue being Vince the rest of my life." Tommy didn't need to look up to know the dubious look Alan was shooting at him. "I know, I know, another one of my stupid ideas."

"It's not stupid, Tommy. It's just not feasible."

"I've devastated her life once, I can't do it again. I need to end all communication with her before she really gets hurt."

"You can't just stop talking to her cold turkey," Alan said.

"You're right," responded Tommy, "I need to let her down easy, so she doesn't think it's her fault. Any suggestions?"

Alan was pleasantly taken aback. Tommy had never come to him for advice…especially on women. "Really? You want my advice?" Alan's heart ballooned with appreciation.

"Well yea," Tommy replied, "You've probably been dumped a hundred times. How did they let you down easy?"

And POP went Alan's balloon.

TRACK 25

As promised, Gina had Tommy over for a special home-cooked meal. The dinner conversation was sparse at best. A nervous energy emitted from each of them; each for different reasons. Tommy knew he needed to find the right words to somehow end things with Gina. Gina's nerves stemmed from knowing she was about to do her best seduction of Vince.

After dinner, Tommy made himself comfortable on Gina's couch and nervously waited for her to join him. He had been there nearly two hours and had yet mustered up the courage to end things with her. The truth was; he still had no clue how to let her down easy. Gina didn't make it easy on him either. From the candlelit dinner, to the sweet-smelling incense, to the quiet music playing in the candlelit living room – Gina created the ultimate romantic atmosphere.

She exited the kitchen with a glass of red wine in one hand and a glass of sparkling water in the other. It was her fourth glass already, and Tommy just assumed it was due to another stressful day at work. In all actuality, her work-day was fine, it was the date that stressed her out. Planning a seduction is very nerve racking. She handed him his water then took a giant sip of her wine. Unfortunately for Tommy, he didn't have the luxury of liquid courage.

"Thanks again for dinner," Tommy said. Your lasagna was unbelievable. It tasted just like my mom used to make."

Gina smiled, "It's the least I can do for what you did for my birthday. I had such a great time." He nodded in agreement. "And as far as the lasagna is concerned, I can't take all the credit for it. I got the recipe a while back from Alan's mother." Tommy's heart sank and a lump formed in his throat. This was going too far. He needed to end it – quick and painless like ripping off a band aid.

Gina pounded down the rest of her wine then smiled at Tommy. "I'll be right back, okay?" She placed her empty glass on the end table and left the room. On her way out, she dimmed the last remaining light. The ripping of the band aid would have to wait a bit longer.

As soon as Gina disappeared up the stairs, Tommy began rehearsing Alan's suggested break-up speech. "Look Gina, I've had a lot of fun, and you're a great woman, but I don't think this is going to work out. It's not you, it's me." He cringed at the thought of saying those tired, cliché lines to her. *Alan was an idiot*, he thought. He needed to come up with something better. Just then, he heard the creak of the stairs. His heart raced. Nervous and panicked, he slowly looked over his shoulder at Gina walking down the stairs…in just a black teddy…and black high heels.

"Oh God," he murmured. "Code red! Code red!" His heart went into overdrive.

Gina's heart was also in overdrive. Partly because she was half naked, but mostly because she was totally not a high-heeled kind of chick. The four glasses of wine didn't help matters either, as she awkwardly moved down the staircase. Tommy did his best not to make eye contact with her. It was as if she was Medusa, and if he looked at her, he'd turn to stone. He knew this to be true, because he already felt parts of himself turning hard.

After tripping down the last few steps, Gina composed herself and made her way in front of Tommy. "You didn't think I'd let you leave without dessert, did you?"

Tommy limited his eye contact and answered, "Dessert? Um, that's okay. I'm still stuffed from dinner."

The next thing he knew, her fingers were running through his hair. "I really, REALLY appreciate your patience with me these last few weeks."

Tommy squirmed and nervously joked, "Patience is my middle name. Yup, good ole Vince Patience Neily."

She leaned in closer. Her familiar scent, combined with the fact he could clearly see boobage down her teddy, caused his breath to quicken. Alan's inhaler would certainly have come in handy right now, he thought.

She whispered in his ear, "You know how I told you that I promised myself I wasn't going to 'be' with someone again unless I completely trusted them?"

Tommy hesitantly nodded. Gina took a step backwards and turned around, and although he couldn't tell, Gina was shaking like a leaf. It had been forever since she'd allowed herself to be this vulnerable. With her liquid courage kicking in, she took a deep breath and slipped her teddy to the floor. Nervously she turned back around.

Tommy's reaction resembled that of a Looney Tunes character. His tongue rolled out of his mouth and hit the floor. His eyes, as if on springs, widened and popped out of his sockets. His full body scan began at her eyes. It then moved to her breasts where it remained for a seven Mississippi count. His eyes started to move down her stomach, but made their way back to her breasts. After the three Mississippi bonus count, his eyes decided to take a vacation down below the equator. It was there that his *kid in a candy store look* became slightly mystified causing him to pause and curiously tilt his head.

Beyond self-conscious, and with the red wine wearing off, Gina made her move. Still in heels, she stumbled forward and began unbuckling his belt. Sweat poured down Tommy's forehead. The clock read 8 PM, but Tommy's sundial was reading high noon!

The battle on his two shoulders was about to be won by the devil. He wanted Gina in the worst way. With the angel seemingly down for the count, the devil ordered Tommy to go for it!

As she continued to fumble with his belt, she whispered, "I want you so bad, Vince."

Vince was the only word in the sentence that resonated with him.

Vince…Vince…Vince…it echoed in his head. And just like that, the angel rose up, forcing Tommy to do the right thing.

"I can't do this! I can't do this! It's not you, it's me," he blurted out.

Caught off guard, Gina stepped back. "Oh my God, you're married."

"No. I'm not married."

"You're gay, aren't you? I knew this was too good to be true."

"No Gina, I'm not gay. God no. It's just that"…

"It's just what?" she insisted. "You don't you find me attractive, do you?"

"Are you kidding? You look"…

"Old?" she lamented.

"No. You look amazing."

"Really?" she smiled, slightly perked up by his compliment.

"Amazingly perfect, actually. It's just"…

Gina's face softened as she sympathetically said, "Aw, I get it. It's been a long time since you've been with a woman, you're nervous, aren't you?" Before Tommy could reply, she once again moved in for the seduction. "You don't have to be nervous with me, Vince." Her hands returned to his belt.

Tommy couldn't take it anymore. He erupted with the truth, "I'm not Vince! I'm Tommy. Tommy Stevens! A crazy doctor faked my death and has been experimenting on me for the past twenty-five years in his laboratory, which is really his basement. And he has a sidekick named Paco. He's a Mexican midget, or dwarf, or little person, or whatever the hell the PC word is. The reason I haven't told anyone yet is because I gave him thirty days to find out what actually cured me." Exhausted from his babble, he let out a huge sigh.

By now, Gina had not only released his belt buckle, but had taken two giant steps back. She reached for a blanket on the chair and quickly covered herself up. Her eyes never left Tommy as she continued staring at him like he was a psychopath. "Who are you?" she quietly said.

"I told you, I'm"...

"Who the FUCK are you!" she yelled. After everything I confided in you about...how could you make up a lie like that? HUH? If you didn't want to be with me, you could have just blown me off like all the others."

"But...I'm not like the others."

"No, you're right. They were just liars, cheats, and assholes. You're worse. You're a fucking demented monster!"

Seeing the tears form in her eyes, Tommy stood up to try to console her. "I swear, Gina, I'm telling you the truth. I know it sounds crazy, but"...

"Get out!" she yelled as she backed away from him.

"But, Gina, I"...

"Get out! NOW!" she screamed and pointed to the door.

Tommy knew this was pointless. His words were only upsetting her more. With his head hung low, he opened the front door and left. Tears flew from Gina's eyes as she curled up on the couch. Out of all the guys in the world to date, she chose a mentally ill, disillusioned nut job.

While Gina balled her eyes out, Tommy was forced to head home on foot. As Tommy walked the darkened streets alone, his internal soundtrack began to play ("Here I Go Again" by Whitesnake). The long walk gave him plenty of time to reflect; reflect on how he had just devastated Gina yet again. He *was* a monster. And a *big, gigantic asshole to boot. Why couldn't he have died when he was supposed to? Why did Doctor Z have to fucking bring him back? Fuck!*

***

When Emma got home the next day and found her mother still sitting on the couch with a glass of wine and tear tracks all down her cheeks, she knew the evening didn't go well. Emma could see her mother was very upset, but she also knew how her mother processed things. Emma knew her mom wouldn't talk until she'd figured enough of it out to say it right. She kissed her on the cheek, gave her a hug, and sighed, "I'm sorry, Mom."

When Emma left the room, Gina closed her eyes and laid her head down on the edge of the couch.

***

Tommy barricaded himself in his room. After getting snarled at the first few times, Alan gave up trying to talk to his brother. There was never any noise coming from the room; no Bon Jovi, no Motley Crue, not even Baywatch or a vacuum cleaner. Every so often, Alan would stand by Tommy's door listening for any sound; the bed creaking or the toilet flushing, just to make sure he was still moving around - still breathing. When Richie happened upon him with his ear pressed against the door, he told him that Vince was 'going through some stuff and just needed time to himself.'

For two days, Tommy stayed in his room. Alan might have thought the room sounded too quiet, but to Tommy, his thoughts were quite loud to him.

During the next few days, he left his room long enough to grab some food from the kitchen, but didn't speak to anyone unless it was to bitch about needing more Chicken in a Biskit.

TRACK 26

When Saturday arrived, it had been a week since the 'Gina incident'. Alan planned on beginning it the way he usually did, with a mocha latte and awkward flirting with Mia. Although, he had to admit, his flirting had improved in the last few weeks, thanks to everything that was going on. Thanks to *Tommy*. "Tommy," Alan sighed. He was not going to let him brood alone in his room any more. He went upstairs and pounded on the bedroom door. "Tommy!" he called out, then corrected himself in case Richie could hear. "Vince! Come on out! You've been in there long enough!"

"Go away!" was the response from inside the room.

Alan lowered his voice a little, but still spoke fervently, "Come on out! This isn't like you!"

The bedroom door swung open and Tommy got nose-to-nose with Alan. "Get real, little brother! I haven't been *me* in twenty-five-fucking-years, and we both know it!"

Alan didn't know what to say to that, but he did know that something had to give. "Go wash your face, put on some *CLEAN* clothes ... and deodorant. We're going out for coffee. I'll be waiting downstairs. Fifteen minutes!" Then he turned away and went down to the kitchen.

Tommy stood in the doorway for a moment then turned back into his room, closing the door behind him. He walked over to his mirror and just stared. *It's hard to see your own face without a mirror.* The words mocked him as he began to understand what that meant. At least he knew where all these stupid sayings were coming from. *Fucking Dr. Phil.*

Alan was sitting at the kitchen table watching the cock clock tick away the minutes ... four ... five ... six minutes passed, and he heard nothing from upstairs. He figured he'd give Tommy four more minutes before he was going to go up to harass him some more, but he didn't have to, after eight minutes he heard the shower running.

Tommy came down twenty minutes later, scowling, but clean and somewhat presentable and *definitely* better-smelling. It wasn't within the fifteen-minute deadline that he gave him, but Alan didn't nit-pick. He was just happy (and shocked) that Tommy actually followed his orders.

***

They sat at the table in the café, neither one talking, both staring at something. Alan's stare was fixated on Mia behind the counter, while Tommy was giving his coffee the evil eye.

Tommy finally spoke, "I really am just like Otto, aren't I?"

Alan turned his attention back to his brother, "Trust me, you're nothing like Otto."

"Then why do I always hurt the people around me? I still can't believe I did that to Gina." Again, Tommy sadly fixated on his coffee. "Especially after all she must be going through."

Alan took a giant sip of his latte (leaving him with a foam moustache) then looked at Tommy a bit puzzled, "Why, what is she going through?"

Tommy looked around to make sure no one was listening then leaned in and whispered, "I think Gina has cancer."

Alan's face dropped. "What?"

"Yup," nodded Tommy, "vagina cancer."

Alan's shock turned skeptical. "Vagina cancer? She told you this?"

"No, but I saw her naked, and she had lost all her hair...you know, down there. Probably from the Chemo." Alan licked the foam off his lip and began cracking up. "Hey! Show some compassion, Alan. It's not funny," Tommy sternly ordered.

"I don't think she has 'vagina cancer,' Tommy. I think she just shaves and waxes down there. Pretty much everyone does it nowadays," laughed Alan.

"Everyone? Even dudes?"

"Yup. But when guys do it, it's called manscaping," Alan answered.

"Sounds pretty weird if you ask me."

"Nah, women loved a well-groomed man. Not to mention, it gives the illusion that it's bigger than it actually is. You know, like a side-view mirror?" All Tommy could do was sit there. And stare. Stare long and hard at his brother... his *well-groomed* brother. He may or may not have thrown up in his mouth a bit.

Alan changed the subject, "Even though Gina didn't actually believe you, did you tell Dr. Zimarchi that you told her?"

"Not yet," sighed Tommy. "I should probably go see him today."

"Maybe he's figured out what cured you. Either way, his thirty days are almost up, right?"

"Whatever," Tommy shrugged. "It doesn't matter anymore."

"Why do you say that?" Alan asked.

"Twenty-five years ago, I was a big jerk to everyone, and now I'm a big, fat liar too. I was actually thinking of leaving town. You can just tell Gina and the guys that good ole Vince went bat-shit crazy from all the years cooped up in the African jungles. Tell them you had to put me in the loony bin or something."

Alan tried to lighten the mood, "Where are you gonna go? Back to the African jungle? Google may help you get there, but it won't help you *live* there."

"It's not funny, Alan. I'm serious. Everyone will be better off thinking that Tommy is still dead. Actually, if the doctor hasn't found the cure, I could just let him use me as his Guinea pig. That's all I'm good for anyway."

"You know that's not true, Tommy. Eventually, everyone will understand why you had to lie to them."

"Alan, you didn't see the look on Gina's face the other night. She was so hurt and upset. It was the same look she gave me on our prom night." Alan had no idea the right words to say to his big brother.

"Speaking of which," continued Tommy, "isn't tonight the big night?"

Alan nodded and looked at his watch, "That reminds me, I need to go pick up our tuxes."

"You're going too?" asked Tommy.

"I'm the principal. It's my duty to be a chaperone." Alan saw that Tommy's gaze was back into his coffee cup. "I guess I don't *have* to go, if you want to hang out or whatever?"

"Thanks, Alan, but I'll be okay. You guys go, have fun."

***

Alan dropped Tommy off at the house and left to pick up the tuxedos. They were going to get dressed a little early so that they would have time to visit and take pictures with Mrs. Stevens before prom.

Tommy hopped on Big Blue with the intention of heading straight for Dr. Zimarchi's house, but instead rode around town for a couple of hours, not really looking at or seeing anything. His mind was going in faster circles than his wheels. *What was he going to do now?*

Who was he? Those were the two questions that would keep interrupting his thoughts. He still had no answers by the time he turned toward the doctor's house.

Out of breath and out of patience, Tommy filled the doctor in on everything. He informed him on how he had blurted out to Gina that he was actually Tommy (he left out his vagina cancer diagnosis).

"She didn't believe me of course, and I wasn't there long enough to convince her. She kicked me out and hasn't talked to me since. Not that I can blame her. I should have just listened to you and Alan and kept a low profile for the month."

The doctor sat stoically and said nothing, making it impossible for Tommy to read his thoughts. The guy was born with a poker face. Tommy assumed the doctor wasn't used to people breaking promises. If he really was in the mafia, Tommy knew there was a chance he could wake up with a horse's head next to him, or worse, maybe he'd make Tommy *disappear*, like that Doctor Hargrove guy.

"I'm sorry, Doc. I know I shouldn't have made contact with my friends, and I know I shouldn't have told Gina the truth. Especially when I promised you thirty days. What can I say, I fucked up…again. But I'm absolutely prepared to make up for it," assured Tommy.

Dr. Zimarchi pulled a cigar out of his shirt pocket and lit it. His stoic face now a bit curious as he awaited Tommy's plan.

"From here on out, I'm all yours, Doc. Do as you please with me. Poke, prod me, run as many tests as you want. Cut open my head and take my brain out, if you think it'll help. I'm better off as your lab rat than being in the real world."

Again, the doctor sat expressionless. Finally, after two big puffs from his cigar, he looked Tommy in the eyes and said, "I think you need to convince Gina of the truth. Convince everyone of the truth."

"You do?" asked Tommy. "As in, you *really* do, or is this your way of saying I'll be swimming with the fishes tonight?"

The doctor chuckled. "You've missed twenty-five years of your life, you shouldn't have to miss another day. I only wish I could have brought you back sooner."

The doctor's response surprised Tommy, and it also pleased him greatly. Not only did he have the doctor's blessing to tell the world, but he wouldn't be used as a lab rat (he really, really didn't want that).

"I still think what you did was pretty shady, Doc. Allowing my family to think I was dead and kidnapping my body. But, the truth is, if it wasn't for you, I wouldn't be here today, and I wouldn't have this second chance with my family, my friends... with Gina. Things probably won't work out with her, and there's a good chance she'll hate me forever, but because of you I at least have a chance."

The doctor took a few more puffs then asked, "Have you thought about what you're going to tell people?"

"To be honest, I don't have a clue. I obviously didn't do so well the other night." Tommy paused a moment then continued, "I do know what I'm *not* gonna tell people though. I'm not gonna tell them anything about your involvement. You're a good man, Doc, I truly believe that," Tommy said, waving the cigar smoke from his face. "And despite my extra pounds, and my new love for Menudo, your Mexican midget is a good lil guy too. Um, I mean, *vertically challenged*

Mexican," Tommy corrected as he remembered Alan's whiteboard. "Anyway, you two don't deserve to take the fall for this."

"I see," the doctor said, "and what are you planning on telling people?"

"That my body was stolen by the Russians. A Dr. Ivan Drago to be exact," Tommy said.

"I appreciate the gesture," smiled the doctor, "but I don't think we need to start the next world war over this. I think you should just stick to the truth."

"But they'll throw you in jail," warned Tommy, "and you'll never get the chance to figure out what cured me."

The doctor took another deep puff on his cigar and quietly spoke, "It's okay, son. I think I already figured it out."

"Really?" Tommy exclaimed.

"I've run test after test after test this past month on all the different things that went into your body that night, and there's no scientific proof that any of it was the reason for your recovery."

Tommy looked confused. "I don't get it. Something must have fixed me."

Dr. Zimarchi extinguished his cigar in a large black ash tray then turned to Tommy, "Sometimes there's only one explanation for things like this - a good ole non-scientific miracle." Just then, Paco entered and stood next to the doctor.

Unsatisfied with his answer, Tommy rolled his eyes and leaned back into the leather couch. "Pfft, I don't know why God would waste a miracle on me."

Doctor Zimarchi looked at Paco then over to Tommy and quietly spoke, "Well, I guess it's up to you to make sure it doesn't get wasted."

He was right. The doctor was absolutely right. Tommy *had* been given a second chance, and it was up to him to make the most of it. And tonight that started with Gina.

Tommy arose from the couch and gave Paco and Dr. Zimarchi a nod. "Well, if not the Russians," Tommy said, "maybe the Canadians?"

The Doctor chuckled and put his hand on Tommy's shoulder. "Don't worry about us, my friend. We'll be okay."

With that, the doctor glanced at the back of the large living room. The back wall was filled with moving boxes. Tommy's eyes followed and quickly began to put two and two together. "You're leaving town, aren't you? You were leaving all along."

Doctor Zimarchi slowly nodded and spoke, "I've spent the past forty years researching, and testing, and researching some more. It's time I face the facts: My son is not coming back to me, and neither is my wife, for that matter."

"I'm sorry, Doc," Tommy said.

"Oh, don't feel sorry for me. This was the life I chose. No regrets. I'm just glad something positive came of it." Tommy hesitantly pointed to himself. "Yes, you, Tommy. Even though I have no idea what actually brought you back, I'd like to think I played some small part in it."

Gratefully, Tommy smiled. "So, what are you gonna do?"

Tommy asked.

The doctor looked around the room then answered, "I think it's long overdue that I"… he looked over at Paco, "that *we* take a nice long vacation."

"Where are you going?" Tommy asked. "Let me guess, you have connections?" Dr. Zimarchi acknowledged him with a wide smile. "I'm sorry, Doc, but I gotta know, are you in the mafia or what?"

The doctor's face turned deadpan as he answered, "I could answer that, but I'd have to kill you."

The room fell silent. Tommy felt a tingle run up his spine. Finally, the doctor broke the silence with a booming laugh. He was quickly joined by Paco. Strangely, no sound came out of Paco, though his body wiggled and jiggled as if he was laughing his little ass off.

Tommy reached out and gave Dr. Zimarchi a firm handshake. "I meant what I said earlier, I really do appreciate all that you've done for me… and my family. Even if things don't work out with me and Gina, I'm eternally thankful that you never gave up hope on me."

As Tommy turned to go, the doctor and Paco shared a look. It was obvious something weighed on their mind. Before Tommy shut the door behind him, the doctor spoke, "Hey, Tommy."

"Yes?" Tommy turned and answered.

"You haven't visited your father since you've been back, have you?"

Tommy was taken off guard. "Umm, no, not yet."

"I really think you should." Tommy offered no response. He just looked down and shrugged. "He's the one you should be thanking for your second chance," the doctor revealed.

Curiously, Tommy's gaze moved from the floor up to Dr. Zimarchi's eyes. "What are you saying?"

"I'm saying he's the one who never lost hope in your recovery."

Tommy was shell-shocked. "Are you saying this whole thing was my parent's idea?"

"No, son, just your father's."

Tommy slumped against the door jam. His face turned white. Without revealing certain sordid details, the doctor explained everything.

"So Alan and my mother never knew?" Tommy asked.

"No. Your father knew the chances were very slim, and he didn't want to get their hopes up. It's bad enough to deal with your death once, never mind twice." He paused a moment then continued, "Ernie was a good man and an ever better husband and father."

"Did he visit me while I was here?" Tommy asked.

Sadly, the doctor smiled, "For the first year or so, he visited you religiously. After a while, though, it got too much for him. His visits became less and less. It certainly wasn't because he didn't care anymore…it was because he cared too much. We both had moments when we questioned if what we were doing was the right thing. He made me promise that no matter what ever happened to him, I should keep the faith. I'm glad I did."

Tommy straightened his posture and as the color came back into his face, he looked Dr. Zimarchi in the eyes and thanked him one last time then left.

About halfway down the walkway, Tommy heard the pitter-patter of tiny feet behind him. He turned around to find Paco standing there. With his little arms outreached, he handed Tommy a book. He took it from him and read the title out loud, *The Power of Positive Thinking'*?

Dr. Zimarchi's voice echoed from the doorway, "Your father would sit and read that to you each time he visited. I thought you might want to have it."

***

With the book tightly in hand, he climbed on his bike and pedaled off. Big Blue seemed to be on auto-pilot, leading him where he needed to go – the cemetery.

The last time he was actually in the cemetery was Easter 1988. That was when they did their annual family trip to pay their respects to their grandparents.

He came upon their headstones first. "Hi, Nana. Hi, Grampa. I suppose it's okay to tell you that it's me, Tommy. Then again, you probably already know that. And you probably know why I haven't visited you in a long time." He thought about that for a moment, and then admitted, "Not that I can say I would have on my own – I was a bit of a shit. I'm sorry. And I still am, I guess; this is my first time coming to see Dad." He sighed, and faced their headstone. "Nana, you died when I was little, so I don't remember much except for the smell of your perfume. I smelled it the other day where Mom lives.

Now I remember why it seemed familiar. That was you, wasn't it? — Grandpa, you raised a good man that I was lucky enough to call my father, even if I didn't always appreciate him. I do now, though. That still carries some weight, right?"

After ten minutes of visiting with them, he knew he was just putting off the inevitable; his true reason for being there. Finally, he took a deep breath and turned to his right and hesitantly approached his father's headstone.

Ernie Stevens 1947 – 2010

Loving Husband & Father

For the longest time, he just stood there, frozen, staring at the engraved words. His heart felt empty yet full at the same time, and he did his best to fight the urge to allow even one tear from his eye. At last, he broke the silence.

"Hey, Dad. It's me, Tommy. I'm sorry I haven't been by sooner. I'm not so good at saying the right things. As a matter of fact, I'm usually only good at saying the wrong things." He took another long, sad pause before continuing. "I still can't believe this whole crazy thing was your idea. I don't think you've ever done an illegal thing in your life. And I really can't believe you were able to keep this from Mom all those years. You never kept anything from her."

The emotions were too much. He couldn't hold back any longer. Tears poured down his cheek. As memories of his dad flashed through his mind, he placed his forehead on the headstone and balled his eyes out. It was the most he had cried since...he couldn't even remember the last time he cried that much. When his cathartic tears came to a stop, he raised his head and gently placed his hand on the stone.

"I'm so sorry for all the crap I put you and Mom through." He took a reflective pause then continued, "Like the time I fed the neighbors' dog ex-lax. How was I supposed to know you agreed to dog-sit that weekend? And I'm really sorry about the time you were fixing the kitchen pipes, and I switched your plumbers putty with the KY jelly I found in your room. The kitchen pipes leaked for a week, and your pipes were stuck for a week." Tommy couldn't help but chuckle out loud. "Anyway, I just wanted to stop by and tell you thanks. Thanks for devising a highly illegal and immoral scheme to leave me in the hands of a mafia dude and his little Mexican sidekick. I'm just kidding, Pops. I'm glad you didn't give up hope, and starting from this point on, I promise to make the most of it. I promise."

Tommy released his hand from the headstone, but before he turned to walk away, he spoke one last thing to his father, "Oh, and thanks for being the best Dad in the world. I'm sorry it took so long for me to tell you that. And I promise, I'm going to read this book. Thank you. I'll keep it forever."

As he turned to leave, something caught the corner of his eye. Off to his right was another gravestone – his gravestone.

Tommy James Stevens 1970 – 1988

Beloved Son & Brother

Tommy felt like he'd been punched in the gut. He was surprised at how hard it hit him. He thought to himself, if it was this hard for him to see his headstone, how hard must it have been for everyone else? For ... *his mother.*

***

Over the last few weeks, Vince had become a recognizable figure at the home. Not only did the nurses and attendants know him by name, but they were touched that this old friend of Alan's voluntarily spent so much time visiting Mrs. Stevens. Depending on the day, she either remembered him as Vince, an old friend of Alan's, or more times than not, as the cable guy come to fix the TV. And on some days, like today, she confused him with both.

When he first arrived, she complained that the television picture was too blurry and that he should gather his tools and fix it before the *Ellen Show* came on. Tommy's tools of choice for this fix – paper towels and Windex. Once again, Mrs. Stevens hailed him as a TV genius, and once again, she pointed out that his boss needed to give him a raise.

Somewhere between then and Ellen dancing her way to her chair, Mrs. Stevens said, "Oh, you just missed Alan and his son." Tommy realized he had been switched from being the cable guy to being Alan's friend Vince once again. "They had to leave for work. I didn't realize he worked in a restaurant." Tommy looked at her blankly then it dawned on him - *the tuxedos.* She didn't notice his confused look as she went on, "I hope he brings something back for me. I love Italian."

As they watched the *Ellen Show*, Tommy played cards with his mother. She liked that. Usually, it was Mrs. Stevens' focus that was a bit scattered, but today, it was obvious that something was weighing heavy on Tommy's mind.

After watching him stare blankly out the window for several moments, Mrs. Stevens cleared her throat and spoke, "If you're going to play cards with someone it's usually polite to actually pay attention."

He turned his attention back to his mother, "I'm sorry," he apologized.

"Girl problems?" she asked.

Tommy shrugged, "More like life problems."

She glanced at her cards then spoke, "Fix your girl problems and your life problems will fall into place. Or maybe it's the other way around. Either way, if you follow your heart you can't go wrong."

"I wish it was that simple," he sighed. They continued playing their card game. A few minutes later, Tommy asked, "Can I ask you a weird question? Do you think a person can change? Like, *really* change?"

Her focus remained on her cards. Finally, she placed them on the table and proclaimed, "Gin! I win again."

It was obvious to Tommy that not only didn't she hear his question, but she was in no frame of mind to answer it anyway - especially since they were playing Crazy 8's and not Gin. Tommy offered up a sad, yet polite smile then stood up.

"Well, I should probably get going," he said as he began picking up the cards.

She clicked off the TV then spoke clearly, "No. No I don't." Tommy gave her a puzzled look as she continued, "I don't think people can change who they really are. Not here," she put her hand to her heart. "I think the true essence of a person will remain the same. Whether good or bad."

He continued gathering up the cards and murmured, "I guess now I just have to figure out which one I am…good or bad." This caused Mrs. Stevens to laugh out loud. "It's not really funny. I'm facing a major dilemma here!" snapped Tommy.

Her laughter slowed and she quietly spoke, "If your dilemma revolves around you figuring out if your essence is good or bad then let me ease your mind. It's good. Definitely good." It was obvious by his fake appreciative smile that he didn't believe her. "What? You don't believe me? You think I'm just a crazy old lady, don't you?"

"No I don't. I appreciate your kindness and all, but the truth is, you don't even know me." Mrs. Stevens stood and walked towards him. Hesitantly, he continued, "I just don't see"… She moved closer, gently placing her hands on his cheeks. Unsure of what was going on, and a bit uncomfortable, Tommy stuttered, "I…I just don't see how you can know for sure that…my essence is good, that's all."

Her eyes looked directly into his, and as she sweetly smiled, her voice broke, "Because a mother always knows. She always knows."

A chill ran through his entire body, leaving him shocked and speechless. He returned her warm smile, and as they both stood there staring, tears formed in each of their eyes. They stared for what seemed like an eternity before resuming collecting up the cards. Finally, Tommy handed her the deck, smiled then started to leave. Before he left the room, he turned back around to offer his mom another loving look. Unfortunately, his look wasn't reciprocated.

"Well?" she impatiently said, "Are you going to fix the TV or what?"

Sadly, Tommy realized her moment of clarity had already passed. He returned to his mother's side, picked up the remote, and turned the television back on. An appreciative smile returned to her face. "They really need to give you a raise," she said. Tommy returned her smile then left.

***

Tommy was drained. Physically and emotionally drained. He didn't have the energy or the strength to continue pedaling around town on Big Blue, so he headed home. The house was quiet. He had just missed Alan and Richie, who had left minutes earlier. As he walked by the bathroom, the pungent smell of Alan's after shave still hung in the air. Tommy knew that smell anywhere. It was Old Spice; just like their dad used to use. The memory of Mr. Stevens teaching Tommy how to shave for the first time also hung in the air. It seemed like a lifetime ago, yet, just like yesterday.

With a full box of Chicken in a Biskit in hand, Tommy entered his bedroom and fell on his bed. His mind was racing a mile a minute; his dad, his mom, Gina. What he needed was to drown out the thoughts. What he needed was to crank on some tunes. He walked over to his wall of cassettes looking for something loud and distracting. When nothing fit his mood, he moved onto a shoebox of random mix-tapes he had under his bed. None of them were in cases, and all of them had unique titles scrawled across the front of one side in his handwriting (if you could call it that): TOMMY'S FUCK THE WORLD MIX, and TOMMY'S ROCK YA HEAD OFF MIX, and BON JOVI RULES MIX. *Unique*, he laughed. Unique and creative. TOMMY'S I WANNA ROCK AND ROLL ALL NIGHT MIX. *Yeah, he came up with that on his own!* A couple of the tapes were useless, the ribbons pulled way out and in a tangled mess together.

One tape caught his eye. *It was in a case.* Without looking closely at it, he knew what it was. It was the last mix Gina had made him. Tommy pulled it out slowly and stared at it. He gazed at the song list – more specifically, at Gina's beautifully perfect handwriting. It had been the same from the first day they met...from the first note she passed to him in math class.

Tommy reached in his drawer and grabbed a handful of old pictures of him and Gina. He popped in the tape, laid on his bed, and listened. Like, really listened. Every song, every word. The songs, mixed with the old photographs, brought tears to his eyes. Gina was the best thing that ever happened to him, and he fucked it up - twice.

Tommy's pity party really peaked when their prom song, "Somebody" by Depeche Mode came on. He rewound and listened to it three times, blubbering like a baby with each listen.

He knew what he had to do. He needed to follow the doctor's advice and go tell Gina the truth again, and this time, make her believe.

TRACK 27

Emma planned on sleeping in the morning of the prom. There was no point in pretending that anything else would get done that day. That suited Gina, because she needed that time to put her parent face on. She needed to mask the pain caused by memories of her own prom night, and she needed to be able to smile fully for Emma and her prom night. She sat at her kitchen table, her forehead propped on her left hand while her right hand idly spun the spoon in her mug, and she watched the coffee swirl round and round.

She remembered everything about her own prom day in full detail. She'd waited so long for it, planned her dress well in advance ...what a beautiful dress ...

When a girl gets ready for a special event, it takes a long time because she needs to feel that every last detail is perfect. That can actually be quite stressful on its own, and it's even worse when she has cause to worry about the event itself. Gina's emotions were all over the spectrum that day, between wanting to look perfect to worrying about Tommy. *Will he have a tuxedo? Will he be high or drunk? Will he even show up?* The sweet thought of *I want to look perfect for him*, the anxious *I hope he likes how I look*, to the brazen, *he better like how I look!* From *I hope he appreciates how much work I put into this*, to *Am I wasting my time putting so much into this?* And underneath all of those thoughts is one recurring litany of *I want this night to be special*, thought both determinedly and as a plea.

That night she'd been so angry with Tommy, and then … and then … *why was she doing this to herself? Vince! Fucking Vince! What kind of fucking asshole would do that to a person? Pretend to be someone's dead boyfriend? And why, of all people, was she ever even interested in him?*

Gina dropped her head down onto the table with a dejected *thump*, then banged it a second time for good measure.

A noise from the other room had her sitting up straight in her chair – *Emma's awake.* She took three deep breaths, ran her fingers quickly through her hair, wiped her eyes, and gave herself a stern lecture. *This is Emma's special day and a great mother/daughter bonding day. That is all that matters today. And no one is going to interfere with that, not if I can help it!*

When Emma burst into the kitchen with an armload of beauty products and dumped them on the table in front of her, the smile she gave to her daughter was real.

"Let's do this!" she said excitedly.

A number of hours later, Gina was scrolling through the pictures she took of Emma and Richie on her phone. Like any good parent in the new millennium, she posted her favorites to Facebook, Instagram, Twittter, etc. Emma, of course, was the most beautiful girl, and she and Richie looked adorable together. Out of the 50 or 60 pictures she took (the kids were so patient with her and Alan while they fussed and gushed and posed them), she only posted ten of them and had it narrowed down to two that she was going to print out and frame. Then she dutifully checked out the pictures her friends posted of their kids on their way to prom, liking and commenting her way down her newsfeed.

This would have been so cool to have back when we were in high school!--

BAM! That one thought was all it took to bring every lost, angry, lonely and painful thought back to the forefront, as if they had been held back by a tensely coiled spring that let them loose all at once. Like the crowds that wait outside a retail store hours before it opens on Black Friday, her negative thoughts pushed and shoved their way in all at once through that small opening, trampling her temporary peace in the process. And just as fast, Gina grabbed her keys and purse and was out the door. Tonight she needed something much stronger than red wine. Little did she know, as she pulled out of the driveway, that Tommy was enroute to her house.

***

By the time Tommy pedaled the 2.7 miles to her house, he was surprisingly *not* out of breath. The past few weeks of riding his bike around town had proved to be just what his body needed. Without over-thinking what he was going to say, Tommy rushed up the steps and pounded on the door. No answer. She must have seen it was him, he thought as he continued to knock. After three minutes of simultaneously knocking and ringing the bell, Tommy decided to peer in the windows. A peeping Tom, if you will. Literally.

The house was quiet and dark. Not one light was on. He rushed around to the driveway. Emma's car was there, but Gina's was gone. *Fuck! What if she was out on a date*, he thought. With his head in his hands, he slumped against a large pine tree, and as he stared at Emma's car it hit him; *it was Prom Night*. Not only was this Emma's prom night, it was the 25th anniversary of his own prom…the 25th anniversary of the accident. There's no way Gina would be out on a date tonight.

The anniversary mixed with the fact that a week earlier Tommy had devastated her by digging up old wounds, there was definitely no way she was on a date. Tommy put himself in her shoes. If a tough day at work drove Gina to partake in a glass or three of wine, then what would a night like this drive her to? Before his thought was even finished, he had jumped on his bike and headed towards the nearest bar.

***

There were three bars spread out across the town, and Tommy was determined to hit all of them, if need be. As luck would have it – it need be. Not only was the third one the furthest, it had the most incline hills to get there. Tommy might have been in better shape than three weeks ago, but the final steep hill did him in. By the time he reached the third bar, he had spaghetti legs and literally fell off his bike into the dirt parking lot. The knees on his jeans were ripped, and his forearm was scrapped and bloodied, but no one saw him fall, so at least his pride was intact.

The bar looked dingy and run-down. The sight of all the mud-covered trucks said all that needed to be said about the type of cliental inside. Tommy's bloodied arm throbbed, but as he scanned the parking lot, his pain quickly disappeared. There, between two Chevy pickups was a dark blue Honda Accord. Gina's Honda Accord.

Inside the dive bar, Gina sat alone, nursing a vodka. She wasn't the only girl in the bar, but she was easily the best looking (and the only one with all of her teeth). She had only been there five minutes, but already put several guy's advances to shame. Her eyes, like daggers, pierced the soul of every pathetic guy who attempted to hit on her. The fifth guy didn't even get a chance to utter a word. Before he spoke, Gina spouted, "Not interested. Fuck off!"

The sixth guy, however, seemed undeterred by her daggers and venom, and strutted his way towards her. It was Otto. He wore his filthy gas station shirt (with his name on it). In one hand, he had his jean jacket slung over his shoulder, in the other, a can of Pabst Blue Ribbon. From the dimly lit pool table in the back, his dirt bag friends watched him in action.

"Aww, drinking all by yourself, Gina?" His voice was like nails down a chalkboard.

"Fuck off, Otto!"

"How about we fuck off together?" he snickered and put his arm around her.

The feel of his touch sent shivers up her body (not the good kind). In one swift motion she pushed his arm off of her shoulder. "Keep your filthy hands to yourself. You disgust me. You always have."

"I love when you get all feisty," he said as he again returned his arm around her.

"The lady said get your hands off of her," a voice boomed from behind. Both Otto and Gina turned around to see Tommy standing there.

Gina wasn't impressed. She simply rolled her eyes and wondered if this night could get any worse. Otto was even less impressed or intimidated. He was actually amused. "Well, well, well, it's Alan Stevens' fat, homo lover. Why don't you beat it, fag, this doesn't concern you. He gave Tommy a poke in the chest then turned his attention back to Gina.

Tommy stood still, mumbling under his breath, "I'm not fat…just a little husky."

"So, where were we, sweetheart?" Otto said to Gina.

Again, Tommy's voice boomed from behind, "You were about to leave her alone."

I've fucking had enough of you look fell on Otto's face as he shook his head in irritation. By the time Otto turned around, his look was replaced with a fake smile. He politely addressed Tommy, "You know what, buddy, you're right. She's not worth my time. I'm outta here."

Holy shit, Tommy thought. I *not only just stood up to Otto Kringeman, but I scared him off.* Tommy fought back a boastful smile as he watched Otto start to put on his jean jacket.

"Do you mind holding my beer while I put my jacket on?" Otto asked. Tommy, still swimming in victory, obliged him by holding Otto's PBR. "Actually, could you hold my jacket for a second while I pay my tab?" Again, Tommy obliged. When both of Tommy's hands were occupied, Otto proceeded to sucker punch him dead in the gut. As he doubled over in pain, Otto smoothly retrieved his beer and jacket.

While Tommy was on his knees attempting to catch his breath, he began mumbling to himself (in a southern accent), "Deep breaths. Deep breaths. Ten, nine, eight"...

Otto pounded his beer then turned to Gina. At that point, she'd had enough. She put money down for her bill and started to leave. She gave Tommy a confused, yet semi-sympathetic look. Otto, on the other hand, received her most venomous stare down.

"What?" Otto smiled. "It's not my fault he's a little slow on the uptake. You've gotta be brain dead not to see that one coming."

Hearing Otto's brain-dead comment, caused Tommy's countdown to stop at three. His embarrassed reddened face was now red with anger. Tommy clenched his fists, slowly stood up, and tapped Otto on his shoulder. When Otto turned around, he was met with Tommy's fist square in his nose. Otto dropped to the floor like a sack of potatoes (Maine potatoes). Tommy's fist throbbed, but it hurt so good. *So fucking good*, thought Tommy.

Tommy turned to see Gina's reaction, but she was already out the door. Before he could go after her, however, he found himself being surrounded by Otto's new minions. It was four against one. Well, five against one…Otto was back on his feet (and pissed). It wasn't long before they had backed Tommy into the corner of the bar by the pool table. The handful of customers who were there, moved to the other side of the bar to give them more room to fight (how nice of them).

Otto wiped the blood from his nose then pulled out a switchblade. Tommy's first thought should have been, *Oh shit, he's gonna cut me up*, but it wasn't. His first thought was, *Who the hell still carries a switchblade? Seriously, even in the 80's that was outdated.* Otto moved closer. His dirt bag friends moved closer. Tommy's right hand clutched at a pool stick. His left grasped a pool ball.

What happened next came as a shock to everyone in the bar - including Tommy. The fight that was about to take place would be talked about for years to come. Let's just say, not only did Paco enjoy *Jeopardy, Dr. Phil*, and Spanish soap operas, but apparently Paco loved him some Jackie Chan.

The dive bar brawl lasted only 3 minutes and 18 seconds, but to those who witnessed it, it was Kung Fu poetry in motion. Chairs, pool sticks, and multiple pool balls were all effectively used by Tommy. He even used Otto's jean jacket as a weapon of mass (and comical) destruction. At one point, Tommy jumped up, and while doing a split in mid-air, kicked two of Otto's minions at the same time. They tumbled to the ground, leaving just Otto and Tommy. Mano a Mano.

Otto still held his switchblade. Tommy held the 8 ball. They stared each other down in anticipation of someone making the first move. Finally, Tommy relaxed his pose and shrugged at Otto. "Ya know what," Tommy spoke, "you're not worth it." With that he gently tossed the 8 ball high in the air to Otto. Of course, Otto did what any moron would do; he took his eyes off of Tommy and reached up to catch the pool ball. Before the 8 ball fell into his hand, Tommy performed a front kick directly into Otto's nuts. Needless to say, all three balls fell onto the floor.

Still stunned by what they just witnessed, the small crowd began clapping. Hesitantly at first, but quickly turned it into a rousing ovation for Tommy. Tommy looked down at his five beaten foes, gratefully whispered a thank you to Paco, then spoke aloud, "Let that be a lesson to you! Tommy Stevens is back, bitches!" And in true cheesy Kung Fu movie fashion, Tommy's words didn't match his lips.

With no time to relish in his victory, Tommy rushed outside, in hopes of catching Gina before she left. He was in luck. She was leaning against her car door with tears running down her cheeks. As soon as she saw Tommy approaching, she wiped her tears and clumsily fumbled for her keys.

"Gina, wait, "Tommy yelled. "I know it's hard to believe, and I know this whole thing sounds crazy, but it's true. I'm Tommy Stevens."

"Why are you doing this to me?" Gina's voice trembled as she fumbled with her keys trying to unlock the door.

By now, Tommy stood directly behind her. "I swear I didn't mean to hurt you again. I swear. What can I say, I'm a fuckin' idiot. I was an idiot to buy you Whitesnake tickets for your birthday. Even more of an idiot to ever let Otto have so much influence on me. I was just scared...scared of losing you...scared of not having a future. Dating you was the only thing I ever did that was right. And I even managed to fuck that up too. And it kills me, absolutely kills me that you blamed yourself for the accident.

With tears still flowing, Gina slowly turned around. "It can't be you. It can't. I went to your funeral. I saw them bury you."

"It wasn't me. The whole thing was my dad's idea. Not even my mom knew. He secretly partnered with some mafia doctor and"... Gina looked at him in disbelief. "I know this all sounds crazy, but it's true. It took many reconstructive face surgeries and twenty-five years of...of *hope*, but all I know is a month ago a miracle happened. And I'm determined not to fuck it up...not this time." Slowly, Tommy wiped away Gina's tears and looked her in the eyes. "I know your favorite flower is the lily. I know your favorite album in junior high was Prince's "Purple Rain". And I know that cabbage makes your farts stink. Like, really stink." Although embarrassed, Gina couldn't help but chuckle. "And I know your favorite movie used to be "Valley Girl" with Nicolas Cage. You always said it reminded you of our relationship. Every time we went to Paras Pizza down at the beach, you used to play "I Melt with You" on the jukebox."

The twinkle in her eyes told Tommy that she was almost swayed. Almost. She still had her doubts. "But what about the other night in my living room? I know I don't have the same body as twenty-five years ago, but I still look pretty good. The Tommy that I knew would have been all over this shit."

Tommy's eyes looked her up and down as he replied, "Trust me, I totally wanted to be all over that shit. Totally. As a matter of fact, I thought about your body all night in bed while I was…um, anyway, what I'm trying to say is as much as I wanted you, I just couldn't. I needed to wait for things to clear up first."

A surprised look appeared on her face as she disturbingly gazed at his crotch.

Tommy quickly realized that she misunderstood him. "Oh God no! Not *disease* cleared up. I meant getting my *life* cleared up." Gina let out a sigh of relief. "And for the record, Gina, your body is just as rockin' as back in high school. More so."

Gina blushed then looked him deep in the eyes, "Is it really you, Tommy?"

"I swear it is," he said. "How else can I prove it to you?"

She pondered a second, then set her sights back on his crotch. "The tattoo," she smirked.

"Of course." he said smacking his head. "The tattoo. Why didn't I think of that?" Tommy scanned the parking lot, and when he saw that no one was around, he unbuckled his pants. He prefaced his undressing with, "Just keep in mind it's a little chilly outside tonight." With his 'shrinkage warning' in place, his pants and underwear fell to his ankles.

Gina's eyes widened, for there before her was the microphone tattoo. "Tommy! It really is you!"

Before they could share in this revelation, a car sped into the parking lot and skidded to a stop. Ricky and Brett jumped out and sprinted towards Tommy and Gina.

"He really *is* Tommy," Gina yelled to them.

"We know!" returned Ricky.

"You know?" Tommy exclaimed.

"Gina came to us last week saying that you were claiming to be Tommy," Brett said.

Tommy looked over at Gina. She shrugged. "I tried contacting Alan first, but he wasn't returning any of my calls."

"Something didn't seem right about you from day one," Ricky said. "And even though we agreed with Gina that you were just a nut job, we had to be sure."

"That's why we broke into your house the other night," added Brett. "To get some samples."

"Samples?" Tommy asked. "Samples of what?"

"Drew some blood. Swabbed your mouth. Took your fingerpri…" Before Brett could get the word out of his mouth, he and Ricky looked down at Tommy. His pants were still around his ankles.

Both guys smacked themselves in the head and simultaneously

exclaimed, "The tattoo!"

"We didn't even think of pulling down your underwear to check," Ricky said.

"Although," interrupted Brett, "we probably wouldn't have anyway. You looked like you were having quite the *happy* dream, if you know what I mean." Gina smirked. Tommy turned red with embarrassment. "Anyway," continued Brett, "we took everything up to the CSI lab and just got the results back. You are indeed Tommy Stevens!"

"It would have been nice if you showed up five minutes ago with this information," Tommy said as he embarrassingly pulled his pants back up. "FYI…it's a very, very chilly night!"

After a few moments of awkward silence, everyone burst out laughing and engaged in a long overdue group hug. Smiles, hugs, high fives, fist bumps, and even tears of joy were exchanged by all four of them.

When their nostalgia-fest subsided, Tommy addressed his friends, "I know I have a lot of explaining to do to all of you, and I promise I will - but not tonight. Tonight we all have plans!" All three friends looked confused. "Tonight, we have a prom to go to!"

All three looked at each other and laughed. "They're not going to let us in," Ricky said.

"Oh yes they will," Tommy replied. "I have connections." Tommy turned to Brett, "Get your wife on the phone and tell her to get her ass down her ASAP! That goes for you too, Ricky." Seeing he was serious, Ricky and Brett smiled, nodded then dialed their phones.

Tommy then turned his attention to Gina. "And you! You need to head home and put on your sexiest dress and wait for me. I have a few things I need to take care of."

Gina's eyes sparkled, and her smile was as big as Tommy had even seen. She still thought she was dreaming as Tommy opened her car door for her. Before she got in, she turned to Tommy and said, "You're not gonna stand me up again, are you?"

"Not a chance, Gina. Not a chance!"

TRACK 28

Considering the late hour and the last minute notice, Ricky and Brett weren't clad in tux's, but rather in khakis, dress shirts, and ties. It was a far cry from Ricky's normal new-age-peace-love and understanding-type attire, and Brett's jeans, and wrinkled-free T-shirt (tucked) look. It was quite the antithesis of their *I don't give a shit look* from twenty-five years ago.

Their wives wore cute dresses, and Alan found them to be 'utterly delightful' (exact words). Their fun, delightful personalities were only matched by their drop-dead gorgeous looks. Alan was impressed. He was also depressed.

As he looked around at all the happy couples in the room, he couldn't help feeling lonely and jealous. Alan, like Tommy, never got to experience the prom. It wasn't that Alan didn't go to his prom, because he did. He just didn't go with an actual date. He went stag with his three best friends.

There was definitely a stigma and double standard attached to this. If a bunch of girls go together, they're admired; the whole *we don't need dates to have a fun time*. When a bunch of dudes show up together, the responses are a bit different. *Look at those fuckin' losers! They couldn't get a date!* Equally as popular back then was the sexual preference type comments. Needless to say, Alan and his friends immediately regretted attending. Unfortunately, they were forced to stay for its entirety because Stuart's mom wasn't going to pick them up until it was over. Yup, none of them had their license. They spent the whole night huddled in the corner talking about video games, comic books, and of course, quantum physics. So basically for them, the prom was just a formal lunch table scene.

Tonight's prom was definitely not as tragic for Alan, nowhere close, actually. Yes he was lonely, but he was also overwhelmed with happiness and gratitude. His little boy had turned into a handsome, good-hearted gentleman, and was dancing with his beautiful girlfriend. Alan was also thankful for his new-found friendship and acceptance with Ricky and Brett. Most of all, Alan was happy to have his brother back, and even happier that the secret would soon be released to the world.

He probably wouldn't admit it, but he was anxiously excited to see Tommy and Gina walk through the doors of the prom together. He knew how much they had been through, and he knew they deserved tonight. Alan's anticipation would have to wait a little longer, for Tommy would arrive fashionably late (literally).

Finally, at 9:32 PM, Tommy and Gina walked hand in hand into the prom. Gina wore a stunning black dress, and her hair and makeup were done to perfection. She looked 18 again (well, maybe 28ish). At first, Emma was shocked to see her mother enter the prom, but after seeing how happy she looked, Emma was overjoyed that Gina and Vince were there together. Emma and Richie didn't find out the truth about Vince until after the prom that night. The rest of the world found out the next day.

Tommy and Gina were met at the door by their friends and family. Everyone was in awe of Gina's youthful beauty, but it was Tommy's *look* that stole the show. He was dressed exactly like Alan (sort of). He wore a white shirt, black bow tie, and a classic black tux. The only difference was that Tommy's tux was three times too small. The sleeves were ¾ length, and his pants looked like he was waiting for a flood (a really high flood).

Tommy smiled ruefully, "It was the only size they had available."

After all the hugs, kisses, and pats on the back, Tommy had a private moment with his brother. "Thanks again, Alan, for letting us all in tonight. It means a lot."

"I know it does," Alan said as he hugged Tommy.

When the two brothers pulled away from their embrace, Alan continued to smirk at Tommy's outfit.

"Not another word, Alan," Tommy ordered.

"I'm just surprised you found a tux store open at this hour."

Tommy smiled, "Luckily, I know someone with connections."

"Ah, Dr. Zimarchi, huh?" Alan said knowingly.

"Yup," Tommy nodded, "but luckily for you, he's not the only one with connections."

"What's that supposed to mean?" Alan asked.

"It means thanks to your big brother, you have an official prom date tonight."

Confused and worried, Alan stared at Tommy and slowly said, "What. Did. You. Do?"

"Just what you didn't have the balls to do – ask your coffee chick to the prom." Before Alan could say a word, Mia entered from behind Tommy. She wore a ruby-red dress, and like Gina, her hair and makeup were flawless. Alan's mouth dropped open. He was surprised, and frozen, and a bit gassy. Tommy had to physically nudge Alan towards her. Once face to face with her, all Alan could do was repeat the same phrase over and over, "Wow, you look amazing, Mia."

It was Mia who broke his sweet, repetitive phrase with, "Would you like to dance?" All Alan managed was an excited nod yes.

Their slow dance consisted of plenty of glowing smiles from Mia as she kept telling Alan how nice this was. Alan just gushed and said, "Wow, you really do look amazing, Mia."

It took nearly a song and a half for Alan to unclench his butt cheeks and relax and have a normal conversation with her. By then, the rest of the gang joined them on the dance floor; Richie and Emma, Ricky and Brett and their wives, and yes, Tommy and Gina. The prom was perfect.

As the night wound down, Tommy excused himself from his friends and walked over to the DJ. The DJ looked like he himself was still in high school. He wore a suit jacket with a Bob Marley shirt underneath. His dreadlocked hair was past his shoulders, and his wrists were full of hemp-made bracelets.

Normally, Tommy would have started the conversation with some wise-ass comment, but he knew he'd need this pothead as an ally. "Hey, any chance you could do me a favor and play a song?"

"Right on, dude. You like a chaperone or something?"

"Yea, something like that," Tommy answered. "Can you play "Somebody" by Depeche Mode? It was my old prom song."

"Sorry, dude, Jamie doesn't have any Depeche Mode. They were never my bag, dude. Jamie could play you some Phish though."

Tommy's irritation level grew. The only thing worse than a hippy-lovin' pothead was one who referred to themselves in the first person. Tommy felt Gina watching him from across the room. Her curiosity was piqued. Tommy's patience wore thin, but before he could tell the DJ where to stick his Phish song, it hit him: Gina's mixed tape! He had it in his pocket.

Without wasting another second, he reached into his tight pockets and pulled out the tape and shoved it into the DJ's face. "Here! The song is on here! Last song. Side B."

The DJ took the tape and began to carefully look it over. His eyes were mesmerized by this archaic plastic thingy that contained music. "Whoa, dude. I've heard about these things, but I've never actually held one."

Tommy noticed Gina making her way over. "Can you just play the song? Please," Tommy desperately urged.

The DJ's eyes widened in amusement, "You want me to play *this*? Is that a joke?"

"No, but your face is!" Tommy snapped. Gina was fast approaching. Tommy knew his time was almost up. In one final attempt, he turned back to the DJ to beg, but when he turned, he noticed the DJ curiously smelling the tape. "You're supposed to play it, not smoke it, ya idiot!" Tommy snatched the tape from his hands.

By now, Gina had arrived. "Everything okay over here?"

The DJ responded first, "I think you need tell your boyfriend dude to get with the times. All of us real DJ's have all of our music on this." He motioned to a laptop. You also might wanna help him with his tux size next time, dude."

"Stop calling everybody dude!" screamed Tommy. It was all he could do from reaching over and ripping out his dreads.

Gina gently placed her hand on Tommy's back. "Calm down, Tommy. What exactly is going on here?"

Reluctantly, Tommy held up the tape. "I was trying to get him to play our prom song."

She took one look at the old mix tape and tears formed in her eyes. "The tape I made you," she whispered in wonder.

Tommy's voice sounded worn out and defeated, "I just wanted tonight to be perfect for you."

Gina placed a kiss on his cheek and whispered, "Why don't you head over to your friends, okay? I'll take care of this." He started to argue, but she put her finger to his lips and motioned him to leave. Tommy shuffled back over to his friends and watched Gina chat up the DJ. The DJ scanned his laptop and gave Gina a high-as-a-kite-nod and thumbs up.

Gina made her way over to a very curious Tommy. Before he could question her, Beyonce's voice faded out and the DJ's voice faded in. "Okay, dudes, time to slow things down with an 80's throwback tune. Here's some classic Bon Jovi for Gina and Tommy."

As "Never say Goodbye" blared out, Gina took Tommy by the hand and led him onto the empty floor, and they began their official prom dance. Emma and Richie warmly smiled at them, then both looked at each other confused and simultaneously said, "Who's Tommy?"

Ricky, Brett and their wives were the first to join them, followed by Alan, Mia, Richie, and Emma. Before long, dozens of other happy couples joined in. Tommy and Gina didn't even notice the crowd, for their eyes were only on one another.

"I know it's twenty-five years too late," Tommy said, "but I'm sorry for being such a jackass back then."

"It's ok, Tommy. I just have so many questions."

"I know, and I promise I'll explain everything to you. I also promise to spend the rest of my life treating you the way you deserve to be. The way I shoulda treated you back in high school." He tightened his grip on her, looking at her from head to toe. "You really do look beautiful tonight, Gina."

"You don't look so bad yourself," Gina said.

"Who are you kidding? I look ridiculous."

"Not at all," smiled Gina, "I think it's sweet you went through all the trouble to get a real tux for tonight. And I'm very touched that you tried to get our old prom song played."

"Speaking of which," Tommy questioned, "what's up with this song choice? I thought you hated Bon Jovi?"

"Eh, their music isn't so bad. Not to mention, he's pretty easy on the eyes. I just hated that you always put them before me."

Tommy looked into her eyes and said, "Never again. Never again." They continued their dance and Tommy added, "Jon Bon Jovi really did age well, didn't he?"

"He REALLY has," gushed Gina. They both laughed then spent the rest of the night on the dance floor in each other's arms.

BONUS TRACK

Just six short months later, wedding bells rang out in the church in York's village. It was a small, intimate wedding; family and close friends only. The church was aglow with smiles and happy tears. Most of the tears were shed by Alan. He couldn't control himself when he saw his beautiful bride walk down the aisle. Luckily, his *two* best men came prepared with a plethora of tissues.

As Alan and Mia said their vows, Tommy's attention was focused on his own future wife, Gina. She sat in the second row looking as radiant and beautiful as ever. They shared a warm, loving look, then, in true Tommy fashion, he shot her a goofy, silly, contorted facial expression. Gina couldn't help herself, she LOL'd. Yup, no one could make Gina laugh like Tommy.

Perhaps the biggest and brightest smile in room was on Mrs. Stevens' face. Sadly, her good days were few and far between, but thankfully, for all involved, today was one of her good days – one of her best days. For there in front of her, stood her two baby boys and her most precious grandson. Her memory only lasted a short while that day, but while it did, she remembered only good memories. And best of all, she remembered her own wedding day – the day she married her sweet, beloved Ernie.

The wedding ceremony was followed by a wild, raucous reception. Well, as wild as a non-alcoholic (coffee bar only) reception could be. About halfway through the celebration, Tommy unveiled his wedding gift to his baby brother. Tommy, Brett, and Ricky reformed their original band and performed a beautiful medley of Richard Marx songs. Alan was deeply moved (as in, more tears).

Of course, about a third of the way through "Hold onto the Night," the band broke into Bon Jovi's "Livin' on a Prayer." The next 45 minutes were spent rockin' out to classic 80's hair band tunes including the original ballad Brett had written back in high school. The whole day was perfect and was only matched by Tommy and Gina's own wedding the following spring.

***

In the months following the revelation that Tommy was indeed alive, the small seaside town of York, Maine was infiltrated with investigators, reporters, and investigative reporters. Mysteriously, Dr. Zimarchi's house burned to the ground the morning after the prom. The story Tommy told authorities didn't involve the Russians or even the Canadians, and there was no mention of kidnapping, the mafia, or bad guys in general. Instead, Tommy talked of true heroes and of guardian angels.

People thought his story was insane, but they ate it up. Tommy turned into a major celebrity. He even replaced that famous astronaut dude as the town's most famous person. He had appearance offers from Good Morning America, the Today Show, the Tonight Show, and every show in between. Graciously, he turned them all down. The only thing he was interested in was spending time with his family, his friends, and of course, with the only true love of his life, Gina.

Countless authors clamored for his book rights, but Tommy rejected them all. There was only one writer he trusted. Gina. "Livin' on a Prayer – The Untold Tommy & Gina Story would be her first official published novel. Producers by the dozens begged for the movie rights to his story. The best offer came from Happy Madison Productions. They wanted Kevin James to star as Tommy, and not only was Adam Sandler going to play Otto, but they got Christopher Walken to play Dr. Zimarchi and Chuy from *Chelsey Lately* to play Paco.

Tommy did allow one exclusive interview. It wasn't Barbara Walters. It wasn't Oprah Winfrey. And it certainly wasn't Geraldo Rivera. The one on one was reserved for one person only – Dr. Phil. The interview was not only prime time, but was live.

Dr. Phil sat engrossed as Tommy told his whole wacky, unbelievable story. He particularly enjoyed the part about how the little person named Paco used to watch his show. Dr. Phil was tickled pink about the whole *verbal osmosis* theory. Tommy finished his tale with a Dr. Phil-esque quote, "…and I was like, don't pee on my leg and tell me it's raining."

A booming laugh emitted from Dr. Phil, "Ooo wee, folks. I'm telling you, you can't make this stuff up! That was one amazing story. Obviously a lot has changed since your accident in 1988, so tell me something you think has changed for the worse."

As Tommy pondered his question, he glanced out at the TV crew. All of them, including the cameraman were sidetracked by their phones. "Communication," he answered.

"Communication is worse now?" Dr. Phil questioned.

"Yea. I mean, it's kind of cool that you can talk or see anyone in the world with just the touch of a button, but this whole cellphone, Facebook Tweeter thing just seems weird to me. Do I really need to see a picture of what you ate for breakfast today? It's like everything is communicated through texts or emails and even then it's done through silly abbreviations or those stupid little picture icons. Nobody talks to each other anymore. Hell, no one even walks with their heads up. It's like their phones are permanently attached to their hands. I used to love hanging out with my friends; talking, joking, laughing. But now when friends get together they spend their time checking their phone for what other friends are doing. Nobody lives in the moment anymore. As a matter of fact, it's become more about capturing the moment on your phone rather than actually enjoying the moment."

Dr. Phil slowly shook his head. "Now that's some deep, deep

stuff, my friend. If this was a text, I'd be giving you a thumbs up and a smiley face emoticon." Tommy blankly stared at him. "Ha, I'm just kidding. How about we end this by you telling us the *best* thing about the world today versus back then?"

Tommy leaned back in his chair, thought long and hard, smiled, then answered, "Yoga pants. Those things are friggin' amazing."

At first, Phil was caught off guard, but ultimately nodded his head in agreement.

SICILY, ITALY

The next morning, in a quaint Italian café, Dr. Zimarchi and Paco sat in a corner booth, drinking. Dr. Zimarchi sipped his tiny espresso as Paco (with both hands), drank his large latte. As they sat and drank, their eyes were glued to the doctor's laptop watching Tommy's interview from the previous day. When it was over, the doctor chuckled then gently closed the laptop. He turned to Paco and said, "We did a good thing."

Paco nodded, but his attention quickly focused on two young ladies standing in line (in yoga pants). Paco's smile widened and he finally spoke, "They really are pretty amazing, huh boss?"

Doctor Zimarchi shared Paco's admiration of the yoga pants, "They sure are, Paco. They sure are."

 The End

ABOUT THE AUTHORS

JODY CLARK

Jody grew up in the Kittery/York area of southern Maine. He originally started out as a screenwriter. As of now, he has written 9 feature length screenplays ranging from dramas to dramedies to comedies. Not only did Jody grow up in Maine, but he makes it a point to utilize and represent his state as much as possible. From Maine's scenic rocky coast, to its remotely pristine backwoods, to its eclectic characters, all serve as backdrops and pay homage to his beloved state. His ultimate goal is not to just sell his scripts, but to have them filmed right here in the great state of Maine.

Unfortunately, searching for the proper financing has been a long, tiring, and at times, disheartening process. Feeling helpless in the whole 'funding' process, Jody decided to reverse the typical Hollywood blueprint. That blueprint being: It's almost ALWAYS a novel that gets turned into a screenplay and not a screenplay which gets turned into a novel. Jody's thought process was simple: It's much easier to self-publish a book rather than self-finance a movie, and who knows, maybe, just maybe, this will be a screenplay that gets turned into a book only to eventually get turned back into a movie! But even if this wild idea never comes to fruition, at least by turning it into a novel, the *story* itself will be able to be shared by the public.

ABOUT THE AUTHORS

SUE ROULUSONIS

Sue Roulusonis is a true child of the 80s, having graduated high school smack-dab in the middle of the decade in 1985. She can name that 80s tune in less than three notes (that's what she says), and has been wearing her leg warmers since they were in style, out of style, and back in again. She lives in Easton, Massachusetts with her two daughters (Deren, 22 and Brynn, 11) and two cats. She also has a great wine rack. She is the author of a coloring journal, "Zen and the Art of Coloring" and the upcoming Volume II. She can be found trolling all over Facebook and blogging as 40-something Breck Girl.

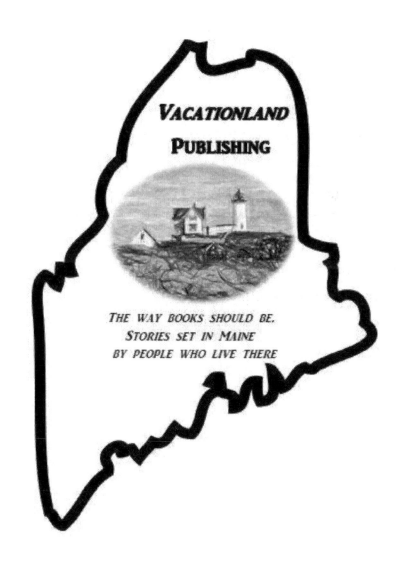

VACATIONLAND
PUBLISHING

THE WAY BOOKS SHOULD BE.
STORIES SET IN MAINE
BY PEOPLE WHO LIVE THERE

Gina's Mix

A1. Just like Heaven – The Cure
2. Melt with you – Modern English
3. Love will tear us apart – Joy Division
4. April Skies – Jesus + Mary Chain
5. Mad World – Tear for Fears
B1. Bigmouth Strikes Again – The Smiths
2. The Killing Moon – Echo + the Bunnymen
3. Bizarre Love Triangle – New Order
4. Blister in the Sun – Violent Femmes
5. Somebody – Depeche Mode

Tommy's Mix

A1. Livin on a Prayer – Bon Jovi
2. Girls, Girls, Girls – Motley Crue
3. Talk Dirty to me – Poison
4. Kiss me Deadly – Lita Ford
5. Here I Go Again – Whitesnake
B1. Round + Round – RATT
2. Sweet Child O mine – Guns + Roses
3. You give love a Bad name – Bon Jovi
4. Don't Know What You Got – Cinderella
5. Home Sweet Home – Motley Crue

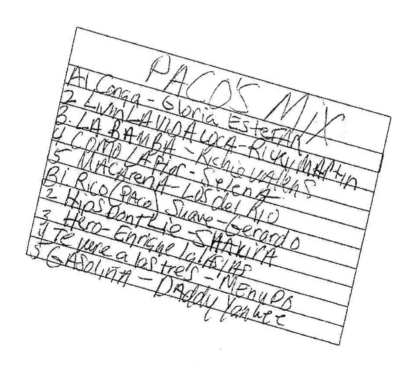

Made in the USA
Middletown, DE
17 October 2016